Since winning the C̶ ̶ ̶ ̶ ̶ ̶ ̶ ̶ ̶ Prize for
Fiction for her first nov̶ ̶ ̶ ̶ ̶ ̶ ̶ ̶ ̶d

Born in the mining town of C̶a̶ ̶ ̶ ̶ ̶ ̶ ̶ ̶ ̶ ̶ ̶ ̶ of
East Yorkshire as a child and has lived in Hull
rural Holderness where many of her novels are set. She
now lives in the market town of Beverley.

When she is not writing, Val is busy promoting libraries
and supporting many charities.

Find out more about Val Wood's novels by visiting her
website: www.valeriewood.co.uk

Have you read all of Val Wood's novels?

The Hungry Tide
Sarah Foster's parents fight a constant battle with poverty – until wealthy John Rayner provides them with work and a home on the coast. But when he falls for their daughter, Sarah, can their love overcome the gulf of wealth and social standing dividing them?

Annie
Annie Swinburn has killed a man. The man was evil in every possible way, but she knows that her only fate if she stays in Hull is a hanging. So she runs as far away as she can – to a new life that could offer her the chance of love, in spite of the tragedy that has gone before . . .

Children of the Tide
A tired woman holding a baby knocks at the door of one of the big houses in Anlaby. She shoves the baby at young James Rayner, then she vanishes. The Rayner family is shattered – born into poverty, will a baby unite or divide the family?

The Gypsy Girl
Polly Anna's mother died when she was just three years old. Alone in the world, the workhouse was the only place for her. But with the help of a young misfit she manages to escape, running away with the fairground folk. Will Polly Anna ever find somewhere she truly belongs?

Emily
A loving and hard-working child, Emily goes into service at just twelve years old. But when an employer's son dishonours and betrays her, her fortunes seem to be at their lowest ebb. Can she journey from shame and imprisonment to a new life and fulfilment?

Going Home
For Amelia and her siblings, the grim past their mother Emily endured seems far away. But when a gentleman travels from Australia to meet Amelia's family, she discovers the past casts a long shadow and that her tangled family history is inextricably bound up with his . . .

Rosa's Island
Taken in as a child, orphaned Rosa grew up on an island off the coast of Yorkshire. Her mother, before she died, promised that one day Rosa's father would return. But when two mysterious Irishmen come back to the island after many years, they threaten everything Rosa holds dear . . .

The Doorstep Girls
Ruby and Grace have grown up in the poorest slums of Hull. Friends since childhood, they have supported each other in bad times and

good. As times grow harder, and money scarcer, the girls search for something that could take them far away . . . But what price will they pay to find it?

Far From Home
When Georgiana Gregory makes the long journey from Hull for New York, she hopes to escape the confines of English life. But once there, Georgiana finds she isn't far from home when she encounters a man she knows – a man who presents dangers almost too much to cope with . . .

The Kitchen Maid
Jenny secures a job as kitchen maid in a grand house in Beverley – but her fortunes fail when scandal forces her to leave. Years later, she is mistress of a hall, but she never forgets the words a gypsy told her: that one day she will return to where she was happy and find her true love . . .

The Songbird
Poppy Mazzini has an ambition – to go on the stage. Her lovely voice and Italian looks lead her to great acclaim. But when her first love from her home town of Hull becomes engaged to someone else, she is devastated. Will Poppy have to choose between fame and true love?

Nobody's Child
Now a prosperous Hull businesswoman, Susannah grew up with the terrible stigma of being nobody's child. When daughter Laura returns to the Holderness village of her mother's childhood, she will discover a story of poverty, heartbreak and a love that never dies . . .

Fallen Angels
After her dastardly husband tries to sell her, Lily Fowler is alone on the streets of Hull. Forced to work in a brothel, she forges friendships with the women there, and together they try to turn their lives around. Can they dare to dream of happy endings?

The Long Walk Home
When Mikey Quinn's mother dies, he is determined to find a better life for his family – so he walks to London from Hull to seek his fortune. There he meets Eleanor, and they gradually make a new life for themselves. Eventually, though, they must make the long walk home to Hull . . .

Rich Girl, Poor Girl
Polly, living in poverty, finds herself alone when her mother dies. Rosalie, brought up in comfort on the other side of Hull, loses her own mother on the same day. When Polly takes a job in Rosalie's house, the two girls form an unlikely friendship. United in tragedy, can they find happiness?

Homecoming Girls
The mysterious Jewel Newmarch turns heads wherever she goes, but she feels a longing to know her own roots. So she decides to return to her birthplace in America, where she learns about family, friendship, love and home. But most importantly, love . . .

The Harbour Girls
Jeannie spends her days at the water's edge waiting for Ethan to come in from fishing. But then she falls for a handsome stranger. When he breaks his word, Jeannie finds herself pregnant and alone in a strange new town. Will she ever find someone to truly love her – and will Ethan ever forgive her?

The Innkeeper's Daughter
Bella's dreams of teaching are dashed when she has to take on the role of mother to her baby brother. Her days are brightened by visits from Jamie Lucan – but when the family is forced to move to Hull, Bella is forced to leave everything behind. Can she ever find her dreams again?

His Brother's Wife
The last thing Harriet expects after her mother dies is to marry a man she barely knows, but her only alternative is the workhouse. And so begins an unhappy marriage to Noah Tuke. The only person who offers her friendship is Noah's brother, Fletcher – the one person she can't possibly be with . . .

Every Mother's Son
Daniel Tuke hopes to share his future with childhood friend Beatrice Hart. But his efforts to find out more about his heritage throw up some shocking truths: is there a connection between the families? Meanwhile, Daniel's mother Harriet could never imagine that discoveries about her own family are also on the horizon . . .

Little Girl Lost
Margriet grew up as a lonely child in the old town of Hull. As she grows into adulthood she forms an unlikely friendship with some of the street children who roam the town. As Margriet acts upon her inspiration to help them, will the troubles of her past break her spirit, or will she be able to overcome them?

No Place for a Woman
Brought up by a kindly uncle after the death of her parents, Lucy grows up inspired to become a doctor, just like her father. But studying in London takes Lucy far from her home in Hull, and she has to battle to be accepted in a man's world. An even greater challenge comes with the onset of the First World War. Will Lucy be able to follow her dreams – and find love – in a world shattered by war?

A MOTHER'S
CHOICE

Val Wood

CORGI BOOKS

TRANSWORLD PUBLISHERS
61–63 Uxbridge Road, London W5 5SA
www.penguin.co.uk

Transworld is part of the Penguin Random House group of companies
whose addresses can be found at global.penguinrandomhouse.com

First published in Great Britain in 2017 by Bantam Press
an imprint of Transworld Publishers
Corgi edition published 2018

A CIP catalogue record for this book
is available from the British Library.

ISBN
9780552173919

Typeset in 11¼/13¾pt New Baskerville by Falcon Oast Graphic Art Ltd.
Printed and bound by Clays Ltd, Bungay, Suffolk.

Penguin Random House is committed to a sustainable
future for our business, our readers and our planet. This book is made
from Forest Stewardship Council® certified paper.

1 3 5 7 9 10 8 6 4 2

For my family with love and Peter as always

CHAPTER ONE

November 1897

The boy, trailing behind his mother, kicked a pebble into the road. It seemed as if they had been travelling for ever. They had, he was sure of it; well, days anyway.

'Come on, Jack!' His mother's voice was irritable. 'Don't dawdle.'

He wanted to ask where they were going, for she hadn't yet told him, but he held back; he could tell when his mother was in the mood for conversation and she wasn't now. She seemed . . . well, not exactly sad, but not very happy.

He had had his tenth birthday last Saturday, the eighth of November, and his mother had announced that they were going to do something special. He had thought that the special thing was the tea party they'd had in Brighton that afternoon with Mr Arthur Crawshaw, who was his best grown-up friend and his mother's too.

His mother and Mr Crawshaw had both played at Bradshaw's that evening and Jack had hung around the theatre until the show had finished. He and his mother had said goodbye to Mr Crawshaw and gone back to their lodgings, and the next day his mother had started to pack their belongings. She had said they were moving on, but she didn't say where they were going.

They left Brighton on Monday morning and took the train to London; he'd asked her if she would be playing in London but she'd said she didn't know until she'd seen her agent. Playing, he thought, kicking another stone. It wasn't playing as he thought of playing. Playing was a game of cards or throwing dice. Playing was hopscotch, chalking squares on the ground and jumping in and out of them, making up your own rules and not caring if you cheated because it was your own game.

His mother's *playing* was standing in the middle of a stage and singing to an audience, who sometimes clapped and sometimes didn't. He liked London and hoped they would stay for a while, and whilst his mother was visiting her agent he walked by the Thames; the tide was out and he saw a group of children down on the muddy shore gathering up what he thought was rubbish and jumped down to join them.

They were not welcoming but he was used to that. They gathered round him, hostile and threatening, saying that this was their patch and everything on it was theirs for the keeping. He argued with them, telling them that they were wrong and that the very ground they were standing on as well as everything on it belonged to the Crown. He knew that for a fact, he said, for Mr Arthur Crawshaw had told him so and *he* knew everything about anything, but in any case he didn't want any of their rubbish. He'd only come down to pass the time whilst he waited for his mother.

'Who's Mr Arfur Crawshaw?' they mocked. 'Never 'eard of 'im.'

'What?' he jeered back in his best imitation of Cockney. 'You ain't 'eard of 'im? He's only the most *celebrated* Shakespearean actor of *all* time.' He put his hands to his hips in a masterful pose and quoted, '*I like this place and willingly could waste my time in it.*' The group of youngsters, three boys and two girls, stared open-mouthed and then as one they pounced and they all rolled in the mud, hitting but not hurting, until he heard his mother calling from above to get himself back up there right now.

'Cheerio,' he called, as he extricated himself from the fracas. 'See you again.'

'Not if we see you first,' they shouted back and, grinning, went back to their rubbish collecting.

His mother wasn't pleased to see the mud on his clothes and brushed him down with a heavy hand before softly cuffing his ear. 'Look at the mess you've made, and there's no time to wash your breeches!'

There was something in her voice that told him it wasn't only his muddy clothes that had put her in a foul humour, but something else; he murmured sorrowfully, 'Sorry. It was just a bit of fun.'

She nodded, but didn't say anything more, and took his hand as they walked on. They caught a horse bus to King's Cross station and she went in to enquire about trains. He sighed as he waited, and rubbed his cold hands together, blowing on them to make them warmer. So where to now? Another town? Not staying in London, anyway.

'Did you get another gaff, Mother?' he asked as they left the concourse. 'Where are we going?' He shivered. It was cold and starting to drizzle with icy rain. 'Can't we stay in London? Are you going to do pantomime?'

'Don't say gaff,' she told him. 'A booking, you mean. No, I didn't and no we can't, except for tonight, and no I'm not. We'll try for lodgings at Mrs Andrews' and then tomorrow – tomorrow!' She took a sharp breath and he looked up at her. Her face was pinched and she looked unhappy. 'Tomorrow we'll catch a train and move on.' She looked down at him, touched his cheek with a cold finger and then looked away. 'We'll move on to another life.'

'Where to?' he asked again.

'Home,' she said. 'We're going home.'

Except it wasn't home to her any more, if in truth it ever had been, she sighed to herself as they climbed aboard another horse bus, and she hadn't yet thought through the next plan. She'd left over ten years ago and had never been back. Every year, just before Christmas, she had sent studio photographs, bought with money she could ill afford to spend: one of her, though not in stage costume, and one of her son so that her parents could see him as he grew from an infant to a hand-some boy of ten. She always sent a forwarding address but not once had they written back to her. It was as if she didn't exist and they could be dead for all she knew, and she'd never find out because no one, not a single person, knew where she was.

4

'Come on,' she said. 'This is our stop.' She lifted her skirt so that it didn't trail in the mud, for this was not a wholesome area, although considered semi-respectable by stage performers who couldn't afford to be choosy. 'I just hope she'll take us,' she murmured.

'If we're going to Mrs Andrews', she said last time that I couldn't stay again,' he reminded her.

'I know,' his mother answered. 'But don't take it personally. She doesn't take any children, not just you.'

A brisk, severe-looking woman answered to her knock on the door of the terraced house. 'Yes? Ah! Miss Delamour.'

His mother stared at her as if she had just remembered something. Delia Delamour. Her real name was Dorothy Deakin, but she never used it.

Mrs Andrews looked down at the boy. 'I thought I said that you couldn't bring the lad again. It's not that I don't like children but it's not a suitable environment for them, unless of course they are performers themselves.'

'I know you did, but could you make an exception just this once?' She hated pleading with the old hag, but it had to be done. 'It's only for tonight. I'm taking him home, you see; we're catching a train tomorrow morning and . . . just need a bed for tonight.' Her voice fell away. She was desperate. What would they do if the woman refused?

Mrs Andrews drew herself upright. 'It ain't right for a boy to share a bed with his mother and I don't have any spare singles.'

'He's only nine, Mrs Andrews,' she pleaded, knocking

5

a year off his age, 'and as I say, I won't bother you ever again. We're heading north, you see.'

'North!' the landlady spluttered as if she had just heard of the last place on earth. 'You'd better come in then.'

Jack bounced on the bed in the shabby but almost adequate bedroom. 'Mother,' he said, 'will there be icebergs?'

'What? What are you talking about?' She was wrapping a warm scarf round her neck. It was freezing in this top-floor room with the draught whistling in through the window.

'You said we were going north.' He threw both arms above him towards the ceiling and pronounced, '*Now is the winter of our discontent.*'

His mother sat on the edge of the bed. 'Oh, Jack,' she said, half laughing and yet wanting to cry. 'Whatever am I going to do with you?'

CHAPTER TWO

The next morning they caught a train going north. His mother had told him there wouldn't be any icebergs, even though it would be much colder than here in the south of England, and they would be near an estuary like the one at the end of the Thames. They were on their way to a town called Hull.

'Kingston upon Hull, to give its proper name,' she told him. 'But all the locals call it Hull.'

'And are we staying there? Have you got a booking?'

'No,' she murmured. 'We're not staying there; we're going into 'country.' She gave a silent laugh. How easily she had slipped into the local dialect.

'Listen, Jack,' she said. 'Going back might be a bit difficult. We're going to visit my parents; they live in a place called Paull. It's a village near the estuary I told you about – the Humber estuary.'

He frowned. 'Paul is a person's name,' he objected. 'It's not a place!'

'It's a different spelling. It's double l. It was called Paghill in 'olden days.'

He grinned. 'Double 'ell! Not a nice place to be, then?'

'Be serious.' She closed her eyes for a second, anxiety threatening to overwhelm her. 'We might not be welcome.'

'At your parents' house, do you mean? Why not? And why are we going if we're not welcome?'

'We fell out. I can't explain; it's . . . complicated.'

'Cos of me, you mean? Cos I haven't got a father?'

'You have got a father,' she said stubbornly. 'Everybody has a father. It's just that . . . I can't say. I'll tell you one day.'

He sat back and contemplated, and then said, 'Why did you call me Jack Robinson instead of Jack Delamour?'

'It's your name,' she said abruptly, knowing that she was lying.

'I don't like it. Folks laugh and say *Before you can say Jack Robinson* if something or other is going to happen, as if it's the first time it's ever been said.' He screwed up his mouth jeeringly. 'It's not funny. Not when you've heard it a thousand million times. And it's always grown-ups who say it.'

'It's a common enough name.' She shrugged. 'Change it if you don't like it.'

'*Romeo, doff thy name.*' The boy thought of Arthur Crawshaw. He'd miss him if they were going to stay in the north. He'd known him for ever. Mr Crawshaw had taught him to read before he went to school; he didn't often go to school, only if his mother had a long run at a theatre and then he was dragged off to a local school where no one knew him or wanted to. He and the gypsy children who occasionally attended were unwelcome. They always stood apart and more often than not played truant.

Arthur Crawshaw wanted him to listen to his lines as he prepared for his performances of Shakespeare or Mr Dickens, and so that Jack could follow his script he had taught him to read, and write too, when he was little. He could also add up and count and occasionally at the smaller theatres he would help to tally the takings in the box office by stacking the coins. I'm a very useful boy, he thought. Everybody says so. He was allowed to paint the scenery and show people to their seats, and because he was so very useful nobody seemed to notice that he should have been at school.

Mmm, he mused. I might change my name. But to what? What name should I choose? A theatrical name maybe, or . . . ? *Deny your father and refuse your name* – I don't know if it's my father's name, but I don't like it when it's made into a joke. He closed his eyes. The swaying of the train made him sleepy. He hadn't slept much. Mrs Andrews' third best bed was very lumpy and narrow and his mother had tossed about; he thought that he'd heard her crying during the night but then she'd turned to him and put her arms around him, just as she used to when he was very little, and murmured something like 'I'm sorry, Jack', and then he'd fallen asleep.

She was shaking him by the shoulder as they steamed into the Hull station. 'Come on. Wake up. We'll have to rush to catch our connection. It's the last train.'

She left the trunk containing her stage costumes in the left luggage office and only carried one bag, which he thought meant that they wouldn't be staying long in this place called Paull. He wondered why they had come, particularly as she'd said they might not be welcome.

They dashed to another platform where a much smaller train was hissing up a head of steam. 'Come on, missus,' a porter called to them as they ran. 'Driver wants to get home for his supper.'

'This is the Hedon train, isn't it?' she asked breathlessly.

'Aye, that it is. Hull and Holderness line. Last train tonight. Sit where you like; there's plenty o' seats.'

They moved off almost immediately and Delia eased off her shoes, exchanging them for a pair of well-worn boots from her bag. 'We've got a two-mile walk when we get off,' she told him, and peered out of the train window. 'It's dark and cold but at least it's not raining.'

'I'm tired,' he whined. 'Can't we get a cab, or an omnibus?'

She smiled whimsically and shook her head. 'No cabriolets where we're going, Jack, except maybe private ones, and no bus either. If we're lucky we might get a ride on a wagon or a carrier cart, but more than likely it'll be shanks's pony.'

'Aw! We've been travelling for *ever*!'

'No we haven't. It just feels like it.'

'You said they might not let us stay.' He looked out of the window into the darkness and saw the dim street lamps briefly shed light on roads and houses as the train rushed out of town. 'Southcoates . . . Marfleet . . .' he murmured after a while. 'Nobody getting on.'

'We're 'next stop,' she said eventually. 'Then the train goes on to Patrington and Withernsea, where it stops. It'll come back in the morning.' She fished about in her bag again and consulted a timetable, then pressed her lips together and replaced it in the bag.

'What'll we do if they won't let us stay?'

She didn't answer at first and just shook her head, and then she muttered, 'I don't know.' He didn't ask again.

'Can you remember the way?' They had left a deserted Hedon station and were walking towards the town down a long cobbled road. It was bitterly cold and quite dark with only a few street lamps and windows to light their way, but he saw small cottages on one side of the road and much grander ones on the other. A man leading a horse from the opposite direction touched his cap to his mother. 'It's a long time since you were last here, isn't it, Mother? Or did we come when I was a baby and I don't remember?'

'I know the way,' she said, and turned to tuck his woollen scarf into the neck of his jacket and pull his cap over his ears. 'Nothing much changes round here.'

A grocery shop was open in the main square and they went inside and bought two currant buns, two scones and a bag of broken chocolate. The woman behind the counter reduced the price of the buns and scones as she said they had been baked early that morning and might be dry. 'They'll fill a corner,' she said, smiling at Jack.

They continued on down the main street through the town, passing inns, butchers, haberdashers and a police station, and then crossed another road, leaving buildings and gas lights behind and continuing on a

11

much longer, darker road. 'It's pitch black!' he said. 'Are you sure this is the right way? We won't fall in the river, will we?'

'No.' His mother gave a brief laugh. 'We won't. We're a long way off the river, though we'll cross over a bridge that goes over the haven in a few minutes. Big ships used to come up the haven in the old days, but it's silted up now and isn't much more than a stream. Look further up on the right; can you see those lights through the trees? That's the Hedon Arms. If we don't get a welcome in Paull we'll come back and spend the night here.'

He felt a rush of relief. 'Perhaps we should book a room now, just in case?'

She took his hand again. 'No, we'll take a chance.'

'We're in proper country now, aren't we?' he asked after about another half hour's walking. 'I can see better now than I could before; and I can smell the sea.'

'Your eyes have adjusted,' she said, 'and you might be able to smell the saltiness of the estuary as we're not all that far away. Not much longer now. You're doing very well.' She squeezed his hand. 'Really well.'

They were passing fences and fields, thickly wooded copses and an occasional dark wooden building or barn; they crossed a bridge over water which his mother told him was the haven, and he thought that if she hadn't been with him he might have been very frightened. A grey-white shape skimmed alongside them and he let out a startled gasp. His mother gave a small huff of amusement. 'Only an owl,' she said. 'Hunting for his supper.'

12

He'd never been in such a quiet and lonely area and wasn't sure if he would like to live in such a place as this, even though the idea of living by a river had at first seemed appealing. He looked up at the sky and it was filled with so many stars that he felt dizzy.

'Mr Crawshaw told me that when there's no street lighting you can see stars called the Plough. Do you know which they are?'

She stopped and pointed. 'You see that line of seven stars that tips up like a tail? That's the Plough. There are millions and millions of stars; too many to count. Navigators find their way by learning which is which and following them to get safely home.'

He didn't answer. He'd seen a light ahead. He pointed into the darkness. 'I saw a light. I think it was moving.'

'Maybe atop a ship's mast,' she said. 'We'd be able to see the estuary if it were daylight. We're nearly there. My parents' cottage is this side of the village.'

'Oh, good,' he breathed. 'Are they farmers? Do they have cows and sheep and things?'

'No, it's a smallholding, not a farm. They've only got a few acres. They keep ducks and hens mostly, and goats. Or used to,' she added.

He heard her wavering voice, and knowing she was nervous he squeezed her hand. 'It'll be all right,' he said softly.

'Do you know why we've come, Jack?'

'No.' He shook his head. 'So they can get to know me? Cos you've not seen them in a long time?'

'Something of the kind,' she sighed. She was clutching at straws, she knew, but she had run out of choices of how to continue. Ahead of them he could see only a few lights and shapes of buildings which he thought could be houses or possibly farmsteads; after another quarter of an hour or so he saw a gleaming white tower which she said was a lighthouse but didn't think was used as one any more, and in another ten minutes, when he could barely see his hand in front of him, she stopped by a field gate and looked over it. An unlit cottage or small house was at the end of a short track. 'This is it,' she murmured. 'Nothing's changed.'

They walked to a smaller gate and she lifted the iron ring and pushed it open; the gate screeched as she did so and she gave a half smile, half grimace. 'It always did need oiling.' A dog in its kennel began barking furiously as the gate grated on its hinges when she closed it behind them. 'They don't oil it so that they can hear if intruders come through. As if they had anything worth stealing,' she muttered as if to herself. 'Nor do they ever think that someone might vault the gate.'

A curtain was opened an inch and lamplight showed through. 'Somebody's home,' Jack murmured; he was beginning to feel nervous.

There was no knocker on the unadorned plank door and his mother curled her fingers into a fist and knocked with her bare hand.

'Who is it?' a woman's voice called out, and the dog continued barking.

Jack looked up and saw his mother's hesitation. He nudged her.

'Dorothy,' she called back in a croaky voice.

Jack's mouth opened. *Dorothy*? Not Delia then?

'Dorothy who?'

'Your daughter Dorothy. Remember me?'

'We 'ave no daughter.'

'Come on, Ma,' Jack's mother pleaded. 'Open 'door, for pity's sake. I've got the boy with me.'

There was no answer for a minute and then they heard the bolt being drawn back and the door was opened a crack. 'You can't come in. You know that.'

Jack came closer to his mother and peered through the opening. A heavy chain kept them out. Someone, an old woman, he thought, with a shawl over her head, was backlit by lamplight as she peered out into the darkness.

'What do you want? Your father's not in; he'll be back soon and you'll not want *him* to catch you here.'

'He'll be at the hostelry, I suppose. Some things don't ever change.' The boy heard the bitterness in his mother's voice as she added, 'Don't you even want to meet your grandson?'

'Why would I?' the woman said.

'I'd like him to meet his family.'

'He has no family, not here at any rate. And it's more'n my life's worth to let you in, you know that.' She began to close the door. 'Try the other folk. Mebbe you'll have better luck with them.'

The door shut and they heard the bolt being drawn across. A moment later the curtain was closed at the window and they were left in darkness.

'Come on.' Jack pulled on his mother's sleeve. 'Let's go. We didn't want to stay here anyway, did we?'

'I should have known better,' she muttered as they walked away. 'Why did I expect anything different?

But I want you to be settled. I want you to go to school every day like other children, and have other children to play with, instead of tagging along with a bunch of mismatched theatre performers.'

'I can read and write,' he said, as she fastened the gate behind them. 'And I know poetry, and – and Shakespeare.'

'It's not enough.' She led the way back towards Hedon. 'It's law that every child receives an education.'

'Are we going to that inn?' he asked, as he tramped behind her.

'Yes,' she sighed. 'I've just enough money for one night. Then tomorrow I'll have another think about what we can do next.'

The woman in the cottage leaned her back against the door and the heavy curtain hanging from it folded about her. She took a deep shuddering breath. She had thought she would never see her again; and she'd dared to bring the boy. She must be braver now than she'd once been. Half an hour earlier and *he* would have been at home and all hell would have broken loose. Her name had never been mentioned since the day she'd left and he never once asked about her or where she had gone. He never saw the photo postcards she sent every year, for she burned them as soon as she'd looked at them. There was no trace of her having ever lived there.

She shivered and went to sit by the fire, recalling the day when she had told Deakin about her own pregnancy; she had held off giving him the news for as long as possible so that he didn't suspect anything, for she had discovered early in their marriage that he had a violent streak. He had slapped her face and told her that she was a fool and should get rid of it, but later he had relented and said she could keep it, but woe betide her if she became pregnant again.

I wasn't brave enough to leave him. I don't know where I would have gone. A stranger to these parts just as Deakin was, and a long way from our home in Brixham; I couldn't understand then why he was in such a hurry to come away, for there was a good living to be made, and a prettier little town you never would find. But now I know why and I suppose he thought that no one would ever find him here.

She glanced down at the mat beneath her feet where the floorboard creaked. He's the fool, she thought in satisfaction, and he'll get his come-uppance one day.

CHAPTER THREE

It was late when they arrived at the hostelry and the landlord looked at them warily.

'I need a room for tonight,' Delia told him. 'Just for the two of us; myself and my son.'

'I've just one room with a truckle bed; it's a busy time.'

It didn't look busy, the boy thought as he glanced round the dimly lit bar, and then the landlord went on, 'We're getting ready for tomorrow, getting 'bar stocked up.' He pointed to where barrels were stacked against a wall.

'What's happening tomorrow?' Delia asked.

'Hah! You're not from round 'ere, I can tell. It's 'iring fair tomorrow. We're in Martinmas!'

'Oh, of course! I'd forgotten,' she said. 'I used to love it when I was a bairn.' She stopped abruptly, thinking she had said too much.

'So you *are* from round 'ere then?'

'Erm, no. Over … York way. That's where I was brought up. We've just come to see some friends in Hedon, but they're away. I must have got the date wrong.' She gave a nervous laugh. 'But I remember them saying this was

18

a hospitable place. You took some finding, though,' she said after another tense hesitation.

'Oh, aye, it can be if you don't know 'way. Come on then. I'll show you up.'

The room was far superior to the one they had shared at Mrs Andrews'. An iron-framed double bed with a flowered bedspread and two soft pillows stood in the middle, with a chamber pot tucked beneath it; there was a matching jug and basin on a marble wash-stand against one wall, a fireplace with the grate ready laid with twigs and coal in the other, with a narrow wardrobe next to it, and a truckle bed under the window. Jack eagerly asked if he might have that.

'Too old to sleep wi' your ma, are you?' The land-lord gave the barest of grins.

'No,' his mother replied for him, 'but he's a wriggler. We'll both sleep better apart. Will it be extra?'

'Nay.' He shook his head. 'And 'price includes break-fast. But you'll have to be out by ten, so's we can get ready for 'rush at dinner time. Will you be wanting to eat tonight?'

Jack saw his mother bite on her lip. He hoped she had enough money for supper. Then she nodded. 'Some-thing simple,' she said, 'so we're not any trouble.'

'It's no trouble,' he said. 'I'll get 'girl to light you a fire,' he added as he left them.

'This is nice,' Jack said, trying out the truckle bed. His mother stretched out on the double bed.

'It is, isn't it? I think when we've had our supper we'll have an early night, so we can be up early in the morning.'

'Then where will we go?' he asked.

'Well, I'll show you the hiring fair in Hedon; there always used to be a lot going on when I was a girl.' Then her animation disappeared and he saw her expression droop.

'You told a fib, Mother,' he chastised her. 'Two fibs. You said you were from York, and—'

'I know,' she interrupted. 'There was a good reason and I'll explain it all to you one day, but I didn't want to tell him where I was from or anything at all, really, because one thing leads to another, and besides, who I was or where I'm from is nothing to do with anybody else.'

'Not even me?' he said in a small voice.

'One day,' she said softly, 'I'll tell you everything.'

'Will there be roundabouts and things at the fair, like in London and Brighton?'

'There might be, though it's not an entertainment fair. It's where people come at the end of a farming year to find new employment or where farmers come to find new workers. Those who are looking for work dress up to show what they can do,' she explained. 'For instance, a dairy maid will carry milk pails on a yoke or bring a three-legged milking stool; stable lads wear a harness round their necks or some horsehair in their caps, and a cowman mebbe carries a piece of cow tail. And although it's a day of fun for those who are not looking for a job of work, it's not for those who are seeking one, cos they have to stand in line whilst employers look them over. Rather degrading, I came to think as I grew up.' She gave a sudden laugh. 'And young lads who are looking for their first job are called *Tommy Owt* and are at everybody's beck and call. Come on. Let's go down and eat.'

The bar was full of customers, but the landlord had set two places at a table for them and brought onion soup with thick slices of bread, and then plates of meat pie brimming with gravy and a dish of mashed potato, turnip and cabbage. They both refused apple pie for dessert, though Jack was tempted in spite of being full.

'Best food I've ever tasted,' he whispered to his mother and she agreed.

The fire was lit and the room warm when they went up, and both fell asleep almost as soon as they got into bed. Jack woke early and heard strange noises, and as a grey dawn began to lighten the sky he could hear birds whistling.

'Mother,' he whispered, 'there are a lot of birds outside. Have they got an aviary, do you think? And I heard a dog barking during the night.'

'It might have been a fox,' she murmured sleepily. 'You're in the country now and the birds are waking up and singing in a new day. In spring and summer they start very early, about four o'clock or so – as soon as day breaks.'

'I like it,' he said, turning over to face her. 'It's better than hearing wagons and cabs trundling past.'

'Oh, you can hear wagons here too, especially at harvest time; the wagoners begin very early.'

He sat up in bed and leaned on his elbow as he looked across at her. 'Why did you leave home? Was it because you wanted to be a singer and your parents didn't want you to?'

She tucked her hand beneath her cheek and gave a deep sigh, blinking her eyes awake. 'That's another thing I'll tell you about one day,' she said. 'When you're older.'

He rolled out of bed and went to the window. It was barely light and a frost had draped fine cobwebs over the branches. A small terrier wandered over the grass and cocked his leg against one of the trees. Terriers were yappy dogs; it wasn't his bark he'd heard during the night. His mother must be right; he liked to think it was a fox he'd heard.

After a substantial breakfast of bacon, eggs and sausages and an enormous pot of tea, they collected their few belongings, paid the bill, thanked the landlord, and went on their way, but first of all they walked along the narrow trickle of a stream that was all that was left of the Hedon haven. Jack found it difficult to imagine that large ships used to sail up it from the Humber.

'It was a long, long time ago,' his mother told him. 'Before my time, or even my parents' time. It was when Hull became a successful port that Hedon's shipping failed and the haven dried up.'

They walked on towards the town and into Market Place and already there was a buzz of conversation and shouts of laughter coming from a crowd of young people gathered there. As his mother had said, there were dairy maids carrying milking stools and servant girls wearing mob caps or carrying feather dusters, trying to impress sour-faced housekeepers dressed in black bombazine and carrying umbrellas and large leather bags. Some of the young girls were not staying in Market Place but heading for the town hall, and his mother said that perhaps the rules had changed about exchanging contracts with only a handshake.

Horse lads chewed on pieces of straw as they joked with their peers, and gentlemen in tweed jackets and sturdy well-polished boots were walking amongst them and asking questions, as were rough-skinned, red-faced farmers dressed in cord breeches and jackets who barked interrogations to determine the suitability of raw and tongue-tied working lads.

He watched as a young boy performed a clog dance, and a small girl tucked into a shop doorway sang sweetly to the accompaniment of her father's concertina and nodded her thanks as people threw coins into a cap on the ground. I'd be able to quote Shakespeare, he thought, except that I don't know the full verses but only parts of them. Arthur Crawshaw only ever asked him to read the first few lines of a speech so that he might prompt him to begin his recitation, as he said that once Jack had started he could remember the rest.

He suddenly missed Arthur; he thought of how he used to turn up, even if he wasn't appearing in the same theatre as his mother, and shake him by the hand as if he were a properly grown-up person. I wish he would turn up now, Jack thought. Arthur would know what to do. He would be able to advise her.

'Come on,' his mother said. 'I'll take you to see the church; it's a very important one.' They walked out of the Market Place and turned a corner and there it was on a slight rise in front of them. 'It's very ancient,' she told him. 'It's called the King of Holderness.'

He nodded. It was very fine, he thought, but really he wanted to go back to the busy Market Place and watch the local folk; the way they behaved and talked. He couldn't understand all of what they were saying. They spoke quite differently from people in the south, especially those from London or Brighton. Those were the places he knew best, even though – he mentally counted where else he had been – he also knew Oxford, where they had stayed for a couple of seasons, and Manchester, where his mother had been booked for a season but left after a week, for it wasn't a theatre at all but a tavern where customers chatted and drank whilst she sang . . . and then there was Glasgow. He had overheard her telling Arthur Crawshaw, when they returned to the south, that she would never in her life go to Scotland again, for the patrons were bawdy, rude and very suggestive.

What the patrons had suggested he never did find out, as his mother hadn't said and Arthur Crawshaw had just shaken his head and tutted and said that it wasn't fitting for a lady to visit such places. Now he wished that he had taken more notice, but then, he reminded himself, he had only been about six or seven years old at the time.

'Would you like to go inside the church?' his mother was asking.

'No thank you,' he answered. 'Can we go back to the market and watch what's happening?'

The town was getting busier and bartering was taking place; they saw some of the young lads who had been taken on strutting about, safe in the knowledge that they had a year's work ahead of them with bed and board provided, and a shilling in their pockets now to spend on whatever they wished for. Most were heading towards one of the inns to dispose of it.

'I'm getting hungry again,' Jack said as an aroma of food from one of the market stalls wafted their way, and he saw a look of anxiety cross his mother's face. 'Well,' he hedged. 'A bit peckish.'

'We haven't much money,' she said. 'I'll be honest with you. But we could afford a slice of bread and beef, how would that be?'

He nodded. 'That would be all right. If you're sure?'

'Yes,' she said, sounding positive. 'We'll go into the Sun Inn. It always had a good reputation and a warm fire if I remember right.'

The Sun Inn was a long narrow red-brick double-fronted building with bow windows and an arched entrance big enough for a coach and horses to drive through. Before they went inside, Jack noticed that at the other side of the entrance were stables and horse boxes. It was a bigger place than he had expected and he went off to explore some of the rooms whilst his mother ordered a portion of bread and beef from the bar, which had a large kitchen behind it. There were a lot of customers in there already, and there was a strong smell of tobacco. In another room was a glowing fire and big tables suitable for large families or groups of friends; just by the door was a small table with two chairs and he sat down on one of the seats and put his cap and scarf on the other to claim it. It was a perfect place to watch from, he decided as he settled himself comfortably.

'There you are,' his mother said over his shoulder. 'Why have you come in here?' She put down a tray holding a plate of beef, bread and a dollop of mustard, and moved his cap and scarf to sit down next to him.

'Cos there are people,' he said, observing those at the long table nearest the fire. A plump and comely woman who was either the mother or the grandmother of several children was divesting herself of numerous woollen scarves, though keeping on her bonnet which covered thick reddish hair; a younger woman with sharp features was chastising a slight, brown-haired girl; an older man with a short grey-streaked beard was looking towards a red-haired man who was ordering food and drink from a serving maid. Around them the children milled about and argued over who was sitting where and next to whom. At the table next to them were more people; both groups obviously all knew one another and even looked alike.

Jack turned to his mother to say something but her eyes were fixed on the man who was ordering food. She had shrunk back into the shadow of the wall as if she didn't want to be seen.

'Mother,' he whispered.

'What?' She gave him a quick glance and then looked again in the direction of the family. She pushed the plate towards him and got up. 'I'm going to the privy,' she mumbled. 'Eat up. Won't be long.'

He put some of the beef between two slices of bread and took a bite. The little brown-haired girl who had been scolded had wandered off and now came towards him. 'Hello,' she said shyly. 'Who are you? I don't know you. I thought I knew all of 'bairns round here.'

'Erm, no, we've just arrived.' He swallowed a large

piece of beef and gave a choking cough. 'Come for the hiring fair, you know.'

She gazed at him, her lips apart. 'Aren't you too young? How old are you? I'm ten.'

'I'm ten as well,' he said. 'When's your birthday? Mine was last week.'

'Mine was in October,' she pronounced gleefully, 'so I'm older 'n you.'

'You don't look older,' he said defiantly. 'You're only a little girl.'

'I know,' she answered. 'Are you on your own? Do you go to school here?' and before he could reply, she added, 'We've got 'day off school cos it's Hiring Day.' She giggled. 'None of 'bairns would turn up anyway, so we all get 'day off. You can come to our table if you like. We're having meat pie. There'll be plenty. Da allus orders too much, and we can start ours straight away. Gran allus lets us when we're here, so that it doesn't get cold.'

He thought of the meat pie they'd had last night at the inn and was tempted; he left the beef and bread on the plate, left his cap and scarf on the chair and followed her across to the table where she was sitting, taking the end seat next to her. None of the grown-ups who were busy chatting or giving a child a telling-off seemed to notice him. A plate of meat pie was put in front of him and with only a fraction of hesitation, before the little girl nudged him as her food was served too, he began to eat.

Delia slipped back into the room and saw him sitting at another table talking to a little girl next to him.

There was a hum of conversation as plates of food were handed round there and she licked her lips. Money no object, then. She cast her eyes to the sharp-faced young woman and saw that she was pregnant. Delia's mouth trembled, and glancing towards the red-haired man she took a bitter breath and muttered an appropriate expletive for the one who had taken a young girl's innocence without so much as a word of love. She turned up her coat collar and buried her face in her woollen shawl. A quick scan round the table saw a clutch of girls; the only boy was her own son. She gave a cynical smile.

But she was frightened. As frightened and desperate now as she had been ten years ago with a decision to make. Her heart hammered, and she felt a pulse drumming in her throat and ears. With trembling fingers she picked up the remains of the bread and beef, sandwiching them together and wrapping them in a serviette, and turned to leave the room. She turned again to look back from the doorway and saw her son tucking in to the hot dinner. Her eyes filled. How her boy loved his food. She put her hand to her mouth and breathed a silent kiss. Goodbye, Jack.

CHAPTER FOUR

The older woman, Peggy Robinson, took off her coat and loosened the warm shawl at her neck. Their table was close enough to the fire to feel the heat on her back. She glanced about her; all the usual regulars were there, the farmers and the smallholders, and some of the estate managers, who didn't sit at the tables like the rest of them but propped up the bar counter with a pint of mild or bitter in their hands. From her position she could see through the open doorway into the main bar, which was packed with customers. There were more people here for the hiring fair than there would be on a normal market day.

She saw people she knew and a few she didn't, and one of those was the back of a young woman in a coat fit for town and not for country, with a flurry of scarves floating behind her and a felt hat on her dark hair, trying to push her way out through the throng. Peggy looked along her family's table. Next to her, her husband Aaron was chatting over his shoulder to an acquaintance; Jack, their red-haired son, was standing at the end of the table, chewing the cud with a mate, his arms folded across his chest. Next to Aaron was their daughter-in-law Susan, with her usual scowl; was she ever happy, Peggy wondered? She persistently spoke with a sharp tongue and a rejoinder to cut anyone down to size; except for me, Peggy thought shrewdly. She had taught Jack's wife a long time ago that she wouldn't stand any nonsense from her.

At the table next to theirs were Peggy's older brothers and sisters and their kin. Her sisters, who had married out of farming, with their sons; her farm worker brothers with their daughters, and their grandchildren a mixture of each. She gave a little grin. All the men had longed for sons to carry on in farming after them but it hadn't happened. She alone of the sisters had been the one to turn a fisherman into a farmer and give him a son, but now Jack couldn't produce a male child either. Serves him right, she thought grimly. He shouldn't have got caught and married that harridan. She had always had her suspicions, and the sweet child Louisa looked nothing like either of them.

Her daughter Jenny wasn't here; she'd escaped from the country as soon as she was old enough, became a teacher and taught and lived in Hull; at twenty-eight she had never married, nor intended to unless she found a man who would treat her as an equal. She said that other people's children were enough for her.

The serving girl was coming with another stack of plates filled with food. The children had been served and now it was the turn of the adults.

'Sit down, Jack,' Susan called harshly. 'Food's coming!'

'I can see that.' His answer was equally abrupt. 'I've

got eyes in my head.' He turned to his friend and muttered something and the other man grinned.

Peggy's eyes glinted and then roamed along the other side of the table where Jack's girls sat. Rosie, the youngest, was bright and sparky with flaming red hair and freckles, and at six could hold her own with her older sisters. Next to her was golden-haired Emma, a year older and as argumentative as her mother. Then Molly, placid and dreamy, but known to stamp her feet if she couldn't have her own way, living in her own eight-year-old world, which would for ever remain the same. They all had the Robinson appearance with shades of red to gold hair and pale skin that burned and freckled; all except Louisa, the eldest at ten, the quiet one, with nut-brown shiny straight hair and cocoa-brown eyes flecked with gold. But who—

Her gaze was momentarily blocked by the servant girl's arm as she reached over her with a plate of meat pie, mash and sprouts, and then a jug of gravy.

'Is that everybody?' the girl asked. 'Do you need owt else? Salt? Pepper?'

'No, that's everything, thanks,' Peggy answered for them all. 'Let's tuck in,' she said pointedly, because Susan had already started hers, not waiting for the others to be served. Peggy was annoyed; she had taught her own son and daughter good table manners when they were young.

She looked again towards the end of the table and wondered who the boy was. He was wiping his mouth on a serviette, listening to Louisa and nodding his head with a grown-up air, which amused Peggy. Who had invited him to eat with them? Not that it mattered, there was plenty, but she was surprised that she didn't recognize him. But children grow so fast, she thought, and he might have changed since I last saw him; perhaps he was one of theirs after all, belonging to one of her sisters. His colouring was certainly similar to her own and theirs, although a darker shade of auburn. That'll be it, she decided. I bet he's our Janet's grandson. He looks like a bright lad; he'll be like his father, who's doing so well for himself. And she turned to the matter in hand: enjoying someone else's cooking for a pleasant change, instead of her own.

The boy glanced over his shoulder from time to time and eventually he murmured something to Louisa, who pointed to the doorway and then sharp left to indicate the yard. He murmured an excuse and went in search of the privy, where his mother had said she was going. Outside in the yard, a rich aroma of hay and straw rose from the stabling at the bottom of the paved area, and he heard the jingle of harness and men talking. He visited the privy and then wandered down to ask the stable lads if they'd seen his mother. They didn't seem to understand him, nor could he make out what they said when they answered, so he murmured his thanks and went back inside. He picked up his hat and scarf from the table by the door and went again to sit beside Louisa, who had ordered a dish of steamed treacle pudding and custard for him.

'I hope you like it,' she said anxiously. 'It was that or apple pie.'

'Oh, I like both,' he said exuberantly. 'Thank you.' As he spooned it into his mouth, he contemplated his situation. Sometimes his mother did disappear; she would perhaps go off to an unexpected rehearsal, or see someone she knew and shoot off to gather information on who was looking for performers, or whom to avoid at all costs. Then she would turn up again at the place where she had left him.

Theatre and music hall people were a *peripatetic* kind, she had once told him. He liked the word; it sounded more important than roaming or travelling, which was what his mother said it meant, and he liked the way it rolled off his tongue. He separated it out into *peri-pat-etic* so that he would always remember it. That's what she's done, he thought, she's gone *peri-pat-eticking* and will come back eventually.

But what should I do now, he wondered as he scraped the dish clean. Should I just wait? Will the landlord let me stay or will he turn me out at closing time if she hasn't come back? Mrs Andrews wouldn't have allowed me to wait in her house; she didn't like children. He looked around the table. The adults were still eating but one of the girls had asked if they might leave the table and go outside and now they were putting on their scarves and bonnets. The children at the next table were doing the same; they all seemed to know each other, so he too got up and put on his scarf and cap. Maybe, he thought, his mother would be waiting outside the inn, or perhaps she had been watching him having a good dinner and didn't want to disturb him or, he thought with a sudden flash of concern, be asked to pay for it.

They played hopscotch because he happened to have a piece of chalk in his pocket and no one asked where he had come from or who he was. He was preparing. for that, for when someone did ask his name. Which they were sure to do. That was for certain. He knew all of theirs because they'd shouted out to each other, and Louisa had told him hers and pointed out her father Jack and her grandparents Peggy and Aaron.

Then they played tig, and just as they were deciding what to play next Louisa's father came outside and whistled to them and beckoned. 'Come on, you lot,' he shouted. 'Look sharp, we're ready for off.'

Louisa tugged at Jack's arm. 'Are you coming with us?'

He hesitated for a second, then: 'Yes, all right, I can do.'

Some of the boys and girls from the other table ran off, but once out in the Market Place at the front of the inn the rest separated and climbed into various wagons and drays and an old brougham. He followed Louisa and her sisters and climbed into one of the bigger wagons. Two of the other girls climbed out of their drays and called to their mothers that they were going with Louisa and would be dropped off, and then another, older boy did so too and sat on a sack of straw next to the little girl called Molly, putting his arm round her and shuffling up close, making her giggle.

Before they set off out of the Market Place he looked back towards the inn, but there was no sign of his mother. They took a wider road out of Hedon than the one he and she had taken yesterday towards the Hedon Arms, and continued in a different direction.

'Will you drop me and Alice off in Thorn, Uncle Jack?' one of the girls called.

'Aye. What about you, Ben? Do you want dropping off in 'village?'

'Aye, please,' the other boy said. 'I can walk up 'lane. You'd not get 'wagon up there anyway.'

'I wasn't offering to tek you to 'door,' Louisa's father muttered. 'You've got a good pair o' legs, haven't you?'

All the children raised their eyebrows and some snorted behind their hands when Ben said cheekily, 'Well, I had a fine pair last time I looked.'

The wagon was drawn to a halt by a road sign marked Thorngumbald and the three children jumped down.

'See 'lasses safe home, young Ben, and go straight home yoursen,' their driver called after the lad, who lifted his arm in answer and ran off, with the two girls trailing behind him.

'Are you all cousins?' Jack whispered to Louisa. 'Or friends?' He thought it would be wonderful to have either. He didn't know any children of his own age; he never attended one school for long enough to make friends. I might like to stay here, he thought, when Louisa nodded.

They took a right turn out of the village and trundled down a very long rutted road. 'Where are we going now?' he whispered again.

'Home,' Louisa whispered back, and then asked, 'Why are we whispering?'

He bit on the side of his thumb where a loose piece of skin dangled. 'Will they let me stay?'

Louisa's lips parted. She clearly hadn't given it any thought. She shook her head. 'Don't know,' she breathed. 'Gran might. Ma won't like it.'

'I'm a very useful boy,' he murmured.

She nodded. 'We'll tell them that.'

'Where do you live? Is it far?'

'Not far now. We live near Paull. On a farm.'

His heart sank. *That's where we went last night; to my mother's parents' house. What if it was the same house? What if Louisa's gran was the woman who had turned them away?* He hadn't seen her well enough to be sure, but he thought she couldn't be the same person as the woman who had sat opposite him at the table. The woman last night didn't like children or she would have let them in, and the woman sitting opposite had seemed very jolly and smiley with everyone.

The road was different too, he thought; the fields and hedges looked well kept to a city boy unused to the country. There was a lowing of cattle and the bleating of sheep, and as the road dipped up and down he saw low shelters over the hedges and heard the grunting of pigs. He was pleased that he could once again smell salt water; the sky was beginning to darken and long silver and purple streaks ran across it. He turned his head to look behind him and saw that the sunset was filling the whole sky, and he gazed at it in wonder.

'Look there,' Louisa whispered and pointed beyond her father's head. 'From here you can see Lincolnshire on 'other side of 'Humber.'

'Oh, yes!' he said. It wasn't like looking across the Thames from the Embankment where there were many fine buildings on the other side. Across this water could be seen a long low landscape with chimneys issuing thick grey smoke into the sky, and on the estuary itself were sea-going ships and trawlers, coal barges and smaller fishing boats.

'Open 'gate, Louisa.' Her father's command was terse as he drew up the horse. 'Come on, look sharp. I'm gasping for a mug o' tea.'

Louisa climbed over the side of the wagon and dropped down to push open a wide farm gate, which she held until they had driven through and then closed after them, dropping a metal bar over the top of the post. An old horse still harnessed to a trap stood in the yard.

The woman with the reddish hair came out of the door of a long and well-built farmhouse. 'Your ma's gone to have a lie down,' she said to the girls as they all climbed out of the wagon, 'so don't mek a noise when you go upstairs.'

The boy waited for Molly, who was last, and helped her to jump down. Then he turned and saw the woman gazing at him, and he glanced at Louisa.

'So who's this then? Are you our Janet's grandson? Richard's lad?'

He pressed his lips together and shook his head; heading towards the door Louisa's father turned when he heard the question, hesitated, and then took a step back.

Louisa came and stood next to him. 'He's come to stay wi' us for a bit, Gran,' she said, taking hold of his hand. 'I said you wouldn't mind. He's a very useful boy.'

CHAPTER FIVE

It was beginning to drizzle with rain and Peggy told them to go inside. They went through a small room where there were cupboards and a small grate with a metal pot set above it, and a deep sink with a water pump at the side. Jack had never seen such things before. Louisa took off her boots and placed them next to others in a box, so he did the same and stood waiting in his socks for further instruction.

'Well, are you coming in or staying out there all night?' The question was brisk but not unkind, and the curly-haired woman gestured to an open door into another room where a bright fire burned in an enormous range. Louisa took his hand again and led him in; there was a large table in the middle of the room, with benches on both sides and high-backed wooden chairs at each end. The grey-bearded man who had been sitting next to the woman in the Sun Inn was reclining comfortably in an old chair by the range, his stockinged feet stretched towards the warmth.

He glanced up as they entered and said, 'Shut 'door behind you, Jack. You're letting all 'heat out.'

The boy was about to obey when he realized that

the command wasn't meant for him but for Louisa's father, who muttered something and closed the door behind him.

'So, young feller-me-lad,' the woman said, looking down on him and smiling, 'I thought you were one of my nieces' bairns, but mebbe you're not?'

The boy shook his head, and said throatily, 'I'm afraid I'm not.'

She raised her eyebrows humorously. 'A school friend of Louisa's?'

Again he shook his head and blinked at her.

'And do you have a name, so that we can seek out your ma and tell her where you are? She'll be worried sick about you, I don't doubt.'

He considered for a moment. 'I don't think she will be worried,' he said. 'She knows I'm able to look after myself. I don't need any supervision.'

Louisa's father, who had taken up a chair by the fire opposite his father, gave a caustic grunt. 'Never met a lad who didn't,' he muttered.

The woman leaned against the table and indicated with her forefinger that the boy and Louisa should come closer.

'You're not from these parts, that's for sure, and 'word is that you're a useful boy. So how is it that you're on your own with no ma or da to look out for you? Bearing in mind,' she added, 'that you don't need any supervision?' Without waiting for an answer, she went on, 'Are we allowed to ask this useful boy's name? And if we do, will he give it honestly?'

This was the moment he had been expecting, and he was prepared. He didn't want to tell a lie but neither did he want to give his real name, especially not now that he had met someone else called Jack. Arthur Crawshaw had said to his mother many times in his presence that the boy deserved a more *redeeming* name than the one she had given him, but his mother had never replied. He wasn't sure what *redeeming* meant, but this woman deserved an answer, for she had been very pleasant towards him so far.

'Robin Jackson,' he said. 'That's my name, and my last abode was in London.'

He saw her try to hide a smile as she asked, 'Well, Robin Jackson. Will your father and mother be at their London abode now, or in this district?'

'My father might be dead,' he said. 'I've never known him. I don't know where my mother is.' And that was the truth, he thought, for his mother could by now be on a train back to London, and he had chosen to say London for there was not a single chance of anyone trying to find anybody in that great city, unlike Brighton where they might.

'Send him off wi' a flea in his ear, why don't you,' Jack mumbled from his place by the fire. 'He's nowt to do wi' us. Why 'you mekkin' such a to-do about him?'

'I wouldn't send a dog out at this time o' night, let alone a child,' his mother said sharply. 'He can stop tonight and we'll mek enquiries at 'Sun in 'morning.'

Robin heaved a deep breath and chanced a smile at Louisa, who grinned from ear to ear.

'Oh, goody,' she said. 'Thank you, Gran. Where will he sleep? He could sleep on 'floor in our room, cos there isn't any room in our bed.'

'No, we'll mek up a bed on 'little sofa in here; he's too big to sleep in a room full o' girls.'

'I'll sleep down here wiv him.'

They all turned at Molly's voice; she had crept downstairs unseen and unheard and was now standing by the door that led to the hall. She came towards Robin and slipped her hand into his. 'I like him,' she announced.

'Do you, my lovely?' Peggy drew the child towards her and sitting down she lifted her on to her knee. 'But you see, big boys have to have their own bed and can't share wi' girls.'

Molly looked across to her father. 'But Da's big and he sleeps wi' Ma 'cept sometimes she don't want him to.'

'That's because they're married, you see, just like me and your grandda,' Peggy explained. 'And we share a bed.'

'Then I'll marry this boy,' Molly said passively.

Robin turned to her. 'We're not old enough to be married yet,' he told her. 'Shall we wait for a bit? We've to finish school first.'

Molly's lips trembled. 'I'm not allowed to go to school.' She buried her head in her grandmother's ample bosom. 'And I want to.'

'But I need you here; you're such a comfort to me,' her grandmother said softly. 'And I'd miss you if you weren't here.'

'And I would too,' her grandfather's voice boomed from his chair by the fire. 'Who'd help us to feed 'hens if you were at school all day, eh?'

Molly slipped off her grandmother's knee and on

41

to her grandfather's, where she snuggled up close to him. 'All right then,' she agreed. 'I'll stop at home wi' you owd folk.'

Robin, watching closely, wondered why the little girl couldn't go to school, and why it was that the grandparents were so loving towards her, whilst her father gazed moodily into the flames and said not a word to her.

He was shown where the privy was at the bottom of the garden and was most intrigued by it; like a little shed, he thought, with a wooden seat with a hole in it. When he came back in, all the girls were waiting to pump water to wash their hands in the deep sink in the room off the kitchen that Louisa called a scullery, and when they had finished he did the same before they all gathered at the supper table.

Robin thought he had never in his life eaten so much food in one day. After having a good breakfast at the Hedon Arms and an enormous midday dinner at the Sun Inn, he was now sitting down to eat a supper of pork pie, cold pressed meat with pickles, and hard-boiled eggs with bread and butter, and in the centre of the table was a huge fruit cake and cheese to go with it. This in itself was a novelty, as he had never had the two together before. Then there was a large brown teapot, big enough to serve an army, which was refilled several times to quench everyone's thirst.

The younger woman, the girls' mother, Robin guessed, although no one had said, had come downstairs for supper and sat down at the table without a word to anyone. Her fair hair was tousled as if she had been asleep in bed and she yawned a lot. After she had drunk her first cup of tea and eaten a slice of pork pie, a portion of meat and a whole egg, she suddenly noticed Robin.

'Who's this?' She looked at Peggy.

'This is Robin Jackson,' Peggy said. 'He's staying wi' us for tonight and tomorrow we'll try to find his mother.'

'So why's he staying wi' us? Do we know him?'

'Aye, I just said,' Peggy said evenly. 'He's Robin Jackson.'

'Well, where's he from?'

'From down London way.' Peggy poured herself more tea, then picked up the cake stand and offered it round the table before taking a slice for herself.

'London! So what's he doing here, eating our victuals?'

Peggy fixed her with a stare. 'I invited him, that's what. This happens to be my house, Susan, and I don't have to ask anyone's permission to invite somebody to eat at my table.'

Robin saw the curl on the younger woman's lips and felt the animosity as she looked his way. Then she gave a shrug and took a second slice of cake and a portion of cheese. 'I'll suffer for this later,' she mumbled.

'I'm going to marry him when I'm old enough,' Molly piped up for her mother's benefit.

'Can we have that in writing?' her mother laughed. 'It might be 'onny chance you get, girl.'

'But I might want to marry him as well,' Louisa said in a small voice. 'I saw him first, and said hello.'

Robin's ears were burning with embarrassment and his face flamed when Louisa's mother said, 'I might have known you'd have a hand in it. Interfering little busybody.' She lifted a finger and shook it at Louisa, who had opened her mouth to speak. 'Just watch it, or you'll have 'hairbrush to your backside.'

'It wasn't her idea,' Robin broke in in Louisa's defence. 'It was mine. I climbed into the wagon with everybody because we were having such fun.'

'Who asked you?' Susan glared at him. 'Just mind your own business, whoever you are.'

Peggy got up from the table. 'Come on, bairns. If you're finished you can leave 'table and go and play for half an hour or read your spelling books ready for school tomorrow. Molly, m'love, you can help me clear 'table and if you're ever so good you can help me wash up.'

'I haven't finished,' Susan interrupted. 'Is there any more tea?'

'Kettle's still simmering,' Peggy advised her. 'And I've never known pregnancy stop any woman from mekkin' a pot o' tea, so help yourself if 'pot's empty.'

The girls got down from the table and chorused their thanks to their granny, all but Emma who moved up to sit by her mother's side. Louisa indicated to Robin to follow her towards the hall door and young Rosie danced ahead of them.

'Thank you very much, Mrs – erm, what should I call you?' Robin asked his hostess.

'I'm Mrs Robinson.' She looked at him and then said, 'But as there are two Mrs Robinsons now, you can call me Granny Robinson if you like.'

He took a deep breath and gave a big grin. So Louisa's father had the same name as his. What a good thing he'd changed his own to Jackson.

44

'I'd like that very much,' he said at last, and felt a warm feeling inside that had nothing to do with the amount of food he'd consumed. 'Thank you for the lovely supper, Granny Robinson. It's the best I've ever eaten.'

She smiled back at him. 'You're very welcome I'm sure, Master Robin. Very welcome indeed.'

CHAPTER SIX

When Robin woke the next morning the first sound he heard was someone riddling the coals in the range and then tipping the coal hod to add more. He put his nose above the blanket and saw it was Jack Robinson busy with the tasks, so he put his head down again and feigned sleep.

Above the rattle of the coals and the gushing of water being pumped into the kettle in the scullery, he could also hear the birds twittering again and marvelled at the way they were so chirpy in a morning in spite of its still being dark. From where he was lying, quite close to the window – but not so close that there would be a draught, for Granny Robinson had been most particular about that – he could see from below the curtain that there was no light at all, but only greyness.

He had slept very well, soothed by the sound of voices by the fireside, Susan's rather shrill one and the rumble of Jack's replies, but Susan was the first of the adults to go to bed and then he heard only the warmer tones of Granny Robinson and an occasional gruffness from Aaron and then Jack saying, 'Well, I

46

haven't 'time to go traipsing over to Hedon. Mebbe somebody saw him come wi' us and will tell his ma where he is. It'll be up to her to look for him, not us to look for her.'

But then he had fallen asleep and hadn't wakened until he'd heard Jack at the range, and now he was drifting off again, lulled into a half sleeping, half waking torpor until he heard someone mention his name.

'Little lad has no worries, that's clear to see. He's settled in very comfortably.' It was Aaron speaking. 'But he can't stop wi'out us asking about him. We have to know where he's come from. You'll have to tek 'trap and drive over to Hedon, Mother, and ask around.'

'Aye, I suppose so,' he heard Granny Robinson answer. 'We'll go as soon as I've got 'other bairns off to school.'

'Their ma should be doing that.' There was a hint of sharp irritation in Aaron's voice. 'She teks advantage of you.'

'I know she does. I also know that 'bairns would go off to school with no breakfast if it were left to her. When she's had this one I'm going to tell our Jack he can start looking for another place to live.'

'Aye, well, but we'll happen keep Molly here,' Aaron said.

'Course,' she answered. 'That goes without saying. I wouldn't trust Susan to look after her; and 'others can come here for their breakfast and tea if they want to.'

Robin stretched and pushed himself up and looked about him, blinking. 'Good morning,' he said. 'Is it late? Have I slept in?'

'Good morning! No, it isn't late,' Peggy answered whilst Aaron looked at him quizzically, before coming towards him and sitting on the edge of the little sofa.

'I was just saying that you don't seem to have any worries,' he said. 'Are you not anxious about your ma?'

Robin folded his arms and considered. 'No, not really. She's used to doing things for herself and going about here and there, you know.'

'She can look after herself is what you're saying, is it?'

'Oh, yes, she can. She's very capable.'

'But what I really meant,' Aaron went on kindly, 'is, won't she be worried about you? You know, she might have slipped out of 'Sun Inn to buy summat, perhaps, or mebbe she'd spotted a friend and went off to have a natter, you know how women do, and then when she came back, you'd gone.'

Robin wanted to answer truthfully, for Aaron did seem quite concerned, but Aaron didn't know his mother at all, whereas he did, and his mother had come with the plate of beef and bread to find him and looked at the people in the room and it seemed to him that she had suddenly not wanted to be seen and that was why she'd said she was going to the privy. She wanted to hide, he thought, but he didn't know who from . . . *from whom*, Arthur Crawshaw would have said in the deep booming voice that he kept for recitals.

But he was almost certain she had come back, because when he and the other children went outside to play in the yard he'd noticed that the bread and beef had gone, and he was sure that his mother had taken it. She wouldn't have wasted the food, not after paying *good money* for it. Money was too hard to come by; he could almost hear her voice and the often quoted remark. He knew he was right, but of course he couldn't mention that now.

'Well, yes,' he admitted, for there was nothing else he could say and after all, he didn't know where she had gone. 'That might have happened, but she's sure to turn up,' he went on, adding, 'sooner or later.'

Aaron nodded but didn't seem convinced and just sat there musing. Then, sighing, he got up, turned to his wife and murmured, 'Well, it's beyond me. She's either abandoned him or lost her way. When you get to Hedon you'd best speak to 'local bobby – or else pop into 'Sun and ask if anybody's been enquiring about a lost boy.'

'Oh, but I'm not lost.' Robin threw back the blanket and got out of bed, clad in his long underpants and vest. 'I know where I am. I'm in Paull and it's spelt with double ell.' He grinned, wondering if Aaron would get the joke, but he didn't appear to.

'Could I have a wash please?' he asked. Granny Robinson seemed surprised but directed him towards the scullery, where he pumped out water and thought what a novelty it was and much more fun than having taps. He swilled his face and scrubbed his hands with a big yellow slab of soap and taking off his vest he washed under his arms in the way his mother had taught him, then went back into the kitchen and climbed into his trousers, shirt and woollen jumper.

'There,' he said. 'I'm more presentable now.'

Peggy, who was stirring something in a pan, laughed, her plump face creasing and her eyes shining. 'So you are,' she chuckled, 'and if you reach on to 'mantel shelf you'll find a clean hairbrush.'

Robin picked up the hairbrush and examined it. The bristles were firm and scratchy and were set into a shiny back with a hard shell-like finish. 'Is this the hairbrush Louisa's mother was going to use on her backside?' he asked in all innocence, and was astonished at the look of fury on Granny Robinson's face and the sharp breath that Aaron took.

'No!' Peggy said sharply. 'It is not and no other child either. Not *ever* in my house.'

Robin smiled. 'Good,' he said. 'Because she's such a nice little girl. My mother says that children shouldn't be smacked because, then, when they grow up they won't smack their children either.' His face grew solemn. 'I think she was smacked when she was young, but she's never smacked me even though sometimes I have been very naughty.'

'Come here to me,' Peggy said.

He went across to where she was standing by the range and stood in front of her, his hands clasped behind his back.

'Do you miss your ma?'

'Yes, I do,' he said in a small quavering voice. 'But I know that whatever has happened or wherever she's gone will be for my own good.'

'How do you know that?' she asked softly.

'Because . . .' Robin stumbled slightly over his words, 'I know that she loves me and wouldn't do anything to make me unhappy.'

She rested the spoon in the pan and pulled it off the heat and sat down on the nearest chair, pulling

Robin towards her. 'And are you unhappy now?'

He paused for a moment, as if considering. 'No,' he said. 'I'm not. I liked it yesterday when I was able to play with the other children, and I like the sounds out here much better than those in the city.'

'What kind of sounds?' Peggy wrinkled her forehead and he saw how her eyes creased as if she were concerned.

'The birds in a morning; they do such a lot of chirping. And I think I might have heard cows; and a fox, I definitely heard a fox barking the first night we came.' He was proud to share the knowledge that his mother had passed on. 'And in cities like London or Manchester there's a lot of noise from traffic and people shouting in markets and suchlike. It can be quite deafening at times,' he added.

She nodded. 'Well, threshing time is a noisy old job here now that farmers are using steam engines and other such new-fangled to-do-ments, and there's a good bit o' banter goes on at harvest time, but nowt that would give you a headache. And we also have to be wary of Mr Fox in 'countryside, so it's a good thing he barks so that we know he's about somewhere. He'll be after our chickens, so we must be sure to lock them up securely every night.'

'Oh, I could do that,' he said eagerly. 'I'm very good at locking doors.'

Peggy heaved herself to her feet. 'Righty ho,' she said. 'You and I will have a drive across to Hedon when 'other bairns have gone to school and see if 'local bobby is around, and then we'll decide what to do about you.'

Then came a clattering of footsteps and a chattering of voices and four little girls came rushing into the kitchen. First was Emma, followed by young Rosie who was rubbing sleep from her eyes, then Louisa shepherding Molly in front of her.

'Can I go to school today? Please!' Molly pleaded with her grandmother. 'I'll be ever so good.'

Peggy patted the side of her nose with her forefinger and whispered, 'No. But there's a treat in store for you.'

'What? What?' The little girl jumped up and down. 'Tell me, tell me!'

Her grandmother shook her head. 'Go and sit down for breakfast with 'others. Sit next to Robin.'

Molly rushed to claim the seat just as Louisa was about to sit on it, and Louisa gave way to her younger sister.

'We go to Thorngumbald school,' Louisa told Robin. 'We walk on our own now that I'm ten. Gran used to take us, but she says that I'm big enough to be in charge.' She looked across at Emma. 'Emma doesn't always behave, though, and runs off in front.'

'Tell-tale.' Emma put her tongue out at Louisa but her grandmother saw her and shook a finger.

'If you don't behave, Emma, and stay with 'others, you won't be allowed to walk with them but will have to wait until somebody's free to tek you and it won't be me. It'll be your ma or da.'

'Ma can't,' Emma said pettishly, 'cos she's expecting.'

'Your da, then, and he'll be pleased, won't he?'

The child didn't answer, but reached across the table

to grab a slice of bread, elbowing Rosie out of the way; Peggy made her get down from the table and stand by the window. She then doled out porridge from the pan for all of them, including Emma, but her dish was left on the table.

Emma's mouth drooped and she glanced at the clock on the wall, but her grandmother ignored her and poured a glass of milk for each of the other children. When they had finished their porridge and milk Louisa asked, 'Please may we get down, Gran?'

'You may, and now go to 'privy all of you – not you, Robin – and don't forget to wash your hands. Come on, chop chop or you'll be late.'

Robin stayed where he was at the table. He and his mother always ate breakfast and lunch together, unless she had a matinee performance when she gave Robin his first so that she could concentrate on her hair and pack what she called her *slap* in a make-up box. He used to laugh when he was little and slap his hands together and pretend to put it into the box, but he didn't do that now that he was nearly grown up. He was astonished that Emma should be so rude and speak to her grandmother as she had.

He looked at her defiant face and wondered what would happen when her father came in and if he would be angry that she hadn't gone to school with the others, but then he saw her mouth screw up, and she muttered, 'Sorry.'

Peggy looked round. 'Did I hear summat just then? Was it a mouse squeaking?'

'Sorry, Granny,' Emma said in a louder voice.

'For what?'

'For misbehaving and answering back,' she said sullenly, 'and not waiting for 'others.'

Peggy nodded. 'Thank you. Now go and eat your breakfast. You've got five minutes. I'll not have 'others late for school because of you.'

'I'll get 'cane if I'm late.' Emma spooned the porridge into her mouth.

'You'll know another time then, won't you? Now no talking, just eat. You can tek 'bread wi' you and eat it at dinner time.'

In the nick of time, Emma finished her porridge and dashed to and back from the privy as Louisa and Rosie were putting on their coats and galoshes. Robin saw the palpable relief on her face as she came back from the scullery where she had washed her hands, just as their father walked through the door. Quickly, she pulled on her boots and put on her coat.

'Off you go, girls,' Jack Robinson said. 'Behave yourselves; don't let me hear of you getting up to mischief. Come on, Emma, look sharp. You're allus such a slowcoach.'

'Goodbye,' Robin called after them, and Molly, glancing at him, put her warm hand in his.

'Where are *we* going, Robin?' she asked. 'Are you staying to play wiv me?'

Robin looked up at Granny Robinson and then chanced a glance at Jack's grim expression. 'I'm not sure, Molly,' he said. 'But I think we might be going on a great adventure.'

CHAPTER SEVEN

Whilst Jack was washing his hands Peggy took his breakfast – bacon, eggs and sausages – out of the bottom oven where it had been keeping warm and put it on the table, then went to the bread crock, brought out a large loaf and put it on a wooden board with a knife.

'Don't let it get cold,' she told him. 'Where's your da? Is he done wi' milking?'

'Aye. He said he'll be in in a minute.'

Peggy went into the scullery to wash up the girls' breakfast crockery and called to Molly to fetch her coat from the hook in the lobby. 'Ask Robin to help you wi' buttons.'

'I can do them by myself,' she said as she went to do as she was bid, 'but he can help me wi' my boot laces.'

Robin followed her into the lobby and helped her on with her coat, whispering, 'You fasten the top buttons, Molly, and I'll fasten them from the bottom and then they'll be done in double quick time and won't Granny be surprised?'

Molly screwed up her face in delight, but struggled to fasten the top one and lifted her chin so that Robin could do it. He tied her boot laces and then put on his own jacket whilst she went back into the kitchen.

'Look Gran! Look Da,' he heard her say. 'I'm ready in double quick time.'

'So you are, honey lamb,' her granny said. 'What a clever girl.'

'Where are you off to?' he heard her father say. 'You don't usually go out at this time of a morning.'

'I'm going on a great 'venture,' she answered. 'Wiv Robin.'

'Are you now?' Jack's chair scraped back from the table as Robin came back into the kitchen and he sat with a sausage skewered on his fork as he gazed at Robin. 'Who says?'

'I do,' Peggy said, drying her hands on a cloth as she came back in. 'I'm going into Hedon and was planning on tekking Molly with me, but if you've got other ideas for her that's all right. Or mebbe your wife will get out o' bed and stop with her?'

Her tone was challenging and Jack turned back to the table to continue with his breakfast. 'You know Susan's not well,' he mumbled.

'You don't have to mek excuses to me about her,' his mother said sharply. 'Pregnancy isn't an illness, and after having four bairns she should know that.'

Jack shrugged and went on eating and then Aaron came in, saw Molly dressed in her coat and remarked, 'Well you look very nice, Molly. Are you going off somewhere?'

She repeated what she'd already told her father and Robin glanced with interest from one to the other, wondering who would be the next to comment, but

Aaron simply glanced at his wife, who said, 'I'll put your breakfast out, Aaron, if you're ready. Molly, why don't you show Robin the chickens?'

Molly at once took Robin's hand, and as they went out of the outer door, he heard Jack arguing with his mother.

The air was cold and damp, the morning mist hovering over the fields, and the bare branches of trees stretched out like dark limbs against the grey sky. Robin looked into the near distance and saw shadowy shapes of animals cropping the ground.

'Are those pigs?' he asked.

'Yes!' Molly laughed. 'They're having their breakfast.'

'Not bacon and eggs?' he joked. 'Like your da's having?'

'No, silly. Course not. They'll be having barley and apple and leftover dinner, and milk! They like everything and they're really, *really* greedy.'

'Yum yum!' Robin grinned. 'Shall we go and have a look at them?'

'If you like,' Molly said. 'But we can't go into 'field cos there're some pregnant ones – that means having babies,' she explained, looking up at him, 'and they don't like being disturbed. My ma doesn't either. She's allus telling me to go away and play.'

They wandered over to the fence and stood on the bottom rail to look over into the field where the pigs were rooting about in straw and apples.

'Those little roundish tin sheds. Is that where they sleep?' he asked.

'You are funny, Robin. Don't you know anyfink?'

'Not about farming, Molly,' he said. 'You'll have to teach me.'

The little girl took a deep breath and then beamed at him. 'I will,' she said eagerly. 'Nobody's ever asked me afore and I know loads o' fings.'

Granny Robinson called them from the doorway to come and get ready to go out.

'I am ready,' Robin said when they reached her. 'Apart from my cap and scarf. I'll get them now.'

'Will you be warm enough?' she said, and Robin saw her glance at his thin and rather worn jacket. 'I'll fetch a thicker scarf for you.'

As Peggy clicked her tongue and urged the old horse on towards Hedon, the thought trickled into her head that if she couldn't find his mother and there was nowhere else for him to stay but with them, then he'd need winter clothes. I don't know what I'm thinking of, she ruminated. We must find his mother.

She'd brought him a woollen muffler and a blanket, which she said they could put over their knees if they were cold.

'This is lovely, isn't it, Robin?' Molly said gleefully, tucking the blanket around hers and Robin's knees. 'Is this our 'venture?'

'You've been to Hedon lots o' times, Molly,' Peggy said. 'We were there for 'hiring fair yesterday, weren't we?'

'But I haven't been wiv Robin afore and Robin asks me fings that he don't know and I do.'

'What kind o' things?'

Molly giggled. 'About pigs and their little huts; they're called pigsties, Robin, or they would be if they were in 'yard and built o' brick; and do you know what, Gran? He asked me if they were having bacon and eggs for breakfast!'

'I reckon he's a town or city boy, don't you, Molly?' Peggy called over her shoulder and wondered if innocent little Molly might find out more about Robin than they could.

'He doesn't know very much, but I'm going to teach him.' Molly smiled disarmingly up at Robin and he grinned back at her.

Peggy drove into the Sun Inn yard from the back lane – Church Lane, she called it – and asked one of the stable lads to keep an eye on the old horse. Robin stroked the mare and said to Peggy how lovely she was, so quiet and calm.

'Does anyone ride on her, or does she only pull the trap?'

'She's old now, so she doesn't get ridden, though she used to.' Peggy patted her too. 'She's a grand girl, aren't you, Betsy?' she murmured and the animal snickered and snorted at her. 'She lives a quiet life nowadays, though she likes to be useful.'

'Just like me, then.' Robin grinned.

They walked into the back entrance of the inn and Peggy called out, 'Is anybody about?'

A grey-haired woman popped her head up from behind the bar counter and groaned as she got off her knees. 'Onny me. Clearing up after everybody. What 'you doing here again, Peg?'

'Come for information,' she said, drawing Robin forward to stand beside her. 'Do you know this young feller-me-lad, Mary?'

The woman scrutinized Robin and then shook her head. 'Don't think so; he's too young to drink in here. Why? Where did you find him?'

'He was in here yesterday at 'hirings and then turned up at our place. I'm looking for his ma and wondered if she'd been in here looking for him.'

'Well, who is she?' Mary frowned.

'That's just it. I don't know and he's not saying much. Just that his name's Robin Jackson,' Peggy said on a huff of a breath.

'Jackson's a common enough name round here, but I can't think that I know anybody wi' that moniker wi' a son; but in any case,' she peered at Robin, 'he's old enough to know who his mother is. Cat got your tongue?' she asked him and he grinned and put just the tip of his tongue out, so that she wouldn't think him cheeky.

'You'll have to tell 'police, mebbe,' she advised Peggy. 'Perhaps he's been abandoned, though it's a bit unusual; it's generally babbies that get left behind if their mothers can't look after 'em, not grown lads that are coming up to working age.'

'He's not old enough to work; he's onny ten, aren't you, Robin?' Peggy said. 'I don't really want to involve 'coppers, though Aaron said I should go to 'cop shop to see if there's anybody there who can help. There never is, o' course, when you want 'em. And anyway,' she added, 'who knows where he'll end up if they get their hands on him, so I came in to say that if you get any enquiries – cos this is where he was left – he's staying wi' us.' She made the statement flatly. It wasn't in her nature to leave the bairn to cope alone. 'And I might pop into 'town hall and see if there's anybody there who might know what to do next.'

'You're a bit soft in 'head, Peggy,' Mary said. 'He's a waif and stray. You might get into bother for keeping him.'

'I'd like to stay,' Robin interrupted. 'I like it where you live, and my mother wouldn't mind; she'll come back eventually.'

The two women stared at him. 'So do you know where she's gone, Robin?' Peggy asked.

'No, I've no idea, but I expect she'll have a plan in mind; and this is only a small place, not like London or Manchester, so she'll soon find me again when she's ready.'

Molly, who had kept silent whilst the conversation was going on, tugged on Robin's jacket. 'Mebbe she's gone on a 'venture, Robin, and knows that you'll be safe wiv us. I'll look after him,' she said to her grandmother. 'He's my best friend.'

Peggy looked down at her and smiled. 'I suppose that settles it then, but I don't know what your da and grandda are going to think about it.'

'Will it make any difference what they think?' Mary folded her arms across her chest. 'If Peggy Robinson's made her mind up there's nowt else to say, is there?'

Peggy laughed. 'I suppose you're right.'

Mary shook a finger at her. 'I've onny known you lose one battle.' She gave a swift glance at Molly, whose attention was wandering elsewhere. 'And that was when your lad got married.'

Peggy sighed. Her expression was cynical. 'Aye, well, he had a shotgun at his head so to speak, didn't he?

Nowt I could do about that, but I reckon he's lived to regret it. It's not a marriage made in heaven, that's for sure.'

CHAPTER EIGHT

Delia held back her tears until reaching the Hedon railway station and then wept and wept on the train back to Hull. She had beaten a hasty retreat out of the Sun Inn when she saw the Robinson family seated at a table, and her own boy chatting to the little girls and tucking into an enormous plate of food.

It was as if he belonged with them, she told herself in justification of leaving him there; and Peggy Robinson is a kind woman, though a no-nonsense type.

She'd hovered outside in the street, hidden within a crowd watching a juggler, and had seen the Robinson family and their in-laws and several children, including her own son, pile into various wagons, gigs and carts. She'd anxiously waited to see if he'd turn to look for her as they pulled away, but he didn't, so busy was he, chatting to the little girls and another boy who had climbed in with them.

Although she knew Peggy Robinson to be a caring compassionate woman, it bothered her that the driver of the wagon, Peggy's only son, wasn't; she had known him since they were children and had thought of him then as a friend, but he had subsequently proved that he didn't care for anyone's feelings but his own. Well, Delia thought, I hope he's got his just deserts with his wife. She concluded with some satisfaction that they hadn't yet had a son, although the wife had definitely looked pregnant; unless, a small doubt crept into her head, the boy who had climbed into the wagon at the last minute – could he be . . . ? No, she decided. He was older, maybe twelve or so. Older than my boy.

My boy! She wept copiously in the empty carriage as the train hissed and steamed noisily towards Hull. Whatever am I thinking of, leaving him with strangers? She excused it by telling herself that she only wanted the best for him: warm clothes, plenty to eat, school, basic essentials that I can't afford. He needs a settled existence, not a nomadic life such as I'm leading now. But how stupid was I to think that my parents would have a change of heart after they turned me out all those years ago? She knew why she'd fooled herself into hoping, though. She was fraught, more so than when he was a baby. I've run out of ways and means to survive.

But how do you know the Robinsons will keep him, her conscience nagged uneasily. Suppose they pack him off to a children's home or somewhere else? How can I find out whether or not he's happy, and how will I know if he stays with them, or, worse, goes off alone to find his fortune? He has so many outlandish thoughts in his head, brought on in part by Arthur Crawshaw, who encouraged him and was forever telling me he deserved a different life. And I know that – she sniffled away her tears – but I can't provide it.

She stood on the platform when the train arrived in Hull, wondering what to do next. It was late; there probably wasn't a train or a connection to take her back to London; besides, she was uncertain whether she wanted to go so far away, out of reach of him. And what will I do without money? The room at the Hedon Arms had been reasonable but she had little left in her purse. I have to get a job. It's as if I've stepped back ten years. She shivered and looked about her. Another train had just arrived and disgorged its passengers, and people were heading for the concourse.

Thoughtlessly she followed them; many of them were chattering as if some had travelled together. She heard their high-pitched laughter, saw the heavy bags that the women were struggling to carry, and a hesitant surge of hope turned up her lips: these were theatre people. But it was mid-week; why were they not at a performance?

She tagged on behind, wondering where they were heading. She had played in Hull, but that was over ten years ago. It had come about quite accidentally: she was working as a cleaner and was brushing the seats and clearing up rubbish after a performance; the theatre manager had heard her singing one of the more sentimental songs from the show and told the director. He had listened to her and had been considerate. He had seen how frightened and nervous she was and had given her an audition and then said he would try her out; she would fill in a gap for a performer who had gone off sick. He had sent her to see the wardrobe mistress for something to wear and she had enjoyed the experience of being on stage. He had given her a recommendation in case she should decide to move on, which she subsequently did – with his company.

'Come on.' Someone carrying a violin case rushed up by her side. 'We can maybe share a cab with someone.'

She looked up at a tall man with fair hair curling on his collar and began to hurry beside him towards the cab stand. When he put a hand on her elbow to help her into a cab with an open door she didn't object but sat down next to a young woman who moved up for her and shifted her bags with her feet.

'Thank Gawd,' the young woman said. 'I thought we'd never get here. If I'd known Hull was such a long way from London I'd never have agreed to come.'

'The theatre audiences are good,' Delia murmured. 'Or at least they always were. I haven't been here for some time.'

'Oh, really? I've never been so far north before but thought I'd give it a try. London's pretty well booked up for the winter season. My agent missed out on a few gigs, so I'm going to sack him as soon as I find somebody else. What's your name? Will I have heard of you?'

'Delia Delamour,' she murmured. 'I'm a singer. What about you?'

'Josie Turner. I'm in a dance troupe – well, we were a dance troupe but our numbers are dwindling so now we're only three. Hope the management don't mind too much.' She looked at the man with the violin case and smiled sweetly. 'You look familiar,' she said archly. 'Are you famous?'

'Giles Dawson,' he said equably. 'No, I'm not famous; I'm filling in for a violinist who has gone off sick. You might have seen the back of my head in an orchestra pit.'

The smile dropped from the young woman's face and she turned away, disappointed, to look out of the cab window. Dawson glanced wryly at Delia and then grinned.

'What kind of music do you sing, Miss Delamour?' he asked.

'Romantic and light opera,' she said quietly. 'Not comedy. I'm not inclined to be amusing.'

'Pleased to hear it,' he said. 'I don't care for music hall songs.'

'I'm . . . not booked,' she murmured. 'I've come on the off chance. Who's top of the bill, do you know?'

He shook his head. 'I don't know. They've been closed for a week doing repairs. I only got the telegram yesterday afternoon asking if I could fill in. I happened to be free so I said yes. I've heard that the management were having difficulty getting performers as most are already committed, so you might be lucky.'

'I hope so,' she said. 'I want to stay in the area if possible.'

'You might be doubly lucky then.' He smiled. 'They might want someone they know will stay.'

Delia was surprised to hear that. 'I've always worked with a contract,' she said. 'I've never ever broken one. It's too risky, and word gets around.'

'I agree.' He looked pointedly in the direction of their travelling companion. 'But not everyone is so committed.'

Delia dropped her voice to a murmur. 'So which theatre are we heading for?' She saw his raised eyebrows and added hastily, 'It's over ten years since I was here and there have been many changes, including the fire that destroyed the theatre I'd appeared in. It looks to me,' she nodded towards the window of the cab, 'that we might be heading towards Paragon Street.'

'We are,' he said. 'It's the newest Theatre Royal and it's been built on part of the old Queen's Theatre. Do you remember it? And,' he said as the cab slowed, 'we're already here! Hardly worth getting a cab, you might think, but it saves a few minutes when carrying luggage. I've played here many times since it opened and I can assure you that it is fire-proofed to a high degree and is a lovely theatre. It holds fifteen hundred.'

'Goodness,' she said. 'And do they fill it?'

'Not always, but they will at this time of year.' He gazed at her curiously. 'Where do you usually appear?'

'London and the south coast,' she said, and was gratified when she saw he was impressed. 'But I need to stay in the north for a while to sort out . . . erm, family commitments.'

The cab drew to a halt and Delia got out and looked up. Her travelling companion was right; the theatre was very impressive. She turned to tell him so and saw him paying the driver. She fumbled for her purse and hoped she had enough to pay her share, but he waved away her contribution and thanked her for offering, 'unlike the other young lady, who didn't give it a single thought,' he said, as they watched the dancer saunter towards her troupe of two waiting outside the theatre.

'She's young and immature,' Delia excused her. 'She'll learn.'

'Perhaps,' he said. 'You're still young, and on our brief acquaintance I couldn't imagine you were ever like that.'

'We all have regrets about what we did in our youth,' she countered. 'Even the most sensible amongst us.'

He smiled and Delia thought he was rather handsome when he did so, the smile lightening his blue eyes and rather thoughtful expression. 'Don't you have any more luggage?' he asked as they walked to the door.

'It's in the left luggage office at the train station,' she explained. 'I didn't know if I'd get a booking so didn't want to haul it round all the theatres with me. It wouldn't have looked good.'

In the foyer waiting for them was the manager of the theatre and a woman who Delia thought might be the wardrobe mistress, and as they were amongst the first in, and some of the other performers were still chattering outside, catching up with gossip and greeting other artistes, Delia made a beeline for the manager.

'My name is Delia Delamour,' she told him, handing him her *carte de visite*, a postcard with a coloured photograph of herself in stage costume on one side and on the other a list of places where she had performed. 'I've been travelling to visit my family since my last Brighton performance, and called on the off chance that you might be able to accommodate me in a role?'

She gave him the name of her agent, who could give him all her references, and said that for family reasons she needed to be in the north of England rather than London or the south coast, where she usually performed.

'I've heard of you, Miss Delamour,' the manager, Dennis Rogers, said, to her delight. 'I worked in the south for a few years, and briefly at Bradshaw's when I was a junior manager.' He rubbed his chin. 'Would you care to wait in my office until I have seen these other performers? The rest will turn up tomorrow, I hope. We're opening on Monday night.'

He opened a glass-panelled door behind the ticket office and invited her to be seated. Giles Dawson was in the foyer chatting to another man, who was also carrying a violin case. He saw her looking out and nodded, mouthing *Good luck*. Which I desperately need, she thought, and she sat back and closed her eyes for a moment.

She was tired, and hungry too; she hadn't eaten since she'd finished off the leftover beef sandwich at the Sun Inn, and that was hours ago. If I don't get this engagement I don't know what I'll do. She felt distressed over her situation, but it was a small comfort to think that she had done the right thing and that her son would be safe for a short while with the Robinsons. Even if we had stayed in the south, she thought, I didn't have an engagement to tide us over. The theatrical profession is so precarious. There's no stability at all, unless you're at the top of the tree.

Her meandering thoughts turned to Arthur Crawshaw and she wondered how he managed to survive; he doesn't have regular work, she pondered, which leads me to think that he might have another income. He's always well dressed, and his boots and shoes are of good leather; he doesn't speak much about his family, just that they are country people and that he has a younger brother who works in an office in London.

The door opened and Mr Rogers rushed in and

sat down behind his desk. 'I'm so sorry to keep you, Miss Delamour. There's always a problem to resolve in this business,' he said, echoing her thoughts. 'But I'm happy to say I am in a position to engage you, but only on condition that you can sign a contract with us for the next three months. We've had such an up and down time of it lately that I do need that assurance.'

Delia's heart soared. What joy! That would give her time to think through what she should do next, or even to take a trip out to Paull and discover if her darling boy really was all right. But Mr Rogers hadn't yet heard her sing! He must be desperate to take someone on without knowing what she could do.

'What kind of role?' she asked cautiously, anxious not to sound too enthusiastic, even though she would have been willing to scrub the stage and auditorium on her hands and knees if necessary. She'd done that before; she could do it again.

He clasped his hands together. 'I'll be honest with you, Miss Delamour. You've been in this business long enough to know the pitfalls, so I will tell you that we have been let down very badly by our lead singer, whose agent has informed us that she cannot fulfil her engagement. In fact, I had already heard a rumour that he had found her a more lucrative role in Manchester, so our lawyers are to sue both of them for breach of contract.'

'Quite right,' Delia murmured, inaudibly blessing the woman and her agent.

'As we are almost into December we are producing a Christmas show. Not the usual pantomime – that

71

will come in the new year – but a show of music, song and dance. We would like you to take second billing as songstress of romantic music. Not music hall songs,' he emphasized. 'We have a singer for those, who of course is further down the bill.'

He mopped his forehead with a large handkerchief. 'I've had to turn down a dance troupe where there should have been six but only three turned up.' He tutted. 'Professional! They don't know the meaning of the word.'

Poor Miss Turner, Delia thought as she shook her head in commiseration, finished before she's begun. But if she's intent on a stage career she'll make a comeback. The offer he had made her was only just seeping through. Second on the bill! She had never been higher than third, and that was only occasionally. In London and Brighton there was enormous competition for starring roles, and theatre managers could pick and choose whom they wanted.

'We shall close for Christmas, and then following the pantomime we are planning another production,' Rogers went on, 'which is why I need to be assured you can accept a three-month contract. After that, well, we'll see how the shows run. Audiences are what we need,' he said in a breath, 'but I'm sure I don't need to tell you that.'

They discussed terms of contract and he asked her if she would like him to inform her agent, to which she replied that she would write to him herself as she had other business to discuss now that she would be staying in the north for a long season. She also asked Mr Rogers if he would be willing to pay her directly rather than through her agent, as he hadn't been involved with the arrangement.

'This will suit me very well indeed,' she said at last, 'and you needn't think I would ever let you down.' Her fingers played about her mouth as if she were considering options, and then she added, 'As I am staying for a longer period, I will want to find a good lodging house where I can be comfortable, and do it tonight before everyone else does. So I was wondering,' again she hesitated as if mulling something over, 'would it be possible for you to pay me an advance so that I can give a substantial deposit and secure the lodgings for the time I'm here? My agent is notoriously slow in passing fees on to his clients and as I am not in London to badger him for what I am owed . . .'

He looked a little startled for a second, and then his face cleared. 'I don't see why not, Miss Delamour. For someone as esteemed as yourself I am sure that can be arranged. If you will wait just another moment longer.' He pushed back his chair and got up. 'I'll see the wages clerk straight away,' and he hurried out of the door.

Delia let out a huge breath. How had she dared to ask such a thing? But if he came up with a substantial advance, or even a small one, she could have a meal and a bed to sleep in that night.

CHAPTER NINE

Giles Dawson recommended the lodging house where he was staying off Church Street. He said that most of the visiting musicians stayed there as it was in a quiet area even though in the centre of town, and the landlady didn't mind if they practised; many of the regular members of the orchestra lived in Hull and didn't need accommodation.

Delia walked with him to see it and it proved to be clean and comfortable. After leaving a deposit out of the cash advanced to her by Mr Rogers, she returned to the railway station to collect her trunk and came back in a cab to find that supper was included in the rent. She sat in the small dining room with Giles Dawson and another musician, a cellist, whose name she didn't catch, and it was then that Giles Dawson told her that he'd recommended her to Dennis Rogers.

'But, Mr Dawson, you've never heard me sing!' she said in astonishment.

He laughed. 'I can tell by the timbre of your voice,' he said. 'But he'll hear you at rehearsal and he can change his mind if he doesn't care for it!'

'But he's given me a three-month contract,' she

protested, and put her hand to her mouth to cover her own amusement when he gave a great guffaw and said, 'He must have been desperate!'

After supper, which was hot and hearty, and saying goodnight to the two men, she went up to her room, for it was getting late and it had been a demanding and stressful day. She opened her trunk and hung up her theatre gowns on the picture rails so that the creases would drop out. Then she sat on the bed and let loose her emotions. What would Jack be thinking about her? Would he be worried, upset? She put her head in her hands. Should she ask the landlady, Mrs Benson, if she could bring him here? And if the woman agreed, what about his schooling? She gave a deep moan. Whatever she thought of didn't seem right. Should she look for other work? What was she fit for, and where would they live?

She didn't sleep well, but tossed and turned and felt wretched the next morning; she tried to concentrate on sorting through her song books to decide which music she might use. She thought that five pieces would be sufficient for her act, perhaps alternating two of them on different evenings for variety.

She liked to use semi-classical operatic arias but had to be careful that the music was within her range and the words light-hearted, unlike some, such as Romani's libretto for *Norma* which she couldn't bring herself to sing, as it conveyed a woman's love for her children. She chose the romantic ballads of Rossini but also included folk songs and gypsy music which the audience would know; she had many pages of sheet music, and although she never thought of herself as a celebrated singer she knew she had a pleasant voice, a mezzo-soprano that was easy to listen to.

After breakfast she visited the theatre to look at the programme on the doors and then took a walk around the town to remind herself how it used to be and see what had changed over the years. From Paragon Street she walked back towards Market Place and Holy Trinity church; and although the weather was cold and wet she retraced her steps to the shopping street of Whitefriargate, where the white-robed monks had lived of old. From there she cut through Parliament Street, skirted the Queen's Dock and walked to the Mechanics' Institute just behind George Street, which she remembered well and was pleased to see was still open as a theatre; she had never played there but recalled how popular it had been. Some of the other theatres were now derelict having been destroyed by fire, a great hazard in theatreland not only here but in many other places too; a stray cigar left carelessly burning and unnoticed could cause devastation within minutes.

Over a pot of coffee in a small café she sat brooding and thinking and wondering if perhaps, now that she had a three-month contract in her possession, she should go back to Hedon and find her son, apologizing that she'd been unwell and hadn't known what she was doing; but, she pondered, that was no excuse, nor did it alter the fact that he needed schooling and she'd still have to leave him alone during her night-time performances and that wasn't good for a growing boy. He would go off to look for entertainment, she thought; I know he did that in Brighton. He must have been bored, poor boy, but it was a dangerous thing to do and he could have got into bad company. She sighed, and thought, not for the first time, that she would be considered a neglectful mother.

I should have taken a different kind of work from the beginning, she thought. I should have stayed as a cleaner, but hindsight is a wonderful thing and at the time I didn't know what to do about my *situation*, and who would have kept me on when they discovered my real reason for leaving home? And then, when I found I could sing for my supper, rightly or wrongly I made the decision to travel to London with the company and disappear altogether into their world. The theatre folk were very kind to me when I needed them most; they seemed to understand, and they accepted both me and my child.

She sighed again, heavily. If only I'd had someone to confide in, her thoughts ran on, but my one true friend had also left home to fulfil her own desires; she was more confident than I was, and more sensible, with good parents to guide her, and would have stood up for herself more ably than I did. I couldn't have told her, of course; it would have been a risk to our friendship, although I almost told her mother, until she uttered those fateful words.

I wonder where she is now and what she's doing. She wasn't in Hedon for the hiring festivity, that's for certain. With that shining beacon of glorious red hair I would have spotted her immediately. I was always jealous of her hair; mine seemed so dull at the side of hers. Delia gave a wry smile when she thought of the secrets they had shared, bar one, and how they had each thought herself plain when they were young, whilst the other insisted no, you're beautiful.

Ah, Jenny, she thought. Where are you now? With a fine husband and children? Or still bent on an independent career of your own?

After the first performance, she sat in a café with Giles Dawson, Fraser Macbeth, a magician, who swore that Macbeth was his real name, and Miriam Edgar, an acrobatic dancer.

'Monday night performances are never expected to have full capacity in the first week,' Delia said in a quiet response to Macbeth's grumble that the house was only half full. 'And I think you'll find that it was more likely three quarters full. I have performed to much smaller audiences than we had tonight and the management still broke even.'

'Tonight was a try-out,' Dawson agreed. 'Monday is the night for ironing out any difficulties and polishing up the acts, the lighting and so on.'

'I happen to know all that, thank you very much,' Macbeth sniffed. 'I've been in this game long enough.'

Delia didn't comment further, but Macbeth was no more than nineteen or twenty and she guessed that his skills with cards, magic boxes and swishing tablecloths had been honed before friends and family and in amateur concerts. Although he was quick and clever with a lively patter, she conjectured that this might be his first professional engagement. She herself was now a seasoned performer; she knew what an almost empty auditorium was like, when you had to imagine that there was a full house below you and not just a few people in the front row.

That night's audience had been warm and appreciative and although she realized that many seats would have been complimentary and some reduced for regular attendees, there would have been an assessment of how the various performances were received and she had seen a genuine smile on Dennis Rogers' face as he had said goodbye and thank you to the entertainers as they left the theatre.

There had been a winter theme throughout the show; the stage had been decorated with sparkling stars and silver trees, and painted reindeer amidst snowy hills on the backdrop, and after seeing it during rehearsal, and knowing how much better it would seem from the darkened auditorium with the spotlights highlighting the artistes, Delia had altered the order of her gowns, wearing a red crinoline with a white shawl for her opening number and second song; then, as the orchestra played, swiftly changing in the wings to reappear in a pure white floaty muslin threaded with silver over a white satin slip. She wore a small silver coronet on her dark hair for her closing song, and received rapturous applause as she returned to the stage and gave a deep curtsy.

'I thought it was very clever of you to switch gowns so swiftly,' Miriam Edgar told her. 'I haven't quite worked out how you did it.'

Delia smiled. Miriam was young too, but not as young as she appeared to be, for she had the slim lithe body of a child. 'Thank you. I'd arranged for a dresser to help me,' she explained.

She didn't give away the secret that she had also spoken to the conductor of the orchestra and asked him to choose a cavatina which would give her time to slip off the scarlet gown to reveal the white muslin beneath and have the coronet placed on her head by the dresser before the musicians began the opening bars of her final song. It was Giles Dawson, the violinist, who had been chosen to play the simple air and it had set the scene perfectly.

She thanked him as they walked back to the lodging house, and he returned the compliment by saying, 'It was a masterly touch. You should be top of the bill instead of the comic; I don't find him in the least amusing.'

'Nor I,' she agreed. 'But he's very popular and will draw in the crowds. They need a big name.'

'Mm,' he said, and Delia could tell he wasn't convinced, but she shivered when he went on to say, 'You know, Miss Delamour, if you're originally from this area, perhaps you should be promoted as *the return of the celebrated local voice of Yorkshire*, or something like that?'

She hid her dread of being so exposed and murmured, 'Oh, I don't think so. Audiences want to hear London stars and I'd prefer to be described as *fresh from London and the south of England*, as if I'd made an effort to come for their personal entertainment.'

He looked quizzically at her as he opened the door to their lodgings and she felt that he was curious about her, but polite enough not to ask.

On Tuesday evening there was a buzz amongst the performers. They had been told a queue was forming outside the theatre and the news lifted their spirits considerably. As the time drew near for the opening, Miriam Edgar slid on her stomach across the stage and lifted the bottom of the curtain to look out. She came back dusting her hands together and announced in a stage whisper, 'It's a full house!' Then, seeing that Delia had not yet emerged from the dressing room they shared with a novelty dancer who performed with shawls and floating scarves, she went to look for her and found her sitting in her dressing robe, in full make-up but not yet changed.

'You were right, Miss Delamour,' she said. 'Last night was almost an extension of the dress rehearsal. Tonight is the real thing.'

Delia smiled and nodded. 'It will be good,' she assured her. 'Enjoy it!'

She had dropped one of her songs in favour of something more lively, but would still make the gown change and end with a romantic number as on the previous night. The audience had appreciated the subtlety and she hoped they would do so again.

She dressed in her gowns, fastened a sparkling paste necklace round her throat and arranged her hair, fixing a few false wisps of curls on her forehead. Picking up the coronet for her final song, she was ready. Don't ever be late, she told herself, but never be too early. Anticipation is a key word.

She received rapturous applause, took two curtain calls and gave one short encore, but bowed off the stage when another was requested. It didn't do to upset the final act waiting in the wings; but neither did it do any harm to leave the audience wanting more.

'You were lovely,' Miriam said, after they had all taken their final curtain call and Delia had been given a rousing cheer when she appeared. 'You have the kind of voice that people warm to; not operatic but not saucy either. I don't know how to describe it.'

'It's kind of you to say so,' Delia said. Praise from a fellow performer was always well received and she always reciprocated in kind. 'I wish I had some of your talent for movement, and yours too, Miss Saunders,' she added to the novelty dancer. 'You are both so graceful and supple.'

'It's cos we're thin,' Miss Saunders said. 'We haven't got your lovely shape. Look at me.' She opened her arms wide. 'No bosom to speak of and straight up and down.'

Miriam nodded in agreement, and Delia was saying that they should all gratefully accept what had been given to them when someone knocked on the door. 'Somebody waiting to see you at 'stage door, Miss Delamour,' the call boy announced. 'Says that she knows you.'

There's no one here who knows me, Delia thought in sudden panic; it must be a member of the audience saying it just to be sure of seeing me. She had given autographs numerous times in Brighton, though rarely in London, but here? Perhaps audiences in Hull liked to meet the performers.

'Tell her I'm just changing,' she called back. 'I won't be long.'

She unpinned the false curls and quickly removed her stage make-up and dressed in her normal clothes, then picked up the picture postcards that she gave out to admirers and headed for the open stage door which led on to the street. Sitting inside on a wooden chair was a young woman with her back to her, and her coat collar turned up.

'Hello,' Delia said brightly. 'Are you waiting to see me?'

The woman turned. She was wearing a neat hat and a warm scarf. 'Dorothy? It is you, isn't it?'

Delia took in a breath. Beneath the hat was a smiling oval face and red hair. 'Jenny?' she whispered. 'Oh, Jenny!'

They both opened their arms to embrace the other. 'How lovely to see you! How I've missed you.'

CHAPTER TEN

It was just after ten o'clock, and Jenny suggested that they go to a small respectable hotel that she knew close by where they could be served with refreshments.

'It's a decent place, owned by a local woman and her family. Her husband is a doctor, and they make sure that it's quite safe for women on their own,' she told Delia. 'It's been here for years and I often use it for meeting friends. And they'll order a cab for me when I'm ready to go home.'

'That's very reassuring,' Delia said, and they walked arm in arm as they used to when they were young girls coming home from school.

The Maritime Hotel was well maintained, with areas of comfortable furnishings where small groups of people could gather for conversation, quite separate from the bar and restaurant.

'Miss Robinson. Good evening! How nice to see you again.' A young manager greeted them. 'Have you been to the theatre? I hear there's an excellent new show.'

'Indeed there is.' Jenny smiled. 'And here is the star of it. Miss Delia Delamour!' She introduced him to Delia. 'This is Mr Gosling.'

'Delighted to meet you, Miss Delamour.' The young man bowed politely. 'Welcome to the Maritime Hotel. Please,' he indicated a comfy sofa. 'Won't you be seated and allow me to offer you refreshments, compliments of the Maritime?'

They both ordered a glass of red wine and a sandwich and sat back with a sigh.

'Tell me about yourself,' Delia began, just as Jenny said exuberantly, 'It's so lovely to see you. Where have you been all of these years? You just disappeared!'

Delia nodded and stretched the truth. 'I did. I was so unhappy that I decided to leave. It was at the time when you'd gone away to York.'

'Yes, it was,' Jenny agreed. 'I'd finally convinced my father that I wanted a career in teaching, and he agreed, at last, that I could continue with my education. My mother was all for it but he'd been afraid to let me go away; you remember what a softie he is?'

Delia smiled wistfully. 'I do.' So unlike her own father, she thought.

'But why didn't you wait until I came back? My mother told me that you had called, looking for me. Or why didn't you write to me? She would have given you my address. We could have discussed why you were unhappy. You never said; why didn't you?'

'I couldn't.' Delia remembered the time so well, probably much better than Jenny did. 'I ran away. My parents . . . well, I never did have much freedom, as you'll recall.' She knew she would have to give a plausible story. I can't tell her everything, she thought. She would then have to take sides.

Jenny frowned. 'I wish you'd told me. I'd thought

for quite a few weeks before I left that you seemed quiet, as if something was troubling you. I was so full of myself and the plans I had,' she said regretfully. 'So you decided to just leave and prove yourself?'

Delia nodded. 'Something like that,' she hedged. 'I didn't want to end up as the family drudge.' She was relieved to see the supper being brought to the table.

'I'm not sure if I can think of you as Delia,' Jenny mused. 'I suppose it's more suitable for stars of the theatre than Dorothy Deakin?'

'I was sometimes called Dolly,' Delia reminded her. 'But I felt that Dolly was more music hall than variety theatre, and a friend I met suggested Delia and I liked the sound of it. So I became Delia Delamour, and Dorothy Deakin has gone for ever.'

'I can see that.' Jenny nodded. 'You are more self-assured than you used to be, and . . .' She paused. 'You're lovely. You looked beautiful up on the stage; and you've shed that nervousness you had when we were children.'

Delia smiled faintly. Wise and clever Jenny really didn't know her at all, and never had.

Jenny was silent for a moment, sipping her wine, and then asked, 'So do your parents know what you're doing or of the change of name?'

Delia heaved a deep breath. 'They don't know and wouldn't want to. They are not in the least interested in me or what I'm doing. I've written . . .' She shrugged, leaving the rest unspoken.

'I'm very sorry,' Jenny murmured. 'I'd be distraught if I thought my parents didn't want to know me, didn't want to hear about my triumphs or catastrophes.

Goodness knows, life always has a share of each.'

'It does.' Delia swallowed hard. 'Everyone needs a confidante. Did you really become a teacher?' she asked quickly before a compulsion to open her heart to her old friend threatened to overcome her.

'I did, and I'm teaching at a national mixed school here in Hull.' Jenny paused. 'I'd like to run my own establishment, but that's a few years away yet.'

'Do you get home very often?' She had to ask; this might be a way of learning how her boy was coping without her, and if he was staying with Jenny's parents or had been sent elsewhere.

'Not all that often,' Jenny admitted. 'Only a few times a year. I'm tied to the school schedule, but to be truthful I'd visit more often at weekends if it were not for Jack's wife, whom I cannot *abide*. They still live with Ma and Da after all this time. Ten years! They have four children and she doesn't lift a finger to help in the house or on the farm; my ma looks after the children most of the time too, especially little Molly. She's a darling, but her mother practically ignores her.'

Jenny beckoned the waiter over. 'Will you have another glass of wine, Delia?' She smiled. 'The name came easily after all! Do say you will, and then I must be off. It's a day of work tomorrow. One glass of red,' she said, when Delia refused. She didn't drink much alcohol, and thought it might prove to be the road to ruin for her.

'Where was I?' Jenny said, when her wine arrived. 'Oh, yes. Susan, Jack's wife. Do you remember her? Susan Barnett as was? She lived at the other side of Hedon? Very flirtatious. I never really liked her, and now she's so lazy . . . well, I hesitate to use the term that would suit her as I'm in such esteemed company. *And*,' she leaned towards Delia and lowered her voice. 'I'm inclined to think that she tricked Jack into getting married; it was done in a rush and their eldest girl, Louisa, is *beautiful* and looks nothing like either of them or any of her three sisters, *and*,' she emphasized again, 'Susan didn't go full term with her. An early baby, she said.'

Delia felt her heart hammering. 'What are you saying? That the child isn't Jack's? Why should you think that? When were they married?'

The sense of betrayal that she had always felt came back full and strong, and yet there was also a sense of triumph that Jack had been deceived.

'Not soon enough.' Jenny sipped her wine. 'I can add up, remember! And my reason for thinking it, and what saucy Susan doesn't know, is that I saw her canoodling a few times with Ralph Pearce, who's a snake in the grass if ever there was one.'

They chatted a while longer and then Jenny sighed. 'I'll visit home for a few days during the Christmas holidays, but not for Christmas itself. I couldn't stand it, even though Ma and Da will be upset. Selfish of me, I know, but I have single friends who don't go home either, male and female, and we'll enjoy a nice meal together here at the Maritime. Will you still be here? If you are you must join us.'

'Perhaps,' Delia said evasively. 'The theatre will be closed on Christmas Day . . . but Jenny, don't tell your family about me, will you?' She saw the look of disappointment on her friend's face. 'Please! I don't want my parents to know where I am. They haven't cared about me for so many years, and they would probably think that theatre work is only suitable for a woman of the lowest kind.'

'They might have regrets?' Jenny suggested, reaching for her coat.

Delia stood and picked up hers too. 'They won't. When I said I was leaving, my mother said don't come back, and my father told me to get out. I was seventeen.' A sob caught in her throat, but she went on, 'Those are the last memories I have of them; why would I think they have changed their minds?'

Jenny leaned forward and kissed her cheek. 'I won't tell,' she said softly. 'But I'm very glad that you've come back. I'll come to see you again, or I'll write to you care of the theatre, but please let's try and spend Christmas Day together. I've missed you; it's been such a long time.'

A cab had been ordered to take Jenny to her rooms in Pearson Park on Princes Avenue. Delia didn't know the district and Jenny exclaimed, 'Oh, you must come and see it. The park is delightful and the housing is new. The owner of the villa I'm in went abroad on business and has never lived in it. He lets off several rooms, only to women, mainly teachers like me or retired elderly spinsters, and we have the use of the kitchen and bathroom. It's almost like being in the country.'

She insisted that Delia should come in the cab and be dropped off at her lodgings off Church Street, and as Delia waved goodbye she worried that she had said too much. In a weak moment, would Jenny mention seeing her to her mother?

Would Mrs Robinson remember my last visit to their house that day? Will she recall how she sat me down with a cup of tea when I became dizzy and almost fainted? I don't know whether she realized that it was what she had just told me that made me feel sick and wretched and totally despairing; that Jack and Susan Barnett had gone to see the vicar about reading the banns for their marriage. I felt that my life was over before it had begun, and I wanted to walk down to the Humber bank and keep on walking into those deep dark waters.

CHAPTER ELEVEN

Peggy and Aaron had discussed what to do on her return from Hedon, whilst Molly was showing Robin around outside. Aaron was uneasy about keeping the lad. 'It's not that I don't want him here, you understand,' he said. 'I'm bothered that we might get into trouble.'

'I've been to 'Sun Inn,' Peggy said defensively, 'and that'll be 'first place anybody would go to enquire. I went to 'police station too and told a clerk but he said I'd have to go back when there was an officer on duty, and then I went to 'Town Hall, but there was nobody about to ask.'

Aaron shook his head. 'It's not enough.'

'Well, I don't know what else to do,' she began, but stopped when Robin and Molly came into the kitchen.

'I've been thinking.' Robin stood in front of them. 'If you're willing to let me stay with you for a short time, I'd like to do some work on the farm to pay for my keep. I don't know anything about ploughing and haymaking and things, but maybe I could feed the pigs or the poultry? The hens seem quite easy, though they are a bit silly and run about squawking when you're near them, and maybe I could progress to the pigs when they've had their babies. Molly said they're having some.'

He looked enquiringly at them and wondered why they were both puckering up their mouths and Aaron was covering his with his hand. 'I wouldn't expect any wages, of course, and I'll try not to eat too much, but I was also going to ask you if I might go to school whilst I'm here? Louisa told me that she went to the school in Thorn-gum-bald, but it's such a funny name that I thought she might be joking.'

Aaron began to laugh and took out a handkerchief to wipe tears from his eyes. 'She wasn't joking,' he chuckled when he could speak. 'That's 'name of 'village. My granfer told me that there was once a country gentleman living in these parts named Thorne and in 'same area were two gentlewomen called Gumbaud and the three of 'em owned most of 'land and estates round here, and over 'years 'village began to be known as Thorngumbald. Do you get my meaning? It's a corruption of their names.'

'I see,' Robin said thoughtfully. 'That's very interesting. Do you think that's how most towns and villages get their names, because of the people who once owned the land?'

Aaron viewed the boy with interest. 'Well, aye, I reckon that's right in 'main, though not allus. I think mebbe sometimes a name might come from summat else—'

'Like French or Latin or something, do you mean?' Robin continued his questioning and Aaron seemed flummoxed.

'Tell you what,' Peggy interrupted. 'Our daughter Jenny will be coming to see us soon; we're hoping she'll come for Christmas too, but we're not banking on it, and we can ask her if you're still here with us. She's a schoolteacher in Hull and very clever. She'll know, I expect.'

'Oh, good.' Robin gave a grin. 'And will she be able to say if I can go to school in Thorn-gum-bald?'

'No,' Peggy said firmly. 'That's something that me and Aaron would have to discuss wi' school and ask if they'll tek you, that's supposing you're still here and your ma hasn't come back for you.'

She looked determinedly at Aaron, challenging him to dispute the matter as Robin said a polite thank you.

Later, after their midday meal, Jack left the table muttering that he'd better get back to the field work; Aaron said he'd join him shortly and Susan slipped upstairs for a lie down, much to Peggy's obvious annoyance. Robin brought up the subject of pigs again as he hadn't received an answer to his question.

'Come on then,' Aaron said. 'Let's go and tek a look, and then I must get off to give Jack a hand.' He found Robin a pair of rubber boots which were rather tight and squeezed his toes, and Robin thought perhaps they belonged to Louisa. Then Peggy gave him a pair of hers, which were too large but more comfortable, and she mumbled something about getting him some of his own if he was going to stay with them.

Left alone, she washed the dinner things and prepared supper, scrubbing potatoes, peeling shrimps and skinning and filleting two large whiting to make a fish pie. When she had finished, she glanced at the clock. Robin and Molly were still outside, and making an instant decision she washed her hands, took off her apron and wrote a short note asking someone to put the pie in the oven at four o'clock as she was going to pick the girls up from school. Then, leaving the note and the pie prominently on the table, she slipped on her winter coat, hat and outdoor shoes and left the house, making for the stable block.

She pulled the trap into the yard and brought Betsy out from her stall, murmuring, 'Come on, old girl, let's you and me have a little jaunt on our own afore anybody misses us.'

The old horse snickered at her as she put her into harness and they pulled out of the yard just as it started to rain.

Good, she thought. I wasn't fibbing after all when I wrote that I'd fetch the girls cos it looked like rain. She drove out of the farm gate and up the track towards Thorngumbald, chuckling as she remembered Robin's pronunciation of the name.

She heard the bell ringing out the end of the school day as she pulled up at the gate. The rain was coming down fast and she reached down to pick up two black umbrellas. Then she saw the three girls coming out, with Louisa hurrying them along and turning up Rosie's coat collar.

'Louisa,' she called. 'Louisa!'

All the girls looked up and the two younger ones squealed when they saw her. 'Oh, Granny, hurray,' Rosie said. 'We thought we'd get soaked.'

'Well, you still might,' Peggy said, 'because I have

to slip into school and have a quick word wi' school-mistress.'

'I'll wait with Betsy,' Louisa offered. 'Emma and Rosie can wait inside until you're finished, Gran.'

Peggy gave one umbrella to Louisa, who stood next to the horse and shared it with her, and hurried back to the school with Rosie and Emma crouched under the other.

'Wait here,' she said as they entered the hall, 'and don't go off anywhere else,' and she scurried off to catch the schoolmistress.

'I won't keep you,' she began, when the woman looked up with a frown that said quite clearly that she didn't welcome the interruption. 'I realize you'll have had a busy day and will want to get off home, but I need your advice.' She quickly went on to explain that they had a relative's child staying with them, and wondered whether he would be allowed to come to school with the other children.

'It's a bit awkward,' Peggy continued quietly. 'The boy's mother is a widow, my husband's late aunt's husband's niece.' She saw the teacher's jaw go slack as she tried to assimilate the relationship. 'They've moved around quite a lot so he hasn't had much schooling, but now his mother has taken a situation in the London area – a very respectable position, you understand,' she added quickly, 'but the hours are long and she's worried about leaving the boy alone and mebbe mixing with undesirables and getting into trouble, as boys so easily can without an occupation.'

She paused for breath. 'She's hoping to come back

to this area once she's found a suitable position, and I offered – well, we have to, haven't we? – to have the boy to live with us until then.'

'Well, the boy should go to school,' the teacher affirmed. 'Strictly speaking his mother is not breaking the law if he doesn't, but by next year there'll be new rules regarding this, although we don't yet know the details. At the moment children in country districts can take time off for haymaking or potato harvesting – of which I do not approve, though Headmaster is more lenient – but it isn't allowed in the towns. Children should be at school, not working.'

'No indeed,' Peggy agreed. 'Our daughter is a schoolteacher and she's in complete agreement with you there.' Which was a downright lie, she thought, because Jenny was a countrywoman, unlike this one, and knew how the children were needed, not only by the farmers but to earn money for their hard-pressed families where every penny counted. 'So, it will be all right for him to come? He's a grand little boy,' she finished. 'Very bright and intelligent.'

The teacher pursed her lips and Peggy thought that if she made a habit of it she would have deep lines around her mouth before she was forty.

'Is there insufficient money in the family to send him away to school?' The teacher seemed to be trying to find another solution before agreeing, but Peggy clasped her hands together and shook her head.

'Nothing!' she whispered. 'All lost. The young woman is practically destitute, which is why she has to work wherever she can.'

The schoolmistress was silent for a moment, and

then said, 'Very well. If there is no alternative solution and no one else to care for him, he can start next Monday. If he's still with you by Christmas I'll discuss it with Headmaster and we'll review the situation after the holiday.'

'Thank you,' Peggy said. 'I'm much obliged.'

'That's quite all right,' the mistress replied in a softer tone. 'We must do what we can; I believe that all children deserve an education. What's the boy's name? I'll make a note in the school register.'

'Robin,' Peggy said. 'Robin Jackson,' and wondered why the name had such a familiar ring.

They arrived home, wet and bedraggled, and the children piled into the house to be greeted by Molly and Robin. Peggy rubbed the old horse down with a clean piece of sacking before putting her into her stall and making sure she had plenty of hay; then, straightening her back, thought, what? What was it that the teacher said? She couldn't quite catch the memory. Something about . . . ? She shook her head and closed the stable door behind her. She couldn't recall. It had gone, but it might come back.

She went indoors to find the fish pie still on the table and no sign of Susan. Muttering to herself, she put the pie in the oven and began to chop up a cabbage and scrape carrots; when she had done that, she quickly mixed up a crumble with raisins and cinnamon and popped it on the oven floor.

She opened her mouth to ask Louisa to set the table and then changed her mind. The child was so willing that it was easier to ask her than Emma, who always made a fuss, but no, the younger girl must learn to take her turn.

'Emma, m'darling,' she said. 'Set 'table, please, and don't forget we're nine now.'

'Nine?' Emma got up without protest to do her bidding. 'No, I'm onny seven, Gran. Have you forgotten?'

Peggy patted the top of her head. 'No, honey lamb, I meant nine of us sitting down to eat. We've got Robin with us now, haven't we?'

Emma nodded and went to fetch a tablecloth from the dresser drawer. Laughing, she said, 'Ma says never mind a robin, he's a cuckoo in the nest! What does she mean, Gran?'

Peggy clenched her teeth. 'I've no idea,' she muttered, but of course she had; and wondered how Susan could consider a small boy as a threat to her own daughters. 'Your ma has some odd notions, hasn't she?' she couldn't help but add.

'She has,' the child unexpectedly agreed as she carefully smoothed the tablecloth that hung lower down on one side than the other. 'Cuckoo would be a very funny name for a boy, wouldn't it?'

As Peggy dished up supper, serving the children first and noticing Rosie pushing the cabbage to the side of her plate, the remark that the schoolmistress had made still niggled at her. She brought a white onion sauce from the range and told the adults to help themselves. Susan, who had come down too late to help, took hers first as always but didn't offer to serve Jack or Aaron.

Peggy sat down with a sigh and glanced at the children, who were tucking in. Even Molly was eating heartily, in spite of having had a good dinner at

98

midday. Smiling, Peggy took up the serving spoon and put portions of fish pie, cabbage and carrots on her own plate.

Whatever it was the schoolmistress had said, she'd forgotten, and it annoyed her. It had been important, she was sure. She put her fork to her mouth and saw that all the girls had cleaned up their plates, except Rosie who had left her cabbage, but she'd excuse her this time, she thought. They've all got good appetites; everyone's allowed to dislike some things. She lifted another forkful to her mouth and then she remembered.

All children deserve an education. That's what 'mistress had said, and she said it sincerely, as if she really meant it. Peggy had not yet told Robin about being given permission to go to school, nor Aaron either, but she had something else on her mind. Molly, dear little Molly, who, they had been told, would never amount to much, would never go to school and learn to read or write, and yet was as bright as a button and knew the names of flowers, how puppies and kittens were born and how long it took for pigs to farrow.

Her meal forgotten, she looked across at Molly now. The eight-year-old wanted to go to school and be with other children and couldn't understand why she wasn't allowed. I'll have words with 'schoolmistress, Peggy thought. I'll ask her about Molly. We don't want a special school, or at least I don't; I don't think her mother has an opinion on the subject. She rejected her right from the start, but Molly needs to be with her family and friends, people she's comfortable with, not shoved off to someplace where she knows nobody.

So that's my next mission, and in 'meantime . . .

'Robin,' she said, and he looked across at her. 'I've got something to tell you.'

CHAPTER TWELVE

Robin's face was a picture of delight when he heard the news, as was Louisa's. Emma and Rosie merely looked at each other and shrugged, but Molly's bottom lip quivered and her eyes filled with tears.

'What in heaven's name are you playing at, Ma?' Jack pushed back his chair and stood up. 'He doesn't live here!'

Susan rolled her eyes and scoffed. Aaron didn't say anything, but he gave Peggy a slight shake of his head and pressed his lips together.

'Schoolmistress says he can until his mother turns up,' was how Peggy justified her decision, although she didn't admit to embroidering the tale she had given the teacher. 'And,' she added, 'he might as well be at school as be here wi' me.'

Molly began to bang the table with her fists. 'But he's my friend,' she howled. 'It's not fair. *I* should go to school. Why can't I?'

Susan was about to answer but Peggy lifted her finger in warning. 'Don't you dare say owt detrimental about that child in my hearing,' she snapped.

'I wasn't going to,' Susan spat out. 'But I think you sometimes forget whose child she is.'

The target hit home, but then Peggy answered in a tight voice, 'And I thought you'd forgotten, as you've so little to do with her. I suppose,' she added cynically, 'that when you and Jack and all your bairns move into your own place after you've had this babby, you'll find her very handy for all sorts of menial jobs that you'll be too tired to manage.'

'Now then, now then,' Aaron said loudly. 'That's enough, all of you.' He too pushed his chair back and stood up, but in his case it was to go to Molly, who was now sobbing with her head on the table. Louisa was patting her back and Robin was looking on in dismay. 'Come here, my lovely. Come to your grandda.'

He stooped down and picked her up as if she were a two-year-old and cradled her in his arms. She made no resistance, but snuffled into his neck, wetting his shirt.

'I'm off out to 'beasts,' Jack muttered. 'Somebody has to earn a living.'

'Aye, well, I'll be there in a bit. It's too dark to do ower much anyway,' his father said.

Jack slammed the door behind him.

Susan got up too, and with an exaggerated sigh pressed a hand to her back and began to slowly clear the dishes from the table.

'Will *you* let me go to school, Grandda?' Molly said, wiping her eyes and her nose on the back of her hand and then cleaning her hand on his shirt. 'It's not fair if I don't, is it?'

'Where's your hanky?' Her grandfather pulled one of his from his trouser pocket and gave it to her. 'Why do you want to go to school? Is it so you can be wi' other bairns? When I was a lad,' he wriggled his thick eyebrows and sat down with Molly on his knee, 'I was allus playing twag and then got 'cane for being absent.'

Molly gulped. 'I won't play twag, Grandda, cos I want to learn to read and play in 'playground wi' other bairns. Louisa and Robin'd mek sure nobody teased me.'

Peggy came towards them. 'We'll find a way, Molly,' she said softly. 'Me and you will go and have a word wi' schoolmistress and see what she says, shall we? Mebbe on Monday when we tek Robin?'

'Molly's coming wi' me on Monday,' Susan broke in, holding dirty plates in her hand. 'I'm visiting a friend and Molly's invited.'

'I don't want to,' Molly pouted. 'I don't like visiting; nobody speaks to me.'

'You're coming whether you like it or not,' her mother said spitefully, which started Molly on another bout of crying.

Louisa came to her. 'Shall we go into 'parlour and read a story before bedtime?' she asked. 'You can choose which one.'

Robin piped up. 'Maybe we can find one with an adventure. Do you have any of those, Molly?'

Molly jumped off her grandfather's knee. 'Yes,' she said, snuffling up her tears. 'Alice in Wonderland. It's on 'bookshelf. I know where,' and she raced out of the kitchen and down the hall until they heard her opening the parlour door.

'There's no fire,' Peggy began, but Aaron interrupted, 'They'll not notice 'cold, and if they do they'll come back in here. Don't fuss, Peg. I'll give our Jack a hand for an hour and then I'm off down to 'village.'

'Meeting your Harry?' she asked.

'Aye.' He shrugged into his working coat. 'If he's about. Find out if owt's happening down by 'river.'

Peggy sat by the table when he'd gone and decided that she'd have to have a serious talk with her daughter-in-law. They'd been at loggerheads ever since Susan and Jack married, never seeing eye to eye and particularly not on issues to do with the children. She would willingly have all the girls living with her, but she knew that wouldn't happen. And neither should it, she berated herself; children should be with their parents, but she was concerned over Molly's welfare. Molly was a special child.

'Peggy!' Susan came back into the kitchen from the scullery. 'I think I'm starting.'

'What?' Peggy looked up.

'In labour.' Susan's face was flushed. 'Oh, how I hate it. Can you get Jack? Ask him to fetch Mrs Glover.'

Peggy got up from the table. 'Already? I didn't think it was due—' She stopped when she saw Susan wince. 'Let me help you upstairs first, and then I'll give him a shout. There won't be any hurry,' she added evenly, 'if you've onny just started.'

'I don't know about that,' Susan gasped. 'I'd rather you told him now.' She leaned on the table. 'I don't feel very well.'

'All right. Try to keep calm.' Peggy recalled Susan's other pregnancies, and telling Aaron that their daughter-in-law's shouts would have been heard on the other side of the estuary. She slipped a shawl over her shoulders and went to the back door, and as luck would have it Jack came out of the cattle shed just as she raised her voice to call.

'What's up?'

'It's Susan. Can you nip up to Thorn and fetch Mrs Glover? You know where she lives, don't you?'

'I should do,' he grunted. 'I've been plenty o' times.'

'And whose fault is that?' she said cuttingly. 'Go on, and look sharp.' As she went back into the house she wondered what had happened to the kind-hearted and merry boy he had once been, and how he had turned into the miserable, discontented man that he was now.

She helped Susan upstairs and stripped the bed before going to the landing cupboard for a pair of old cotton sheets and a rubber one and making it up again. Then she went downstairs, filled the kettle and a pan with water, and put them over the fire to heat.

All the children were laughing when she listened at the parlour door. She made out Robin's voice, and then Louisa's, and smiled. They were entertaining the others and she heard Molly shouting and chortling. They'll be all right for a while, she thought. Another hour before bedtime, and then Robin had better sleep in the kitchen again. Tomorrow he could help her to clear the attic room and after that he could have it as his own.

She knew she would have to argue her case for allowing him to stay, but what else can I do, she asked herself. He's turned up here; I can hardly turn him away, but I'll make more of an effort to find his mother. Why did she leave him? No mother would willingly leave her child behind with strangers. Did she see him with us?

Did she know us and tell him to sit with us? Was she so desperate that she would do such a thing?

A shout from Susan startled her. 'Peggy! Can you come up?'

It's the only time she ever wants me, she thought as she hurried up the stairs. Susan was kneeling by the bed. 'I can't get up,' she said, her voice strained. 'I want to walk about; oh, God, I hope this'll be 'last one I ever have.'

'It probably won't be.' Peggy bent down and hooked her arms under Susan's to bring her to her feet. 'You're onny a young woman; just thank your lucky stars you're healthy.'

'I onny hope it's a lad,' Susan muttered, 'and mebbe Jack'll think that's enough. Five bairns are plenty for anybody. Oh!' She groaned, and bent over the bed. 'Did he get off to Mrs Glover's?'

'Yes. Come on, let's walk you about. I don't suppose they'll be long. Just tek nice long deep breaths. It won't be here yet.'

'What would you know about it,' Susan burst out. 'You onny had two! This is my fifth and I'm telling you it's on its way.'

There was a quiet knock on the door. Louisa with huge saucer eyes said, 'Can I do anything, Gran? Is Ma's baby coming?'

'No you can't! Get out,' Susan shouted.

Peggy put her finger to her lips and said quietly, 'Watch out for your da and ask Mrs Glover to come up straight away, will you? Then will you look after 'other bairns just as you have been doing?'

Louisa nodded, turned about and went down again, quietly closing the staircase door behind her.

106

Peggy put her arm around Susan. 'Shall we walk, or do you want to lie down?'

'No, I'll walk.' Susan leaned heavily on Peggy, and then muttered, 'I'm sorry, Peg. I know I'm bad-tempered sometimes, but I want our own place as much as you want us to get out from under your feet. But,' she went on even though Peggy had begun to protest, 'it's your Jack. He doesn't want to move. He says this is his home.'

She stopped and gave a yell. 'Oh! God . . .' She bent over again, and Peggy couldn't make up her mind whether or not she was playacting. It seemed to be happening too fast.

There came another quiet knock. 'Tell that little—' Susan uttered an expletive, 'to stay downstairs and stop bothering me.'

But it was Aaron outside the door. 'Sorry,' he whispered. 'Shall I wait a bit afore going out in case you need owt?'

'Just stop till our Jack comes back wi' midwife, will you?' Peggy whispered back. 'And then you get off, but don't let 'kettle and pan boil dry!'

'Righty ho!'

Peggy gave a rueful smile as she pictured Aaron tiptoeing back down the stairs, anxious to be doing the right thing, which was impossible with a woman like Susan. No matter how sorry she says she is, Peggy thought, she always manages to blame somebody else.

They both heard the rattle of wheels in the yard. 'Here they are,' she said with relief. 'Here's 'midwife.'

'Yes, I heard,' Susan said impatiently. 'They took their time.' She straightened up again. 'I'm ready to get back into bed if you'll help me in.' She sat on the edge of the mattress and Peggy heaved her legs up and put a pillow behind her back.

'I'll go and ask if she needs anything,' she said. 'Do you want me to stop, or—'

'No, I'll be all right now she's here,' Susan said. 'She's been to all of my confinements. She knows what she's doing. I wouldn't mind another cup o' tea, though, if you're mekking one,' she added.

Peggy saw her making herself comfortable, covering her legs with a blanket and shuffling on the pillow. 'I'll mek a pot,' she said. 'Mebbe Mrs Glover will have one too, if there's time for you both to drink it!'

If her last words were meant to be sarcastic, Susan didn't respond, but just lay back on her pillow and closed her eyes.

The midwife had taken off her coat and was washing her hands in the scullery sink. 'I hope you don't mind, Mrs Robinson,' she called out to Peggy. 'Your son said it was urgent.'

'No, not a bit,' Peggy said. 'There's a clean towel in 'top drawer. I can't tell if it's urgent or not. Susan says it's coming, but' – she glanced up at the clock – 'it's less than an hour since she felt 'first pain.'

'Less than an hour! Well, that's far too soon. Somebody'll have to tek me home if it's a wasted journey.'

'Don't worry about that,' Peggy said. 'I'll tek you myself if Jack can't.'

Peggy heard Mrs Glover mumbling to herself as she huffed and puffed up the stairs. The children were still chattering and laughing in the parlour and she decided she'd let them play for a little longer before bedtime if the birth of Susan's baby was imminent.

She'd made the tea and put a cosy over the teapot when Jack came in.

'Is owt happening?' He took off his jacket and sat down.

'Midwife's gone up. We'll know in a minute.' She poured him a cup of tea.

He took a deep gulp of his drink and then wiped his mouth with the back of his hand. 'I'm fed up wi' this, Ma,' he muttered.

She gave a small scoff. 'You're the one who's father-ing 'em!'

'I don't mean just 'bairns; it's all of 'bickering that goes on.' He lifted a finger to stop her sharp rejoinder. 'And I don't mean between you and Susan, I mean between me and her. She's never satisfied wi' owt I do or say, and even if we get another place it won't stop.'

'You'll still have to move, Jack,' she said softly. 'You chose her as your wife and she's your concern. You must find out why she's unhappy; it might be different in her own place. But we'll talk about 'bairns. You know we'll do right by them, and—'

But Mrs Glover was calling from upstairs, and Peggy got up to answer her. 'And especially Molly,' she concluded, going to the door.

'Can you come up, Mrs Robinson?' Mrs Glover said in an urgent whisper. 'Bring a bowl of hot water and a clean empty one and some clean cloths. Ask her husband not to go out. I'm afraid we have some difficulty here.'

CHAPTER THIRTEEN

Peggy collected the items that the midwife had asked for and told Jack not to go out as he might be needed. He nodded, but didn't ask if Susan was all right. As Peggy approached the bedroom door she heard the midwife say, 'You're a silly, stupid woman.'

'I've told you, I haven't done anything.' Susan abruptly stopped speaking when Peggy came in.

'What is it? What's wrong?'

Mrs Glover shook her head, her lips pinched tightly together, and then took a heaving breath and said, 'I don't hold out much hope for this babby, Mrs Robinson, and that's a fact.' She carefully took the bowl of hot water and cloths from Peggy. 'And 'other bowl?' she asked.

'I couldn't carry 'em both. I'll just get it.'

'Leave it outside 'bedroom door, if you please,' the midwife said. 'I'll get it when I'm ready.'

'Did you mek that tea?' Susan said from the bed. Her face was flushed and her hair wet with perspiration.

'You can have tea when we're done here,' Mrs Glover told her abruptly, reaching for her large black bag. 'You can have water for now. Bring a glass up and leave it with the bowl, will you?' she asked Peggy, who said she would and hurried away again.

What's happened? she thought. Why is Mrs Glover so sharp with her? Has Susan taken summat to bring 'child on?

She scurried downstairs again and an eruption of laughter came from the parlour as Rosie opened the door and headed for the kitchen. 'Oh, Gran, I need 'privy now. Quick quick. Can I have a wee in 'yard?'

'Yes, go on then. Don't wet your drawers.'

Peggy drew water into a glass and then, picking up the empty bowl, wearily climbed the stairs again and left them outside the door as instructed. Downstairs she poured herself tea and sat down at the table.

'I don't know what's happening, Jack,' she said. 'But there are complications.'

Rosie dashed back in again and he waited until the parlour door was closed behind her before he said, 'What sort o' complications?'

'I don't know.' She wasn't going to tell him what she feared, but then came an anguished cry from upstairs, followed by another, and they both got to their feet as they heard the parlour door open again. Peggy dashed out to warn the children to stay where they were.

It was Robin who stood in the hall. 'Is something wrong?' he asked, his face anxious and alarmed.

'No, it's all right,' Peggy told him. 'Nothing to worry about.'

'I said I'd come to ask,' he said bravely. 'The girls were frightened.'

She tapped her mouth. 'I'll explain later,' she whispered. 'Tell them it's all right.'

Jack stood at the bottom of the stairs as she went up again. 'Should I come up?'

'Not if you value your life,' his mother said grimly. 'You're likely to have something aimed at your head.'

When she went in the bedroom, there was a smell of blood and urine and Susan was stretched out on the bed, covered from the waist down by a bloodstained sheet.

'I don't want you here,' she snapped. 'Where's Jack?'

'Downstairs keeping out of 'way. What's happened?' Peggy's question was to Mrs Glover.

'Stillborn,' the midwife answered. 'Poor little mite was brought too early for him to tek a breath.'

'A boy! Oh, I'm sorry, Susan. I know it was what you and Jack wanted.'

Susan turned her head away. Rather oddly, Peggy thought, Mrs Glover turned her head too and concentrated on what she was doing.

Peggy put her hand on the midwife's arm and mouthed, *Where is he?*

Mrs Glover looked up and shook her head and indicated the dry bowl, which now had a towel over it, and then put her hand up to indicate that Peggy shouldn't look.

'I'll just clean up the patient,' she muttered, 'and then her husband can come up.'

'I want him here *now*.' Susan turned towards them. 'Men should see what women have to go through, 'stead o' strutting about and boasting that *they've* had a child.'

'Well, he's not coming up whilst I'm in charge,' Mrs Glover retorted. 'And if you want him here when, or

112

if, you have another bairn, then you can find some-body else to deliver it. In fact,' her face was red with anger, 'you can find somebody else anyway cos I'll not be coming back.'

Peggy crept out of the room. She wasn't wanted, Susan had said, although she was only going to offer to help clear up; she would have liked to see her grand-son, but she was fairly sure that he had been very early, so maybe that was why he hadn't lived and not because of her imaginings that Susan had in some way ushered the proceedings along. That, she thought, was far too dreadful a deed to contemplate.

'I'm sorry, Jack,' she told him. 'The bairn came too soon. Too early for him to tek a breath, the midwife said.'

'A lad! Oh, and I was banking on its being a son this time.'

'If you don't mind me giving you some advice, Jack,' his mother said carefully, 'I wouldn't say to Susan that mebbe next time . . .' She paused a second before adding, 'You might need to be a bit more careful for a while, let Susan recover.'

Jack stared at her. 'A bit more careful!' he burst out bitterly. 'Rosie's six, isn't she? How careful do I have to be, for God's sake? Am I to be completely celibate, or go off and be a blasted hermit?'

'I wouldn't know, Jack, and neither do I want to.' More than ever Peggy determined that they must find their own place and leave. 'You're to go up when 'mid-wife's finished, and then will you tek her home?'

Jack spent no more than a few minutes with his wife whilst Mrs Glover waited silently in the kitchen, refusing a cup of tea or a chair. When he came down, she simply nodded to Peggy and murmured 'Goodnight' as she followed him out of the door.

Whilst the kitchen was quiet, Peggy made up Robin's bed on the sofa, then collected the girls' nightgowns from upstairs and brought them down. She called them from the parlour and sat them down in the kitchen and told them that sadly they would not be having a little brother or sister after all, as the baby had been called to heaven.

'Your ma and da will be very sad for a while and your ma especially will want some peace and quiet, so I'm expecting that you will all be very good and not disturb her too much until she's recovered.'

'We heard a big shout,' Rosie said, and Molly interrupted to say she had heard it too. 'We'll be good and give her a big piece of quiet,' Rosie went on, 'and mebbe you could make her a big piece of chocolate cake as well, Gran, cos that will make her very happy.'

'She likes your chocolate cake, Gran,' Molly said. 'But she said we hadn't to tell you.'

Peggy controlled a sigh; she hated to think that her daughter-in-law might be trying to turn the children against her.

'Robin,' she said, 'be a good lad and tidy up in 'parlour; put 'books and everything away whilst 'girls are getting into their nightgowns, and then you can all have a cup o' cocoa afore you go to bed.'

'Ooh, lovely,' he said. 'Thank you. It does seem to have been a long day, doesn't it? And do you know what, Granny Robinson? It feels as if I've been living here for ages.'

'So it does,' she murmured. 'But tomorrow, Robin, I think we must go back to Hedon to find out if there's any news about your mother.'

Aaron and Jack were still out and Peggy guessed that their son would have followed his father down to the village hostelry to drown his sorrows. She felt tired herself and after checking that Susan was all right and making her a cup of cocoa and a cheese sandwich, which she said was all she wanted, Peggy banked up the fire and put up the fireguard, smiling when she saw Robin fast asleep on the sofa. He was a silent sleeper, just as Jack had been when he was little, and she remembered how when she was a young mother she used to put her hand on his chest to make sure he was breathing. Jenny had tied her sheets in knots as she tossed and turned in her bed, filled with dreams and imaginings and always with a bright idea as soon as she awakened.

She peeked in at the girls before going to her own bed but didn't fall asleep immediately; a wind was getting up and she heard the patter of sleet on the bedroom window. Winter's here with a vengeance, she thought; better get prepared. Mentally she ran through her head all the items they had in the larder, and what extra would be needed. Tea, sugar, flour, soap and soap flakes. We've enough vegetables; there's a sack of potatoes in the barn and plenty of onions. She was just nodding off when she heard the clop of hooves and the clatter of wheels and knew the men were home.

Aaron's feet were cold when he climbed in beside her and she grumbled at him and said he should have kept his socks on. 'Did our Jack tell you about the bairn?' she asked.

'Aye. It's a bad job, isn't it? He's right upset.'

'Is he?' She heaved a sigh. I suppose all men want a son. We were lucky to have one of each, but unlucky that there were no more. 'Did you see your Harry?'

'Aye, I did.' His voice brightened considerably. 'He asked if I wanted to go fishing on Sat'day and I said yes. A few of 'other shrimper lads were there at 'Humber Tavern. Two of 'Wilkin brothers, Fred Starkey, Frank Parrott, we'd a right old natter. It was good to see them.' His voice had a wistful quality and Peggy knew he missed his old cronies.

'You should go fishing more often,' she murmured.

'Mebbe I should.' He turned on to his side and put his arm round her, drawing her towards him and kissing her cheek. 'But I made a choice, didn't I? My place is on 'land now, not out on 'estuary or at sea. I've no regrets.'

She turned and returned the kiss on his stubbly cheek, which once had the tang of the sea and now smelled of the earth and the sweet scent of tobacco, and knew that in his heart he must once have had a few misgivings. 'Goodnight, m'darling,' she said sleepily, and was glad that he was safe by her side and not battling the deep waters of the Humber.

The next morning Peggy was up earlier than usual. She baked a batch of bread, then prepared some beef and vegetables for a stew and put it in a cauldron to cook over the fire. She began to fry ham rashers, knowing that the aroma would rouse everyone, before setting the table for breakfast. As soon as the children were off to school, she decided, she'd check on Susan and give her her breakfast, and then she and Robin would drive to Hedon and ask again at the police station about his mother.

I must be sensible, she told herself. She must be found. Then a thought struck her. I hope in heaven's name she hasn't done away with herself. Who knows what desperate straits she must be in to leave her son with strangers? Unless, of course . . . Odd notions began to run around in her head. Perhaps we're not strangers. Mebbe she knows us somehow. Has she met us at some time? I must ask my sisters, see if they can shed any light on the matter.

Jackson? Is it her married name or is she a single woman? Would a single woman leave behind a boy of ten? She would if she had a very pressing problem, but why here, if, as he says, they'd lived in London? Surely she'd have folks there who would have him. It doesn't mek sense. No sense at all.

It was extremely cold and she wrapped the girls up well with warm stockings, bonnets and scarves. She told them to go upstairs one by one to see their mother before going off to school, and this they did, and then Molly went up too, to tell her mother she was going out to Hedon with Granny.

'I didn't tell Ma that you were going as well,' she told Robin when she came down again, 'because I didn't fink she was very happy.'

'I'm sorry about that,' Robin said. 'Perhaps she's not feeling very well.'

Aaron popped his head round the door. 'I'll tek

'bairns to school,' he told Peggy. 'It's starting to snow; they'll be soaked afore they get there if they walk. I'll harness up owd Betsy, so tell them to wait. And I forgot to tell you last night that Barney Foggit has died. Funeral's at 'end of next week. His wife's going to live in Preston wi' one of her daughters so there'll be a smallholding going beggin'.'

Glory be! Peggy praised beneath her breath, though she was sad to hear of the old man's death. It'll be just the place for our Jack. It's a good house, and that land reaches ours so he can still easily work with his da. Her mind began planning: they'll be able to keep their own hens and grow vegetables and Susan can learn how to be a farmer's wife in her own home instead of feeling like a spare part in mine. Ten years – she must be as fed up wi' me as I am wi' her. We might even get to like each other once they've moved, though I wouldn't tek any bets on it.

Too early to begin enquiries, she thought as she prepared a breakfast tray for her daughter-in-law; we'll let old Barney be put to rest afore we put 'question, but there's nowt to stop us planting 'idea in Jack's and Susan's heads.

The children kissed her goodbye and she knew she'd miss them if they weren't living with her, but they'd pass by on their way to school and being only next door they could come and stay whenever they wanted. But there was Molly to think of; what to do about her? Would they accept her at school, and would Susan do right by her? Was she capable of understanding this special little girl?

CHAPTER FOURTEEN

Peggy took Susan's breakfast up and placed it on the bedside table. 'I've cooked a rasher and made you a cheese omelette. I thought you'd digest it better than fried eggs.' She'd also brought her a pot of tea and a slice of toast.

'Thank you.' Susan pulled herself up, wincing as she did so.

'I'm going to slip down to 'village and then go on to Hedon. Will you be all right?' She thought that Susan looked very pale and mentally added to her list some calves' liver from the Hedon butcher. 'I'll tek Molly wi' me.'

'Yes, I'll have another sleep after I've had breakfast,' Susan said. 'Thanks, Peggy. I'm – sorry I was so stroppy yesterday. Midwife was a bit rough; didn't seem to care.'

'She was concerned, I think.' Peggy offered up the excuse.

'I didn't do anything to hurt babby,' Susan assured her. 'I admit I took something to bring it on quicker; somebody I know had used this tincture of something and it had worked for her and she had an easy time and a healthy baby.'

'Ah!' Peggy was relieved to hear it, though not wholly approving. 'Mebbe he wasn't meant to be,' she murmured. 'Not all of them are. I had a miscarriage after Jenny. That was a great loss to me. But you must rest up now and think that mebbe it was for 'best. And you've got four beautiful girls,' she added, 'so count yourself lucky.'

Susan gave a droll laugh. 'Three,' she said, 'and Molly. She'll never come up to much, that's what 'doctor said, and he should know.'

'He was wrong,' Peggy said defiantly. 'She's a lovely, bright little girl and we must do our best for her.'

Susan nodded but didn't seem convinced, and pulled the tray towards her. 'Could you get me something from 'Hedon pharmacist while you're out?' she asked. 'I've got a pounding headache.'

'Yes.' Peggy turned to leave. 'I'm going down to 'village to ask about 'day of Barney Foggit's funeral. Did Jack tell you he'd died? He was a good age, as is his widow. She's going to live with one of her daughters, so I heard.'

'Is she?' Susan began her breakfast, so Peggy left, saying, 'I'll tell Jack to look in on you, but I'll be back by dinner time in any case.'

Well, I've dropped a hint, she thought as she gathered up Molly and Robin, her shopping basket and an extra shawl to put over her coat; whether it will drop on stony ground or flourish will remain to be seen. She called to Aaron as she drove off, to tell Jack to look in on Susan, and ignored his shout asking where she was going.

'We're going a different way,' Robin said as they took

a left turn out of the gate. 'I thought Hedon was that way?' He pointed back over his shoulder.

'It is,' Peggy told him, 'but I need to go to Paull first.'

'Oh, so will we see the estuary?' he asked eagerly. 'I haven't seen it yet, at least only from a distance. I'd like to compare it to the Thames.'

'What's the Thames?' Molly said.

'It's a river like the Humber,' he replied. 'Except, well, they're not just rivers – well, they *are* rivers, but when the Thames is in London it's a river, then it flows on all the way to Kent and becomes an estuary; I think that's right,' he said thoughtfully. 'It's because a lot of other rivers and streams and tributaries run into it, and then the estuary runs into the sea.'

'*Our* estuary runs into 'sea as well,' Molly said. 'I've seen it when we went to Spurn Point.'

'Have you?' Robin exclaimed. 'You lucky thing! I'd love to see that.'

'We can only go when 'tide is right,' she explained, 'cos sometimes when 'spring tide is very high, or in winter, Spurn is washed ower wi' seawater and we can't walk on it.'

'Why is it called Spurn Point?' he asked her.

She chuckled. 'Cos it's got a point at 'end of 'road; it's like a bent finger, and Grandda said its shape changes cos of 'sand and clay allus shifting.'

Peggy was listening to their chatter and was astonished at how much Molly had remembered from their visit to Spurn, which must have been at least two years ago. She *can* learn, she thought. She shouldn't be consigned to the scrap heap. She just needs someone patient enough to teach her.

'Oh, look! The estuary is right there.' Robin stood up in the back of the cart as they clip-clopped into the village. 'I didn't think we'd be able to get so close.'

The muddy brown choppy waters were right in front of them. Here was the road, there a fence, and below it the estuary. To their left was a lighthouse and Molly pointed out some houses and said they were coast-guard's cottages. To their right was a long street of houses and an inn on the corner, all with their backs to the water.

'I just need to pop into 'post office,' Peggy said. 'If I tie Betsy up here so you can see the estuary, can you both be trusted not to wander off, and *definitely* not go on to 'slipway?''

'Yes, of course,' Robin said. 'But can we walk by the fence and watch the ships and fishing boats?'

'I'll look after him, Gran,' Molly proclaimed. 'Cos I know how careful you have to be when you're near water. Even when you can swim. I can swim, Robin. Can you?'

'I've swum in the sea at Brighton and Eastbourne,' he said, 'but only in the shallows.' He was about to say more when he realized he would be giving away some vital information. 'When we were on holiday,' he finished.

Peggy told them they could walk by the fence, and then set off towards the main street, calling back that she wouldn't be long.

'Grandda used to be a fisherman.' Molly stood on the bottom rail of the fence and stretched up on her toes to look over into the deep water. 'He said when I'm bigger he'll tek me out in his boat.'

'Has he got a boat?' Robin asked in surprise. 'Where does he keep it?'

'It's tied up in Paull creek wi' some of 'other boats. You can't see it from here. Sometimes he lends it out.'

They walked alongside the fence until they came close to the slipway and the Humber Tavern, and Robin thought that had he been alone he might have walked down the slipway and nearer to the water where dark viscous seaweed gathered in tangled brackish clumps; but he had promised, so he wouldn't. But how exciting it was to know that the estuary was so close; he loved it, the smell of it, and the smack and slurp of the choppy waves dashing and splashing against the retaining wall, throwing up a salty spray that wasn't brown as he would have expected but a sparkling crystal shower.

It wasn't long before Peggy was on her way back. She had gleaned what she wanted to know from the post office, the time and day of the funeral, and having expressed her sorrow at the old man's death and agreed that he had had a long lifespan, had casually asked what was happening to the homestead.

'Our Jack and his wife are looking to move. They need a place of their own with four growing bairns; they want somewhere near to ours, of course, as Jack works with his da.' Dropping her voice, she imparted the news that they'd just lost a baby.

Peggy Robinson had a respected standing in the village. Her father, Bill Foster, had been a canny man who had bought up odd pieces of land that large land-owners didn't want and small landholders couldn't afford; eventually these parcels of land joined up and some he farmed himself, or his sons did, and others he let out to tenants.

The farm that Aaron and Peggy ran had once been one of these parcels of land. When eighteen-year-old Peggy fell in love with a Paull fisherman, Aaron Robinson, she knew that the only way she would be allowed to marry him was if he showed that he was deserving of her by agreeing to work the land. Peggy, sharp and decisive, had told him that it was the best piece of land her father possessed, and that he would still be able to go shrimping, since she would help him on the farm until their sons were old enough to help as well.

Aaron was an amenable young man and the idea of running his own farm had appealed to him; he had become a fisherman because his father and grandfather had been Paull Shrimpers too, and only sometimes after their marriage had he longed for the camaraderie of his fellow shrimpers and the smell of the sea as it flowed into the estuary bringing in its briny harvest. But he loved Peggy more than he loved the sea and it hadn't been a difficult choice to make.

'Right then,' she said, as the children climbed back into the cart. 'What do you think of Paull, Robin?' She clicked her tongue to urge old Betsy on.

'I like it a lot!' Robin said enthusiastically, adding, 'I wish I lived here.'

'Well, you are living here, aren't you?' Peggy said over her shoulder.

'Yes, but we're going to Hedon again.' His voice dropped. 'So I suppose you're going to try and give me away to a policeman.'

Peggy half turned her head. 'I'm doing no such thing!

Didn't I tell you that I've spoken to 'schoolmistress?'

'Yes, but . . .' He spoke in a teary voice. 'I'm used to being moved on. I don't think I'll ever be in one place for very long.'

Peggy drew the horse to a standstill; they had driven down the main street past the post office and the small school that served the children of Paull, and were about to turn along another road. They could hear the creak of masts and the rattle of rigging.

'If I don't enquire whether they've heard of 'whereabouts of your mother,' she told him, 'and she comes looking for you and then thinks I've kidnapped you, what kind of hot water will I find myself in? Eh? What if I find myself in trouble with 'law?'

Molly began to whine. 'Will you go to prison if you're in trouble, Gran? I won't like it if you do.'

'No. No, she won't,' Robin broke in. 'I'll tell them. I'll say that I wanted to stay.'

'And what will your ma say then? Won't she be upset if she thinks you prefer living wi' strangers rather than her?'

'I don't prefer it, but I don't feel as if I'm with strangers,' he said, putting his arm round Molly's shoulder and patting it. 'I wish she could be here too, but she's not, and,' he hesitated, 'I think she'd understand.'

Peggy explained the situation to the duty officer at the police station, and he said that posters would be distributed to outlying villages as well as round Hedon. Peggy hoped that the schoolmistress wouldn't see them, or she'd be caught out in a lie.

'They'd be better placed in Hull,' she told him.

'No, Mrs Robinson,' he said patiently. 'It's too soon for that. We have your details; we know where to come if she turns up. If she hasn't come back after a few months then we'll have to do something about the boy. We'll alert 'authorities and he'll be sent on somewhere, mebbe to a children's home or an orphanage.'

'I won't go,' Robin said firmly when they came out into the street again. 'I'll run away if I think they're coming for me.'

Peggy blew out a breath. 'It won't come to that,' she said. 'We won't let that happen, will we, Molly?'

Molly sniffled, and then shook her head. 'No we won't. I know a good hiding place, Robin, and we'll go and hide together if people come looking for you.'

Peggy smiled. 'So that's settled. Now we'll pop to 'draper's shop and see what we can get you for school; you'll need new breeches, a couple of warm jumpers and shirts, socks – let's have a look at your boots.'

Robin dutifully lifted a foot. 'Mm,' Peggy said. 'We can get away with a sole and heel, I think. Let's ask 'cobbler if he can do them now, while we wait.'

An hour later they were on their way home laden with parcels; commodities from the grocer, tender liver from the butcher for Susan, and an extract of willow bark that the pharmacist recommended for headaches rather than a laudanum tincture.

Not a bad day's doings, one way or another, Peggy thought as they trundled into the yard, and for some reason which she admitted to herself she couldn't put into words, she had a very pleasurable sense of warmth and satisfaction coursing through her veins.

CHAPTER FIFTEEN

'I'm going home at the weekend,' Jenny told Delia. She hadn't been to see the show, but had come to the stage door when she knew it would be finished to invite Delia out to supper to meet some of her friends who had gathered at the Maritime Hotel. They had had an enjoyable evening, but the others had gone now and the two of them were having a quiet chat.

Delia hesitated. 'Ah! That's nice,' she said, rather feebly, and Jenny gazed at her in puzzlement.

'I won't tell them I've met you again, if that's what you're thinking,' she told her. 'I've already said I won't. Though I don't know why you'd be scared of them *or* your parents knowing, for heaven's sake. You're a grown woman. You can do whatever you like; you're like me, you've no ties. We're practically, but not quite, emancipated.'

'That'll be a long time coming.' Delia gave an ironic laugh to cover her nervousness. 'But you're right; one day women will be able to choose what they do with their own lives.'

'We'll have to remain single until then,' Jenny said. 'As soon as a woman marries she's merely an appendage to her husband.'

Delia shook her head. 'You're such a cynic, Jenny. I feel enormous pleasure and exhilaration when I'm on stage and I'm as equal there as I want to be.'

'It's true that I might be a cynic,' Jenny agreed. 'I shall marry only when I meet a man who thinks the same as I do and I haven't found one yet. But what about you, Dorothy? Is there no man in your life?' she asked more softly, not noticing that she had reverted to her friend's real name. 'I always thought that you of all people would settle down to a comfortable life with a husband and children.'

Delia gave a bittersweet smile. 'To be truthful, so did I. I used to have these youthful fantasies that it would be hearth and home for me, with someone loving and caring. But,' she added brightly, 'it wasn't meant to be.'

'So,' Jenny persisted, 'there isn't anyone? What about the good friend you mentioned, or the violinist?'

'The violinist? No, I've only just met him. There's no one. I do see my friend from time to time when I'm in London or Brighton; he gives readings of Shakespeare and sometimes Dickens, and he's very good, very clever and amusing. But there's no romance.'

She thought wistfully of Arthur Crawshaw and wondered if he had asked anyone about her. Perhaps he hadn't missed her yet. Weeks would go by sometimes between their encounters, and only her agent knew where she was at present, for she had written to tell him that she was staying in Hull for the time being but wished to be kept on his books. I might need him one day, she thought, for the three-month contract would soon speed by. She thought how lucky she had been to be given this breathing space. But I don't want to move from the area yet, not until I've decided what to do about my boy, and at the moment I just don't see how I can resolve it.

Jenny had written a postcard to her parents telling them she would be on the Saturday morning train to Hedon and could someone meet her. Her father was waiting in the trap, with Louisa and Molly behind him.

'Your ma is preparing a banquet,' he joked. 'She's slaughtered 'fatted calf, brought in a full field of sprouts, carrots, cabbages and potatoes, and is cooking half a beast and Yorkshire pudding that looks fit to overflow the oven.'

'Have I been away so long?' She laughed. 'Hope she's making a sweet pudding too, cos I'll still be hungry even after second helpings.'

'Aye, apple pie and gooseberry crumble, so you've got a choice.'

'Will anyone else be eating, or is it only me?'

'I'll help you, Auntie Jenny,' Molly piped up. 'I like apple pie.'

'You do, don't you, Molly? I remember.' Jenny turned towards the girls. 'What have you been up to since I last saw you?'

'I might be going to school,' Molly told her excitedly. 'Gran's going to ask if I can.'

'And we might be moving,' Louisa said quietly. 'And I don't want to.'

Jenny turned to her father and raised her eyebrows. 'Really?'

'Aye, mebbe.' They trotted through Hedon Market Place and on to the long Thorngumbald road. 'Old Barney Foggit next door died recently and his wife's moved to her daughter's. Our Jack's got 'chance of 'house and land if he wants it. House needs a lick o' paint and a few other things but it's generally sound, I reckon.' He paused. 'It'll be convenient, being so close, but I'm not sure if he wants to move either.'

'He's a home bird is our Jack, but Susan must want her own place, doesn't she?'

Aaron lowered his voice. 'Don't know if she does. She'll be tied if she's to cook and clean, won't she? She's got plenty o' time now for gadding about cos your ma does everything; allus has done since they were first married.'

'But Da, that's ten years ago! Why does she expect Ma to do everything?'

He shrugged. 'Dunno. She's lost the bairn; did your ma write and tell you? A lad it was; never drew breath. The midwife blamed her, she blames the midwife. Anyway, now that she's up and about, she and Jack are going to have a look round 'house. It's got about two acres so they could keep some hens and pigs and a couple o' goats to keep 'grass down, grow some veg.'

'And do the girls want to go? Is it only Louisa who doesn't?' she asked quietly.

'Molly might stay wi' us. Your ma wants her to.' He dropped his voice further. 'She's bothered that she'll be neglected otherwise and I'm inclined to agree wi' her. And it's true that she might be going to school. Schoolmistress and 'headmaster are in discussion about it.'

Jenny nodded but didn't comment. She'd speak to her mother privately about Molly so that Peggy was under no illusion about the girl's education, or lack of it.

'I've got a new friend.' Molly leaned over towards Jenny, breathing heavily into her ear.

'He's my friend as well!' Surprisingly for Louisa, her comment sounded like a complaint. 'I met him first, Molly, before you did.'

'Yes, but he's my special friend now,' Molly insisted, 'cos he's teaching me to read Alice in Wonderland.'

'Is he? Who is this clever person?' Jenny turned back to the little girls again.

They both began to speak at once and Jenny said, 'Whoa, whoa! Louisa, you can tell me; you've had a turn already, Molly.' She saw Molly's lips turn down but ignored it; the child was too used to getting her own way with her sisters.

'He's called Robin Jackson,' Louisa told her. 'And I met him at 'Sun Inn in Hedon on Hiring Day and he had some dinner with us and then came home to play. And he's staying with us,' she said in one long breath. 'And he's started at school as well 'n' that's why Molly wants to go too, but she won't be able to sit with him cos 'boys sit at 'back of 'class.'

Molly started to wail that it wasn't fair and Jenny reminded herself that this was why she didn't want children of her own. Not because they might be born with a frailty such as Molly's, but because she valued her freedom, which she recognized as being totally selfish in many people's eyes.

'Stop that now, Molly,' she said firmly. 'If you're grown up enough to go to school, you also have to be obedient and do whatever the teacher tells you. Do you understand?'

'Yes,' Molly muttered reluctantly. 'But I can see him at playtime.'

'Why is he at our house? Your house, I mean,' she added quickly. 'Where are his parents?'

'Gran said we hadn't to say,' Louisa said before Molly could speak. 'Gran's going to tell you herself.'

Jenny looked at her father and he answered in a low voice. 'We don't know. His mother seems to have abandoned him, but you know your ma, she's intent on keeping him safe until she turns up again. She's tekken a liking to 'lad.'

'Oh, dear.' Jenny was beginning to wish she hadn't come. 'She can't just keep him. She'll have to report the situation to the authorities.'

'She's done that and they've put posters up, but there's been no response. His ma seems to have vanished. Odd thing is that 'little lad doesn't seem to mind. He says she'll turn up sooner or later.'

'Has she done this before, then? Gone off and left him? She needs locking up if she has. That's child neglect.' Jenny wrapped her scarf more closely round her neck and pulled her hat over her ears. 'Ooh, but it's cold,' she muttered. 'I hope Ma has a good fire.' They'd turned down the long road to Paull and the wind hit them with full force as it blew off the estuary. She glanced over her shoulder and saw that the two children had huddled beneath a blanket.

'Aye, she has. We've plenty o' logs, coal and kindling. We're well prepared for winter. Spades and salt at 'ready.'

'Have you been fishing, Da? Or is it too cold?'

'I've had a couple o' Sat'days wi 'lads. Enjoyed them; went out last night, caught sea trout and shrimps. We'll probably have them for dinner today.'

'Yum yum,' she said, and the little girls laughed behind them.

The house was as cosy as Jenny expected it to be. A fiery red blaze in the range, a simmering cauldron of fisherman's soup hanging from a hook over it and a good smell of roast beef coming from the oven. She thought how fortunate they were in their comfortable home compared with some of the children's families that she knew.

Laura and Molly ran upstairs to find their slippers while Peggy put her arms out to greet her daughter.

'Oh, Ma, there's no better smell than the one in your kitchen,' Jenny said, giving her mother a hug. 'I'm sorry I've been so long in coming.'

'Well, I hope it's us you come to see and not just a good dinner,' her mother joked. 'It was summer when you were last here.'

'I know.' Jenny divested herself of her outdoor clothing. 'There's always so much to do at weekends, but I should make more effort.' She glanced round the kitchen. 'No Susan?'

'Jack's tekken her and Emma and Rosie to look at Barney Foggit's old place, did your da not tell you?' Peggy lifted the kettle on to the bars of the fire. She gave a great sigh. 'I do hope she agrees,' she said. 'It's time they had their own home.'

'You make it too comfortable for her, Ma, doing everything yourself instead of asking her to give a hand.'

'Yes, but she doesn't do things 'way I like, so it's my fault as much as hers. And when she was pregnant . . . and then there's Molly, so I let her off.'

Jenny got up to fetch a teapot and cups and saucers from a cupboard, put them on the table and then took the tea caddy down from the shelf above the range. 'Da said she'd lost the child she was carrying,' she commented as she spooned leaves into the teapot. 'A boy? They must have been disappointed.'

Peggy sat down at the table and watched her daughter make the tea. She nodded. 'Jack was,' she said. 'He's not very happy. A son might have made things right.'

Jenny found a tin of biscuits, and bringing it to the table she sat down too and began to pour the tea. 'If it's not a happy marriage, having more children isn't going to put it right,' she murmured. 'But they've got to make the best of it, having made their bed, as they say. There's nothing to be done about it.'

'Aye. Problem is that they made their bed far too soon. He was too young and immature to be married, and then having a child so quick—' She stopped.

Jenny sipped her tea and chose a shortbread biscuit. 'Mmm. Nobody makes shortbread like you do, Ma. You're right, he was too young. Nineteen, but he got caught, didn't he?' She helped herself to another biscuit. 'When you've got a girl's parents breathing down your neck, what can you do?'

They heard the sound of voices outside and looked at each other. 'Speaking of angels,' Jenny said. 'Good thing I made a large pot.' She put the lid back on the biscuits. 'Don't want anybody spoiling their appetites,' she grinned.

Peggy laughed. 'I'll mek you some more to tek back with you. How long can you stay?'

'I'll have to catch the two o'clock train tomorrow,' Jenny said. 'Sorry!'

'And you won't be here for Christmas either?' her mother said resignedly and wasn't surprised when Jenny pressed her lips together and shook her head as the door opened and Susan came in.

'Oh!' she said. 'I'd forgotten you were coming, Jenny. We don't see much of you.'

Jenny gave a small smile. 'I have to work,' she reminded her. 'How are you, anyway? I'm sorry to hear about the loss of your baby.'

Susan pulled out a chair from the table and sat down. 'I'm all right. Disappointed and a bit sad. It was a boy, so Jack's cut up about it.' She gingerly lifted the teapot lid. 'Is there any tea left?'

'Yes, plenty; help yourself,' Jenny said. 'I'll have a top up, please, whilst you're about it.' She pushed her cup towards her. 'How did you get on with the Foggit place? It will make a good smallholding, I should think.' She laughed. 'I remember that Dorothy and I used to take a short cut across it between her house and ours when we were little, and he always used to yell at us!'

'Jack wants it,' Susan said. 'It needs work on it. Chimney needs sweeping. Distemper is flaking off 'kitchen walls.'

'There's still a sweep in the village, surely?' Jenny asked. 'There always used to be. So is that all that's needed? They've looked after it, then. And enough bedrooms? I've never been in it, have you, Ma?'

'Aye, many years back, before Foggit took it. It's a

good house,' Peggy said. 'Well sheltered by hawthorn hedges. Don't know about upstairs.'

'Three bedrooms,' Susan told them. 'One of them is onny small, but teks a single bed and a chest of drawers. That'd do for Louisa. Other two could have bigger one.'

'Three, you mean.' Jenny smiled. 'Didn't you have four daughters at the last count?'

Susan swallowed and looked at Peggy. 'Your Jack said . . .'

'That Molly could stay with us,' Peggy finished for her. 'Yes, we did offer. Depends on whether you'd want her to.'

'And does Molly have a say in this?' Jenny asked quietly. 'Won't she want to stay with her sisters?'

Susan gave a non-committal shrug. 'She might want to stay here now that she's tekken a liking to that stray lad Ma's tekken on.' She looked down at her fingernails, which were clean and short. 'But as we don't know his history or anything about him I'm not too sure about that. I'll not trust him with any of my girls, at any rate, until we know more about him.'

CHAPTER SIXTEEN

Outside the farmhouse the wind was beginning to howl and the windows rattled.

'Stray lad?' Jenny murmured as if she hadn't heard him mentioned before. 'Strayed from where?' she asked, always precise.

'Strayed away from his mother, or she's strayed away from him,' Peggy explained. 'At any rate, he's stopping here until she turns up, rather than be shipped off to a children's home or somewhere. Cos that doesn't seem right.' She rose from the table to give the soup a stir.

'And you don't know who he is?'

'We know his name!' Peggy stood with her back to them and behind her Jenny glanced at Susan, who gave an offhand shrug.

'Well, I'll not trust him,' she repeated.

'He's ten, Susan!' Peggy turned back to face them. 'He's a child, 'same age as Louisa and she's trusted wi' Molly even though she's vulnerable. But if you think that Aaron and me are not dependable enough to tek care of her after 'last eight years of doing so, then so be it.'

'I don't mean that, Peggy, you know I don't.' Susan looked flustered. 'I didn't say—'

'But you think that boy's a threat to the girls?'

Jenny could hear her mother's temper rising and knew that any minute now Peggy's normal good nature would blow and she'd say something she might regret.

'Let's calm down,' she interrupted. 'Let's talk about it responsibly. It makes sense for him to stay here, rather than be given up to the police, if you don't mind, Ma. I suppose you've notified the authorities?'

Her mother didn't answer, but merely nodded and stood with her eyes flashing and her lips clenched.

Then they heard the crash of the scullery door opening and a great draught came wafting through, along with the sound of men's and children's voices; Aaron was telling the youngsters to take their boots off and wash their hands before going into the kitchen and a minute later Emma and Rosie came through and headed straight for Jenny, followed by their father and then a boy with hair the colour of dark sand and a merry grin on his face.

Rosie wriggled on to Jenny's knee whilst Emma stood next to her. 'Hello, girls,' Jenny said, adding the obtuse remark which she hated when other adults said it when speaking to children. 'I do believe you've grown since I was last here.'

'Aye, well, you'd hardly expect 'em not to have done.' Jack bent and gave his sister a brief pat on the shoulder. 'Seeing as we haven't seen you since summer!'

'I know,' she sighed. 'It's work that gets in the way of doing what we'd like to do. And who is this young man?'

Robin came forward and put out his hand. 'Hello,' he said. 'How do you do? I'm Robin Jackson. I'm – erm,' he glanced towards Peggy, 'staying here for now.'

Jenny shook his hand. 'Are you? Well, how very nice to meet you. I heard you've made good friends with Molly and Louisa?'

He smiled rather bashfully. 'Yes,' he said. 'We have good fun. They like to hear me read.'

Rosie looked up. 'He does White Rabbit in a funny voice,' she chortled. 'Do it, Robin. Do it for Auntie Jenny.'

'Oh, it isn't the same without reading the whole chapter,' he claimed. 'Maybe we'll read it later, shall we?'

'Good idea,' Jenny agreed. 'Maybe before bed-time, or will you get too excited?' She appeared to be asking Rosie, but was actually looking at Susan, who was clearly unimpressed by this charming boy. Jenny wondered why she had taken against him.

'I won't get excited,' Rosie began, but was cut off when Molly and Louisa came into the room.

'I've found some duck eggs under 'hedge,' Molly complained, holding two dirty eggs in her hands, 'but Louisa says they'll have gone off and we can't eat them.'

'No, you can't,' her father said, and went to take them off her. 'They'll have been there for weeks. You know that ducks go off lay in winter.'

Molly shrugged away from him and dropped one of the eggs on the flagged floor. It broke and a stink of sulphur rose up.

'You see!' he said. 'Now give it here.'

Molly threw the other egg on the floor in front of him and began to wail.

'Oh, Humpty Dumpty sat on a wall,' Robin began.

'Humpty Dumpty had a great fall,' Louisa continued, and Molly began laughing through her tears, whilst Peggy hurried off into the scullery to get cloths to clear up the mess.

'Happy days,' Jenny said to no one in particular as Aaron scooped up Molly and sat her on his knee in the chair by the fire, and they continued with the nursery rhyme. Then she turned to Susan. 'I don't think you need have any worries,' she murmured. 'It seems to me that the boy might be a good influence on Molly.'

Susan heaved out a breath. 'I wish somebody was,' she muttered. 'She's beyond me.'

'It's not Molly's fault, Susan,' Jenny said softly. 'No amount of chastising will change her. It's simply a misfortune of birth that she's not the same as other children, and no one's to blame.' She looked up at Jack as she spoke, and intercepted an ice-cold stare at his wife that made her shiver. I wonder how they'll survive in their own place without the distraction of all the family here, she thought, but it's unreasonable to expect Mother and Father to deal with their marriage difficulties. That's something Jack and Susan have to work out for themselves. Till death us do part, she thought. She gave a deep inward sigh. Definitely not for me, thank you very much.

The wind became stronger and sleet came down heavily as they ate their midday meal; Jack checked on the fire in the parlour, putting on more logs and coal to make

140

a big blaze, whilst Aaron built up the fire in the range. When they'd finished eating they both got up to put on their coats before going outside again.

'I'll need to chop some more logs,' Jack said. 'It's a constant job.'

'Can I help?' Robin asked. 'I've never done it before but I could try.'

'Dunno about that,' Jack muttered. 'What will your ma say if she turns up and you've got toes missing?'

Robin didn't realize that Jack was being sarcastic and he responded seriously that she might say that he'd been careless.

'You were splittin' logs afore you were ten,' Aaron reminded Jack. 'Every lad should learn.'

'Aye, every country lad. Don't suppose town lads need to,' Jack retorted.

'Oh, they do,' Robin said earnestly. 'I've seen them, and bringing coal up from a cellar.'

'From a cellar?' Susan commented. 'So you've always lived in a town, have you?'

Robin nodded, but it seemed to Jenny that he suddenly looked uneasy. 'Yes,' he murmured. 'Or a city.'

'Aye, well mebbe,' Jack said. 'But I'm not doing it right now; we've plenty for 'time being. I've got 'livestock to feed first.'

'I'll give you a hand,' Aaron said. 'Then I'm off down to Paull, see who's about.'

'You were there last night,' Peggy admonished him. 'Your daughter's come to see you.'

'Oh, aye. Sorry,' Aaron said apologetically, grinning sheepishly.

Jenny laughed. 'Go on,' she said. 'We'll chat later

and you can tell me all the gossip when you come back. Here.' She reached for her bag and took out a small packet of something sweet-smelling and pungent.

'Ooh, thanks, love,' he beamed. 'Rotterdam Shag, my favourite baccy. I won't be more than an hour or so.' He headed off, the children disappeared into the parlour and Jenny stood up to help her mother with the dishes. Then Susan got up too.

'I'll see to 'dishes,' she said, and Peggy looked at her in astonishment. 'You and Jenny go and have a chat. I don't mind, honest.'

'If you're sure? Are you feeling up to it?' Peggy unfastened her apron before she changed her mind. 'That'll be nice. Come on, Jenny. Let's sit in 'parlour and catch up with what you've been up to.'

They hoisted Emma and Rosie out of the chairs by the fire; Molly, Louisa and Robin were sitting on the floor playing pick up sticks and the younger girls joined them.

'They play well together,' Jenny murmured. 'I've said to Susan I don't think she need have any worries about the boy.'

Her mother nodded. 'Susan's a bit on edge at 'minute, as we all are since she lost 'baby.' She shook her head sadly. 'If anything, they don't squabble when Robin's there. The trouble is,' she dropped her voice, 'Molly tends to monopolize him and wants him to play only with her. He listens to her and explains things to her; he's very patient.'

Jenny watched the children before speaking. 'I think he's more used to being with adults than with children,' she said thoughtfully. 'How many children do you know who shake hands with an adult on first meeting them?'

'None,' her mother said.

'I don't understand why his mother would leave him; and why here? He doesn't have a Yorkshire accent – has he said where he's from?'

'They came from London, so he said. Though he's also mentioned Manchester, and Eastbourne, and Brighton,' Peggy added, 'so they've been around a lot. Don't seem to have stayed in any one place for long, and he told me that they were always moving on. But it's a mystery why they should turn up here, unless they were visiting someone.'

'Do you have a deck of playing cards?' Jenny heard Robin say. 'I could teach you how to play Patience.'

All the little girls laughed. 'Patience,' Emma said. 'That's not a game! That's what you have to have, that's what our ma says.'

Jenny turned back to her mother. 'Sorry,' she murmured. 'What did you say?'

'About what?'

'About where they'd lived.'

'London and Manchester—'

'Yes, and where else?'

Peggy thought. 'Erm, Eastbourne and Brighton. Why?'

'Oh, I just wondered.' Jenny thought for a minute. Something stirred in her mind. What was it she was recollecting? Then she murmured again, 'He's definitely spent time with grown-ups. Only an adult would teach a boy to play Patience, but why?'

'No idea,' her mother said. 'Who has the time to do such a thing?'

'Somebody with time on their hands? Or maybe so that he could entertain himself.' You might think it could be a grandparent, Jenny pondered, but not one like my parents, who are working people. Somebody retired, perhaps, or not in regular work. They sometimes had gypsy children in the school where she taught and they were sharp and knowing and intelligent, but not all could read or write and she doubted that Patience would be the kind of card game that their parents would play.

She looked across at him now. He wasn't from gypsy stock, that was for certain: fair-skinned and that reddish, brownish hair; he could almost be a brother or cousin to the girls.

Her mother was speaking, asking what she would be doing for Christmas. Was she staying with friends? Who was cooking Christmas dinner? 'We'll have most of 'family here on Boxing Day,' Peggy went on. 'We'll all be to-ing and fro-ing between each other's houses, I expect; your aunts and uncles and all of 'bairns.'

And that's precisely why I won't be here, Jenny thought. I know I'm being selfish but it's like being with the Spanish Inquisition. All the aunts want to know why I'm not married with a houseful of children and the men eye me up and down and wonder why I haven't got a man in tow and what's wrong with me.

'I'm meeting a group of friends at the Maritime Hotel in Hull. We've booked a table. We're all independent and don't have to rush off anywhere. In fact I've booked a room.' She thought her mother looked rather forlorn, so she added, 'And the day after Boxing Day I'll come home and help you eat up all the extra food you cooked and didn't eat, and as everyone else will have gone home you and I and Da can have a nice cosy time together.'

Peggy smiled. 'Oh, I'm so pleased, and your da will be too. And you do know, don't you, that you can bring a friend with you at any time?'

She had said the same thing every year since Jenny had left home, and Jenny said again, as she always did, 'I do know that, Ma, but there's no one special that I'd want to bring.'

But then she remembered Dorothy – or Delia as she now called herself – and wondered how on earth she had managed not to mention her name.

CHAPTER SEVENTEEN

It was on the return journey to Hull that Jenny began to put two and two together and remembered who it was who had mentioned Brighton. No one around here would know much about the seaside resort on the Sussex coast. A young Prince of Wales had infamously made the fishing village a fashionable resort a hundred years before, and with the coming of the railways the coastal town had become popular with London day trippers; that in turn led to the building of hotels and theatres and made the town even more attractive.

It was a long way from the north of England, but Delia had been desperate to get away from her parents and would have wanted to travel to where they would never find her. But it must surely be a coincidence, Jenny mused. From his accent the boy was definitely from the south, but still . . .

She couldn't think straight. It was such a long time, ten years or more, since she and Delia had been close. They'd done everything together: romped in the playground, walked home from school, strolled by the estuary whenever Delia was allowed out . . . she didn't have the freedom that I enjoyed, Jenny remembered.

She always had jobs to do, serious work: cleaning the cottage, cooking, tending the vegetable garden, feeding the goats and hens – well, I fed our hens too, of course, but it was never my sole responsibility.

Both Jack and I had to help out on the farm, Jack because it was expected that he would work there when he left school, and me because it was assumed, wrongly, that I would eventually become a farmer's wife. But school work and playing with friends was of paramount importance too, for us, and our parents knew that, but it wasn't the same for Delia. She wasn't allowed any opinions and her free time was strictly curtailed.

And then she remembered that if she called for Delia she wasn't allowed into the cottage if Mr or Mrs Deakin was there. I had to stand on the doorstep and more often than not I was told that Dorothy – Delia – couldn't come out until she had finished whatever it was she was doing.

But why did she run away? What was the final hurt that made her decide that she couldn't stay at home any longer but must plough her own furrow, to use a farming term? Jenny had often worried that her father might have beaten her; quite often she had a bruise on her legs or arms. She sighed. Perhaps one day she might tell me.

Jenny had thought of walking from the train station to her rooms in the park; it was a pleasant walk along the Spring Bank and not too far, but as she left the concourse she saw that it was sleeting hard and it was quite dark so she decided to hire a cab and was home in just under fifteen minutes.

Bliss, she sighed as she climbed the stairs, which were dimly lit by gaslight from a ceiling lamp in the hall, unlocked her door on the first-floor landing and reached for the box of matches that she kept inside the door to light her own lamp. She turned up the wick and as the flame glowed brighter she glanced around in satisfaction at her living room with its comfy sofa, the fireplace where she had left the grate filled with paper, kindling and coal ready to light, her table covered with a chenille cloth with a space to place the lamp, the ornaments on the side dresser, the paintings on the wall and her precious bookcase filled with her favourite books.

She was a neat and tidy person and everything was in its place. 'I love to visit my family, but I don't think I could ever live with anyone else again,' she murmured. 'It would upset my equilibrium.'

It wasn't until she had changed from her travelling clothes into something more comfortable, put on her slippers, and eaten the bread and ham her mother had insisted she should bring home, along with a bag of shortbread biscuits just made that morning, that her thoughts drifted back to the boy.

'Where was I with that?' she mumbled, breaking into the habit she had of talking to herself. 'What was the connection?'

She sipped a cup of tea, nibbled on a biscuit and stretched her feet towards the fire. I don't think there is one, she decided. Delia didn't say that she had lived in Brighton, just that she had played in a theatre there. Perhaps his family were Londoners and they'd been to the coast for holidays. Then she sat forward. But why did they arrive in such an out of the way place as Paull? Even people from Hull don't know where it is.

Ah! Of course! She put down her cup. He wasn't taken there deliberately; he had been in Hedon at the hiring fair and simply joined the children when they went home. He could just as well have turned up anywhere. Thorngumbald or Camerton, Burton Pidsea or Burstwick, or any of the villages round about. There's no mystery about it – I must write to my mother and tell her she's got hold of the wrong end of the stick.

The show was in its final week before the theatre closed to prepare for the annual pantomime. Delia had written to her agent to ask if there were any short gaps she could fill in this area, but he'd replied to say there was a vacancy in Leeds, but nothing closer.

I was lucky to find this booking, she thought as she curled up on a chair in her lodgings one evening. But what shall I do now? I have to earn some money; I won't be paid whilst I'm not appearing even though I have the contract for the next show. Do I take the Leeds booking to tide me over?

She put her head in her hands. I don't know what to do. I'm no further on than I was before. She took a deep breath. I must tell Jenny when I see her that I can't join her and her friends on Christmas Day. I don't have that kind of money to spend. Jenny has a regular salary, and although I don't suppose it's huge, it will be a lot more than I can earn. I really do have to sing for my supper.

She began to undress and brush her hair; her stage make-up she had removed before she left the theatre.

Giles Dawson had been waiting to walk with her to their shared lodgings.

'It's good of you to wait,' she'd said.

'Not at all.' He'd smiled. 'Can't have a lovely lady walking alone at this time of night.'

'You're very gallant, Mr Dawson.' She'd accepted the offer of his arm. She felt comfortable with him, as she always had done with Arthur Crawshaw; there was no flirting or flippant dalliance from either of them, just straightforward friendship, which she regarded as unusual but what she was happiest with.

She'd asked him what he would be doing next. Would he be staying on with the theatre orchestra?

'Yes, if they want me,' he'd said. 'What about you?'

'Well, I don't do pantomime, so I must find something else. There's a vacancy in Leeds if I want to apply, but . . .'

'That's not far,' he was quick to point out. 'You might not want to come back to Hull every night, even if there's a late train, but if you're called back for any, erm, family problems you could be here the next day.'

She'd been almost on the point of telling him about her son, but she had held back. What would he think of her? He would of course immediately guess that Jack had been born out of wedlock, which was true, but his view of her would then be warped.

So I didn't, she thought as she lit a candle beside her bed and drew back the covers, but there are times when I would like to take *someone* into my confidence. I was often on the edge of sharing my story with Arthur, but I didn't want to lose his friendship either.

And the odd thing was, she pondered, that he had

never asked. It was as if he accepted me as I was, a young woman with a son and no husband in tow. Perhaps he was typical of theatre folk, used to the vagaries of characters who choose to hide behind a mask rather than reveal their real selves.

But what to do now? I'll ask Mr Rogers if he's still planning a show after the pantomime, as he told me. Of course, he might want a different cast entirely, but I'm fairly sure he won't break my contract. He seems an honest man.

She drew her legs into bed and put her head on the pillow. I just need something to tide me over. I could apply to be a temporary shop girl, just to earn enough for my lodgings. Other ideas flitted through her mind, and she thought too of the story she must spin to Jenny when she told her that she wouldn't be at the Maritime for Christmas Day lunch.

Unless . . . she suddenly sat up as a notion – a plan – broke into her meandering thoughts. Just suppose . . . what if . . . ? The Maritime was a lovely hotel. It had a comfortable lounge, and a very select dining room with a grand piano; she had run her fingers over the keys when she'd been there with Jenny. She couldn't play – she'd never been taught; they hadn't had the luxury of a piano at home – but she knew a few notes of several songs.

Perhaps – the idea took hold – perhaps I'll call tomorrow. Her self-esteem was often very low and she was inclined to be pessimistic, but she forced herself now to consider how she would offer such a concept, with herself as the prize.

* * *

The rain was heavy the next morning and after breakfast she asked the landlady if she could loan her an umbrella.

'You're never going out in this?' Giles Dawson asked. He had only just come down for breakfast, leaving it until the very last minute before the kitchen closed.

'I am,' she assured him. 'I thought of something last night and I must strike whilst the iron's hot.' She smiled. 'Otherwise I might change my mind.'

He looked at her and grinned. 'Perhaps you'd iron a couple of shirts for me whilst you're about it!' he said.

She raised her eyebrows. 'I'm out of practice,' she parried back. 'Maybe the landlady will oblige!'

From Church Street to the Maritime wasn't far, but nevertheless in spite of the umbrella she was soaked by the time she got there. The hotel was only just opening and she asked if Mr Gosling was available. Whilst the porter went to fetch him, Delia tidied up her hair, tucking it beneath her hat and checking herself in one of the mirrors in the lounge where she had been asked to wait.

'Miss Delamour! Good morning.'

Delia was pleased that he remembered her, and when he asked how he could help her she told him that she had a proposition.

'Please, won't you take a seat. Would you like a pot of coffee?'

He was most affable, she thought as she refused his offer, and her tension began to ease. He can say yes or no, she thought. That's all.

'You may know that the theatre where I am performing will be closing at the end of the week to prepare for the pantomime season,' she told him. 'And I'm in rather a quandary as to what to do next. I have the promise of another contract for next year and I would quite like to stay in this district until then, rather than go back to London. I am sure you will be having extra guests over the Christmas holiday, and I wondered how you would feel about having a singer to entertain them? Say in the afternoons and evenings?'

She saw by his expression that he was considering the proposal with interest and not dismissing it out of hand, and she added, 'I can sing without music, although you have a piano on which I could play a few notes as an introduction, although I'm not a pianist.'

'It sounds like an excellent idea, Miss Delamour,' he said, 'I will have to ask the owners of the hotel as I can't make the decision. There would be your fee, of course, but—'

Delia saw another opportunity. 'Are you fully booked?'

'Almost,' he said. 'We have clients who come for Christmas lunch or evening meals, but some do stay for a few days.'

'Well, I wonder how the owners would feel about paying a smaller fee and including my bed and board in lieu of my entertainment?' She smiled. 'So I would sing for my supper, and lunch and tea as well?'

'What a marvellous idea,' he said enthusiastically. 'I'll ask them. Mrs Lucan and her family are always open to ideas and suggestions to enhance the attractions of the hotel. Where are you staying? I'll slip round with a note as soon as they decide.' He smiled. 'Are you sure you won't have some coffee?'

'Perhaps I will after all,' she agreed. 'Why not, indeed?'

153

CHAPTER EIGHTEEN

As Christmas drew near and the children at school practised their carols, Robin began to feel rather sad. Although he was loving being at school and being given challenges in the lessons, he'd never been away from his mother at Christmas before, he thought as he sat in the schoolroom with Louisa to eat their midday bread and beef. Louisa called it dinner, but he couldn't work out why, when they had another hot dinner when they returned to Granny Robinson's house after school.

It had been decided that Louisa, Emma and Rosie and their parents would be moving to the other house after Christmas. Jack was cleaning and painting it with the help of Aaron, and Susan had been sewing curtains from material that Granny Robinson had found in the bottom of a cupboard. Granny Robinson said it was good hard-wearing material and would be suitable for keeping out any draughts; Susan hadn't liked the colour but when it was suggested that she could dye it she said it would do for the time being.

Robin had thought that perhaps Susan was rather lazy, and that if Louisa's granny had offered to do it for her she might have agreed, only Granny Robinson didn't offer.

He knew that he would miss Louisa when they went. Molly was staying with Granny Robinson and Aaron and not moving with the others, and although he thought she was a nice little girl he liked Louisa better than anybody, even more than Ben, who was Louisa's cousin and sat next to her in class.

Molly was starting school for a trial period after Christmas. The headmaster had told Mrs Robinson that he would make an announcement in assembly before they broke up for the holiday, to tell the children that no one must tease Molly or call her names. Robin wondered why anyone would do such a thing, but sometimes Molly could be difficult if she didn't get her own way. She was also telling everyone that she was going to sit next to Robin and he was a little worried about that too. She was such a chatterbox that he thought he might not be able to concentrate on his schoolwork.

When the girls' Auntie Jenny had come to visit, he'd seen her give a cardboard box of wrapped parcels to her mother and he'd guessed that they were Christmas presents for her nieces. Then she'd glanced at him and although he pretended not to notice he saw that she was whispering that she hadn't brought anything for him, but then she shuffled about in another bag and handed her mother something else. He hadn't expected a present, because after all she hadn't known he was there, but he knew he would feel outside the circle when parcels were being handed out if he didn't get one too.

Then he wondered if he should leave and try to find

his mother, for he thought that she might be lonely without him, but he had no idea of where she might be. 'Louisa,' he said. 'Where do *you* think my mother might have gone?'

Louisa was about to take a bite of bread, but she stopped. 'I don't know,' she said. 'I don't know anything about her. Does she work? Some ladies do, especially if they haven't a husband to give them any money.'

'Yes,' he said, 'she does. Or at least it's a kind of work, although it isn't *hard* work, not like scrubbing floors or working in a shop.' He wondered if she'd got a booking in one of the Hull theatres, but then thought that he'd better not mention it to Louisa in case she accidentally told someone who then might tell a policeman and he didn't want his mother to get into trouble for having left him behind.

I'd be quite happy to stay here, he thought, as long as I could see my mother sometimes and know that she wasn't unhappy.

'We could go and search for her in the school holidays if you like,' Louisa said. 'But where would we start looking? I don't think she'll be in Paull. She might be in Hedon, but I think Gran would have found out. She knows *everybody* in Hedon, so somebody would have told her.'

'I don't know what my mother would do in Hedon. I don't think it's her kind of place.'

'What is her kind of place?' she asked, and then took a large bite of bread and beef so she couldn't speak again for a few minutes.

'Somewhere like London or Brighton,' he said gloomily. 'But that's no good, because they're both a long way away and I haven't any money for the train.'

'If it's such a long way, why did she come?' Louisa asked eventually, chewing on a piece of meat. 'Does she know somebody who lives round here?'

He nodded. 'Erm, yes, I think she did, once.'

It wasn't quite a lie, he thought as he continued to eat, although the old woman that they had called upon couldn't have been her mother, because he had heard her say quite distinctly that she hadn't got a daughter; so either Delia had gone to the wrong house or else her parents had moved to live somewhere else. And maybe, he thought in sudden clarification, she's gone to look for them.

He felt slightly happier now that he might have solved the puzzle, because it meant that she would eventually return. Except, he thought guiltily, I like it here and don't really want to go back to living in lodgings, not even in London. I like the countryside; I like the smells and the animals, and seeing the ships on the estuary, and yesterday morning I saw *hundreds* of ducks and geese flying towards their feeding ground; at least that's where Louisa said they were going, and she also said that some birds live abroad in the summer and come back here in the winter.

Louisa knows a lot about the countryside and flowers and plants and animals and things. She said that when she grows up she'd like to grow plants and flowers to help people if they had a headache or a pain anywhere and it would save them from having to go to a doctor, especially if they were very poor and couldn't afford to pay to visit one. But she said that first she would have to study botany and learn more about it

157

and she didn't know if her mother or father would let her do that. They might send her to work in service which means cleaning someone else's house and waiting on table and things like that.

I don't often get a headache, he considered. I'm very healthy. Mother always said that I was, so that makes me healthy as well as useful; Mr Arthur Crawshaw told me that both of those were most worthwhile *attributes*, which he said meant qualities. So really I don't have much to worry about, he pondered, and took another bite of his bread; but that doesn't mean I don't feel sad sometimes.

Jenny went to the final Saturday performance of the show before it closed. Delia was in good voice, she thought as she listened from her front row seat, and she wondered who had taught her; except at school, she couldn't recall ever hearing her sing when they were young, but then she maybe didn't have much to sing about. However, she did remember that at the school Christmas carol service, when their parents and the vicar and the Sunday school teacher came to hear them, Miss Scrowston who taught them music and games always told Delia to stand at the back of their group so that her voice carried over the top of everyone else's.

She never sang at any other time, Jenny thought, never hummed a tune, never in my presence anyway. Poor Delia. I wonder if she was always unhappy and never said.

She waited for her at the stage door and saw her hunched into her coat as she came towards her.

'Jenny,' Delia said as if surprised. 'Have you been to the show?'

'Yes, didn't you see me? I was in the front row.'

'No,' Delia said. 'The lights are very bright and I tend to look into the distance, which makes most members of the audience think I'm looking directly at them.'

'Are you joining me for supper?' Jenny asked. 'I've booked a table.'

'Just for the two of us? Yes, all right. That will be nice.' She hesitated. 'I'll just tell Giles, then he won't worry that I'm walking back alone.'

She re-joined Jenny a few minutes later and together they set off for the Maritime. They both huddled into their coats and scarves, as the weather was turning bitterly cold.

'Is Giles becoming a special friend?' Jenny asked.

'No, I told you, I only met him when I first came to Hull. I'd just got off the train from Hedon and saw him – on the – station platform . . .' Too late she realized that she'd given herself away.

Jenny turned to her as they walked. 'You went to Hedon? When was that?'

'When – I first came back – I went to Hedon, and then walked to Paull to see my parents.' She swallowed hard. 'Well, only my mother. I suspect my father was down in one of the village hostelries, but in any case it doesn't matter where he was because my mother didn't want to speak to me. She didn't even open the door more than a crack.' Her voice was choked and she felt as if she couldn't breathe. 'She told me I wasn't welcome.'

'For heaven's sake!' Jenny exploded, and shepherded

Delia down towards the Maritime. 'What on earth is the matter with the woman? Did you commit a crime or something?' She pushed the door open into the hotel and they were greeted by warmth and chatter and then a welcome from Mr Gosling.

'Good evening, Miss Robinson. Good evening, Miss Delamour. How lovely to see you both.' He gave Delia a complicit smile and a raised eyebrow and nodded his head very slightly.

'Good evening, Mr Gosling,' Jenny replied for both of them. 'We're in fearful need of a brandy to warm us, if you please. Miss Delamour is frozen through and she mustn't catch a chill; it will play havoc with her voice.'

'Oh, indeed!' He pushed first one chair and then another towards a fireplace where a bright fire was burning. 'Come,' he said. 'Sit down and warm yourselves. Perhaps some hot punch might be acceptable?'

'Lovely, thank you,' Jenny said, whilst Delia gave him a weak smile of acceptance.

When the punch and a plate of biscuits had been brought Jenny urged Delia to take a drink to calm her before she said quietly, 'Why didn't you tell me before? You've been holding this in ever since we met again. Surely you could have trusted me?'

Delia turned moist eyes towards her friend. 'I'm sorry,' she whispered. 'I've kept everything to myself for such a long time that I've forgotten how to trust. My friend down south is the only person I could have confided in, and I haven't told even him everything about myself.'

Something niggled at the back of Jenny's mind.

'Why would I tell him?' Delia continued, her tongue

loosening from the effect of the punch. 'Why would I risk losing his friendship merely to unburden myself?'

'If he's a true friend you wouldn't lose it,' Jenny said confidently. 'You wouldn't lose mine if you unburdened yourself to me.'

Delia felt totally miserable. Was that true? Could she risk losing Jenny's friendship if she confessed when they had just found each other again? Jenny would be torn in two, unlike Arthur who could simply walk away. But then, would he? He was very fond of Jack; often called him *my boy* when they met.

'Arthur is a gentleman,' she said. 'A real gentleman, I mean. He's different from anyone else I know. I think he's been brought up by a different set of rules. In fact I doubt if his parents even know that he appears on the stage. He certainly doesn't do it for the money, but for the pleasure of telling a tale.'

'He sounds fascinating,' Jenny said and took a proffered menu from a young maid. 'I'd like to meet him one day.'

They chose food from the menu, Delia selecting something light and not too expensive, which Jenny noted but didn't remark upon. Instead she said, 'I was going to tell you about my visit home.'

Delia held her breath. What was she about to hear? Is my boy still there? Because if he isn't, if they've sent him on somewhere else, then I must go and look for him.

'What?' Jenny said. 'Are you all right?'

'Yes, yes, perfectly,' Delia mumbled.

Jenny gave a slight frown, and then went on. 'It was the usual frenzy, but the good news is that Jack and Susan are moving out. Do you remember Barney Foggit? Well, he died and his wife has gone' – she waved her hand vaguely – 'to a daughter's, I think, and Jack applied for the house.'

'Oh, I do remember them. The farm was between your house and ours.'

'They're moving after Christmas,' Jenny went on. 'Susan lost the child she was expecting, unfortunately, and now they're all busy getting the house ready, painting it and sorting out furniture and so on, but listen to this. They're taking three girls with them, but leaving Molly with my ma and da. She's a *special* child, shall we say. She needs more attention and kindness than I think Susan has to offer. Ma's asked the headmaster of the Thorngumbald school if he'll allow her to go for a couple of days a week and he said that he would.' She pondered for a moment before saying, 'I think he might be obliged to, when I think about it.

'But here's the other thing,' she went on. 'There's a young boy living with my ma and da. He's about Louisa's age, and he just turned up after the hirings; he came home in the wagon with the other children and, well, you know my ma – she told him he could stay until his mother came looking for him. He's an absolute charmer, entertains the girls, and Molly says he's teaching her to read. He does the White Rabbit in a funny voice and the girls fall about laughing.'

She paused. 'Are you sure you're all right, Delia?' she said, leaning towards her. 'You're looking very flushed!'

'Yes!' Delia said in a strangled voice. 'I'm fine. The – the punch has gone to my head.'

'Anyway, Ma has informed the police; Da said they had to in case they were accused of abducting him or something,' Jenny went on. 'But it's what, over a month, and there's no sign of his mother.'

'What's his name?' Delia managed.

'Robin Jackson.' When Jenny saw the expression on Delia's face, a fusion of misery, relief and overpowering emotion, she realized for the first time that her friend had been playing a part ever since they had met again. The calm face and behaviour had been merely a mask; this was the real Delia, a woman in distress.

'Delia,' she said softly. 'What is it?'

'Help me, Jenny.' Delia began to weep. 'I'm drowning!'

And then everything fell into place. 'My God,' Jenny whispered. 'He's yours, isn't he? Robin is your child!'

CHAPTER NINETEEN

Mr Gosling came to say their table was ready and looked enquiringly at Jenny; she gave a gentle shake of her head and mouthed *Five minutes*. He brought a pot of coffee which they hadn't asked for, but were thankful to drink.

'Do you want to talk about it?' Jenny whispered. 'I think you should.'

Delia nodded; her hand trembled as she picked up the coffee cup. 'In a minute,' she said. 'When I think of the best way to explain.'

Jenny waited. What a plight to be in, she thought. This must be why her parents won't talk to her, and the reason for throwing her out all those years ago. How could they? Their only daughter! She must only have been seventeen when – when . . . How did she keep it secret from me? And who was the reprobate who violated her, for I'm quite sure that she was innocent. We both were. Neither of us knew any boys to talk to, apart from the ones who'd been at school, and there was never one of them with anything but farming or fishing on his mind. Both girls had left the school when they were thirteen, Delia to help her mother at home

164

and Jenny to a day school in Hull, travelling back and forth on the train every day.

'I couldn't . . . I can't go on,' Delia began at last. 'We have no permanent home; we move from one set of lodgings to another, living from hand to mouth on the pittance I earn. Being in the theatre isn't the glamorous life that you might imagine, and although I managed when he was a baby and he was always a good child and someone would keep an eye on him whilst I was on stage . . .' It was as if the floodgates had opened and her words poured out without stopping. 'But now that he's older he needs to go to school and although he's been whenever I've had a long run he can't settle because he knows that we'll soon be on the road again—'

'So you came back because,' Jenny interrupted gently, 'you thought your parents might have relented?'

'I didn't know where else to go or what to do. Perhaps I thought they might have relented; I don't know why I should have, not after being told all those years ago never to show my face again. I was stupid. They didn't want any explanations; my mother had heard me being sick and knew immediately, even before I did; she told me to get off and tell the lad's parents and ask what they were going to do about it, and then later that day she told my father and he leathered me with his belt and my mother said nothing.'

'I'm so very sorry,' Jenny said, putting her hand on Delia's arm. 'But why didn't you come to see me or my mother? Ma would have helped you.'

Delia stared at Jenny. This was the crux of the matter; now she would know whether or not they would remain friends.

165

'I did,' she whispered. 'But you weren't there; you'd stayed in Hull with someone from your school and – and I spoke to your mother. She said that you and your friend were doing exams together and you'd been invited to stay with her and her family. I think your mother thought I was unwell and she made me sit down and gave me a cup of tea – and then – and she told me that . . .' She swallowed hard. 'She said that Jack and Susan had gone to church to see the vicar about having the banns read because they were getting married.'

She took a breath and her next words came out on a shuddering sob. 'And I knew then that my life was completely over.'

They sat in silence for a while. One of the young porters came and put another log on the fire and then they got up and sat at their corner table, waiting for the food to be brought.

'What do you mean?' Jenny asked quietly. 'Why did you think that? Did you not consider going to the man – boy – who had committed this . . .' she let out a sigh, 'outrage, and confront him or his parents?'

Delia turned her face away; a small frown knitted her forehead.

'Delia?' Jenny bent towards her.

Delia lifted her moist eyes to Jenny's. 'Do I really have to spell it out for you?' she whispered, and her voice was bitter. 'I was a virgin. I'd never even kissed a boy.'

Jenny ran her tongue over her lips. I hope this doesn't mean – surely not. He wouldn't – would he? 'What – what is it you're implying, Delia?'

'I think you can guess and I'm not implying anything.' Delia held back another sob. 'I'm *telling* you and you did say I should unburden myself and that's what I'm doing at the risk of losing our friendship.'

She lowered her head and fell silent again as their soup was brought. When the waiter had gone she took a deep breath and said quietly, 'I'm telling you that one late afternoon in February eleven years ago I was walking back from the village with some shopping. It was dark and raining and as I came to your farm I thought I'd call on your mother and tell her that I'd received a letter from you, and then I was going to take a short cut home across Foggit's land.

'Jack answered the door and told me she had gone to Hedon. He was – well, he looked different, I don't know what it was, and he looked at me oddly and then he said . . .' She took a heaving breath and clutched her chest. 'He said did I have time to go with him to the barn before I went home. I'd always liked Jack, he'd always been friendly towards me, and I thought he was going to show me a litter of puppies or kittens, so I said all right and he carried my basket and I went with him. He led me to the back of the barn behind a stack of straw and took hold of me and began kissing me. I told him to stop but he said he couldn't because he'd always liked me.'

She couldn't go on; couldn't tell Jack's sister of the things he'd said to her, of how soft her skin was next to his; or of how he'd torn her skirt and petticoat in his haste and how the straw had scratched her and she'd cried, and he'd said don't cry because other girls liked it and she would too, and put his mouth over hers so

167

that she wouldn't scream out that he was hurting her.

And then, when I thought he would break me in two, he'd suddenly given a groan and rolled off me and looked at me and said I was lovely and he was sorry if he'd hurt me and I couldn't speak because I was so ashamed.

She sobbed and sobbed, all the humiliation, distress and anxiety that she had bottled up for so long released like air from a balloon.

Jenny moved her chair back from the table, and putting her arm about Delia's shoulder she led her towards the ladies' room. She didn't speak until they were inside; it was as if she was trying to make sense of what she had just heard, and wondering also what words could be used to help or comfort, while knowing that there was no expression of commiseration that could possibly put the situation right.

Her brother at nineteen had been arrogant, knew everything there was to know about everything, or so he thought, but he was also naïve and gullible and easily led astray.

He wouldn't have been led astray by Delia, or Dorothy as she was then, for she wouldn't have known how to begin to lead a boy on; but he was friends then with Ralph Pearce, who had an eye for the girls and wouldn't have hesitated to gloat over his conquests to someone as susceptible as Jack, goading him on to find prey of his own.

Not that it excuses him, she thought, and he deserves the come-uppance that I think he's had with his darling wife – and perhaps he led her astray too.

'I'm so sorry, Delia,' she murmured. 'So very sorry that it was my brother who did this to you.'

Delia lifted her tear-stained, red-eyed face to hers. 'You believe me?' she said hoarsely.

'Of course I believe you.' Jenny handed her a clean handkerchief. 'Why would you make up a story like that? What I don't understand, though, is why, after living down south for so long, you brought your son here and left him with a family he had never met – with the man who had ruined your life?'

Delia blew her nose. 'I didn't intend to,' she said thickly. 'I went home first to see how the land was lying. I didn't even know if my parents were still there.' She heaved a breath. 'And I suppose I really did hope that they might have had a change of heart, felt sorry for being hasty, you know, and would help me in some way. How green I still am. Then we stayed overnight at the Hedon Arms and I was told about the hiring fair so I took Jack – my Jack, I mean; that's his real name – to see it. It used to be the highlight of my year; I didn't have much fun in my life. Afterwards we went into the Sun Inn for something to eat. I had only a little money left.' She swallowed hard. 'I went to get a plate of bread and beef and when I came back with it Jack had gone into the snug and was sitting at a table watching all the families with their children and I knew what he was missing; and then I saw *him*, your brother Jack, and I was so upset I had to go out for some air. When I came back again there was *my* Jack sitting with them and tucking into an enormous plate of food.'

She gave a choking, weeping laugh. 'I saw your mother and your father, and I remembered how kind

Peggy had been to me that day, as if she knew there was something wrong that I couldn't tell her, and – and I thought that she wouldn't turn him away. It was an instant decision, impetuous, *stupid*, and I regretted it the minute I got back on the train.'

She turned to face Jenny again. 'But it was too late. A step too far. If I'd gone back I'd have had to face them all, confront your brother and accuse him in front of everyone – and what if he'd denied it? Who would they have believed, and what would I have done then?'

Jenny nodded. What indeed? She remained silent for a moment, and it seemed to Delia that Jenny was pondering on a problem, analysing the facts as she saw them without any emotion involved, as Delia was unable to do.

'Very well,' Jenny declared at last. 'Rinse your face and then come back to the table and finish your meal. Don't try to run away, as I'll be watching.'

She left the ladies' room and returned to the dining room; the soup dishes had gone and a waiter was standing near. She apologized and said he could bring the next course, which he did just as Delia returned with her hair tidied and a touch of powder to calm her flushed cheeks.

Neither of them said very much for the rest of the meal, Delia eating little and both declining a dessert or coffee. Jenny asked for the bill, which she paid, then looked round for a porter. There was just one, standing by the inner door, stifling a yawn, and she signalled to him.

'Order a cab, will you please?' She smiled sweetly

at him. 'So sorry to keep you, we've been catching up with news.'

She turned to Delia. 'We're going to sleep on it; I'm dropping you off at your lodgings and you're not going to think about anything tonight, and tomorrow we'll meet for lunch – or no, I know, I'll come here to meet you and then I'll take you back to my place and we'll have lunch there. How does that sound?'

'Thank you,' Delia whispered, feeling humble and not knowing what else to say. 'Are you sure, Jenny? I feel as if I've put all my problems on to your shoulders.'

'We'll share the weight,' Jenny said. 'And it isn't only your dilemma, Delia, it's also someone else's, but as he can't help at this stage it's up to the rest of us to help out if we can.'

'Robin!' Delia whispered. 'Is that really what my Jack calls himself?'

'Robin Jackson,' Jenny said. 'What is his proper name? Deakin? Delamour?'

'Jack Robinson Deakin on his birth certificate,' Delia murmured. 'But I never told him about the Deakin. He thinks it's only Jack Robinson and said he didn't like it as people were always saying *Before you can say Jack Robinson*. I told him to change it if he didn't like it. I should never have given him that name. It was a perverse act on my part to prove his birthright, even though an outrage had been committed against me.'

She shook her head and gave a wry grimace, but Jenny suddenly laughed. '*Robin Jackson*! What a smart boy!' she chuckled. 'I've just realized, Delia, that Robin Jackson alias Jack Robinson is my nephew!'

CHAPTER TWENTY

Jenny lay sleepless in bed. She tried to put herself in Delia's position; what would she have done in similar circumstances?

For a start she would have told her mother what had happened, but she understood why Delia couldn't do that with hers; she would have been too frightened and ashamed. She'd always thought that Delia's mother was a mean woman. She would and obviously did blame Delia; Jenny had disliked her even when they were young, and she doubted whether Delia's father would have troubled himself to go off after the perpetrator when it was easier just to throw his daughter out, and the shame with her.

Unlike her own father, she thought, who, although a moderate placid man, hated injustice and had a strong sense of what was right and proper and would have seen justice done even at his own hands; and that might now be a problem, she told herself, for our Jack is his son and married with children whom Aaron adores; so what can be done in reparation? Her father would most certainly turn against her brother if he heard what had happened.

What a can of worms. She turned over on her pillow, bashing it with her fist to make a comfy nest for her head. I think I'll have to tell Mother and I'm certain she'll accept Robin – and then, of course, she thought suddenly, she'll no longer be anxious about him, for as she's his real grandmother no one will be able to say she can't keep him. But I won't tell Father. I'll let Mother decide on that.

She fell asleep, and woke again an hour later. And then, if Delia stays in Hull, perhaps Robin could come here and see her. That's it, she thought sleepily, her mind befuddled. That's the way round it. A conundrum; there's always a solitary – no, a *soli-solvable* – solution, if you think hard enough.

When Delia waved goodbye to Jenny, she felt drained of energy; the telling of her story had completely emptied her out and she knew she wouldn't sleep. She turned her key in the lodging house door and, after locking it behind her as requested on the placard inside, opened the door into the small sitting room which the landlady called the theatricals' lounge. A low fire was burning behind a fire guard and Giles Dawson was fast asleep in an easy chair in front of it.

Carefully she moved the guard to one side and with the coal tongs placed a few pieces of coal on the embers. He didn't stir, and she sat down opposite and observed him.

In repose, his forehead was smooth, unlike when he was playing, when a small frown of concentration creased between his eyebrows. He had fine features, smooth skin and a generous mouth, rather like Arthur

Crawshaw, she thought, except that their colouring differed; Arthur was dark-haired and dark-eyed and very aristocratic, with a short beard and a penetrating gaze, whereas Giles was fair, with friendly blue eyes and a clean-shaven chin.

He suddenly opened his eyes and smiled sleepily. 'Miss Delamour, hello,' he said. 'Isn't it odd that even when asleep you can sense when someone else appears?'

'Can you?' she murmured. 'I don't know.'

He gazed at her. 'Mmm. Perhaps women don't fall asleep as easily as men do. You take care not to be caught catching flies or snoring.'

'You weren't snoring,' she told him, 'and you had your mouth firmly closed.'

'Really?'

Delia blushed even though she knew he was teasing her by suggesting that she had been watching him, which she had.

He sat up in the chair. 'Have you had a pleasant evening?'

Delia hesitated; she probably looked a wreck, eyes reddened, drained. 'I met my friend Jenny Robinson,' she said. 'We're still catching up with all our news.'

'Is she a married woman?' he asked. 'Or independent like yourself?'

'She's a single woman, a teacher.' She looked at him curiously. 'Why do you ask?'

'Forgive me if I seem inquisitive. It's just that you meet late in the evenings and not during the day, but of course if she's a teacher that explains it. She's busy following her profession.' He nodded thoughtfully. 'I

174

admire the strength of women who follow a chosen career, as you have done too. There are so many pitfalls for women, who generally are expected to marry and have children rather than live a life that they choose for themselves.'

Delia turned her gaze away from him. 'Life doesn't always allow you to choose what you do with it,' she said slowly. 'Sometimes it's thrust upon you and there is no option but to follow one path.'

He leaned forward and rested his elbows on his long cord-clad legs. 'Isn't there sometimes an alternative?'

She gave a short sardonic scoff. 'Oh, yes,' she said, thinking of her lowest ebb when she had contemplated the deep waters of the estuary. 'An alternative indeed, and often the only solution.'

'Miss Delamour!' he said. 'Are you – do you have troubles? Can I – can I help in any way? Listen to your problems? Be a shoulder to cry on?'

She lifted her head and turned to him. 'Is it so obvious?'

He nodded. 'Yes,' he said honestly. 'You have been through some difficult times, I think. You have a deep sadness within you.'

'You're very observant.' There was a slight bitterness in her tone.

'I am. When I see a beautiful woman who rarely smiles, I wonder why. Has she suffered great sorrow, been through some deep crisis in her life? Forgive me,' he said again. 'Life is often difficult and I don't wish to pry.' He put out a hand towards her. 'But if I can help with anything, I would like to. I'd like to think that you would consider me as a friend.'

Delia stood up, ignoring the hand that he proffered. 'There's nothing,' she said, her voice tight and strangled, and she felt the sharp stone of rancour lodged within her. 'Nothing to be done. My life is what it is.'

He rose from his chair too and studied her perceptively, the small characteristic frown furrowed between his eyebrows. 'I'm sorry,' he began, but she raised her hand in rejection.

'Don't be,' she said, turning away. 'Goodnight.'

She was sorry, of course; she was not usually so abrupt or ill-mannered and the next morning, as she ate breakfast alone, she wondered if he had left and hoped that he hadn't. It was nine o'clock, the latest time for breakfast, and he was usually down early. He hadn't said if he was going on to another booking; in fact she knew nothing about him. She had become so wrapped up in her own miserable life that she hadn't thought to ask him anything about himself; and he hadn't offered any information voluntarily.

I don't know anything about anyone, she realized as she drank the weak and tasteless coffee. I never enquire in case anyone, in return, asks about my situation. She put her hand to her forehead. A headache was hovering. I know nothing about Arthur either, she sighed. In all the years I've known him I've never asked why he doesn't have a regular spot, or where he has been recently, and he never questions me either, though he must have drawn his own conclusions.

She pushed away from the table and glanced through the net curtains and out of the window. The outlook was grey but it wasn't raining, and she decided to take a walk to clear her head. She went upstairs for her coat and on impulse knocked on Giles Dawson's door as she passed. She had noticed the number on his key, which they always laid on the table as they were too big for pockets or handbags.

There was no immediate answer and she was about to walk away when she heard the key turn and he looked out. His hair was tousled and he was wearing a dressing gown.

'Oh, I'm so sorry to disturb you.' Delia was embarrassed at finding him in a state of undress.

'That's all right. I was up, just being lazy.' He smiled. 'I didn't sleep well.'

'Nor I,' she admitted. 'Mr Dawson, I'm ashamed of being so abrupt when you were only trying to be kind.'

He lifted his hands in a careless dismissal. 'Where are you going now?' he asked. 'Have you had breakfast?'

'Yes, I'm – just going for a walk to clear my head.' She touched her forehead, signifying a headache.

'Can you wait? We could perhaps have coffee and muffins; that would be nice, wouldn't it? Breakfast on me! And I'll promise not to ask questions.' He raised his eyebrows.

'I'm sorry,' she began again, but he shook his head.

'Give me ten minutes and I'll be down.'

In ten minutes exactly he appeared in a warm overcoat, scarf and hat. 'Where would you like to go, Miss Delamour? I know a place, but if you have a preference?'

'No, wherever you say. I . . .' She hesitated. 'Last night Jenny and I went to the Maritime Hotel.'

He took her elbow as they walked and she felt strangely comforted. 'You don't have to tell me anything,' he assured her.

'I know, but I want to explain.' She felt the icy cold of winter on her cheeks and huddled into her scarf. 'We were at school together, and were great friends, but when I left the district I . . . we lost touch. My fault entirely. I could have written to her, but I chose not to.'

He steered her towards Market Place, and as they crossed over the bells of Holy Trinity began to peal. 'We could go to church first, if you wish?'

She glanced up at him to see if he was serious, but his face was impassive. 'I don't – as a rule.'

He smiled. 'Forced to as a youngster were you, as I was?'

'Oh, no! My father said it was mumbo-jumbo and I wasn't allowed. The only time I went was from school, Easter and Christmas, you know, and he didn't know about that. I would have liked to go more, because then I could have sung.'

'Couldn't you sing at home?'

'No. There wasn't anything to sing about.'

He pushed open a door to a small café on the edge of the street and the steamy warmth closed around them, as did the aroma of roast coffee beans and frying bacon.

'I'm going to have coffee, bacon, eggs and sausage,' he declared. 'And then muffins.' He greeted a woman behind the counter, who indicated a table in the corner already set with cups, saucers and cutlery.

Delia sat down. 'This is very cosy. I think I might

have the same. The breakfast that Mrs Benson supplies is all right but not very sustaining.'

He unfastened his coat and scarf and put them on the high back of his chair. 'I quite agree. But as lodgings go it's quite good. Shall I take your coat?'

Delia undid the buttons of her coat and handed it to him but kept on her scarf. She was so cold; how she hated winter.

They were brought coffee instantly and ordered breakfast, and Giles murmured, 'It's a role reversal here. The woman deals with the customers and her husband does the cooking.'

'That's the kind of husband I'd like,' Delia answered, 'and for him to sweep the floors and do the dusting as well.'

He picked up her hand and examined it carefully. 'Doesn't look to me, Miss Delamour, as if you've ever done any!'

'Not lately I haven't' – she retrieved her hand – 'but I used to when I was a girl.' The statement slipped out without her thinking. 'It was expected of me,' she added lamely. 'Families like ours – that's what we did.'

'Of course, and that's the way it still is for many.' He poured them both a cup of coffee and with practised ease put hers at her side of the table. 'And you'd per-haps have been expected to go into service if you hadn't chosen the theatre, wouldn't you? It's the way of life unless you were born into the upper classes.'

Delia poured milk into her coffee. 'No,' she muttered. 'I was expected to stay at home and be the household drudge, just as I had been since I was old enough to hold a scrubbing brush or a duster.'

He paused in the act of taking a sip of his black coffee and put the cup back on the saucer. 'Then – well done in making your escape,' he said slowly. 'How very brave of you. Were you the only one at home?'

She felt her throat tightening again. 'Yes,' she croaked. 'I was, but I wasn't brave. I was told to leave.'

Why am I telling him this? We don't know each other, and now that the theatre's closed he'll probably take up other engagements and I'll never see him again. That's the life we lead.

Yet she felt compelled to talk. The catharsis of her discussion with Jenny was not yet complete. 'You see, a young man I knew – he – assaulted me – and . . .'

'You became pregnant,' he said in a low voice. 'And your parents thought it was your fault? A classic tale.'

Numbly she nodded. 'Yes,' she said hoarsely. 'And now I have a son, a handsome beautiful son.' Tears welled in her eyes and coursed down her face and she brushed them swiftly away. 'And that's why I'm in the state I'm in.'

The breakfast was brought and put in front of them. Two plates of bacon, eggs, sausage, tomatoes, fried bread and black pudding, and a separate plate of freshly baked bread and muffins.

'Eat up,' he said firmly, topping up her coffee cup. 'And then we'll talk. If you want to.'

CHAPTER TWENTY-ONE

'I think I'm all talked out,' Delia said, looking down at the food on her plate and wondering if she could eat it all. 'I had a long discussion with my friend Jenny last night. In fact,' she glanced at the clock on the wall, 'she insists on coming back today to take me to her rooms so we can try and make some sense of my situation.'

'Which is?'

'I'm a single woman, not earning much, with no home to call my own and a son to support.'

He poured her more coffee from another jug that had been brought to the table, and she thought how nice it was to have something done for her, even something so simple as being poured a cup of coffee. It might seem trivial to some, but it gave her a wonderful sense of warmth and cordiality.

'And where is your son now?'

'He – erm, I left him with some people I know,' she hedged. 'He's staying with them for the present, until I decide what I should do next.'

He nodded and went on eating. Then he patted his mouth with a table napkin. 'Is he old enough to be at school?'

'Yes.' She dropped her voice and traced a pattern on the plate with her fork. 'He's ten. That's my main dilemma. I want him to go to school; he's a bright boy and he deserves an education.'

'The man who did this to you should be helping you,' he said in a terse whisper, 'but I suppose he didn't want to know?'

To give Jack Robinson his due, she thought, he was quite ignorant of my pregnancy. He had been a youth whose only thought was of taking his pleasure, not of any consequences that might ensue; and as he was committed to marrying someone else, what could he have done? She had never before given thought to what havoc would have been caused if she had confessed to Peggy Robinson that long ago day.

'I never told him,' she answered bleakly. 'He was about to marry someone else.'

They finished their breakfast in silence, and then Giles said, 'It's a predicament, I quite agree, and I wonder how you've managed to survive for the last ten years. What you need now is some kind of work that is stable and regular and where you can stay in one place.'

She nodded. She knew that already. It was easy enough to work out the answer, not so easy to carry it out. To change the subject, she told him about the arrangement she hoped to make over Christmas with the Maritime Hotel and he congratulated her on the plan. Then she glanced at the clock again. 'I hate to rush, but I should be leaving,' she said, and reached for her purse. 'I said I'd meet her at the Maritime.'

Giles called for the bill and paid, ushering away her

offer to pay half. 'I'll walk with you, if I may?' he said. 'And I'm sorry I haven't come up with an answer, but I'll work on it. Put on my thinking-cap.' He smiled.

Delia was relieved, and thought that her confession hadn't been as difficult as she had feared; perhaps some people were more broad-minded and tolerant than she'd previously thought.

From Trinity Square they cut through Posterngate and walked alongside the warehouses on Princes Dock, pausing to watch a ship come in to berth. The gangplank was lowered and the crew came down, some heading towards the Seamen's Mission, others hurrying towards the nearest hostelry; then Delia and Giles turned away from the icy wind blowing up the dock from the estuary and cut down more sheltered streets towards the hotel.

'Won't you come in and meet Jenny?' she asked him. 'She'll be here fairly soon.'

He agreed that he would, and they had only just taken a seat when Jenny arrived. They both rose to greet her and Delia said, rather shyly, 'Jenny, I'd like you to meet Giles Dawson. You've heard me speak of him. Mr Dawson, this is Miss Jenny Robinson, a friend I have known since childhood.'

Giles Dawson took Jenny's outstretched hand and gave her a short bow. 'Delighted to meet you, Miss Robinson. It must have been very agreeable for you and Miss Delamour to meet again. I am glad that she has your friendship and support in her present dilemma. If I can help in any capacity, then do tell me.'

He turned to Delia and gave her a short bow too, and wishing them good day he took his leave.

Jenny watched him go and then turned to Delia. 'Well! You told him! How brave you are after all.'

'I – I didn't intend to. It was just that last night, when I got back from our meeting, I was so distressed that I'm afraid I was rather rude when he asked if he could help. This morning I apologized and he invited me out for breakfast, which is where we have come from. I haven't told him everything, but he guessed why I'd left home. I suppose it was obvious.' She turned to look towards the door where Giles had departed. 'He was very understanding,' she said quietly. 'He's rather nice, isn't he?'

Jenny smiled and raised a quizzical eyebrow; was Delia coming back to something like normality? 'He is,' she agreed. 'Do you know anything about him, his background, his credentials?'

Delia looked astonished and it showed in her voice. 'No!' she exclaimed. 'I don't. Why would I ask?'

Jenny gave a little shrug. 'Just wondered; assessing his worth, you know.'

'With what intention? As a suitor, do you mean?' Delia's voice dropped to a breath.

'Possibly,' Jenny teased. Really, Delia was so innocent; so guileless.

'So, do you – erm – that is, do you like him? Do you think that you and he . . .?'

'Oh, not for *me*, you darling girl,' Jenny exclaimed. 'I'm a dyed-in-the-wool spinster. For you, of course!'

Delia was very envious of Jenny's rooms in Pearson Park. She had a lovely living room with a view over the park, a separate bedroom, and a bathroom just along the landing, and everything was in pristine condition.

'It's a new house,' Jenny explained. 'They all are, and all built to a certain standard. Zachariah Pearson bestowed the land on the people of Hull so that they could have a park to walk in and enjoy the trees and flowers and have picnics on the grass. Don't you recall hearing about it?'

Delia nodded. 'Vaguely.' She sighed. 'It's over ten years since I was last here and I didn't stay very long. I made our escape to London as soon as I was given the chance. I didn't want anyone to find me.' She gave a bitter grimace. 'But I don't think that anyone was looking!'

'That's behind you now,' Jenny said briskly. 'Now, this is what I suggest.'

She outlined her proposal of telling her mother everything but not until after Christmas when Jack and his wife and daughters had moved out to their new house.

Delia was unsure about it and again wondered if she would be believed. After a long discussion, they finally agreed that Peggy would simply be told that Delia had borne Robin out of wedlock and she needed a home for him for a short time until she found regular employment.

I don't know if it will work, Jenny thought. Delia is so afraid of rejection again. But my mother isn't stupid; nobody can pull the wool over her eyes, and if she guesses Jack's the father I don't know if she will agree not to tell Da, but I won't tell Delia that. Let her just remain confident that Robin is being well looked after, which is what she really wants.

They ate sandwiches and cake with a pot of tea, and as the day drew on and the sky began to darken they strolled across the park to the main road where Delia would catch the omnibus back to town.

'You see how convenient it is,' Jenny said. 'I can get into town easily on this side of the park or on the other. I love it. And it's really rather grand living in such an impressive house, even though only in part of it.'

They said their goodbyes as a horse tram arrived and Delia climbed aboard. 'Don't worry,' Jenny called after her. 'Everything will work out well.' She immediately thought of another plan that she wouldn't tell Delia about, and added, 'I'll try to call in to see you at your lodgings next Saturday.'

'What?' Delia called back as the vehicle moved off, but Jenny just waved her hand.

The following Friday after school Jenny hurried to the railway station to catch a train to Hedon. She hadn't written to say she was coming in case she changed her mind, having thought about the visit, and wondered if she might be acting hastily, but having decided that she would go she'd written a note to Delia asking her to meet her for lunch at the Maritime the next day.

Dusk had fallen as she arrived in Hedon and she knew she'd have to walk quickly if she were to get home before the skies completely darkened. She left the station and saw one of her cousins stepping into a trap.

'Richard!' she called. 'Are you going home? Can I beg a lift to Thorn? I made a last-minute decision to come home for the weekend!'

'Course you can. I've just come to put a parcel on

186

board the train. How are you? It's nice to see you. Will you be coming for Christmas?'

'It's nice to see you too, but I won't be able to come at Christmas.' Her cousin glanced at her curiously.

'Can't abide the interrogation, is that it?' he asked. 'I know the feeling. I'm always being quizzed about my business plans.' He shook the reins and they moved off. 'We'll be doing the usual rounds of visiting, I expect. It's quite exhausting, and I sometimes think I'd like to stay at home by my own fireside, but my mother would be upset. Has your mother still got that young lad staying with them? He and Ben have been hitting it off at school; they've become good pals. Ben said he makes all 'other bairns laugh.'

'Does he? Yes, I think he's still there. You know my ma, she loves having children to stay. Did you hear that Jack and Susan are moving out after Christmas?' she said to change the subject. 'Ma will miss having the girls there.'

'But they're keeping Molly with them, I understand? Susan told us she's a handful to deal with.'

Jenny prickled. 'No she's not! But she needs someone firm who understands her, and Susan plainly doesn't.'

'Ooh, touched a nerve there, did I?'

'Yes, actually you did. Molly needs a chance, just the same as any other child. She's very bright and eager to learn.'

'Is she?' he said in astonishment. 'Not backward, then, as we've been led to believe?'

'No!' Jenny said. 'Most definitely not. But she has a condition that means she's slower than other children at doing things and that frustrates her.'

They reached Thorngumbald and he insisted on driving her to the farm. 'It's rather boggy down there, and besides, it's dark. You're a town girl now, aren't you? Used to street lights?' he teased her.

'I am, but I'm not afraid of the dark of the country-side. I was born to it, don't forget.'

She invited him in when they reached the gate but he said he would get off home, for there would be a meal waiting. She thanked him for the lift and waved him goodbye as he turned the horse and trap round.

Her mother was dishing up supper and all the children were sitting at the table waiting for it, but with the exception of Robin they all got up and rushed to give her a hug.

'Well, what an unexpected treat,' her mother beamed. 'Have you walked from Hedon?'

'No,' she said, unwinding her scarf and slipping off her hat and coat. 'I saw Cousin Richard at the station and he gave me a lift. It's a short stay, but, well, I wanted to come and discuss something.'

She turned back to the table. 'Hello, Robin,' she said. 'My cousin Richard who gave me a ride home is your friend Ben's father. He said how well you're get-ting on together.'

'Did he?' Robin's face lit up in delight. 'Yes, we're best mates. After the girls, I mean,' he added hastily as Louisa and Molly turned to look at him. 'It's really, really nice to have so many friends.'

Jenny smiled at the *best mates* description. He had quickly picked up the local expression. She made a pot of tea whilst the children were eating; her mother said that her father and brother were in the barn repairing something and would be in later for supper.

'What was it you wanted to discuss?' Peggy asked.

'I'll tell you later,' Jenny murmured, 'when the children aren't around.'

'Please may I get down?' Rosie piped up, quickly followed by Emma and then Molly.

'You must wait until Robin has finished eating,' Peggy told them, but Jenny interrupted.

'I want to ask Robin something too, when he's finished.'

'So can we go and play for a bit while you're talking?' Emma asked.

'Go on then,' Peggy said. 'You too, Louisa.' Robin glanced cautiously at Jenny and then Peggy and put his knife and fork together.

'Thank you,' he said. 'I've finished now. It was very nice.'

'It's all right, Robin,' Jenny assured him after the girls had disappeared into the parlour. 'You don't need to be apprehensive. I want to suggest a treat for you.'

She sat at the table with him and her mother sat opposite, her arms folded across her chest. 'What sort of treat?' Peggy asked.

'I wondered if Robin would like to come on a little trip with me tomorrow. It will be a sort of Christmas present.'

Peggy looked at her, and Robin beamed. 'Oh,' he said. 'Thank you. Will I like it?'

'I'm fairly sure that you will. We'll be taking the train into Hull and you'll get your present there.'

He glanced at Peggy, who was looking baffled, and then back at Jenny. 'Will I be coming back?'

'Of course!' she said. 'You'll want to come back, won't you? It's just that there's something I want you to see, a special kind of something.'

He glanced again at Peggy, but she shook her head and shrugged. 'I've no idea,' she said. 'None at all. First I've heard of it.'

'Well, it's a secret,' Jenny told them. She bent her head towards them and lowered her voice. 'I'd like to keep it a surprise until we get there.'

Robin heaved a breath. 'All right,' he said. 'Thank you. I feel very excited.' He didn't sound excited, she thought, but still rather anxious. He moved his chair back from the table and got to his feet. 'I'd better see what the girls are up to.'

'What's this about?' Peggy asked, when he had left the room.

Jenny blew out her cheeks. 'I hope I'm doing right,' she said, 'and *please*, promise that you won't tell Da or Jack. Not yet anyway.'

Her mother shrugged. 'You always were one for intrigue,' she said. 'You'd better spit it out and tell me afore the men come in.'

'We're going into Hull,' Jenny said carefully and quietly, 'for Robin to see his mother.'

CHAPTER TWENTY-TWO

Jenny reassured Robin several times on the train journey that they would be coming back. 'What's for supper tonight?' she'd asked, and, 'I expect you'll miss Louisa and the other girls when they move to the other house after Christmas? You'll still see them at school, of course,' and so on, all remarks designed to reinforce his confidence that he would be returning to the farm.

'I do like being at the farm,' he told Jenny. 'I love Granny Robinson and the girls, especially Louisa. She's my very best friend.'

'I'm very pleased to hear it,' she said, and thought that of all the little girls Louisa was her favourite too, though she tried not to be biased. Perhaps it's because she was my first niece, she pondered, or more likely because I don't understand Susan's attitude towards her, nor my brother's either.

'Here we are,' she said brightly as the train pulled into the Paragon terminus. 'Let's go and find your present.'

'Do I have to close my eyes?' He reached for her hand and she gave his a gentle squeeze and thought she could become very fond of this young boy.

'Not yet,' she said practically. 'You should look around and see the town. We're not walking far, and we are a bit early, but I'll tell you when to close your eyes.'

He looked about him as they walked through the railway station. 'It isn't as big as King's Cross,' he said. 'But it has very long platforms.'

'It was built more than thirty years ago,' she said, 'and when Queen Victoria, Prince Albert and the royal children visited Hull their train came in to this station.' She indicated the rear of a building as they turned towards the exit. 'And they stayed in that very hotel. A special throne room was built for the Queen so that she could receive the notables of the town.' She could never resist giving children a history lesson; it was the teacher in her. 'Her Majesty then allowed it to be called the *Royal* Station Hotel. I'll show you the front as we pass. It's a very fine building.'

She felt very apprehensive as they came out into the street. I hope I'm doing the right thing. Suppose Delia wants to keep him with her when she sees him? He'll be right back to where he was before, leading a nomadic life; he'll become a drifter himself, or a wandering actor, never settling down to anything much. I could just take him into one of the shops and buy him a present and then we could go back home again.

But that would be unfair, she told herself, and I do believe that although he is only a child still, he's capable of knowing what he wants. The choice should be his, and I hope, I really hope, that he chooses to come back with me to Paull – where he really belongs.

She added this defiant thought, justifying herself for interfering.

The Maritime Hotel was close to the railway station, and as they arrived it began to rain.

'We haven't brought an umbrella, Auntie Jenny,' he said, as she pushed open the door. 'We might get soaked going back.'

She smiled, instantly cheered by his positivity. 'We'll borrow one,' she said, and opening the door into the foyer she saw Delia sitting by the fire with her back to them. Fortunately there were no other guests there. 'Close your eyes now,' she said quickly, and moved in front of him.

'Hello,' she called out. 'Close your eyes, I've got a surprise for you!'

Delia turned, saw Jenny and closed her eyes as commanded. 'You were always such a tease, Jenny. What are you up to?'

Jenny heard Robin take a sudden breath as he heard Delia's voice, and as he rushed past her she felt a prickling in her eyes and knew she had done the right thing as the boy charged towards his mother and wrapped his arms around her.

'Mother,' he sobbed. 'It's you. It's really you!'

Delia wept. She couldn't believe that here was her boy, sturdy and rosy-cheeked. Grown too, in the short month since she had left him.

'Do you forgive me?' she said, hugging him and kissing his cheek as he sat on her knee, something he hadn't done in many years; now it seemed that he couldn't get close enough to her.

'For what, Mother?'

'Leaving you behind.'

'Oh, I knew you'd come back eventually,' he said earnestly. 'I had every faith in you.'

Delia heard Jenny give a strangled laugh at his solemn assertion.

'And I'm having such a splendid time with Granny Robinson and Aaron and all the little girls. Aaron calls them *bairns*,' he chuckled. 'Isn't that such a nice thing to say? Is that what your parents called you?' he asked in all innocence.

Brat, more like, she thought, but lied and said yes, glancing at Jenny as she did so.

Jenny ordered coffee for her and Delia and hot chocolate for Robin, whom Delia kept calling Jack until eventually she said, 'I understand you've changed your name to Robin?'

He nodded. 'It wasn't because I didn't like the name Jack, it was because it was linked to Robinson and you remember what I'd said about it before?'

'I do,' she said. 'And I said that you should change it if you didn't like it.'

'It's a good thing I did,' he went on, 'because there's another Jack Robinson living in the house, so it would have been very confusing.' He frowned. 'I don't think he likes me being there, but I don't think he likes children much anyway; but they're moving after Christmas,' he added, 'so it won't matter. I'm going to have the girls' bedroom upstairs after they've gone.' He sounded excited. 'And you can see the estuary from up there and great big *enormous* skies.'

Delia took a deep breath, and, unnoticed, so did

Jenny. 'So are you happy to stay there for a little while longer?' Delia asked cautiously.

'Oh, yes please,' he said, and glanced at Jenny. 'Jenny said I could go back.' He paused. 'Is – that all right, Mother?' He bit on his lip. 'You won't be too unhappy without me?' and added without waiting for an answer, 'And if you're staying in Hull for now, I'm sure I could travel by train on my own to come and see you.'

'I'll be staying until the end of February,' she said. 'I have a contract until then, but afterwards I might have to move on elsewhere. You know how it is, don't you?'

He nodded. 'I'd like to know where you'll be going,' he said earnestly. 'Perhaps you could write to me?'

'Of course I can.' She gave a sad smile, and then said, 'But I want to ask you something. Can you keep it secret about who I am, just for the time being? A secret, maybe, between the three of us?' She glanced at Jenny for confirmation.

Jenny shook her head. 'Four of us,' she said. 'I must tell my mother. It wouldn't be fair otherwise. At the moment all she knows is that I've found Robin's mother and she's living in Hull.'

'Of course!' Delia put her hand to her chest. 'Of course you're right, Jenny. I'm sorry; your mother is so kind that it would be unfair to take advantage of her generosity. And I must recompense her for Jack's – Robin's, I mean – for his care and board, and the new clothes that I see he's wearing.'

'I'd grown out of my breeches because of all the lovely food,' Robin told her, 'and also it's much colder now than it was when I arrived, so I've got new jumpers as well.'

'My mother won't take any payment, Delia,' Jenny said firmly. 'I'll tell her you've offered, but I know she'll refuse. Besides,' she said feelingly, 'she's had Jack and Susan and their children living with them all these years,' and she raised her eyebrows so that Delia would understand the unspoken allusion fully. 'There's much making up to do, I think.'

Jenny ordered lunch, and whilst they were waiting for a table Robin went to have a wander around the hotel.

'I can't thank you enough, Jenny,' Delia said fervently, and if Jenny had had any reservations about her friend's having left her son with people who were virtual strangers to him, they were now dispelled. Delia obviously loved him so much that she had felt compelled to take such a drastic step to assure his well-being.

'I ought to buy him a Christmas present,' Delia murmured. 'But will it be questioned?'

'There's no need,' Jenny responded. '*You* are his Christmas present; I told him that was why we were coming to Hull, to give him a present. He won't want anything else now that he knows you're safe and that he'll see you again. He's a lovely boy, Delia. I love him to bits and my mother does too, and she will all the more if I tell her that he's her grandson.' She paused. 'The difficulty will be keeping it from my father. But I'll wait until Jack and all of them move out. Then we'll have a heart to heart.'

'And Robin?' Delia said quietly. 'I don't want him to know everything; not yet. Not until he's old enough to understand. I don't want him to feel hostility at such a young age; not as I've known it. And I don't want him to know about my parents either; people who could be so cruel as to disown their own child.'

Jenny had asked her father to pick them up in Hedon and he was patiently waiting in the station yard.

'Thanks, Da,' she said, and kissed his cheek. Now more than ever, she was appreciative of the fact that her father had always cared for her and would have done anything to make her life as perfect as possible, spoiling her with little favours in the way that fathers did with daughters; some fathers, she corrected herself. He would have been appalled if he had known how Davis Deakin had treated his. No one would have known; she hadn't and she was Delia's closest friend.

When they arrived back at the farm, Robin shot out of the trap shouting 'Thank you, Aaron' and ran into the house, while Jenny lingered to add her thanks again as her father pulled away towards the barn.

'What's this, then?' Peggy had turned away from the range, having given the stew in the pan a stir, and was almost bowled over by Robin, who hurled himself at her and buried his face in her comfy body, his arms around her ample waist.

'I can stay, Granny Peg,' he said, his voice muffled. 'I can stay! Tell her, Auntie Jenny.'

Peggy looked down at the boy whose face was flushed and whose eyes were moist. He looked up at her with elation. Then she glanced at Jenny who was watching from the doorway, smiling broadly.

Jenny nodded, and then, as the back door clicked again and she heard children's voices, she said, 'Robin and I have lots to tell you.'

'Loads and loads,' he blurted out.

'But we want to tell you later, don't we, Robin?' She dropped her voice. 'Because some of it is secret and we only want to share it with Granny Peg, isn't that right?' She put her finger to her lips.

'Oh, yes,' he breathed. 'I almost forgot because I was so excited.'

The girls all tumbled into the room, and he whispered, 'But I can stay, Granny Peg. I can stay!'

The youngest girls were tired as they had all been backwards and forwards to Foggit's farm for most of the day, helping to take some of their own things over and squabbling about who should sleep where. Molly had been helping and was slightly disgruntled that she wouldn't be going to live there too; Louisa, on the other hand, was delighted with her single room. It had been used as a store room when the Foggits had lived there and smelled rather damp, but Grandpa Aaron had said he would bring wood and coal and light a fire in the grate, and distemper the walls to make it look nice and put up some shelves for her books.

Robin longed to tell Louisa about his mother, but Auntie Jenny kept giving him a secret wink and tapping her fingers on her lips so that he would remember they shared a secret, and then he began to think that it was rather fun.

After the girls had gone to bed and Granny Peg had made up his bed on the sofa, he thought that they would be able to talk, but they couldn't because although Aaron and Jack had gone down to the hostelry Susan was still there, going on about what they needed to do at the other house, and Jenny and Granny Peg were offering suggestions. Robin tried to keep awake in case Susan went to bed early, as she sometimes did, but it wasn't long before he drifted off to sleep, worn out by the excitement of the day.

'Just look at him,' Susan chided. 'Onny just gone off to sleep. He's been trying to keep awake, listening to our conversation.'

'Well, we weren't talking about anything he shouldn't hear,' Peggy pointed out. 'It's generally wholesome conversation in this house.'

'I'm not saying it isn't,' Susan huffed. 'I'm onny saying—'

'Shall we have another cuppa?' Jenny rose to her feet. 'And then I'll be off to bed. I'm catching the morning train, Ma. I've some work to do on school reports before Monday morning. Then we finish at the end of the week and hurrah, I can have an extra hour in bed in a morning.'

'I'll make 'tea,' Susan offered, 'and I'll take mine up. I'm ready for my bed. I'm exhausted with all the jobs we've done, and there's still more to do.'

She brought in a tray of tea and some biscuits and cheese, and then, having made cocoa for herself, said goodnight and took her drink upstairs.

'Getting into practice?' Jenny murmured, her lips against the cup. 'Or was it something I said?'

'I think she finds you rather forbidding.' Her mother gave a wry smile.

'Me!' Jenny said in mock astonishment. 'Never. I'm such a soft touch.'

'I think not,' Peggy said. 'But don't prevaricate with

me, young woman; you forget I brought you up. I know just what you're like, so come on, let's hear how you and young Robin got on in Hull and why he's so sure he can stop with us.'

'Well,' Jenny recognized that this was the ultimate challenge, 'if you say he can't, then that's an end to it, but he really wants to.'

'You know what I mean, so tell me,' Peggy said quietly, 'and also tell me why it's a secret. I don't keep secrets from your father.'

'I realize that, Ma,' Jenny said softly. 'But there are other people who shouldn't know, so the fewer people who are told the better, for the time being anyway.'

'Go on then, get on with it,' her mother urged impatiently. 'Don't shilly-shally.'

So be it. Jenny heaved a big breath. 'Robin's mother – is Dorothy Deakin.'

CHAPTER TWENTY-THREE

'No husband?' Peggy asked, her forehead creasing in bewilderment.

Jenny shook her head; 'No,' she whispered. 'Ma, whilst I was away at school and taking my exams, some – lad assaulted her! She didn't tell anyone and didn't even know she was pregnant, but her mother guessed and when her father was told he took his belt to her, and I don't think it was the first time either. They turned her out of the house and told her never to come back. Her father was a tyrant, and I never even guessed; never had an inkling of the kind of life she'd been living since she was a child.' Jenny's voice broke. 'She never once said. She kept everything to herself.'

They heard the scullery door open and the sound of the men talking and taking off their boots. 'She doesn't want them to know where she is or what she's doing,' she added swiftly. 'Seemingly she wrote to them every year, God knows why; but they never replied.'

She stopped talking as her father and brother came in. 'Still jawing, then?' Jack muttered as he unfastened his coat and took off his cap. 'Beats me what women find to talk about.'

'Men usually,' Jenny said icily; she could hardly bring herself to look at her brother. 'And the reasons why some women choose to stay single.'

'Oh-oh!' Aaron sucked in a breath.

'Not every man, Da,' she said gently. 'Not men like you.'

Peggy took herself into the scullery and pumped water into the kettle, giving herself time to digest the information she had been given. She shivered, the cold air of the scullery giving her goose pimples after the heat from the kitchen fire. She heard the dog bark from his kennel, probably in response to a fox. She peered out of the window but could see nothing but blackness and the reflection of the small paraffin lamp that sat on a shelf behind her.

How could anyone turn their own daughter out of her home? Their own flesh and blood. It wasn't right, especially if it wasn't her fault; they should have got 'police out searching for 'culprit. Or perhaps they thought they'd be tainted by her shame; that it would be a reflection on them. I remember her as a sweet young lass, rather shy. Who could have done that to her? Some lad – or maybe even a grown man from 'village who caught her as she was walking home. She was always on her own, running errands, shopping down in 'village; anybody might have noticed her.

She picked up the kettle to take to the range. That last day she called here, she was in such a state; why didn't she tell me? Was that 'same day it happened – or later? Was she running here, to 'nearest place? Frightened? Did she ask for our Jenny, or did she know she wasn't at home? I can't remember what she said; I thought she was going to pass out. I brought her inside, made her a cup of tea, I think. She sighed. It was a long time ago.

She placed the kettle on the hook over the fire and as she turned to sit down she glanced across at Robin, fast asleep on the sofa. Poor bairn. So where've they been all this time? And where's his mother staying now? There's more to this than I've yet been told.

'Davis Deakin was in 'Humber Tavern,' Aaron said abruptly, which made Jenny and her mother jump; it was as if he had been reading their thoughts. 'He's a miserable owd beggar! Never has 'time of day for anybody. When you think how long he's been fishing in these waters alongside all 'other Paull Shrimpers, you'd think he'd have summat to say, wouldn't you? And even if' – his rare anger surfaced – 'even when they say how do to him, he onny nods, never looks anybody in 'eye.'

No one commented until Jack asked suddenly, 'Where did their daughter go? Dorothy? Did she leave 'district? I don't remember seeing her in years.' And then, just as abruptly, and it seemed to Jenny, who was watching him as a cat might watch a mouse, that he might have been reminded of something, he asked if Susan had gone to bed.

'Only just missed her, have you?' she said slyly. 'Isn't that just typical of men, conveniently forgetting their womenfolk?'

Aaron tutted gently. 'Our Jenny's got a bee in her bonnet about summat, Mother. Have you worked out what it is?'

Peggy shook her head. 'It'll be a honey bee, I expect,' she murmured.

'She's mebbe turning into one o' those men-haters, Da,' Jack chipped in. 'That's why she's never married.'

'Kettle's on 'boil.' Peggy rose swiftly to her feet. 'Who wants tea, and who wants cocoa?'

Peggy was the last to go up and sat pondering, gazing into the banked-up fire. Outside the wind blowing in from the sea began to whine and whistle and she glanced across at Robin, then got up and put her hand on the windowsill above him to check if there was a draught. Although there wasn't, she went to fetch a thick towel from a drawer and tucked it along the bottom of the pane and drew the curtains closer.

His face was in calm and quiet repose, and as she gazed at him she felt the urge to weep. If what Jenny had told her was true, then by rights this child should be at the Deakins' house; he was their flesh and blood, their only grandchild. And what would they make of him? If they took him would they treat him as badly as they'd treated their daughter? Why, she thought fiercely, they'd probably turn him away just as they'd turned her away all those years ago.

I'll keep him safe here, she decided, making the commitment without any qualms or reservations, until such time as his mother is able to give him a proper home.

She smiled down at him as he uttered a deep sigh and tucked a hand beneath his cheek. I'll love him as my own, just as I do 'other bairns, and I won't make any discrimination between 'em and I won't listen to any argument from our Jack either. Aaron won't mind; I think he's tekken a liking to the lad.

She moved away and turned down the lamp on the table, leaving only the flickering firelight from the range to give the room a soft warm glow.

'Night night, Robin,' she said softly as she lifted the latch of the staircase door and smiled as she heard him murmur in his sleep.

'*Mmm*, Granny Peg.'

When Jenny arrived back in Hull she made a quick visit to Delia's lodgings and discovered from Giles Dawson that she had gone across to the Maritime Hotel to rehearse the songs that she would sing over Christmas.

'Could I discuss something with you, Miss Robinson?' Giles asked. 'Something that I think might add to the holiday atmosphere at the Maritime and even make it feel romantic – not that it is,' he quickly assured her. 'It's a piece of theatre, that's all. But not to tell Miss Delamour! I would like her to show surprise, not pretend to it.'

She'd arched her brows at this, but smiled when he explained and said yes, she agreed.

'Are you staying here over Christmas, or going home?' she asked, indicating the lodgings.

'I'm staying here, but I'm taking a leaf out of Miss Delamour's book and having Christmas Day lunch at the Maritime.'

'Oh, really?' she said. 'Then why don't you join us? A small group of friends and I are sharing a table with Miss Delamour. You are very welcome.'

He seemed startled for a moment, and then said, 'That's most thoughtful of you, but . . .' He hesitated. 'I wouldn't want Miss Delamour to think I was taking undue advantage. We barely know each other.'

Again she lifted her eyebrows. 'Therefore an opportunity to rectify that oversight? I will go across now and find out if she has any objection, and if she has,' she said, as she swept out of the door, 'I will of course tell you immediately.'

He gave a little chuckle. He liked this positive young woman who wasn't in the least daunted by anyone, unlike the gentle Miss Delamour. Miss Robinson would be a force to be reckoned with. No one would take advantage of her.

Delia had run through several classical songs to decide which would be appropriate for the various days. Christmas Eve, something light, she thought; Christmas Day something a little richer in tone to begin with and ending on a celebratory note; and for Boxing Day, the final day of the holiday, music with a lilt that would send the guests home with a melody ringing in their ears to remind them of a happy time.

She guessed that many of the guests might be lonely, which was why they were there and not with their families; although for some, like Jenny, it might have been their choice, for whatever reason.

Loneliness she would know, for this would be the first Christmas she would not spend with her darling son, and she would have wept but for knowing that he was safe, well fed and with friends. He will miss me too, some of the time; she consoled herself with the thought, but she also knew that a child could be cheered by good company and she had known on meeting him that he wasn't unhappy.

Jenny breezed into the dining room where Delia was fingering the keys of the piano. 'How are you getting along?' she asked. 'Have you chosen the music?'

'Y-yes, I think so. Will you listen to this? I thought perhaps for Christmas Eve.'

Delia struck a note on the keyboard. 'I wish I could play,' she murmured. 'I think I have the ear, but not the time or the wherewithal to pay for lessons.'

She sang a verse of 'Greensleeves' and Jenny clapped approvingly, as did a young porter who was listening as he brought in a wood basket.

'Lovely!' Jenny said admiringly. 'I can't believe that I never heard you sing except at school or in church.'

Delia gave a wry laugh; there was a discernible note of bitterness. 'I've said before, there wasn't anything to sing about. I never told anyone, not even you, Jenny, just how miserable I was. I saw you with your lovely ma and your understanding father and wished with all my heart that I could be their daughter too.'

She stopped. Once again she had said too much, and wouldn't go on to tell Jenny that another reason why she sometimes ran like the wind on her errands was so that there was time to call at the Robinsons' home on the way back without being missed or scolded by her own mother on her return home.

'I've come to tell you something,' Jenny began.

'About Ja— Robin?' Delia asked, immediately anxious.

'No, not about Robin; he was perfectly happy when I left and he whispered to me that I should tell you so. He's keeping the secret and I've told my mother about you, but not about your new name or what you're doing, and she didn't ask. No, it's about Mr Giles Dawson. He said he was coming to the Maritime for Christmas lunch and I suggested that he join our table. You have no objection, have you?'

Delia shook her head. 'No, why would I?'

'He seemed to be rather embarrassed about the idea, as if he might be intruding.'

'Nonsense, of course he wouldn't, and it would be rather nice for me, for then I would have someone I know to talk to, for I don't know your friends, Jenny.'

'I find it incredible,' Jenny sat down on the arm of a sofa, 'that you can be shy of meeting new people and yet can stand up in front of an audience and entertain them.'

'Ah, well, you see,' Delia's face lit up and Jenny thought how lovely she was when she smiled, 'when I'm on stage it's not me, but someone else entirely. It's a trick I learned a long time ago.' Her voice dropped. 'But when I sit down to eat with strangers it's only me.'

CHAPTER TWENTY-FOUR

Delia was as ready as she could possibly be and couldn't believe how lucky she was with her accommodation at the Maritime Hotel. She had been given a small bedroom, adequate for a short stay and beautifully decorated with thick hangings, a very comfortable single bed, a large mirror on the wall, a wardrobe, a washbasin, a pile of thick towels for bathing and a bathroom next door on the landing.

The agreement was that she would receive a small fee and her meals, bed and board, as the manager had put it, in return for her entertainment on each of the three days.

She was delighted when he said, 'If it goes well, Miss Delamour, then perhaps we could repeat the arrangement over the Easter period, depending of course on whether you are free?'

And she agreed that she would look in her diary and check with her agent. Not that she had any intention of asking her agent, for she was managing her own affairs at present.

She changed into her red gown for Christmas Eve supper. It was showier, more extravagant than anything

209

she would have normally worn, but, she reminded herself, you are entertaining. Pretend you're the hostess, Delia, she told herself nervously; be charming, you're on stage. She could hear the voices of other guests going downstairs and hoped that Jenny was already there so that she could introduce her to her friends, and wondered too if Giles Dawson was coming tonight or only on Christmas Day.

She waited another ten minutes and gave a final tweak at the combs in her hair; then she pulled on her long silk gloves and opened the door, locked it behind her and slipped the key into her purse before descending the stairs into the reception area.

Some of the guests, gathered around the fire with drinks in their hands, turned to gaze at her as she paused on the bottom step with her hand on the balustrade, and then Jenny emerged from the throng.

'Delia!' Jenny put out a gloved hand to greet her. 'How lovely you look! Come and meet everyone.'

She escorted Delia to a smaller group of people who were standing by the window, and said gaily, 'Here we are, everyone, this is a *very* special friend of mine. Miss Delia Delamour!'

Delia gave a slight dip of her knee and two of the ladies did the same, but the others reached out their hands to touch hers; the men came across and gave her a short bow or nod of their heads and said they were delighted to meet her. Including Jenny there were seven of them, four women and three men, and she made the eighth in the party.

'Miss Delamour!' One of the gentlemen brought her a glass of champagne without waiting for the serving staff to bring a tray. 'How is it we haven't met before if you are a special friend of Miss Robinson?'

Delia glanced at Jenny. What had she told them about her? Jenny just smiled and sipped from her glass.

'I've lived in the south of England for the last ten years,' she said huskily, 'and only recently returned to my home area.'

'So what have you been doing with yourself in the south of England?' he asked merrily. 'Not getting married, I hope? Our group are all single bodies, completely dedicated to the solitary state.'

'Speak for yourself, Charles.' Another man came to join them and pressed her hand. 'After meeting Miss Delamour, I might well change my mind about that.'

'Don't take any notice of either of them, Delia.' Jenny waved them away and led her out of their hearing. 'They're only teasing. They are both dedicated bachelors and *very* good friends.' She nodded her head significantly, and Delia smiled. She wasn't quite as naïve as Jenny imagined. Living amongst theatricals she had learned much about personal idiosyncrasies and accepted people for what they were. Jenny might consider her friends to be a novelty, and they were certainly a complete contrast to how she had been brought up in her traditional home, but they were not unusual.

Canapés were brought round and more champagne, which Delia refused; she must keep a clear head, at least until she had finished her performance. She slipped into the dining room and wandered over to the piano, where a single silver candlestick bore a flickering white candle, and, as if idly, she ran her fingers over the keys.

211

She had decided she would begin with 'Greensleeves', a delightful tender melody that most people would know which would put them in pleasant humour.

Ten minutes more and a gong sounded to alert the guests that supper was about to be served and they began to saunter towards the dining tables. Delia took her place, conveniently situated close to the piano. She waited for the hors d'oeuvre to be served and more wine poured and discreetly rose to her feet without anyone from her table immediately noticing.

She began to sing the first verse of the romantic Tudor folk tale – *Alas my love you do me wrong to cast me off discourteously* – and guests turned round from the tables and then looked at each other, smiling at the unexpected treat. As she took a breath she heard a faint refrain from a violin. It came nearer, and when she turned her head there was Giles Dawson in his evening dress tails and crisp white shirt walking slowly towards her, with the violin tucked beneath his chin and a twinkle in his eyes. Smiling, she continued, her voice soaring with the accompaniment: *Greensleeves was all my joy, Greensleeves was my delight; Greensleeves was my heart of gold . . .*

Her second song was 'Flow Gently Sweet Afton' and again Giles accompanied her, playing softly in the background. After one more melody she took her bow, as did Giles, and then he bowed to her too and taking her hand led her back to her seat at the table. His own seat, which she hadn't previously noticed was empty, was immediately opposite hers.

'Thank you very much, Mr Dawson,' she murmured

across to him. 'That was lovely. How did you know what I was going to sing?'

'I didn't,' he said. 'But I guessed it would be something that you've already performed at the theatre. Did you mind?' His eyebrows rose. 'I could have made a terrible mistake by playing without being asked. You might have been annoyed with me for pitching in.'

'Not at all. I was actually more comfortable with the sound of music in the background.'

They both ate their hors d'oeuvre and the soup was brought, after which more wine filled their glasses and the main course of pheasant and duck was served. Delia finished her conversation with her neighbour, a gentleman who had introduced himself as Godfrey, and once more spoke across the table to Giles, murmuring that she would sing again before the dessert.

'Are you planning on playing again, or was the idea just for the beginning of the evening?'

He shook his head, leaning forward to whisper, 'It's your evening, Miss Delamour, not mine. I'd be quite happy to sit here and listen to you, as the other guests will.' He paused. 'But if you'd like me to join you it would be a very great pleasure.'

She ran the tip of her tongue over her lips and said, 'I was planning to sing "Scarborough Fair", changing "she" to "he" and so on, and then "The Last Rose of Summer", finishing with "See Amid the Winter's Snow" and "Oh Little Town of Bethlehem" to remind us that tomorrow is Christmas Day. What do you think?'

'Excellent,' he pronounced. 'All favourites of mine. Perhaps invite the guests to join in?'

'Then – would you? Although it seems unfair when

it's your holiday time.' She laughed. 'The Maritime will be delighted that they're getting two performers for the price of one!'

'You are charging a fee?' he whispered again.

She nodded. 'I said I would accept just a small fee and my bed and board, but I think I might waive the fee as I've been given such a lovely room. And an excellent dinner.'

'Nonsense!' he said, his voice still low but adamant. 'Miss Delamour – Delia! You must believe in your worth. You are a professional performer and have a living to earn. They will expect to pay you just as they will expect to pay the staff serving dinner. I won't require a fee, of course, because I asked them if I might accompany you as a surprise for you, and it will be a bonus for them if I continue playing; but sometimes,' he added seriously, 'by giving, you also receive in kind.'

Delia took a sip of water. 'You're right, I know.'

Jenny interrupted their conversation. 'What schemes are the two of you planning? Your performance was delightful, incidentally. You make a splendid duet. You, Mr Dawson, are lost in the middle of an orchestra.'

'I'm not proficient enough to be a solo artist,' he explained. 'I know my limitations, but I think that Miss Delamour's voice brings out the best in my playing.'

'And your playing in my voice,' Delia said, surprising herself at her boldness; and rising from the table, she added, 'I would be delighted if you would consider accompanying me once more?'

He rose to his feet and put his hand to his chest, declaring, 'My pleasure.'

There was spontaneous applause as they took their

places by the piano. The candle had been replaced by a fresh one and another candlestick had been brought to stand at the other side of the piano. The lamps in the room were turned down and Giles began playing the old folk tune "Scarborough Fair". Delia was warmed by the sight of the guests mouthing the words and moving their heads in time to the music.

She began to sing, and the loneliness and sadness of being apart from her son dissolved as she lost herself in the music.

CHAPTER TWENTY-FIVE

Robin gazed at the kitchen table in astonishment as he took his place between Louisa and Molly. He was dressed in new dark blue cord trousers that came down to his ankles and a pale blue shirt with a collar that showed above the navy blue jumper, all presents that he had opened that Christmas Day morning. He had also received two volumes of *Sixpenny Dickens* that Jenny had found in a Hull bookshop and posted to him in a parcel bearing the message *Not to be opened until Christmas Day*. He couldn't wait to begin reading them.

All the children had played with their new toys in the parlour whilst their grandmother prepared the Christmas feast, and Robin too had received additional presents as well as his new clothes: bonbons, puzzles and games. But it was what lay on the table that enraptured him now, for he had never seen anything like it in his life. An enormous roast goose resting on a large plate in the centre of the groaning white-clad table was decorated with holly, and clustered around it were chestnut stuffing balls and golden brown sausages that Molly said were made from their own pork, by which he supposed she meant pigs. Two large jugs of home-made wine and another of lemon-ade sat on a side dresser.

'Oh, Granny Peg,' he said, as she came to the table bearing a tray on which dishes of crisp roasted potatoes and more stuffing jostled with bowls of redcurrant and gooseberry jelly. 'I want to stay here for ever!'

She set down the dishes and wiped her warm forehead. 'Just for the food?'

'No!' he said. 'Because I love you all.'

'Robin loves me best,' Molly declared. 'Because I'm special!'

Robin turned to glance at Louisa, who shyly lowered her eyes but smiled as if she knew that he loved her best, for he had told her so.

'Oh, well that's a relief then.' Peggy smiled. 'I thought it was only because of my cooking.'

Aaron was sharpening a carving knife with a steel. He looked up and said, 'But what would your ma say about you staying for ever, Robin? Would she mind?'

Robin emitted a deep sigh. 'I don't know. I wish she could have been here for Christmas Day.'

'Mebbe we'll ask her next year, eh?' Peggy said, and then lifted her voice to where Jack could be heard bringing in another basket of logs for the parlour fire. 'Come on, Jack. We're ready to dish up. Where's Susan?' Her lips turned down as she spoke her daughter-in-law's name.

'I'm here.' Susan came through the door into the kitchen. 'Sorry, can I do anything?'

'Yes, sprouts and turnip in 'bottom oven,' Peggy said briskly. 'Set them on 'table whilst I whisk 'gravy. Aaron better start carving 'goose. We don't want everything getting cold. Emma, Rosie, sit down now, please.'

There was a contented silence as everyone tucked in. Then Jack raised his glass of elderberry wine to his mother and said, 'Thanks, Ma. You've worked wonders as usual.' All the adults raised a glass, and the children waved their lemonade tumblers.

'Thank you, Granny Peg,' Robin said in a trembling voice. He suddenly felt sad and his eyes were moist. This was the first time in his life that he had been away from his mother at Christmas, and he was now more aware of her absence than he had been in ages because of seeing her so recently. He held aloft his lemonade and in a quavering voice said, 'Happy Christmas, everyone.'

'Happy Christmas to you too, Robin,' Peggy said quietly, lifting her glass to him. 'And here's to your mother too.'

'Whoever she is and wherever she is,' Susan sniffed, and took a large gulp of wine that emptied half her glass.

'Go easy with that, Susan,' Jack told her. 'Ma's elderberry packs a punch.'

'I know! I've had it before.' Susan took a slice of goose. 'Nice goose,' she commented. 'I suppose *we'll* have to fatten one up for next year.'

Jack looked up. 'Why? You're not thinking o' cooking Christmas dinner, are you?' His gaze crossed to his mother, but her face was impassive and she lifted her shoulders slightly and went on eating as if she had no idea what anyone was talking about. 'We always have Christmas here,' he insisted. 'It won't be 'same if we don't.'

'Mebbe Susan wants to have it at your own house,' Peggy said quietly, handing a dish of buttered carrots to Aaron. 'Every woman likes to be in her own home at Christmas time, and you'll be all set up by next year.'

'Or we could go to my parents.' Susan finished her wine and reached for the jug. 'They've asked us plenty o' times, but your Jack never wants to go.'

Jack ran his tongue around his teeth in search of a stray piece of sausage. He found it and swallowed it. 'No,' he said. 'I don't.'

The following morning, relatives of Peggy's and Aaron's called. First came Peggy's sisters and brothers with their husbands and wives, children and grandchildren, and they were served tea, coffee, beer and lemonade – of which Peggy had made gallons – and scones, hot out of the oven. No sooner had they left than Aaron's unmarried sister, his three brothers and their wives and children, five granddaughters and three grandsons arrived, and they were served wine or beer, ginger ale and mince pies. Robin was in his element when he heard that some of the men were fishermen as Aaron used to be, and he told them that he would like to go out on the estuary as soon as he was old enough.

'I go out fishing with my da,' one of the grandsons boasted, 'but I'm twelve, so I've finished school already. I don't remember seeing you afore. Are you Uncle Jack's lad?'

'No.' Robin shook his head. 'I'm Robin Jackson. I'm just staying here for a bit.'

He was bewildered that anyone could have so many relations. He knew some of the boys from school but only Ben had become a friend. He had no idea how any of the other children were related to Jack's daughters and he whispered to Louisa asking her if she knew them all and she laughed and said, yes, she did. They were all cousins.

After a while, he picked up his Dickens books, sidled out of the parlour where they were sitting and went into the kitchen to claim what he thought of as his sofa; there were some women talking to Peggy as she made tea and coffee, and as nobody seemed to notice him he eased off his shoes and tucked his legs beneath him and opened one of the books.

'No, he's staying wi' us for 'time being,' he heard Peggy say. 'Just until his ma sorts herself out.'

'So who is he?' one of the women asked. 'Susan said that his mother had left him on his own.'

'She hardly did that when she left him wi' us,' Peggy said sharply. 'She knows where we are.'

'She'll not be wed, I suppose?' another one said.

'That's neither here nor there,' Peggy answered. 'I'm happy to have him stay here for as long as he wants. Tea?' she said. 'Or coffee? There are shortbread biscuits on 'table.'

'Oh, thanks, Peggy. You're a marvel as always.'

After they had eaten a late dinner of cold goose and ham and re-heated mashed potatoes, turnips and carrots, then leftover Christmas pudding, Aaron took all the children for a walk to stretch their legs and get some fresh air.

'Where to, then?' he asked them as they headed down the track towards the estuary.

'The river,' Louisa and Molly said eagerly and Robin said, 'Oh, yes please.'

'It's too far to walk,' Emma complained. 'I want to go home!'

Then Rosie said the same, adding, 'Cos then we'll have to walk back.'

'No, we're going out to give Gran a rest,' Aaron told them. 'She's been very busy cooking and feeding everybody and she's going to put her feet up for an hour while we're out. You can have a piggy-back on 'way home, Rosie, but you're big enough to walk, Emma. What shall we look for, Louisa?'

'What will be flying in, Grandda?' she asked. 'Greylags? Or pink-footed geese? Plover?'

'Greylags? Mebbe not; word is that they've been over-hunted and there's not many about. Pink-feet, I reckon, and if we walk along 'bank we should see plover and shelduck, and we'll listen for curlew, and a penny for who hears 'em first.'

'Pink-feet?' Robin queried. 'What are they?'

'Geese,' Louisa giggled. 'They've got pink legs and feet.'

'Pink legs and feet!' Robin exclaimed. 'You'll have to show me.'

'We'll hear them afore we see them,' Molly said, anxious to impart her knowledge too. 'Won't we, Grandda?'

'We certainly will; now come on, best feet forward.' They soon reached the Humber bank and turned left to walk away from the village. 'No playing about; Rosie and Molly, tek my hands, and 'rest of you come in front where I can see you.'

They walked past the lighthouse and the coastguard cottages, where Aaron acknowledged someone in one of the cottage windows; they climbed a few rough steps on to the river bank and walked along a well-trodden path. The wind was sharp here and everyone drew their scarves closer to their necks and the girls pulled their bonnets over their ears. Aaron was already wearing a tweed cap, and seeing that Robin hadn't brought his he released one of his hands from Molly's grasp, dug deep into his coat pocket and brought out a woolly hat.

'Here you are, lad,' he said, looking down at him. 'You'll find you're much warmer with a hat on, even though you've got a thick head of hair.'

Robin took it gratefully. 'I won't forget another time,' he said. 'Not now that I'm living in the country.'

'Aye, there's generally a chill wind near an estuary, and we're not that far from 'sea here at Paull,' Aaron told him. 'Not as 'crow flies, any road. Now then.' He had spotted a horse and rider coming towards them. 'Come inland a bit to let him pass. And keep still and quiet so that you don't spook 'hoss.'

They all stood still as instructed, and as the rider drew abreast of him he lifted his crop. 'Many thanks,' he said. 'Much obliged.' Then he tightened the reins. 'Mr Robinson, isn't it?'

'Aye, it is.' Aaron looked up at the horseman. 'Beggin' your pardon, but have we met?'

'Ralph Pearce,' the man said. 'Your Jack and I were friends when we were young. Not seen him lately. I suppose we're both busy with business and families. How are they, he and his wife . . . Susan, isn't it?'

It sounded as though mentioning Jack's wife by name was almost an afterthought.

'Aye, they're all right. We've all enjoyed Christmas together.'

'Ah! Jack and I got married about the same time.' His gaze ran over the children. 'I hadn't realized he had a son.'

Aaron glanced at Robin and then up at the rider. 'He hasn't,' he said. 'This is a friend's son come to stay wi' us.'

'Ah,' he said again. 'I've four sons. I imagine daughters are easier to manage.' He gathered up the reins and prepared to move off. 'Give my regards to Jack and his wife, and the season's greetings to you, sir, and your family. Jenny,' he added swiftly, 'your daughter. Does she still live in Paull?'

'No,' Aaron answered brusquely. 'She doesn't. Good day to you.'

Aaron doesn't like him, Robin thought perceptively as they walked on. He was being rather nosy, I think, asking questions. And that's twice today that someone thought I was Jack's son. Hah! Jack's son. Jackson, that's my new name, and he grinned to himself.

They walked on, and soon turned their backs on the Humber. 'This will interest you, Robin,' Aaron told him. 'We'll go and have a quick look at a site of history while we're here. The girls have been many times but I'm sure they won't mind showing it to you, and then we'll head home, cos it's getting much colder.'

And indeed it was; an icy wind was blowing off the estuary, and tossing the shining silver-steel wave-crests crashing against the river wall. 'You've seen the lighthouse back there,' Aaron went on, 'except it's in use as a telegraph office now since 'new lights were built further along 'river. There's allus been a beacon here. Some were washed away, but what I wanted to show you was 'Paull Battery, built hundreds of years ago to protect Hull from its enemies.'

'Oh, a sort of fort, do you mean?' Robin asked eagerly.

'Exactly that.' Aaron warmed to his theme now that he sensed a willing listener. 'When I was a lad we used to play there, climbing on 'walls and pretending we were sodgers on 'lookout for enemy ships coming up 'river.'

Sodgers, Robin thought. I must remember that. 'I'd like to do that,' he said. 'Maybe in the spring when it's a bit warmer.'

So he intends to stay, Aaron thought. He's not considering leaving us.

'So who built it?' Robin asked as they walked up the track towards the fort.

'Ah, well. Who built it, girls?'

'King Henry!' Louisa said promptly, as if she'd been waiting for the question. 'We learned about it in school. He thought there was going to be a war with . . . erm, France or Spain I think, and he was building forts all around 'coast.'

'That's it! He did, and he built a battery here for twelve cannons to warn off any of his enemies and let the town of Hull know of 'danger.'

'So Paull was really important?' Robin asked.

'Oh, aye, it was, and over a lot of years 'battery was rebuilt so it's still standing today.'

The weather was worsening; sleet was beginning to fall, sharp as needles on their faces. The girls were starting to shiver and Rosie to cry and Aaron decided to cut their journey short.

'I'll bring you another day, Robin,' he told him, 'and give you a proper look round, but right now we'd better mek tracks for home. Come on, Rosie, I'll give you a piggy-back.' He bent low and Robin helped her on to his back. 'Come on then, all hold hands, two-be-two, and off we trot.'

Robin smiled and pensively wished that Aaron was his grandfather, and wondered if he had ever had one.

CHAPTER TWENTY-SIX

Delia had thoroughly enjoyed Christmas at the Maritime, yet apart from when she was immersed in the music she was constantly aware of a deep loneliness within her. Her precious son was with another family and she wondered if he was missing her as much as she was missing him.

After Boxing Day luncheon she asked Jenny if she thought he would have been all right and not unhappy. Jenny assured her that he would have been.

'It seems to me,' she said, 'that Robin is a very sensible boy, and although yes of course he'll miss you – he's bound to when he's had your constant company for all of his young life – he's also level-headed and I think he'll see the advantages of being with a family. I know children, even though I haven't any of my own. It will be good for him, Delia,' she was quick to point out when she saw Delia's expression of pain. 'I know it was an impetuous decision on your part to leave him in the first place, but it's worked out to the advantage of both of you.'

'But it was wrong of me to land him in your parents' laps without even thinking about it. It's true, it was impulsive. When I saw him sitting with the little girls and chatting as if he'd known them all his life, I knew just what he was missing and I couldn't give it to him.' She restrained a sob.

'And my mother loves him already,' Jenny said gently, 'and if I know my father at all, then he will too.'

At Boxing Day luncheon she had sung unaccompanied, as Giles had taken his leave after supper on Christmas Day to attend, he said, to other matters. At supper there were fewer guests, mainly local; others with a longer distance to travel had already left.

Jenny and her friends drifted off the following morning and Delia packed up her theatre gowns, carefully folding them so that they wouldn't crease. She had buttoned up her boots, put on her hat and tied a warm cloak over her woollen dress when a chambermaid knocked on her door.

'I'm sorry to disturb you, ma'am; Mr Giles Dawson is downstairs enquiring if you were still here and I said I'd check.'

Delia thanked her. 'Would you tell him I'll be down in five minutes, and would you ask a porter if he would bring my luggage down, please?'

'Oh, I can do that, ma'am,' the girl offered. 'I'm used to carrying things.' She picked up Delia's already fastened valise. 'Not heavy at all,' she said.

When Delia arrived downstairs, Giles was sitting comfortably in an armchair drinking coffee and reading a copy of the *Illustrated London News*. He rose when he saw her.

'Good morning, Delia,' he said. They had agreed

over Christmas that they could stop being quite so formal and use their first names.

'So how was your Boxing Day?' Delia asked. 'Did Mrs Benson feed you leftovers?'

'She did, as a matter of fact. There were just two other guests, and for supper we had chicken broth followed by chicken and sausagemeat rissoles. And then, as she had joined us at the table, she brought out a bottle of port which we had with a very ripe Stilton and Christmas cake. I went up to my room to get a bottle of whisky, one of the other men had been given a box of chocolates and cigars, and we had quite a merry time over a game of crib.'

Is he making it up? she wondered. Or perhaps he's used to that kind of festivity during the Christmas holiday. She thought of the many times when all the other theatre folk had gone home or to stay with friends and she and her son had made the best of whichever lodging house would take them in over Christmas. She had felt sorry for the older people who had shared their lodgings and eaten the same meagre Christmas dinner, and often wondered if the same fate awaited her.

'Would you like to take a walk?' he asked. 'Or do you consider it too cold?'

'I would like to walk,' she said. 'I need some air after being inside for so long. But I should take my luggage to Mrs Benson's first.'

'Let me carry it. We'll drop it off on our way. I think it's going to snow so we must make the most of the day before it does.'

Having left her valise in the lodging house hall,

at Giles' suggestion they continued through Market Place, where there were fewer stalls than usual and not many customers buying, and on towards the pier, glad to be outside after being cooped up over the holiday. The sky was blue and almost cloudless but it was bitterly cold.

'This has been the coldest year for years,' he remarked. 'They're saying it could be the coldest winter ever.'

'I'm sure that it is.' Delia huddled further into her collar and shawl. 'Perhaps the pier wasn't such a good idea.'

'A quick turn only,' he said, 'and then we'll find a cosy tea house or coffee shop.'

'This is our life, isn't it?' she murmured. 'Or mine at least. Borrowing warmth from every possible source.' She looked up at him. 'Or perhaps it isn't for you, Giles? It occurs to me that you might have known something better?'

He paused, and then, taking her arm, he said, 'And you would be correct. I have known something else, though not necessarily better. Certainly the company I have today far excels any other I have known in recent years, and I must add,' he said hastily, for perhaps he felt her flinch, 'I am no flatterer.'

They turned away from the pounding waves on the estuary, which were plunging into the horse wash and dashing a surging swell of high water against the pier walls, and he steered her towards a small coffee shop in Queen Street. The window was steamed up so that they couldn't see inside, but the warmth hit them as he opened the door and they claimed a table tucked into a corner where it would be free of draughts.

'You might be full of good food from the Maritime, but I'm sure you can manage a pot of coffee or tea?' he asked.

'I can,' she said, 'and although I had a hearty break-fast, I could probably manage a slice of cake as well!'

'I know most of the coffee shops in the town by now, and this one I might tell you produces delicious cakes.'

She glanced at him surreptitiously as he ordered and wondered if he would expand on the statement he had made earlier. He didn't seem aimless, as she thought she must appear, but rather he had an air of determin-ation and confidence that appeared to tell the world that the way he lived was his choice and not a necessity. But she wouldn't press him; she had always avoided any cosy unburdening of personal matters. He poured the coffee and cleared his throat.

'I, erm, I thought that as you have given me the honour of your confidence over your personal troubles, it is only right that I should reciprocate with my own.'

'Oh, but you need not,' she broke in quickly. 'I wouldn't expect you to.'

'I'd rather like to,' he said calmly, 'because at some time in the future you might find I have gone off on business of my own somewhere, and you might per-haps wonder where.' He put down his cup and turned to her, speaking softly. 'We have known each other for only a short time, Delia, but I have come to value our friendship, for such a thing is rare between a man and a woman unless there is the prospect of some-thing more.'

Delia nodded. He was quite right, and she had had a similar relationship with Arthur Crawshaw, except that he often disappeared from view without feeling the need to explain, nor she to ask why or where he had gone.

'I'm comfortable with our friendship,' she said. 'I make no demands on you.'

He took a sip of coffee. 'I know. But I would like to tell you that I hired a cab yesterday morning and was driven to York.'

She raised her eyebrows in astonishment and he gave a wry smile. 'It cost me a lot of money during the Christmas festivities, but it was necessary. I went to visit my wife.'

Delia drew in a breath and covered her mouth with her hand. Her first response was to flee, but he lifted appeasing hands and said, 'If I might explain?'

She took up her cup and found her hands were trembling. She had no romantic aspirations towards him, but this might alter their friendship.

'My wife and I were married when we were very young, at the expectations of both our families,' he began. 'Neither of us wanted it, but we had such pressure from them that unwisely we gave in. She was in love with someone entirely unsuitable in the eyes of her family, whereas I wanted to continue with my musical education, which was only possible if my father supported me, which he agreed to do if I married Marion, the daughter of his best friend.'

He lowered his voice. 'Our marriage was and is in name only and a source of unhappiness to us both. She continues to see her lover and I . . . well, I completed

231

my music studies and after a few years decided that the best thing for me to do was join an orchestra and travel, which gave us both a chance to live our own lives, unhindered by each other.'

'I'm so sorry,' Delia breathed. 'And she lives in York?'

'She does, in our family home, except that we have no family. I don't usually see her over Christmas, but in the New Year we visit both sets of parents together, to give our marriage a veil of respectability. However,' he went on, 'I received a message asking me to call as she was unwell and needed to discuss certain issues, which is why I visited her.'

'Is she very unwell?' Delia asked.

'I'm not sure. She has unexplained illnesses from time to time. She is still a relatively young woman but she appears fragile, though whether or not she is I can't determine. I feel that it is our situation that makes her ill. She complains now that she has a sickness and is convinced she is dying.'

He put his chin in his hands and gave a deep sigh. 'I have an uneasy suspicion that she might be carrying a child.' He sighed again. 'And it isn't mine.'

'And the issues she wished to discuss with you?'

'Well, she wishes me to spend more time there, and to inform our parents that we can't travel to see them during the New Year because she is ill.'

'She could write to tell them that,' Delia suggested.

He gave a grimace. 'She can be a cunning minx. She knows it will be believable coming from me. Her parents know her very well, my parents less so. I believe that when she asked me to spend more time with her it was her way – if in fact she *is* expecting a child – of showing that it will naturally appear to be mine. And it most certainly is *not*!'

Delia gazed at him. 'Yet if there isn't any proof that she is carrying her lover's child, it will be natural for everyone to think it is yours. Your only hope is that you are mistaken. It seems unlikely, doesn't it, after so many years, that she would now conceive a child?'

They were both silent for a few minutes, and they were brought fresh coffee and biscuits. It was as if the woman who served them realized they were in serious conversation. Delia gave her a warm smile as she thanked her.

'And so what will you do?' she went on.

'I don't know what to do. If she's expecting a child and I deny it is mine, she will be classed as a fallen woman. If I accept it, I will be expected to bring up a son or daughter I haven't fathered.'

'What tangled lives we lead.' Delia shook her head dejectedly. 'We're like actors in a play, or characters in a book. And yet . . .' She paused. 'It's real life and it can be tragic or sad, comic and – unbelievable.'

CHAPTER TWENTY-SEVEN

Robin felt sad when the day came for the girls to move to the other house, but he kept busy, helping to pack bags and crates into the wagon, sitting on top of them with Louisa as Jack drove the short distance round to Foggit's farm, and then passing them down to Jack and Aaron when they pulled up in the yard where the agent was waiting with the keys.

It was a long, low, boulder-and-brick house with a pantile roof facing the estuary. Off the large kitchen, which had a range and a stone sink, was a short staircase to the first floor where there were three bedrooms. It had a scullery similar to Peggy's and a parlour behind the kitchen. At the end of the building a barn was attached and behind it, across the back yard and set apart from the house, were a privy, a pigsty and a cow-shed; beyond that a paddock, a kitchen garden and a large field for livestock.

Over the fence was a smaller field where two goats cropped round a stunted apple tree. By the fence a short-haired terrier-type dog was barking frantic-ally and hoarsely at them. A woman with a shawl over her head stood at the door of a rundown cottage, shouting at the dog to come in, but it took no heed.

'Who lives there?' Robin asked Louisa. 'That's a very noisy dog.'

'It's Mr Deakin's house,' she said, her voice low. 'That's Mrs Deakin calling the dog. You're best not speaking to them, Robin. All 'bairns in Paull are scared of them.'

'Why?'

'Don't know,' she said. 'They just are. Mr Deakin's a fisherman but he doesn't talk to any of 'other fishermen and he doesn't like bairns. That's what Grandda says, anyway.'

'Have you just got one grandfather and granny?' It had struck Robin that there was only one set of grandparents helping with the move.

'No, Ma's mother and father are our grandparents as well, but we don't see them much, cos they live 'far side of Hedon. Ma takes us sometimes and they give us a penny, or a bonbon.'

Peggy and Susan arrived in the trap with boxes and bedding, bringing the other children along for the ride. Robin and Louisa followed them into the house.

'You'd best light a fire, Jack,' Susan said when she put her nose inside. 'It smells damp.'

'It'll not be damp,' Peggy remarked. 'It's not been empty that long. It's just a bit cold, that's all. There'll probably be kindling and logs in 'barn, and you ordered coal, didn't you?'

Jack ignored Susan's request to make a fire; the agent had gone and he and Aaron were bringing in the heavier furniture like the kitchen table and benches; Robin carried in a box and Louisa did too.

Peggy looked up. She had no intention of making a fire. She decided that Susan's lessons in homemaking should begin immediately. She began to unpack a box of saucepans and put them on a low cupboard shelf. 'I'll leave these here, Susan, and you can put them wherever's best for you when you're ready.'

Susan ignored her. 'Jack, are you going to mek that fire? It's freezing in here.'

'Fetch some kindling in, then,' Jack said. 'Did you bring some paper or old straw to start it?'

'No, I didn't,' she answered sharply. 'I've been busy, in case you haven't noticed.'

Peggy banged down a heavy pan, her resolve failing. 'Look, you finish unpacking and I'll mek 'damned fire, and when I've done that I'll nip home and bring a pan of stew. That'll save you having to do anything for supper.'

She put on the coat she'd just taken off and her rubber boots and went out to the barn, bringing back kindling, a small bundle of dusty straw that she'd gathered up from a corner, a few logs and some pieces of coal, and within minutes a fire was blazing in the range.

Peggy was livid as she went home, not driving but going out of the gate and climbing the fence into their property and muttering to herself about the inadequacies of her daughter-in-law. Contrary to what Susan had said, she didn't consider that the younger woman had stirred a finger for this move apart from stripping their beds to take the sheets and bedspreads with them. 'And those are my sheets if everybody had their own,' she raged.

She carefully packed the casserole dish into a box, wrapped a loaf of bread that she'd made fresh that morning and put that in as well. 'I'll not have those bairns going to bed hungry,' she muttered. 'And I suppose I'd better make 'beds up whilst I'm about it.'

When she got back, Susan had filled the kettle and put it on the fire, which was now burning steadily. Aaron had been into the barn and brought in a basket of logs, then returned to fill an old bucket with coal that the Foggits had left behind.

Peggy put the casserole in the side oven. It was only just warm, but she knew it would be hot enough by the time they were ready to eat.

As the afternoon drew on, Jack and Aaron carried the beds and chests of drawers upstairs and she made up the beds for the children, but not for Jack and Susan; that was something that Susan could do herself, she decided.

'Right,' she said. 'Robin and Molly, you'd better come home with me. We'll tek 'trap and Grandda can bring 'wagon back later.'

'I'm stopping here tonight,' Molly told her. 'I want to sleep here in 'new house.'

'We haven't made up a bed for you,' Susan said abruptly. 'I thought you were stopping with Gran.'

'Not tonight I'm not,' Molly said inflexibly, without looking at her mother. 'I'll go back to Gran's tomorrow.'

'She can sleep in my bed with me,' Louisa offered. 'I expect you want to know what it feels like, don't you, Molly? You won't have to mind being at 'bottom of 'bed, though.'

'Will you mind your own business, miss,' Susan snapped. 'Nobody asked for your opinion.'

'She can stay if she wants,' Jack interrupted, coming inside with a box of crockery. 'She doesn't want to be left out, do you, Molly?'

'No I don't.' Molly pressed her lips together determinedly. 'If I like it here I might stop wi' other bairns.'

Susan heaved a deep angry breath. 'Well, don't anybody bother to ask me.'

Peggy glanced from one to another. 'All right, honey,' she said to Molly. 'Come and give your gran a big kiss, all of you. I'll see you sometime tomorrow, won't I? You all know where we live.'

'Course we do, Gran.' Molly put her arms round Peggy's waist. 'You won't be lonely wivout us, will you? You've got Grandda and Robin to look after you.'

Peggy was choked as all the little girls came to give her a kiss and said they'd see her the next day, and then Emma and Rosie shot off upstairs to their shared bedroom and the next instant Molly did too. Only Louisa stood with doubt written on her face.

'Bye, Gran,' she said quietly. 'Bye, Robin. I'll see you tomorrow.'

Peggy kept her eyes firmly ahead as they drove down the track and Robin didn't speak. He guessed that she was upset at leaving the girls behind and he was too; he'd have to read to himself now and he'd enjoyed reading to the girls and acting with funny voices. He knew he would miss his mother more now that there would be fewer interruptions.

I'll do a batch bake, Peggy thought, enough for two

families; just until they get settled in, though it's time that Susan and Jack learned about their own family life. I'll prove some bread tonight and mebbe mek a couple of apple pies; I should have given Susan some apples. She decided to send some over the next day, but as they pulled into their yard she recalled that she hadn't much sugar left for baking.

By the time she'd put Betsy in her stall and come into the kitchen, Robin had filled the kettle and put it over the fire.

'I thought you might like a cup of tea, Granny Peg,' he murmured.

'Aye, I would.' She smiled. 'That's thoughtful of you, Robin. There's nothing quite like a cup in your own home, is there?'

'I don't know,' he said, and there was a catch in his voice. 'I've never lived in my own home. My mother and I have never had one.'

She sat down on a kitchen chair and drew him towards her. 'Well, consider this one yours for 'time being,' she said softly. 'Until such time as you feel you want to move on, and there's absolutely no hurry at all to do that.'

'Thank you,' he said in a low voice. 'I'd like that very much.' He paused, and then added, 'I expect you'll feel rather lonely without the girls here.'

'Yes, I think I might, so it's a good thing that you're here, isn't it?'

He brightened up considerably. 'Is there anything I can do for you?'

'Well,' Peggy glanced out of the kitchen window and saw that it was not yet dark, 'there is, as a matter of fact.

I was going to bake but I've realized I haven't much sugar.'

'Oh, I can go to the shop for you,' he said eagerly. 'I've always been very useful at running errands and I'm very quick.'

'It will take ten minutes to run there and ten back, so if we allow half an hour you'll be back easily before it turns dark. You won't dawdle, will you, or go near the slipway?'

'Oh, no, I promise,' he said. 'I'll just put my coat and cap on. Was that all you wanted? Just a bag of sugar?'

'Yes, please.' Peggy reached for her purse to give him the money. 'And here's a penny extra for you to buy something for yourself; do you like aniseed balls or liquorice?'

'Oh, yes, I do.' He handed back the penny. 'But I don't need a reward, thank you.'

She took back the coin and smiled. 'All right, off you go then. You know which shop I mean, don't you?'

He put on his cap. 'Yes,' he said, and headed for the door. 'I won't be long.'

He wants to repay me, she thought, and looked out of the window as he went out of the gate and carefully shut it after him. What a well brought up child he is. His mother did well in spite of the circumstances she found herself in. Poor girl. She must miss him.

Robin ran all the way down the track towards the village and vowed that he'd try to get there and back within the twenty minutes. I won't even stop to look at the river. But as he reached the road he saw it in front of him and noticed that today as the light was fading

240

the water looked leaden and forbidding, the white crests dull and subdued rather than frolicsome as they had been when he had last been down here. Gulls were flying low, close to the surface.

Fishing smacks and tugboats were heading towards Hull; some coal barges and larger ships were steaming in the direction of the estuary mouth and the open sea. Some, he thought, were cargo boats but there were also two-masted schooners with their sharply pointed bows, and one graceful tall ship with three masts and billowing sails like the ones he'd seen on the Thames. Others were smaller and sailing towards the far end of Paull, and he wondered if these were the shrimp boats that the Paull fishermen used. Then he saw another boat in the middle of the river heading towards the slipway and he ran swiftly down the village street to the shop so that he might see it close up on his way back.

There was no one else in the shop and he asked for a bag of sugar for Mrs Peggy Robinson, please, and the shopkeeper weighed it and bagged it, took the money and gave him change. He touched his cap and thanked her and wished her good day and she gave him a wide smile.

He ran back again towards the slipway. The boat had lowered its sails and he noticed a foreign name on the side of it; a man on board was reaching out to hand a parcel to another man, who was standing on the slipway with his back to Robin and his boots almost in the water.

As he paused to see how the sails would be hoisted, the man on shore turned round and saw him. 'Hey,' he shouted. 'What do you think you're doing?'

Startled, Robin turned his gaze to him. 'I'm – I'm watching to see how the sails are raised.'

The man strode towards him. 'Come here.' He indicated brusquely with his hand and Robin moved closer. The next second he yelped as the man clipped him on the ear and then grabbed his earlobe between a rough and cold finger and thumb.

'Ow,' Robin yelled. 'That hurts.'

'Aye, it was meant to.' The lobe was pinched again and he felt something sharp before he was let go. 'Who are you and why you hanging around here?' A fist was shaken in his face and he stepped back.

'I – I'm not!' His ear was stinging and his eyes smarting from the pain of it. 'I was – just watching the boat.'

A florid face beneath a peaked cap was pushed close to his. The eyes were mean and the lips narrow. 'You're up to no good. Who are you? You're not from round here!'

'I'm – Robin Jackson, sir, and I'm staying with Mr and Mrs Robinson.'

'Aaron Robinson, do you mean? Them with a house-ful of brats?'

He nodded and saw no reason to tell him that the children were not living there as from today.

'Go on, clear off then, and don't let me see you down here again. Do you hear?'

'Yes, sir.' Robin started to back away, and when the man raised his stick to him he turned and fled.

Peggy glanced up at the clock as Robin flew in the door and stood with his back leaning against it, breathing hard. 'There was no need to break your

242

neck,' she said. 'I onny wanted you to be back afore dark.'

Robin breathed out and went to put the bag of sugar on the table, then sat down on the bench.

'What's up?' she said, and took his cap off. 'You're bleeding; did you catch on a branch or something?'

Robin flinched as she touched his ear and he shook his head. 'No,' he muttered, and wondered whether or not to say anything else, but a tell-tale tear slid down his cheek.

'What happened?' She frowned, her eyebrows drawing together.

'A man,' he croaked. 'He was standing on the slipway and I only looked at a sailboat as I was passing to watch how the seaman would raise the sails, and I think he must have thought I was watching him but I wasn't, I was watching the man in the boat.'

'And what did he do?'

'The man on shore told me to come to him and when I did he hit me across the head and grabbed my ear.' Tenderly he touched his ear and realized it was sticky. 'He must have nipped me with his nail. It hurt,' he said tearfully. 'And I wasn't doing anything, honest, and I barely stopped because I'd promised. I was only looking as I went past. The seaman on the boat was handing him a parcel.'

'Was he now? Well, first things first. I'm going to bathe your ear with some warm water and then put some antiseptic on it in case his nails weren't clean.'

She went to the cupboard and brought out a tin, then filled a bowl with warm water from the kettle. 'Did you get a good look at him?'

'Oh, yes. He put his face right into mine and said I wasn't from round here and that I was up to no good. He had little piggy eyes and hardly any lips. He was wearing a cap with a peak, like the one that Aaron wears when he goes fishing. Oh, and he had a stick which he shook at me; and he knows Aaron because I told him I was staying with Mr and Mrs Robinson and he said did I mean Aaron Robinson.'

He decided that he wouldn't mention what the man had said about the houseful of brats because he didn't think it was a very nice thing to tell her. 'He wasn't a very nice man and I wouldn't like to meet him again,' he said. 'Can you think of who he might be, Granny Peg?'

'Oh, yes,' she said, carefully cleaning his earlobe with a damp flannel to wipe the blood away. 'I certainly can, and rest assured he'll be getting a visit from me in 'morning if he doesn't get one from Aaron tonight. Now, this might sting a bit, but I know you'll be brave.'

CHAPTER TWENTY-EIGHT

Aaron pushed open the squeaking gate, which set the dog in the kennel barking, strode to the cottage door and hammered it with his fist.

As expected, for Davis Deakin never answered the door himself, Mrs Deakin called through it in a quavering voice. 'Who is it?'

'Aaron Robinson. I need a word with your husband.'

'He – he's not in.'

'I think he is. Tell him to come to 'door or I'm going to 'Hedon cop shop to mek a charge against him.'

There was a whispering and scuffling inside and then a bolt was drawn back and a key turned and the door opened a crack. 'What!'

'Open 'door, Deakin. I'm not going to stand here and talk through a plank o' wood.'

Davis Deakin opened the door wider and then shouted at the dog, who was still barking. 'Stop that row or you'll feel my stick!'

The barks stopped instantly and Aaron wondered how often the dog had felt the stick.

'Easy to bully anybody, animal or child, isn't it?'

he said, his voice curt with sarcasm. 'Especially when you've got a weapon in your hand.'

'What 'you talking about?'

'You know what I'm talking about, but I'll remind you if your memory's amiss. You assaulted a child in my care, hit him on his head, made him bleed and threatened him wi' that stick you're holding on to right now. Perhaps you'd like to step outside instead of hiding behind 'door and your wife and try it on wi' me.'

'I've got no grudge against you,' Deakin muttered.

'Not somebody your size, eh, onny young bairns and dogs? Well, come outside,' Aaron persisted, 'and let's see just how brave you are. Oh, and mebbe leave your stick inside, eh? How about that?'

Deakin grunted, pushed the heavy door curtain aside, leaned the stick against the door jamb and stepped out.

'What's this all about, then?'

'It's about my nephew that you met a couple of hours ago.' Aaron decided that he would claim a further connection between himself and Robin, so that Deakin would realize the seriousness of the issue. 'Not only did you threaten him, you assaulted him and drew blood.'

'I never touched him,' Deakin blustered. 'I told him to clear off because he was up to no good hanging about near the estuary.'

'He'd gone on an errand for my wife and happened to see a sailboat coming to shore. A shrimp boat was it, or . . . ?'

Aaron let the question hang and then grabbed

Deakin by the scarf he wore round his neck. 'If you so much as lay a finger on any bairn that belongs to me, or even any that doesn't, you'll find yourself in 'deep water of 'estuary. And then' – he tightened his grip on the scarf – 'and *then* I'll go to 'cop shop in Hedon and I'll drive very very slowly cos our hoss is very old, and by 'time they get back here to fish you out it might be too late.' He shook him. 'Do you hear me?'

'Aye, aye, it were a mistake. I never meant to hurt the lad,' Deakin snivelled, showing Aaron that he was the coward that he'd always thought he was. 'I just accidentally—'

'And another thing.' Aaron hadn't quite finished. 'Do your dodgy business away from Paull. Don't give our shrimpers a bad name with your nefarious activities. If they should find out that you're up to summat, you might be even sorrier than you are now.'

He gave him a shove away and Deakin turned for the door. 'I don't know what you're talking about,' he muttered, and went inside. Aaron heard the bolt being drawn across and the key turn. He brushed his hands together as if to rid himself of any vestige of Davis Deakin.

The dog cowered in the kennel as he went past, but didn't bark. Aaron took a few strides towards the gate, then paused and turned back and bent down. He picked up the thick rope that bound the animal and spoke soothingly to him as he unfastened it. He set the dog free and threw the rope into the yard. The dog peered at him as he straightened up.

'You can come if you want,' Aaron offered. 'It's up to you.' He turned and walked towards the gate, but

247

instead of opening it he climbed over to avoid the creak giving notice of his departure. He watched the dog watching him and then walked away. Within a minute it had raced after him, jumping through the bars and following him down the track. He climbed the fence into Foggit's field and crossed the new homestead of his son.

'You came of your own accord, don't forget,' he told the dog as he headed for home. 'And not a word about what happened tonight.'

The dog trotted beside him and followed him over his own fence and into the yard.

'We're a dog missing, you see,' Aaron went on. 'Our Jack has tekken our other dog cos his bairns are used to him, but we'll have to be sure that you don't nip. Is that clear?'

The dog looked up, and on reaching the door sat at the side of it.

'You didn't get into a fight wi' Deakin, did you?' Peggy asked when he went in and she helped him off with his coat.

'Me! No, that's not my way, you should know that, Peggy Robinson,' he grinned. 'Where's young feller-me-lad?'

'He's taken some stuff upstairs; he's desperate to have 'small front bedroom so that he can see 'estuary from 'window, but I think he's rather scared that he's caused trouble wi' Deakin. He told me that Louisa said that all 'young bairns in 'village are frightened of him.'

'They needn't be,' he said. 'Not now he's had a warning.'

'Why, what did you tell him?' Peggy stood anxiously with a thick cloth in her hand, ready to take something from the oven.

'Oh, nowt much.' Aaron parked himself in a chair by the fire. 'Onny that I'd tip him into 'Humber if I should hear a whisper of his laying a finger on any other bairn. If anybody's scared it'll be him, especially if he thinks that 'other shrimpers might get to hear about what he's been up to.'

Robin slowly opened the door into the kitchen and looked cautiously at Aaron.

'Ah!' Aaron said. 'I nearly forgot. Just open 'back door, will you, Robin? I left summat on doorstep. I hope it's still there.'

'It's a dog,' Robin called out as he opened the door. 'Shall I let him in?'

'We don't have dogs in 'house,' Peggy began, then as the dog came trotting towards the fire said, 'That's Deakin's dog, isn't it?'

'Aye, I believe it is. He must have followed me.' Aaron bent to fondle the dog's ears. 'We'll let him out in 'morning and see if he wants to go home.'

'What was that about?' Mrs Deakin drew the door curtain tight. 'What did he want?'

'Nothing much.' Davis Deakin took his usual place by the fire. 'The old gaffer was crewnting and complaining that I'd whopped one of his lads.'

'They don't have any lads, only little lassies.'

'His nephew or some such.' He cleared his throat and spat into the fire. 'I don't know, nor do I care. I ain't afeared of him.'

'Better watch out, though. I wouldn't put it past him to get the police.'

She was worried. He shouldn't hit anybody else's children. Bad enough to hit their own, and if the police came there could be trouble.

'The dog's quiet,' she said.

He didn't answer, and reached for his pipe.

Delia's small amount of money was running out. The payment she had made for her lodgings would only last until the final week of January. She decided she would call on Mr Rogers at the theatre to ask if he definitely had a role for her once the pantomime was finished.

'Oh, Miss Delamour,' he said, when she dropped by after a matinee. 'I was hoping that you might come in. Mr Dawson suggested that you might be interested in a proposal.'

'Oh? What kind of proposal?'

'Our leading lady, Cinderella, has been told that she must rest her voice as she has laryngitis. It's a very long pantomime, as you know, and she has several numbers which are too taxing for her. She can manage the speaking parts but her voice isn't strong enough to carry for the whole performance. It keeps breaking up. I really don't know what to do, as it will be impossible to find another performer to take on the role at this late stage.'

He looked exceedingly worried and she appreciated his dilemma, but she didn't see how she could help. 'I've never played in pantomime,' she told him, 'and I think that I'm too old for the part in any case.'

She looked round as a swarm of children headed past her towards the auditorium.

'Those are local children who are playing the village children,' he explained.

She laughed. 'What, all of them?'

'Yes, about fifty of them. That's as many as we can accommodate on stage. Miss Delamour, would you be interested?' He clasped his hands together. 'Not to play the part, but to sing?'

'I don't understand.'

'Cinderella – Miss Stannard, that is – would mouth the words and you would stand in the wings and sing. You have a good carrying voice. You would both have to rehearse, of course, so that it would appear that she was singing, but I'm sure it could be done. It was Mr Dawson's idea and I thought it an excellent one.'

Oh, bless him, she thought. He's saved my life again.

'We have many special effects,' he went on. 'Lighting, and mirrors, and we can darken the stage where appropriate so that the audience won't guess that it isn't Miss Stannard singing. What do you think?'

'Well . . .' She hesitated. 'I suppose . . .'

'And of course we would pay you the same rate as if you were top of the bill.'

'Well, why not?' She smiled. 'It might be rather fun, and it would be something quite different for me. Would my name be in the programme?'

He rubbed his fingers over his stubby beard. 'I'm afraid the programme and posters are out already, of course, as the show is under way. Perhaps at the end of the final show we might introduce you . . . or perhaps offer you some kind of recompense?'

She hesitated a second or two before saying, 'Of course. I quite understand. It would be awkward for Miss Stannard, too. Yes, we'll work something out between us, Mr Rogers. When would you like me to start?'

He gazed at her, took a breath, and said, 'Tonight?'

When she agreed, he took her hand. 'Miss Delamour. You've saved the show!'

She went back to the lodging house immediately to change into something warm for rehearsal. Giles was just leaving for the theatre, and she thanked him profusely for his suggestion. 'I can't tell you how grateful I am. I was so worried about what to do next.'

'I've seen it done before, when the main act had a terrible voice and they brought someone else in to sing in her place. I don't think the audience guessed, because they dimmed the lights and the leading lady did several little dances round the stage when she was supposed to be singing. He mentioned a fee, of course?' he asked anxiously.

She nodded enthusiastically. 'Top of the bill rate, but no name in the programme; but Mr Rogers said he'd make some recompense for that and that's fine. I don't want to be known for pantomime.'

'When your ship comes in, Miss Delamour,' he teased, 'you will take singing lessons and become known as a classical singer.'

She took a breath. 'I wish I could believe that.'

'Go on,' he said. 'Get changed and I'll wait and we'll walk to the theatre together. And wear a warm scarf,' he called after her. 'We don't want you ruining your voice and your fortune. It can be draughty standing in the wings.'

All things considered, Delia thought, the first week had gone very well. Miss Stannard was young but experienced, having been on stage since she was a child, and she was more than happy to have someone sing for her if it meant she could continue in the role. As they rehearsed together she'd listened carefully to Delia, to the tone and pitch of her voice and the way in which she breathed or paused on some of the words of the songs, and she was then able to follow her, sometimes raising her clasped hands to her face over a poignant verse, or swaying and dancing around the stage when she was happy.

There were distractions too, as Mr Rogers and Giles had said: lights were dimmed, or the comic lead somer-saulted across the stage in an effort to cheer Cinderella during wistful verses.

It was a very long pantomime and Delia was not needed the whole time, but inevitably, as she watched the children, she thought of Robin.

'Could he come to see the show, do you think?' she asked Jenny when they met for an early lunch at the Maritime one Saturday before Delia left for a matinee performance. The hotel had become their regular meeting place. 'Am I asking too much of you?'

'I was thinking the same thing, as a matter of fact,' Jenny murmured. 'Except that I was thinking of all my nieces as well.' She paused and looked at Delia. 'They've never seen a pantomime. I suppose Robin has seen many?'

Delia shook her head. 'Not all that many as I don't play in them, but sometimes if he was given complimentary tickets he would go off and see them on his own.' She laughed. 'Sometimes he was rather scornful about them and said they were far too childish for him; and besides, he knew how all the special effects worked!'

But then the implication of what Jenny was saying made her hesitate. 'Would Robin still be able to keep our secret if the girls came, or would he be tempted to tell them who it was who was singing?'

Jenny got up from the table to put on her coat. 'I don't know,' she confessed. 'But I wondered too, in all seriousness, Delia, just how long you are going to keep this secret? Is it fair to Robin? Is it fair to my parents? And shouldn't my brother be told? He sees Robin most days, though he doesn't have a lot to do with him. Nor with his daughters either, for that matter. He doesn't interact with them as our father did with us. Da was unusual, I suppose, for not all fathers do, certainly not the fathers of the children I teach. It's always the mothers who have to find a solution if there's a problem.' She sighed. 'Like many people who don't have children of their own, I have views on how parents should be involved with their offspring.' She gazed at Delia, who appeared to be totally unprepared for such a conversation. 'And I believe that the most important thing of all to teach a child is truth and honesty.'

CHAPTER TWENTY-NINE

'I'll tek you out in 'boat tomorrow,' Aaron told Robin one Saturday morning as they were having breakfast.

Robin drew in a breath. 'Will you? Really? Oh, thank you.'

'You'll have to do everything I say,' Aaron went on. 'Fishing can be a dangerous business.'

'Oh, I will,' Robin said earnestly. 'I'll sit perfectly still unless you tell me to do something.'

Molly was spooning porridge into her mouth. When she had swallowed, she said, 'I'm coming as well.'

Robin turned to look at her with a question on his lips, but Aaron said, 'No, not this time, Molly. I can't look after two of you.'

'I don't need lookin' after,' she maintained. 'I've been in 'boat before.'

'You have,' her grandfather said patiently. 'And now it's Robin's turn.'

'That's not fair.' She clattered her spoon into the empty dish. 'I want to.'

'Now then,' Peggy said, having heard the conversation from the scullery. 'What's all this din? I want doesn't get. I thought you were a grown-up girl, old enough to go to school?'

'I am a grown-up girl.' Molly defiantly folded her arms in front of her. 'And that's why I'm going fishing as well.'

'Not this time,' Aaron said. 'So no arguing. You can go another day, mebbe when 'weather's better, and I'll tek you to Paull Creek.'

Molly pouted and sulked, but neither of her grandparents gave in to her. She had not been well behaved since her night at Foggit's farm or whilst she was there either, and Peggy was inclined to think that both Jack and Susan had given in to her just to pacify her.

'Perhaps you could practise your reading,' Robin suggested. 'Won't the schoolmistress be surprised if she finds you can read before she has had the chance to teach you?'

The suggestion seemed to appeal to Molly, and after asking to be excused from the table she rushed off to find her reading book. When Robin had finished his breakfast he asked Aaron if he could help him to feed the pigs.

'Pigs have been fed already,' Aaron told him. 'You've to be up early when you keep animals, Robin, but you can clean out sties and then you'll know whether or not you'd like to be a farmer.'

Peggy smiled. She recalled when Jack was told the same thing at about the same age and he couldn't decide whether to be a fisherman or a farmer, but two trips out on the Humber in the shrimp boat on squally days had decided him. He would be a landsman, to his father's disappointment and his mother's relief. She watched as Robin climbed into his rubber boots and warm coat and wondered which he would choose. Of course, he might not choose either; might not even be given the choice, since it was his mother's decision whether he stayed with them or left. She felt the pull of her heart strings and knew this wouldn't do. She was becoming very fond of the boy and it wouldn't do at all. He wasn't hers.

Sunday morning Robin was up early and by seven o'clock was fully dressed and had finished his breakfast and was ready to go out. Peggy had left socks and gloves, a flannel vest, a woollen jumper and cord trousers in front of the range so that they would be warm to put on.

'We'll be back by dinner time,' Aaron told her, kissing her cheek.

'With some shrimps,' Robin added eagerly.

'Aye, well mebbe.' Aaron grinned. 'Or a whiting or two.'

'See if you can catch a joint of beef and we'll have that wi' Yorkshire pudding,' Peggy answered back.

They were halfway down the track to the village with Betsy pulling the trap when they spotted a familiar figure coming towards them carrying a sack over his shoulder. Robin immediately hunched down so as not to be seen.

'Sit up, lad,' Aaron told him. 'You're not to be afraid of him. We've had a few words. He's been warned. He'll not touch you or any other bairn again.'

Robin glanced at Aaron. 'How did you know it was him?' His voice was low, even though the man was not yet near enough to hear them.

'Onny by description. And there's no other man in 'village who'd strike anybody else's bairn.'

As they drew near, Aaron pulled over slightly to let the man pass, and Davis Deakin scowled and nodded, glancing at Robin before looking away again.

'I've forgotten his name,' Robin said.

'Deakin,' Aaron said. 'Davis Deakin. He lives in 'cottage next to Foggit's farm.'

'We've got his dog!' Robin said nervously.

'Aye.' Aaron whistled through his teeth. 'So we have, but 'dog's not fastened up. He can go back any time he wants.'

'I think he'd like to stay in the house.'

'I expect he would, but he can't. If he's stopping he's got to earn his keep and keep foxes out of 'hen-house. Besides, we've made him that fine kennel, haven't we?'

'We did,' Robin said proudly. 'That's the first time I've ever helped to make anything like that.'

The day after the dog had followed Aaron home and had apparently decided to stay, Robin and Aaron had gathered some wood and felt together and built a sound, rainproof kennel, and even before Peggy had found an old rug and blanket to put inside it the dog, whom Robin had named Charlie, stepped inside and claimed it as his own.

'I've never had a dog before,' Robin told Aaron now. 'Well, I know he's not mine, but I mean I've never lived beside one.'

'I see,' Aaron said thoughtfully. He pulled into the main street, glanced at the estuary and turned old Betsy's head towards the creek. 'Well, to mek him yours, you have to be responsible for feeding him and giving him water and teaching him to come to heel, that kind o' thing. A dog has to be taught just 'same as bairns have, otherwise how can they learn?'

Robin pondered. 'So could I do that?'

'I don't see why you shouldn't,' Aaron said. 'It'd be a job less for me.'

'But I think you'd always be special to him, cos you rescued him.'

'Well, mebbe we'll share him then, shall we? How would that be?'

'Splendid!' Robin enthused. 'My mother will be so surprised when I tell her!'

Aaron didn't answer, but only nodded. From the manner in which Robin had answered, it almost seemed as if he was expecting to see his mother fairly soon. He wondered if there was something he didn't know.

He told Peggy later that he would have said that Robin had taken to sailing like a duck to water, but that the expression was over-used by everybody who lived by a river.

'It's 'fishing that's important,' he had told Robin. 'Aye, you've to know how to handle a boat and keep yourself safe, but you still need that knack of knowing where shrimps or fish are and you have to watch out for 'signs.'

'What kind of signs?' Robin had asked. He kept his hand on the bulwark to keep himself steady but he was sailing the boat; Aaron had shown him how whilst they were still in the creek, just to get him used to the feel of her. He'd told him that the back of the boat was the stern and if he looked forward the left side was the port side and the right side was starboard.

'*Starboard* comes from 'old Viking ships, so I'm told,' he had said. 'They called it steerboard.'

'Perhaps they steered their ships from the right side?' Robin suggested. 'And what's the front of the boat called?'

'That's the bow.'

'Oh, I know that word,' Robin said excitedly, and he felt the exhilarating pull of the wind on the sails as they reached the estuary waters. 'That's what performers do when they've finished their act on stage.'

Aaron glanced at him; he knows such odd things, he thought as he strode over to help him. 'Keep her steady,' he said.

'What kind of signs?' Robin asked again. 'In the water, do you mean?'

'Aye,' Aaron pointed. 'Look for 'shimmer on top of 'water. That way you'll know that there's fish about.'

'But not shrimps?'

'Not shrimps because they stay well below and feed from 'bottom, but then so do cod and halibut and eels. That's why we use trawl nets for catching shrimps, so that we can scoop them up. I'll show you how another time. But for now, do you fancy a sail down 'Humber as far as Spurn?'

'Oh, *yes*, please.'

Aaron had told him that the shrimp boats were easy to use and the smaller ones like his could be handled by one man. 'We can boil 'shrimps on board and 'boat will still remain steady.'

'You can boil the shrimps? Do you mean whilst you're out on the water?' Robin was astonished.

'Aye, it saves time, you see, especially if you're selling shrimps commercially like some of 'shrimpers do. Then when you get back to shore you can send them off straight away to the buyers.'

'And do you still do that, Aaron?' Robin was keeping his eyes on the water for signs of fish.

'Nay,' he answered on a sigh. 'Not any more. I keep 'boat for recreation or bringing summat home for supper. I'm a landsman now. A farmer. But sometimes I'll go out for a day with my brothers.'

'I don't know which I'd like to be,' Robin said abstractedly. 'It's a hard decision to make, isn't it?'

Aaron nodded and smiled. It had been for him, but in the end there was only one choice; he'd been young and he loved Peggy and if it meant pleasing her parents and receiving permission to marry her he had thought then so be it; and there had been no regrets, except for the odd time when he had seen the sails of the shrimp boats heading down on the tide towards the Humber mouth and had drawn in a deep breath of the salty sea.

'So do you think you'll be stopping, then?' he asked Robin.

'Oh, aye,' Robin answered, and Aaron grinned at his expression. 'I think so,' Robin went on. 'I feel as if I belong here.' He pressed his lips together. 'That's if you and Granny Peg don't mind. You see, before I came here, Aaron, I didn't know where I belonged. I felt as if I came from nowhere.'

* * *

261

When they arrived back at midday, Robin was full of enthusiasm for sailing and fishing too, except that they had only brought home two whiting and two flounder. Then, triumphantly, he held up the bag that contained the fish and took out his prize.

'Look, Granny Peg,' he crowed. 'Look, Molly. Look what I caught.'

Molly lifted her head from where she was crayoning a picture at the table, and then looked back at her drawing again. Peggy turned her enquiring gaze to him. 'Salmon?' she guessed.

'It's like a small salmon,' Robin told her from his new-found store of information. 'But it's called a smolt. Aaron says it's a juvenile salmon and tastes just as nice.'

'So would you like to have it for your supper whilst it's fresh?' Peggy said. 'We're having roast beef for dinner.'

'I know, I can smell it.' Robin slipped off his coat. 'I'm starving, but I'd better get washed first.'

'You'd better,' Peggy agreed, 'especially as we're expecting company. We don't want you stinking of wet fish. And then later on I'll show you how to take the head off the fish and fillet it.'

He screwed up his face, but didn't object. 'I suppose if I'm going to be a fisherman I'll have to learn how to do that sort of thing. I'm learning such a lot.' He continued the conversation as he scrubbed his hands in the scullery sink whilst Peggy put the fish on a cold slab and covered it with muslin.

'When we were coming back in the cart, a man in Paull touched his cap and said, "Ow do, Aaron?" I asked what it was he'd said and Aaron told me he'd said how do. I didn't understand it until Aaron told me that it means *How do you do?*' He put his head back and laughed. 'And then Aaron touched his forehead and said back to him, "Awright, Fred, 'n' you?" It's much friendlier here, isn't it? And as soon as I learn the language, that's how I shall speak.' He rinsed his hands and face and asked as he dried them, 'Who's the company that's coming for lunch, Granny Peg – I mean dinner? Do I know them?'

Peggy's mouth twitched. 'Yes, indeed you do, Master Robin. It's a company of little girls.'

And before she could say more the back door opened and Louisa, Emma and Rosie burst inside, and Robin felt as happy as he had ever been in his life.

CHAPTER THIRTY

It was just the girls who had come for Sunday dinner. Jack and Susan were still making the farmhouse more comfortable and Susan had asked Jack to paper the parlour with mock flock wallpaper with a red floral design. He hadn't liked the pattern and said it was difficult to match, but Susan had insisted and said it would cover up some of the cracks in the walls. Her mother had had her parlour papered in a similar pattern and she wanted it too. She had also bought thick red woollen material to make a curtain to hang from a pole over the door to keep out any draughts and had also made some dark red curtains for the window. The curtains that Peggy had given her were going on the upstairs windows.

'It'll look like a damned bordello,' Jack had muttered to his father a few days earlier.

'Eh, eh! What?' his father had demanded. 'What do you know of such places?'

'Nothing,' Jack grunted. 'Never been in one, but I can imagine!'

'Well, you'd better not let your ma hear you talk about them as if you have, or you'll get a warning shot across your bows.'

Jack scoffed. 'I'm not a little lad any more, Da. I'm a grown man; I know about 'em, even if I haven't ever visited one.' Then he added, 'Are you going to offer to help me wi' papering on Sunday?'

'No. I've promised to tek young Robin out fishing.'

'He's got his feet well under 'table, hasn't he?' Jack commented. 'Somebody must know who he is and where he's from.'

His father had nodded. 'I think you're right, Jack; I expect I'll find out sooner or later. There's some reason why it's such a big secret and if your ma knows she'll tell me eventually.' He'd put his hand on his son's shoulder. 'Good luck wi' the decorating!'

Aaron walked the girls back home across the field to Foggit's farm after dinner and lifted them over the fence, reminding himself that he must make a gate so that they could come and go as they pleased.

The house was quiet when he came back and he asked Peggy where Molly and Robin were.

'They're in 'parlour. Robin is trying to teach her to read ready for school tomorrow. I'm a bit bothered about her,' she admitted anxiously. 'I hope she'll be all right; she doesn't take easily to other people telling her what to do. I hope 'schoolmistress and 'headmaster will understand her.'

'They'll be used to children's behaviour,' he said calmly. 'I'm sure there's no need to worry.' He sat down in one of the fireside chairs. 'Come and sit down,' he said. 'I want to ask you summat, Peggy love.'

Peggy knew that coaxing voice well and cautiously sat down. He was always so patient, always prepared to wait for the right moment to ask a question that she knew would eventually come.

'It's about Robin,' he said. 'It's 'way he talks about his mother. As if he knows where she is. Does he? And do you?'

Peggy took a deep breath; she knew that she couldn't keep this from him any longer. 'I don't know where she is, Aaron, except that she's somewhere in Hull, and you know I'd never lie to you; but I now know who she is, and it's a sad story.'

'Go on then,' he said quietly. 'I'm listening.'

'Do you remember Jenny's friend from when she was onny little?'

He lifted his chin and his eyes to the ceiling as he cast his mind back. 'I onny recall Jenny ever having one close friend and that was 'Deakins' daughter. Dorothy, wasn't it? They went to school together and came home together, and she sometimes came here but never had time to play and allus had to rush off home.' His forehead creased. 'Where did she go off to? I think I asked you a time or two back if she'd gone into service.'

'Aye.' Peggy nodded. 'I think we all thought that, but of course neither of 'Deakins ever spoke to anybody, and now I come to think of it there was talk at 'post office wi' folk trying to guess where she might have gone.' She gave a slight shake of her head. 'She could've been dead for all we knew, but none of us thought to tek it any further; shame on us!'

'So – what!' Aaron leaned forward, his elbows on his knees. 'She's not dead, is she? Not that young lass?'

'No, no, she's not. Some lad . . .' She faltered. 'Some

lad took advantage of her, and . . . well, she got caught wi' a child.' She gazed straight at Aaron. 'And when her ma and da found out she was expecting, they told her to leave; turned her out of their house.' Peggy's voice caught in her throat and cracked. 'She called here one day; she must have wanted to talk to Jenny but she wasn't here. It was during 'time she was studying in Hull.'

Peggy took a handkerchief out of her skirt pocket and wiped her eyes, and was about to continue when the hall door burst open and Molly rushed in brandishing a book.

'I can read,' she said triumphantly. 'Will you listen to me?' and without waiting for an answer she sat crosslegged on the floor, her skirt up to her knees and her drawers showing, and proceeded to read, slowly and laboriously, and Aaron and Peggy listened patiently until she got to the bottom of the page.

'Well done, Molly,' Aaron said kindly. 'Can you learn 'next page?'

'Yes,' she said. 'Robin's going to teach me.' She got up and went back into the parlour, carefully closing the door behind her.

'So where did she go?' Aaron asked, continuing their conversation.

Peggy shook her head. 'I don't know. But she had a son and that young son is now in 'parlour teaching our Molly to read.'

Aaron got up from his chair and gazed down at the top of Peggy's head. 'How long have you known?'

'Not long,' she murmured. 'When our Jenny came home last time and took Robin into Hull, do you remember? She said she was going to give him a present. She must have met Dorothy somehow or other and I don't know all 'ins and outs of it, cos there never seems time to talk when she comes.'

She looked up at him. 'But Jenny told me that day when they came back from Hull that he was Dorothy's child and that she, Dorothy, was at her wits' end trying to find work and bring him up. Jenny was about to tell me more when you and Jack came in and she clammed up. She asked me to keep it secret for 'time being.'

Aaron sat down again. 'So 'Deakins don't know owt about her or her bairn being in 'district?'

Again Peggy shook her head. 'No, and neither does she want them to know.'

Aaron muttered beneath his breath. He didn't often swear but she knew he was swearing now.

'What would you like to do?' she asked.

He looked at her. 'What do you mean, what would *I* like to do?'

'I mean, does it make a difference as to how you feel about him being here with us?'

Aaron contemplated her but seemingly without comprehending her words. Then he said, 'Well, where else would he go? You're not suggesting we tek him down 'track and leave him wi' – with . . .' words seemed to fail him before he stuttered, 'that *blackguard* that we call a neighbour – or his wretch of a wife? No,' he said fiercely. 'He'll stop here where we can keep him safe.'

Which was exactly what Peggy expected him to say, but she still heaved a silent breath of relief now that she had told him.

He sat staring into the fire, only lifting his head

now and again to look at her, before saying softly, 'So where've they been for 'last ten years? How has she managed? What kind o' work has she been doing? Little lad's been well brought up; good manners, polite. She's done a good job on him – but has she had a man in her life to help her?' His forehead creased worriedly. 'Women can go to 'bad when they've been left in such a situation.'

'They can, that's true,' Peggy admitted, 'But I honestly don't know, Aaron. I'm hoping that when Jenny comes again she'll be able to tell us. If you'll agree I'd like to invite her here to see us so we can talk things over.'

'Invite . . . ? You mean 'lad's mother? Dorothy?'

The door opened again. 'Sorry for disturbing you,' Robin apologized. 'Is it all right to get some logs from the basket? The fire's burning very low.'

'Aye, yes, course it is.' Aaron half rose from his chair.

'It's all right, Aaron, I can get them.' Robin gave a merry grin and lowered his voice. 'Molly's doing very well with her reading, but I think she's just remembering a lot of the words. She might have forgotten some of them by tomorrow.'

Aaron nodded and watched him go into the scullery and come back with several logs in his arms. 'Mebbe you'd mek a teacher when you're grown?' he suggested.

'I think I'd rather be a fisherman.' Robin paused, and then said seriously, 'I used to think I'd like to be an actor, but I loved it out on the estuary this morning. I suppose I'll know for sure when I've been out in rough weather.'

When he'd gone back into the parlour, Aaron scratched his beard. 'I'll tell you what, Mother,' he murmured. 'No matter that I'll never forgive that rogue Deakin for what he's done, I'll say this much: he's a good sailor and fisherman, allus was and still is, and you can be sure that when he teks out a sailboat he'll bring it safe home.'

'What 'you on about, Aaron?'

'Why, Deakin o' course.' He spoke quietly, almost in a whisper. 'And that's where 'lad gets it from. This morning I took him almost to 'mouth of 'Humber and although 'tide was strong he nivver turned a hair. Sailing or fishing, it's in his blood. That's for sure.'

CHAPTER THIRTY-ONE

'You're very quiet,' Giles said as he and Delia walked back to their lodgings after a show. They had left the theatre earlier than the other performers; Delia had no need to stay for a final bow and Giles had quickly put on his hat, coat and gloves. They had left by the stage door and were heading down Paragon Street before the audience came out.

As it was almost midnight they avoided the darkened Princes Dock and passing by William Wilberforce's towering monument crossed over Junction Bridge into Whitefriargate, where the shops were in darkness and the only light came from the flickering gas of the street lamps. It was quiet, save for the rattle of a brougham's wheels as it passed on the cobbled street and the muffled ribald laughter coming from a nearby hostelry.

Delia admitted that she was tired. But that wasn't the sole reason why she was quiet. She had been pondering for a few days on what Jenny had said about her owning up about Robin and even confronting Jack. It seemed to Delia that Jenny was furious with her brother over his youthful behaviour and thought that his whole manner had been and still was despicable; it was as if she couldn't wait to challenge and punish him on Delia's behalf.

'It will ruin his marriage,' Delia had said to her. 'His wife won't ever forgive him if she learns what happened, and . . .' She had hesitated. She always evaded arguments – perhaps because in times past she had expected a physical blow if she was too plain-speaking – and tended to step away from any confrontation. 'I have Robin to think of.'

And that was the root of the matter. She had seen for herself what a difference a settled existence had made to Robin; he had made friends and he seemed happy and that was what she wanted above all else. She didn't want to disturb him, even though it broke her heart to be away from him. But the thought that she had abandoned him to the care of others worried her. That wasn't what a good mother did. And if Jack Robinson should be told that his unknowingly begotten son was living in such close proximity, would he turn against him or even deny him?

'You're thinking about your son?' Giles murmured as they turned towards Church Street and the chimes of midnight began to ring out.

'I am,' she admitted. 'I want to see him. I want to be with him.' Without any prior warning the situation suddenly became too much and she began to sob. 'What kind of mother am I – what kind of mother can leave her child with someone else?'

Giles took her arm and tucked it under his. 'One who had reached rock bottom, perhaps, and couldn't see a way forward? What would have happened to him, or indeed either of you, if you hadn't done what you did?'

Delia fumbled in her pocket for a handkerchief and Giles handed her a clean one of his own; she could smell the slight fragrance of eau de Cologne and realized it was the one he used when resting his chin on his violin during a performance. The perfume was comforting and soothing.

'I don't know,' she mumbled. 'The unknown! That has always been my greatest fear.' She recalled so clearly her shock when her agent had said he had nothing to offer her for the near future, and suggested she took a break and came back to him in May, when he'd try to book her for a summer show; and her panic as she wondered how they would survive until then. She had watched her son down on the edge of the Thames play-fighting with the young London mudlarks and realized that although he could mix with adults he enjoyed the company of other children and she had to do something to change their lives.

'I don't generally offer advice, Delia,' Giles said softly, 'for I'm not in a position to do so, considering my own situation, but I think you'll have to visit this family who are looking after your son. You must acknowledge your circumstances, and' – he hesitated – 'face up to the man who put you in this situation.'

Delia swallowed hard. He was right; but she was afraid. Afraid of being turned away; she knew how that felt, but if she was turned away again her position would be even worse than it had been ten years ago; this time she would have not an unborn child but a young intelligent son who would be asking questions.

And as for facing up to Jack Robinson – well, he might deny every word of her accusation.

'I have no proof that he's the father,' she faltered. 'How can a woman confirm who is the father of her children?'

He steered her towards the lodging house; she was malleable beneath his touch, as if unable to move of her own accord. 'She cannot,' he answered ironically, 'and yet she can *claim*, as indeed I'm sure my own wife will assert, if what I believe is true, that the child she carries is mine and not another's; and although I can dispute it, there is no proof.'

He opened the door and ushered her inside. 'Go into the sitting room,' he said, pushing her gently in that direction. 'I have a small bottle of brandy upstairs and I think you're in need—'

'Oh, but I'm not,' she began, but he waved her protests away and opened the door to the sitting room, which was still warm from the now extinguished fire.

'Sit,' he ordered. 'I won't be more than five minutes.'

Delia sat as instructed. She seemed unable to help or think for herself; what on earth was the matter with her? How had everything become so impossible when she had such a short time and previously thought that there might be a solution? It had been Jenny, she decided. Jenny, who had always been so sure of herself, always able to make her own decisions, who had finally told her that she must face up to life, must show herself to the Robinson family, including the very man who had made her life so difficult

I will. She trembled at the mere thought of it, and couldn't decide who or what she was afraid of.

Humiliation? Being branded a liar? And if she did visit the Robinsons, what if she should by chance meet her own parents? Would they recognize her, and if they did, would they walk by? It would perhaps be best if they did.

The door opened and Giles came back with two glasses, a small jug of hot water and the brandy bottle. 'Here we are; just what the doctor ordered.'

He pulled a small table forward and placed everything on it, then sat down to pour. He measured a generous amount of brandy into one glass, topped it up with hot water and handed it to Delia. 'Drink up,' he said, and then poured himself a smaller tot, but without the water.

He lifted the glass. 'Here's to us and our predicaments,' he said wryly, and as Delia lifted her glass she was surprised to find herself cheered by the thought of their shared dilemmas.

She slept soundly until eight o'clock the next morning, Giles having topped up her brandy again, and roused herself with the decision that she would face up to her problem and go to Paull on the following Sunday. She wrote a postcard to Jenny telling her of her resolution and asking if she might be able to visit her family that day; she was unsure whether she could be brave enough to face them alone.

As she dressed she saw that an envelope had been pushed beneath her door. She opened it; the note was brief, and from Giles.

I have received correspondence from York, he wrote, *and am leaving immediately as it seems there is some*

urgency which could precipitate any decision I might need to make. I trust you are in a more positive state of mind this morning?
Yours most sincerely, Giles.

I wonder what has happened, she thought. A telegram must have arrived.

Her resolve over her decision began to waver. Can I get to the weekend without changing my mind, and must I be prepared to bring Robin back with me if the family refuses to have him any longer once I tell them who his father is? They will of course believe their son rather than me.

There was no matinee that afternoon, which meant she had a whole day to kill before the evening performance. She couldn't even take a leisurely breakfast, as Mrs Benson discouraged any lingering but swept, dusted and polished as soon as her lodgers had finished, and prepared the tables for the next meal.

Delia went back up to her room, looked out of the window, and seeing that it wasn't raining put on her coat, hat, shawl and outdoor boots and went downstairs again and out of the house.

Her feet took her back through Trinity Square, and on impulse she turned towards the ancient church, walking up the path and finding the doors open as if expecting her. How beautiful it was, how calming, and she sat in one of the pews and folded her hands on her lap. For seven hundred years the church had stood on this site, and as she gave thought to all the people who had sat here before her, perhaps to give thanks, or, as she did now, to find some kind of peace or resolution, the sun came out momentarily, lighting up the stained glass windows and sending beams of colour sliding towards her, lifting the greyness of her mood. She had removed her gloves, and when she looked down at her bare hands she saw motes of rich blue, the gleam of gold, and splashes of opulent purple dancing on her pale skin.

Her thoughts drifted from one thing to another, settling on her son and finally on his father. Did Jack Robinson ever wonder about her? Did he ever regret what he had done? Why had he behaved in such a manner if he was already planning to marry someone else?

She gave a deep sigh. His actions didn't make sense. He had always been friendly towards her when they were young, but never especially so; she suspected that like her he might have been shy. So what had got into him as a young adult to make him so shameless? Could she ever forgive him? *Would* she ever forgive him?

I don't know if I can, she thought as she rose to her feet; and yet – and yet . . . She looked towards the altar and felt her throat tighten and tears begin to well. I have a son whom I love dearly. Without him I would be nothing, just an empty shell, and in spite of my present dilemma I wouldn't, couldn't, ever imagine a life in which he did not exist.

CHAPTER THIRTY-TWO

Jenny wrote back to Delia, congratulating her on her decision to visit her parents and suggesting they travel together on Sunday. She would write to her mother to tell her they were coming.

I realize it won't be easy for you, Delia, but I feel that you are right and that it is time you grasped the nettle. Even if nothing is resolved, you will know that there is no need to hide away any longer.

Easier said than done, Delia thought on reading her friend's reply. I don't know how I'll get through the rest of the week until Sunday. Giles had not yet returned from York so she couldn't talk to him, and when she asked Mr Rogers when he was expected back, he told her that he had received a telegram to say that Mr Dawson would be away for an indeterminate time. 'I have brought in a replacement violinist,' he told her.

Strangely, she found some relief from her anxiety when she was singing, particularly as she was hidden in the wings and not on stage; there she was able to soothe her own apprehension by imparting more pathos and emotion to the Cinderella role. Her sincerity shone through, and during one interval Miss

Stannard sought her out, finding her sitting quietly having a cup of coffee. 'Oh, Miss Delamour, you have such a beautiful voice,' she said. 'It made me cry, just in the right place. Thank you so much.'

Delia smiled and thanked her for the compliment. It was certainly much easier to convey great joy or sadness from the wings than it was to show it on stage in front of an audience.

Sunday morning she dressed carefully, wanting to create a good impression on Mr and Mrs Robinson and show that she was neither a frivolous theatrical performer who had abandoned her child without a thought, nor a ruined woman with no means of looking after him. She chose her ankle-length navy blue fitted tunic dress with its high lace-edged collar and flounced hem, and only a small bustle; over it she wore her grey woollen coat which for the winter season she had trimmed with a fur collar, one she had found some years ago in a haberdasher's shop. Her fur hat was trimmed with velvet, and looking in the mirror she saw a respectable young matron.

She met Jenny at the Maritime Hotel, and they walked together to the Paragon railway station to catch a train to Hedon.

'It's a fine morning,' she said nervously as they went. 'The walk to Paull should be pleasant enough.'

'Oh, I think my father will probably meet us in the trap,' Jenny said. 'I hope he will, anyway; it will give us more time to talk.'

Delia turned anxious eyes to Jenny; she hoped Jenny wouldn't try to take charge. This was her predicament and hers alone, and she must explain in her own way her reasons for leaving Jack with the Robinson family.

Jenny must have understood Delia's expression and immediately apologized. 'I'm sorry, Delia,' she said. 'That's what comes of being a teacher. You become used to being in control and saying what should be done.'

Delia gave a sudden laugh; she recalled now how she had always followed in Jenny's shadow, trusting that whatever Jenny said or did would be right. 'No,' she teased her. 'It's not just since you've become a teacher. You were always confident, and if you said that black was white I believed you.'

She tucked her arm under Jenny's. 'I always trusted you. But now it's my turn.' They turned on to the station concourse and headed for the platform where the Hedon train was waiting. 'I must decide what to say and do. I'm so glad of your support, Jenny, and I can't thank you enough for what you've already done to help me.' She took a breath. 'But it's my life and my son's at stake and whatever the outcome of this meeting, I must make the final decision.' She turned to her friend. 'Tell me that you understand.'

Jenny nodded. 'I do,' she said, 'and I don't mean to meddle.' Her lip trembled and Delia knew that Jenny, who wasn't usually an emotional person, cared enough for her to go out of her way to help her. 'I just want to make up to you for what happened. I feel responsible,' her voice broke, 'because it was my own brother who caused this havoc in your life.'

Delia shook her head, and as they entered the train and sat down in an empty carriage she said softly, 'I've been thinking about that. In fact I've been thinking a lot over this past week since I decided to *grasp the nettle*, as you described it, and I came to the odd conclusion that your brother Jack, although ruining the life that I had, gave me another, and one that is preferable to the former.' She hesitated. 'And if necessary I'll bring my Jack – Robin – back with me and give him the life he deserves. I will give up the theatre and I'll work at anything, just as I did when I was expecting him. I'll be a shop girl, a mill woman; I'll even scrub the stage where once I was a star.'

As Jenny had predicted, her father was at Hedon station to meet them off the train. He kissed Jenny's cheek and took Delia's outstretched hand and clasped it in his, then leaning forward he kissed her cheek too.

'Now then, Dorothy,' he said softly. 'It's been a long time.'

'It has, Mr Robinson,' she said, moved by his friend-liness and affection. 'You do remember me, then?'

'Aye, I do.' He shepherded them towards the trap. 'You were allus a quiet little lass from what I recall. Not a chatterbox like our Jenny.'

'I was,' she admitted, 'and I suppose I still am, to some degree.'

'And her name is Delia now, Da,' Jenny told him.

'Oh? What's wrong wi' Dorothy then?' He gave her a friendly grin. 'Too plain for them London folk, eh?'

'I changed my life, Mr Robinson, so I changed my name as well.'

As they drove, Delia realized that she had almost forgotten about the wide skies of Holderness; it had been dark when she and Jack arrived all those weeks ago, and the following day she had been too concerned about their situation to notice; but now, on seeing the pattern of clouds scudding across the blue-grey sky as they began their journey towards Paull, she was reminded of the joy a sunrise or a sunset could give her when she was a young girl. She would stop briefly and wonder at it; a pale golden dawn over the Humber or a deep suffusing purple sunset over the flatlands of Holderness. The skies were often like vivid paintings moving at speed, changing colours as the light rose or faded depending on the time of day, or the season. Each silver-rimmed drifting cloud brought a small miracle of beauty, miraculously creating castles and mountains for those who cared to find them.

'Look at the sky,' she murmured as they continued along the road towards Thorngumbald. 'How wide it is without any buildings to block the view.'

'Aye,' Aaron agreed. 'Holderness skies allus give me a sense of peace, except when they're dramatic and full of impending weather. Your lad came fishing wi' me, by the way,' he added. 'He's a natural.'

'Really?' Delia was astonished. 'He's never been out in a boat.'

'He has now,' Aaron told her. 'He loved it. Says he's going to be a fisherman.'

That must mean that he wants to stay, Delia thought. Am I ready for that? Do I really want him to? When will I see him? I can't give him up completely! She breathed heavily. It seemed that whichever way she turned brought an added quandary.

They pulled into the yard outside the house and Peggy opened the back door to them as they stepped down from the trap.

'Hello, Ma, here I am again.' Jenny gave her mother a kiss and Delia felt a pang of envy, recalling the greeting she had received from her own mother when she had called back in November and been turned away at the door. 'And here is Delia,' Jenny said more soberly. 'Dorothy as was.'

Delia went towards Peggy. 'Hello, Mrs Robinson,' she said quietly, feeling again like the shy girl she had been.

Peggy put out her arms to embrace her, putting her warm cheek against Delia's cold one and saying, 'Come in, come in, do. It's very good to see you again, Delia. It's been far too long.'

The kitchen, with its warm range and a table laid ready with places set for the midday meal, looked exactly as always, and the same delicious aroma of roast meat wafted from the oven.

'Nothing's changed,' she said, looking round. 'It's exactly as I remember it; so cosy and warm – and welcoming.'

She felt her eyes filling with tears and there was a tightness in her chest. It was no wonder that her son wanted to stay; she could wish the same for herself if it had been possible.

'Let me take your coat, m'dear, and come and sit down by 'fire. The kettle is on 'boil. I expect you'll be ready for a cup o' tea?'

'Yes, please,' she said, trying to hold her emotions together but unable to check the tears that trickled down her cheeks as other memories came to the fore. 'You're very kind. Extremely kind.'

'I'll make the tea, Ma,' Jenny said. 'You sit down and chat to Delia. Where are the children?' she added brightly, and Delia sensed that she was trying to make their situation as normal as possible.

'Molly and Robin have gone across to see 'other bairns at Foggit's,' Peggy said. 'I suggested they should, but said to be sure to come back before twelve o'clock as we were having something special for dinner.' She laughed. 'Robin asked if we were having Yorkshire pudding and I said he'd have to wait and see.'

At the mention of Robin's name, Delia burst into tears, unable to contain them any longer. 'I'm so sorry,' she wept. 'I'm so very sorry.'

Peggy patted her shoulder and drew up a chair near to her. 'That's it,' she murmured. 'Weep it all out. I expect you've been holding in tears all 'morning. Don't worry about me, m'dear. We'll sort something out between us, one way or another.'

'I don't see how we ever can,' Delia could hardly speak, she was so choked. 'You don't know the half of it, Mrs Robinson, and when you do you won't want to know me, any more than my ma or da did all those years ago.'

'Now then, now then,' Peggy protested. 'I onny know that somebody took advantage of you when you were onny an innocent young girl, and you must stop blaming yourself. You've made a good job of bringing up your son under what must have been very difficult circumstances, and I can tell you, from what I've discovered about him, he's a boy to be proud of.'

Delia wiped her eyes and blew her nose. 'Thank you,' she snuffled. 'I am proud of him. I've been lucky; he's never been a minute's trouble since the day he was born.'

'That's not luck,' Peggy said firmly. 'That's 'way that you've taught him. You don't get good manners and politeness from luck, but onny by what you've been taught. Now come on, dry them tears. Here's our Jenny wi' a cup that cheers, which is just what we all need.'

Jenny was carrying a tray with teapot, milk, sugar, and four cups and saucers. She put it down on the table and called to her father, who was hovering in the scullery. 'Come on, Da. I'm going to pour the tea.'

They sat quietly as they drank, Peggy and Aaron making desultory conversation about the weather to fill in the expanse of silence. Finally Aaron put down his cup. 'Now then, Dorothy,' he said, looking straight at Delia. 'Sorry – Delia. That's a pretty name, by the way. I like it. It suits you, the young woman you have become and not 'quiet scared little lass you once were. You were, weren't you? Frightened of your own shadow?'

Delia hesitated for a moment and then said, 'I was never afraid of the dark; only of people. I was always afraid of doing or saying the wrong thing. That's why I was quiet, so that I didn't make any mistakes.' She gave a slight shrug. 'The odd thing is that I'm not afraid of standing up to sing in front of an audience.'

'Well, just fancy that,' Aaron commented. 'Why's that, do you think?'

'Because I'm now someone else. I'm not the family drudge who can do no right, but a singer, and people pay to hear me. A friend explained it to me; he said that I was wearing a sort of invisible cloak or mask to hide behind.'

'Well,' Aaron muttered. 'Would you believe it? I've nivver heard of such a thing, have you, Mother?'

Peggy shook her head. 'No, I haven't, but I can believe it. We all act differently in front of different people.'

Aaron looked up from the contemplation of his knees. 'I don't. At least I don't think I do.'

Jenny smiled at her father. 'No, I don't think you do, Da. You're always the same, no matter what. Thank goodness,' she added. 'It's reassuring to know that some people never change.'

'So what now?' Aaron asked. 'What 'we going to do about 'little lad? No matter what we think or do, he's the one who's important. It's his future that's at stake. I tek it that you'll stay in 'same profession, which can't be all that reliable, I suppose, though I know nowt about it.'

'It isn't reliable, Mr Robinson,' Delia said. 'Performers are lucky to get a booking from one season to the next, and tastes change. Audiences often like something new, although fortunately they still like the old songs.'

'So you can't stay in one place for long?' Peggy asked. 'You have to move to a different area for a new audience?'

'Like a travelling troubadour?' Aaron put in.

'Yes, something like that,' Delia admitted and put down her cup. 'Which was why – which was why . . .' She could feel her eyes filling up again. How could she explain the desperation she had finally felt? No prospect of work, no prospect of a roof over their heads without money to pay for lodgings, but worst of all no prospect of an education or a proper home for her son.

'No place to call home?' Peggy said gently. 'Is that why you came back; in the hope that your parents would help you?'

Delia bent her head and nodded. How stupid she had been to think such a thing; they had turned her away at the beginning of her troubles, so how could she have been so senseless as to think they might have had a change of heart? As Jenny had just said, some people never did change and her parents could be included in that category.

Aaron was about to say something when they all heard the click of the latch on the scullery door and the sound of children's voices.

Delia wiped her eyes and patted her cheeks and gave a wide smile as first a little girl and then Robin tumbled exuberantly into the room. Robin stopped dead on seeing his mother and then flew into her arms.

'Oh, Mother,' he said, kissing her over and over again. 'I never expected—' He turned to Peggy. 'Is this the special treat you said, Granny Peg, and nothing to do with our dinner?'

At Peggy's nod, for she was too emotional to speak, Robin hugged his mother again, saying, 'You're much better than Yorkshire pudding, Mother, even though I could eat you up.'

None of them heard the click of the latch a second time or heard Jack's tread as he came into the kitchen, or even noticed him standing there, staring, until Molly piped up.

'Da, do you know who this lady is? Cos I don't.'

CHAPTER THIRTY-THREE

Jack came forward, shaking his head at Molly's question. 'I – I don't think so, though I'd guess it's Robin's ma.'

'You're right, Jack.' Robin got to his feet. 'This is my mother, Delia Delamour.' He gave a huge grin. 'She's come on a visit to see me.'

Delia looked up at Jack as he slowly came forward to meet her, holding out his hand to greet her. He hasn't forgotten his manners, then, she thought, and murmured, 'You'd perhaps remember me as Dorothy Deakin.' Robin looked at her with interest, and then at Jack, and frowned slightly as if recalling something.

Jack released her hand and a slow flush suffused his neck. He cleared his throat. 'Aye? I – doubt I would've known you, Dorothy.'

'Delia,' she corrected resolutely. 'Dorothy is long gone; dead and buried.'

'Mother, what do you mean? I've heard you say that before.' Robin looked confused.

'You did,' Delia reached for him, putting her arm round his waist. 'It's all right. I'm Delia. I changed my name a long time ago; you won't remember. I like it better than Dorothy, don't you?' She spoke quietly and confidently, wanting to reassure him that there was nothing amiss.

'Oh, yes, I remember now.' Robin's face cleared. 'It sounds better for the stage, doesn't it? Molly,' he said to the little girl who was watching and listening, 'come and say hello to my mother.'

'You're on 'stage?' Jack seemed puzzled. 'H-how come? I – we often wondered what had happened to you. You just disappeared.'

'I did.' She turned to Molly and said hello, and then returned her gaze to Jack. He seemed like a different person from the one she remembered, as she must seem to him.

He blinked and suddenly looked away from her and spoke to his father. 'I, erm – I came to ask if I could tek owd Betsy and 'trap,' he said awkwardly. 'I've heard of a hoss and trap for sale over at Preston; it's a good price, and we can do wi' another.'

'I'll have to have them back by this afternoon,' Aaron told him. 'I've to run our Jenny and Delia back to Hedon to catch 'last train. I can't tek them in 'wagon.'

'I'll onny be an hour.' He seemed anxious to be off. 'Susan's coming wi' me to drive back if it's suitable.'

'Aye, all right then,' Aaron agreed. 'Who's selling?'

'Rudge. His wife wants an older hoss; the one they're selling is a bit too lively for her.'

Peggy commented that they could certainly do with another, younger horse and a bigger trap to fit everyone in. She called after him to bring the girls over before he left and Jack swiftly made his exit, muttering something about not being long. Molly, bored with the conversation, followed him out.

Peggy got up to take the beef out of the oven and prepare the vegetables. 'I'd better crack on if we're eating at midday.'

'Granny Peg makes lovely Yorkshire pudding,' Robin told his mother, and put his arms akimbo to show his waistline. 'That's why I needed bigger breeches.'

'I'm sure she does.' Delia trembled with relief now that Jack had gone; she hadn't wanted to confront him and thought he'd been aware that there was something not quite right. 'Are you happy?'

'I am!' Robin said. 'I love it here, but . . .' He looked into her eyes. 'I mean – if you're sad without me . . .' Looking down, he picked up her hand and played with her fingers, '. . . then I'll come back with you. Because I don't want you to be sad and you seem sad now.'

Peggy turned from the range; Jenny looked across at her father, who in turn gazed at Robin with his lips parted.

With her other hand, Delia stroked her son's face. 'You're the best boy in the whole world,' she whispered. 'The person I love more than anyone else, and the reason I'm here today is for us to decide what's best for you.' She swallowed. 'And the only way to do that is to talk to Mr and Mrs Robinson and ask them if they'll forgive me for leaving you here without asking their permission.'

'But you didn't know I'd come back with them that day at the hiring fair,' he argued. 'I should have waited for you.'

'No, I didn't know, but I guessed that you might,' she murmured. 'Or that they might take you with them if I didn't turn up. I saw you with the family at the table in the Sun Inn and saw how you fitted in, and I left you, Jack.' She spoke his given name without realizing it. 'I left you, hoping that they'd look after you in the way that I couldn't.'

Peggy sat down with a thump on the nearest seat, and Aaron put out his hand to find his easy chair without actually looking for it.

Robin smiled at her. 'You've given the game away,' he teased. 'Now they'll know my name's not Robin.' He grinned up at Peggy and Aaron and then Jenny. 'You didn't know that I'd swapped my name round, did you? Robin Jackson from Jack Robinson. It's a good thing I did,' he blithely and innocently went on. 'It would have been confusing otherwise, wouldn't it?'

Delia's throat tightened; this wasn't what she had planned, and she was about to tell him that his name was also Deakin. Then she decided that that was a step too far and would be too much for him to take in, as well as raising more questions.

'I like it,' Jenny chipped in to fill an awkward pause. 'The robin's a very cheerful bird, isn't it, with its merry tune, and I think the name suits you very well.'

'Robin,' Aaron broke in, shakily, 'could you build up 'fire in parlour? When all 'little girls get here we'll have to spread out a bit.'

'Yes, of course.' Robin detached himself from his mother and went into the scullery to collect logs.

'I think we need to have a discussion,' Aaron suggested in a low voice. 'If what I'm hearing and 'conclusion I'm coming to is true.' He took a deep breath. 'And we can't do that in front of 'lad; not yet, at any rate.'

'After we've eaten,' Peggy said huskily. She seemed shaken to the core.

'I'm sorry, Mrs Robinson,' Delia whispered. 'I hadn't intended it to be this way. Although I didn't know what I was going to tell you until I got here.'

'There's no need for you to apologize for anything, Delia,' Aaron butted in, and now there was steel in his voice. 'But somebody has to answer for himself afore this day is out.'

The house was filled with little girls as Louisa, Emma, Rosie and Molly returned. Robin introduced them to his mother, murmuring to her that Louisa was his very best friend. Molly overheard him and butted in to add that she was Robin's special friend too and that he was teaching her to read.

'I hope you don't all spoil him,' Delia said quietly.

They didn't seem to know what spoiling meant, and Louisa piped up that Robin was like a new brother; and then Molly added that they'd had a baby brother but that he'd died and they'd never even seen him.

Delia glanced at Peggy, who nodded. 'Stillborn,' she said quietly. 'Came too early.'

Dinner was almost ready and Delia asked, 'Can I do anything?' as Jenny put on an apron to baste the roast potatoes. 'Although I'm out of practice,' she confessed.

'No, you take it easy,' Peggy said. 'You're our guest today. Mebbe another time when you come again?'

Inwardly, Delia felt an easing of tension. They weren't going to ask her and Robin to leave, even though she was sure they had now grasped the whole situation.

Aaron had gone out into the yard. Through the window she could see him pacing.

'Have you never had a proper home since you left 'village?' Peggy asked her when all the children had disappeared into the parlour.

'No,' Delia said croakily. 'I—' She looked down into her lap and confessed, 'When my mother found out, she told my father, and . . .' She hesitated. There was no need to tell of the leathering or the harsh things he had said or threatened her with; neither did she want to drag up the sickening memory.

'He said I should leave immediately, but Ma persuaded him that I could stay the night and leave next morning. He agreed to that but said I shouldn't be there when he got back from fishing or it would be the worse for me.

'It's a long story. I'd just enough money to pay for the train into Hull and lodgings for one night, and the next day I began looking for work.'

The scullery door banged and they could hear Aaron pulling off his boots. He came into the kitchen in his thick socks. Peggy changed the subject, saying that it was a pity she and Jenny couldn't have stayed the night, but conceding that they both had commitments, before adding anxiously, 'But you'll let Robin stay, won't you?' Then Aaron interrupted to say, 'Of course we want him to stay, but we must talk this over, and it'll be Delia's decision in 'long run.'

Peggy looked worried at his remark but busied herself with checking the vegetables. Delia got up and went to stand by the window looking out at the yard. There were ducks and hens scratching about in the dust and

293

a terrier-type dog sitting by the fence watching them as if he might round them up if they attempted to escape or misbehave.

She recalled that the Robinsons had always had a dog that could be patted or stroked, unlike the dogs that her father had kept on a metal chain in the kennel near the door. They were either cowed or vicious, and she thought that he had made them so by his ill-treatment.

'That's a nice little dog out there.' It was a throwaway remark of no consequence to anyone in particular.

'That's Charlie; he's Robin's dog,' Aaron replied, coming over to her side. 'I rescued him from a bad home and Robin took a fancy to him. Our old dog went to 'new house.'

'Robin has a dog?' she murmured. 'Oh!'

'That's all right, isn't it?' Aaron turned to her. 'I was going to get another dog to keep here. The other dog is used to 'bairns, that's why he went wi' them. But then I came across this one and he sort of followed me home.'

'And you gave him to Robin?'

'We're sharing him,' he said softly. 'We've built him a kennel.'

'You and Robin?'

'Aye, that's right.' He looked at her kindly and put his large hand on her shoulder. 'It's 'sort o' thing I'd have done if I'd had a grandson. Done things together, you know.'

She nodded but couldn't speak. Such a simple act of kindness brought tears to her eyes. Aaron hadn't known then that Robin had any connection to him, and yet he still treated him thoughtfully and generously. They were good people, she thought, and the knowledge should make her decision easier, but it didn't. Even though she had left him with them, every day that passed she missed him more and more.

'Are you all stopping for some dinner?' Peggy asked the girls. 'Or is your ma cooking when she comes back?'

'Don't know, Gran,' Louisa said.

'I want to stop,' Rosie said. 'I couldn't smell anyfing cooking at home.'

'We're having cold ham and mash, Ma said.' Emma chipped in. 'And she'll cook later. She's really busy cos she's had to go over to Preston to look at this new horse.'

'Right,' Peggy said evenly. 'Wash hands, everybody, we're about ready. Jenny, will you put out extra cutlery?'

There was a mad rush to the scullery and Delia smiled; it didn't seem to perturb Peggy in the slightest that there'd be three extra mouths to feed.

They were finishing off their apple sponge pudding when Jack arrived back and announced that he hadn't bought the horse after all. 'He was difficult to handle,' he said. 'There's no wonder Rudge's missis didn't want him. Susan wouldn't have been able to hold him. We'll look for another.'

He looked at the girls sitting at the table with clean dishes in front of them. 'You've had your dinner, then. Don't suppose you've left any for me?'

They all solemnly shook their heads. 'You're too late, Da!' Molly said.

He heaved a big sigh of disappointment that made the children laugh, and Delia wondered how they would react if they found out the truth about their father and her and Robin. And what about his wife? How would she take the news? Delia didn't know her except by name, but she'd heard Jenny's unfavourable comments about her.

'You can tek 'remains of 'joint home if you like,' Peggy offered in an offhand kind of way. 'Susan can mebbe serve it up cold with some fresh vegetables.'

'Thanks, Ma,' Jack murmured. Then he bestirred himself. 'Are you staying here for a bit or coming home?' he asked his daughters.

'Staying,' they chorused. 'We've got games to play,' Rosie explained; then Louisa stood stock still and looked at Delia.

'You're not taking Robin home with you, are you, Mrs Del—' She hesitated over the name. 'Mrs Delmore?'

'Not today,' Delia said quietly. 'Not unless your gran and grandda say so.' She silently uttered a plea that they wouldn't; what would they do, now that they knew, or almost knew, the truth? 'Would you like him to stay?'

It was unfair to say that, she realized. She was playing on everyone's emotions.

'Yes we would,' Louisa and Molly spoke as one, and Emma and Rosie both nodded their heads.

'Where do you live?' Jack interrupted abruptly. 'In Hull, or . . . have you come back to live wi' your folks?'

He must have seen the shock and dismay on her face and his eyes widened. 'You haven't been to see them?' He looked from Delia to Robin, who was standing tense and confused and looking at each grown-up in turn; then Jack looked back at Delia. 'Why not? They're your kin. Surely . . .'

He doesn't understand, she thought. He has no idea whatsoever. Do I explain now or leave it for another day? Peggy and Aaron were watching her, waiting with bated breath for her answer to their son's question. It had to be now.

CHAPTER THIRTY-FOUR

'Go and play, then,' Peggy told the children. 'We'll have a cup of tea.'

The girls trooped out but Robin stood looking at his mother until Louisa tapped him on the arm, urging him to join them. He followed her, but gave a last backward glance to Delia.

She picked up her shawl and draped it around her shoulders. 'I'll explain if you like,' she said to Jack. She pointed through the window to where a pale sun was attempting to break through the cloud. 'Shall we go outside, so we don't bore everybody else?'

Jack looked curiously at her, clearly wondering about her motive. 'Aye, if you like, then I must get back home. Susan'll wonder what I'm doing.'

'Will she?' Delia asked as they went to the door. 'Does she keep you on a tight rein?'

He closed the door behind them, and gave a wry laugh. 'Ma thinks she does. There's not much love lost between them two.'

'Why's that?' Delia walked across to the fence, away from any view from the house, and leaned upon it. The dog had gone to his kennel and the hens were clucking around the barn. She looked towards it and gave a little shudder as she remembered.

From where they stood she could see the edge of Foggit's land, where she and Jenny had once dashed across to reach one's house or the other's. She could see the corner of her parents' old cottage and the light glinting on a window, and knowing that her mother sometimes spied on her neighbours she turned her back to it.

'Not sure, really.' He stuck his hands in his jacket pockets, then with his boot he idly scraped at a weed growing beneath his foot. 'Goes back a long way. Ma thought I was too young to get married. She said it was a shotgun wedding.'

'And was it?' she asked quietly.

He gave a slight nod. 'Yeh, I suppose.' He was silent for a moment, and then muttered, 'I had no sense back then – easily led.' He chanced a look at her. 'I did a few things wrong; things that I'm sorry for. You know that I did, Dorothy.'

Here it comes, she thought. 'I'm Delia,' she reminded him. 'It was Dorothy who was violated; Dorothy who was beaten by her father when he found out she was pregnant. It was Dorothy who was turned out of the house. Dorothy who ran away from everything and everybody she knew.' She paused. 'Because of you.'

He lifted his head and looked at her, his mouth open. 'No!' he said in a low voice. 'Oh, God! No!'

She held his gaze. 'Yes.'

'Why didn't you say?' His voice was hoarse. 'Why didn't you come and tell us?'

'I did,' she said softly. 'I did come.' Her voice shook.

'I spoke to your mother; I'd hoped to see Jenny but she wasn't here; she was still in Hull. And then . . . your ma – Peggy – told me that you'd gone with Susan to talk to the vicar about reading the banns for your marriage.'

Tears streamed down her cheeks; it suddenly seemed like yesterday that it had happened to her other self, and she was sorry for her.

Jack turned his back to the house and with his elbows on the fence he covered his eyes with his hands. 'I'm sorry,' he mumbled. 'I'm so very sorry. How could I do such a thing? Where did you go? What did you do?'

'When my father heard he took his belt to me and said I had to get out, but then he said I could stay until the next morning, so it was then that I slipped out and went to your house. When your mother told me about you and Susan, I didn't know what to do or who to turn to, but I knew I had to get as far away from home as possible if I valued my life. He'd told Ma that he was going fishing and taking the boat out early dawn, and I had better be gone before he got back.'

She remembered sitting up in bed willing herself not to fall asleep, and then whilst it was still dark hearing him plod downstairs; she'd listened for his routine of picking up the bread and cheese that her mother always left ready for him, unhooking his coat from behind the door and his grunt as he pulled on his boots, then the wrench of the door bolt and the click of the latch. She'd waited five more minutes, listening to hear if her mother was rising, but then on hearing her rattling snore had scurried downstairs in her bare feet.

She had known for a long time where her father

kept his money; she it was who kept the house clean, the floors swept and the little furniture that they had dusted and polished, and every morning she shook the mat that covered the loose floorboard under which he kept the tin box. She didn't know where the money came from, but assumed it was from selling shrimps; she and her mother never saw any of it. She didn't know if her mother knew about the hiding place. Her father paid any bills and handed out coins to buy groceries when they asked, and he always demanded the receipt.

'I stole money from his secret tin,' she confessed. 'I knew he wouldn't give me any and that my mother had very little, but I was desperate to get out of the district so that he wouldn't ever find me and I could only do that by catching the train from Hedon to Hull.'

She wiped her eyes and gave a grimace. 'There was more money in that tin than I'd ever seen in my life, but I didn't dare take much in case he counted it and came after me.'

She'd wrapped the coins in a piece of clean rag that she used as a handkerchief, knotted it and placed it inside her bloomers, gone back upstairs to dress in her warmest clothes and gone downstairs again to eat her breakfast of bread and dripping. Her mother had come down too but didn't speak to her, not even when she was putting on her coat and boots ready to leave, but then she had put her hand into her apron pocket and handed her a penny, and said it was all she had.

Jack listened quietly, and then began his own justification. 'I – I'd – Susan told me that she was expecting,' he stammered. 'I hadn't been – I mean, I'd never

301

. . . well, it was cos of Ralph Pearce. I'd met him at Patrington hirings 'year before. He allus had plenty of money, his folks have a big farm somewhere round there, and I knocked about with him and we sometimes went to hostelries together.'

He looked down at the ground. 'He used to tell me about 'girls he'd been with and how . . . you know, how they were allus willing. I didn't really believe him, but he kept on about it every time we met, and—' he swore to himself, calling himself a fool. 'Well, I suppose I'd got all worked up, and then a bit later Susan was waiting for me; she told me that she'd been talking to Ralph Pearce and he'd told her that I was looking for some excitement.'

Delia turned in astonishment. Why was he telling her this? Where was it leading? 'I don't think you should—' she began.

He ran his fingers through his thick red hair, making it stand up in tufts, and grunted, 'It's *relevant*, Dorothy. It's relevant!'

She wanted to scream at him that she didn't want to know about his sordid escapades, that it didn't excuse what had happened to her.

'Don't you see?' he pleaded. 'She came to me! And I was green and inexperienced and – and it was so disappointing and I thought that it was supposed to be special, and then about a week later you called and there wasn't anybody at home . . .' He paused. 'I liked you, Delia. I'd always liked you, but you were allus shy and quiet, and – and I took advantage of you that day, and I'm really sorry. I was sorry as soon as you'd run off home.'

He took a handkerchief from his pocket and blew his nose. 'I didn't mean to hurt you.' He took a deep sighing breath. 'And if I'd known about . . . well, I would have done 'right thing by you.'

'Except that Susan got there first,' she muttered. 'Quite a Lothario, weren't you?'

'What?' He gazed at her, not understanding her sarcasm. 'So where did you go?' he asked again. 'How did you manage on your own? Did you get work?'

'Yes,' she said wearily, 'I did.' She was tiring of telling this story. There could be no end to it, no conclusion, and she was beginning to form the opinion that she was glad she hadn't told him of her pregnancy before Susan told him of hers. Had she and Jack married, she would have had a loving family in Peggy and Aaron, and a comfortable existence, but would she have been happy in a marriage with Jack?

Delia slowly shook her head; her life alone had been very difficult, but she'd survived and had the constant love of her son to sustain her. She wanted nothing from Jack for herself, but she wanted a loving family life for Robin. He had missed out, just as she had done as a child, but she could do something about it: she could ask Peggy and Aaron if they were still willing to let him stay now that they knew the truth; to let him enjoy the security of a family around him until such time as he wanted to move on or return to an uncertain life with her.

'I found work as a cleaner in a Hull theatre,' she said softly, giving him only the bones of her story. 'I even slept there, hiding in a cupboard until everyone had gone, and I stayed there until after his birth. People were kind . . . then I joined a theatre company and travelled. I had my son,' she said slowly, still wondering if he fully understood. 'It was ten years ago. He's the same age as your daughter Louisa, and he looks just like you.'

Except, she thought, he's more handsome, intelligent, funny and adorable. She continued to gaze at him until she saw the dawn of comprehension.

'Yes,' she whispered. 'Robin. Did you not guess? I named him Jack Robinson Deakin. I gave my maiden name for his birth certificate.'

Jack stood staring at her as if a thunderbolt had struck him.

'The bright boy that he is,' she said proudly, 'he decided that he didn't want to be called Jack Robinson because—'

'Everybody meks a joke about it,' he mumbled.

'That's why he called himself Robin Jackson.'

'He's my son!' Jack's words were husky and low. He swallowed hard but the tears came anyway and his voice broke. 'I'm so very sorry, Delia, that I put you through so much because of my – my brutal behaviour. I'm not usually – I mean, I never – *don't* – normally behave in that way. I wasn't brought up to be unfeeling. Ma and Da are going to be that mad at me and I – I don't want them to be ashamed of me. I *am* ashamed,' he said, weeping with emotion, and rubbing his eyes and nose with the back of his hand, 'and I'll do what I can to mek it up to you.'

He took a deep breath and muttered, 'God knows what Susan's going to say about it. She'll mek my life unbearable.'

Delia gave a wry grimace. 'Serves you right,' she declared.

They went back inside and Delia waited in the scullery whilst Jack went through to face his parents and sister. She leaned on the stone sink and looked outside through the small paned window at the yard where she had disclosed the truth of what had happened all those years ago. Beyond the fields lay the estuary, a deep wide turbulent highway carrying barges, ships and fishing boats, and a fleeting thought came to her that her father might be out there on one of them. The thought was followed by another: she did not care if he were alive or dead.

Then she heard the sound of someone sobbing. It was Jack, and she took a heaving breath and went to join them in the kitchen.

Peggy stood holding Jack wrapped in her arms and they were both crying; Aaron sat stony-faced in his chair with Jenny perched on the chair arm with her hand gently patting his shoulder.

As tears flooded Delia's eyes, she realized that now wasn't the time to ask if Robin could stay. His presence might cause even more conflict within the family; loyalties would be divided, and no matter that Jack had said he would make it up to her for the difficulties she had gone through, his commitment must be to his wife and children.

As she stood, uncertain of what to say or do, the scullery door opened and a voice asked, 'Is anybody at home?' Delia turned to see a woman who she guessed was Susan, who glanced at her and then at Jack, blowing his nose and obviously distressed, standing next to his mother.

Her lips turned down and she folded her arms in front of her. 'Just what is going on? Is this something I should be privy to, or am I excluded?'

CHAPTER THIRTY-FIVE

Jack muttered to Susan that they had to go home and he would tell her there what had happened.

Susan glanced at Delia and nodded as they left; they hadn't been introduced and it was clear that Susan had no idea who Delia was, although her gaze passed over her curiously as she asked Peggy to send the children home when she was fed up with them.

Jenny got up from the chair arm and went to the scullery to fill the kettle to make more tea.

Delia cleared her throat. 'Should we catch the earlier train, Jenny?' she ventured quietly as Jenny came back and hooked the kettle over the fire. 'Perhaps enough has been said for one day.'

'No!' Peggy, sitting by the table with her fingers clasped tightly together, answered for her daughter. Her thick hair had become tangled and hung in unruly curls across her forehead and around her cheeks. 'Let's talk this through now.' Her voice was hoarse. 'No use leaving it for some other time; we need some sort of – idea of what to do next. A plan.'

'Aye, we do.' Aaron got up from his chair, his stupor receding and a look of determination forming in his expression. He went to Peggy and patted her cheek. 'Come on now, honey; let's get a grip on this situation.' Then he turned to Delia, who still stood in the middle of the room, wondering what to do and whether or not to sit down. Was she going to be rejected for the second time in her life?

'I'm going to speak for 'rest of my family,' he said, 'especially that blackguard who is my son.'

Delia's blood ran cold and Peggy looked up at her husband in alarm.

'It behoves me to apologize for what's gone before,' he said soberly. 'We brought our Jack up to be a caring young man, to be kind to others, to do and be done by 'same as he would expect from other folk. Or so we thought. But it seems . . .' He drew himself up straight and took a breath. 'It seems that we didn't mek a very good fist of it; we failed somehow to learn him. In fact we failed miserably.'

Delia hurried into speech. 'Mr Robinson, it was a long time ago. He was young and impetuous; he didn't kill anybody and I haven't come for revenge.'

He looked across at her; she had interrupted his flow and he was unsure of how to continue. 'That's all very well, but we have to mek recompense somehow.'

'You've already done that,' she said softly. 'You took my son, a boy you didn't know, and kept him safe in your home.'

'Aye, well,' he murmured. 'We'd have done that for any youngster to keep 'em from harm.'

Delia nodded. They would, she understood that, and she felt a tightness in her throat at their kindness to a child they hadn't known was their blood; and I, she thought wretchedly, I did wrong by just leaving him with people he didn't know.

'Come and sit down, Delia.' Peggy patted the chair next to her. 'Kettle's boiling, Jenny. Mek tea and bring 'biscuits out of 'barrel, would you?' Her voice was hoarse after her weeping and Delia guessed that she would be worrying about what was happening between Jack and Susan. 'We might not resolve everything today,' she went on, 'but mebbe we'll mek some headway.'

'Mrs Robinson,' Delia began, 'I didn't come with the intention of causing trouble.' Inside her head, she could hear her former self, the shy insecure Dorothy, contrite and apologetic and taking the blame for any mishap, even when not of her making. She sighed out a breath to dispel the image of that young girl. She had gone; she was no more. 'I came to thank you for looking after my son, and to say that I couldn't wish for better grandparents for him.'

'So does that mean that you'd be happy for us to continue looking after him?' Aaron chipped in; he seemed close to tears. 'For a bit longer at any rate?'

'Cos we'd like to,' Peggy added. 'It would break our hearts to watch him go and never see him again.' She pressed her handkerchief to her nose. 'Cos he's a grand little lad.'

Delia swallowed, and wondered how it was that Peggy and Aaron had both come to the same conclusion, for it didn't appear to her that they had had any discussion. Perhaps that was what happened when two people had had a long and amicable marriage: each understood the other's needs and intentions.

Jenny silently poured tea and took the lid off the biscuit barrel. She had kept very quiet and seemed quite shaken by the turn of events. Maybe she's not quite as brave as she makes out, Delia thought. Perhaps she hadn't realized the impact the disclosure would have on her brother; they were very close when they were young, Delia remembered. Jenny had said some harsh things about him and his wife, but perhaps now she regretted them.

Silently, they drank their tea, Peggy topping hers up again from the teapot, and then Jenny said quietly to her parents, 'You've agreed that you'd like Robin to stay with you, and I think, Delia, that you'd be happy with that?'

Delia nodded, unable to speak, and Jenny continued, 'So do you think that before making any final decision, you might like to find out what views Jack and Susan might have?'

'What's going on?' Susan asked as she and Jack crossed the yard and unfastened the gate that led on to Foggit farm; they had unanimously agreed to keep the name as everyone local knew it as that. Jack and Aaron had created a pathway from cracked old stone and rubble to make it easier for the children to walk across the grass if it were wet or muddy when going between the two houses. Eventually, Aaron and Jack had decided, they would open up some of the joint fields to make better grazing for more sheep and pigs.

'Let's wait till we're inside,' he muttered. 'There's a lot to say.'

'Who was that woman? Was it Robin's mother?'

There was a long pause until he managed eventually to say, 'Aye, it was.'

'Really? She's not as I expected,' Susan said. 'I thought she'd be – well, disreputable, a bit of a slattern, you know?'

'I don't know why you'd think that; the lad was clean and tidy and well-spoken when he first came.' Jack took off his boots as they entered the kitchen and gazed round. It looked cosy; the fire was glowing in the range and there was a good smell coming from the oven. Susan had obviously prepared food before coming over to find out when he was coming home.

She shrugged. 'Yeh, but she left him, didn't she? Left her son with complete strangers.'

'Except that we weren't.' He flopped down into a chair by the fire and Susan thought pensively how like his father Jack was, with similar mannerisms and habits.

'What?' She was opening the oven door and had only loosely grasped his comment.

'I said that we weren't. We weren't strangers. Delia knew us. She used to live in Paull.' Jack put his hands to his head and closed his eyes.

She came and sat opposite him. 'What's up, Jack? Why were you and your ma so upset? She was crying.' She gazed at him, and then leaning forward she took his hands away from his face. 'And so were you,' she whispered. 'What's happened? You've got to tell me.'

He clenched his eyes shut and took a shuddering breath. 'You're never going to forgive me, Susan, but you're stuck wi' me till death us do part, isn't that what we promised?' He opened his eyes, which were red and swollen, and Susan looked away, unable to meet his gaze.

'I'm sorry.' His words were choked. 'I was young and stupid and I didn't really know you well back then, afore we married, but I knew Delia, Dorothy as she was then, and – I took advantage of her.'

'What 'you talking about?' Her voice rose. 'What do you mean you didn't know me well? We had—' She stopped, hesitating as if not knowing what to say. 'You took advantage of her? What's that supposed to mean?'

He stood up and began to pace about. 'It means that cos of my actions – my *callous* behaviour – that young lad, Robin, whose real name it seems is Jack, is my son.'

Susan sat in total silence, as if struck dumb, and then suddenly stood up and went out of the kitchen. Jack heard her running up the narrow stairs and into their bedroom overhead. He could hear her pacing.

I'll pay towards his keep, he thought as he sat down again. Delia's had to manage alone all these years; how has she coped, looking after a child and having to find work to pay rent and put bread on 'table? Unless – he was struck by a thought – has there been another man in her life? Mebbe one who doesn't want her son around any more so she decided to off-load him? But then he dismissed that idea. She wouldn't have brought him all the way from London, or wherever they were living, and just left him in the way that she did. He didn't seem scarred at all; he was a well-adjusted lad, and didn't he always say that she would come back when she could, as if he was totally sure of her? And, he thought again, she wasn't to know that we'd be in the Sun Inn that day.

Then he thought of his parents; had they suspected something? Did Ma put two and two together? Delia said that she'd come to our place when she'd found out she was pregnant. She'd be in a state, I expect; she'd not have had any sympathy from her parents. Davis Deakin is nowt but a bully, everybody knows that, and his wife . . . well, who knows what she's like, for nobody ever sees her.

He heard Susan's footsteps on the stairs and she came back into the kitchen. She looked pale and shaken but she'd brushed her hair and tied it into a bun at the back of her neck. It looked nice like that, he thought.

'I'm sorry,' he said again, but she just gave a shake of her head.

'Can you be sure?' she asked. 'She's not just looking for somebody to blame?'

He grimaced and huffed. 'I'm sure. Would she have waited ten years? And 'timing is right; he's not far short of Louisa's age. Besides, I remember it clearly and I remember how ashamed I was afterwards. She was frightened, poor lass.' He looked up at her. 'Not like you,' he said. 'You weren't frightened.' He paused. Quite the opposite, in fact; it was Susan who had made up to him, enticing him just as Ralph Pearce had said that girls did.

Susan licked her lips. 'I was frightened,' she said, 'but not for 'same reason. I thought you might reject me.'

Jack frowned. She'd been eager to kiss and cuddle

and then offered more, and he couldn't believe how lucky he was. It was his first time, but it was unexpected and awkward and not quite as marvellous as he'd been led to believe, and Susan seemed in a hurry for it to be over and done with. It was not long afterwards that Dorothy happened to come by and he was tempted because Susan hadn't come back as she'd promised. At least not until later, when she came to tell him she'd been caught and was expecting and he'd have to marry her.

'We've had our ups and downs, Jack,' Susan's voice cut into his thoughts, 'but I have to say I'm shocked. I thought I'd married 'perfect man, which you are in your ma and da's eyes.'

'Not any more,' he said grimly. 'I'm right at 'bottom of 'barrel now.'

'Well, once you were,' she said impatiently, 'and I was 'girl who'd led you astray, so in a way it's a relief to know that you're not perfect after all, but just as weak and flawed as 'rest of us.'

He got to his feet and took hold of her hands. 'I've never considered that I was perfect; I'm just an ordinary man trying to get through life without mekkin' too many mistakes.'

Susan looked him in the eyes. 'I've something to tell you, Jack. If we're to make our marriage work without hating each other, we're going to have to be honest with one another.'

'I thought I was,' he said miserably. 'To my shame I'd forgotten about Dorothy – Delia. I never gave her a single thought after 'first few weeks when I was racked by my conscience; she was 'sort of girl who blended into 'background. I think she must have been frightened of her own shadow, poor lass.'

'Well, I wasn't honest and I tricked you,' she said softly. 'Like Delia I was terrified, but in my case it was of being found out.'

'What do you mean?' He frowned. 'How did you trick me?'

'With Louisa. She isn't yours, Jack. Her father is Ralph Pearce.'

Fear showed in her eyes, but relief too, and it was as if a cloud had lifted. 'That swine! He told me he loved me and forgot to mention that he was already engaged to be married to someone else; someone more suitable, from a better family than mine. When I told him I was pregnant he said he couldn't get out of it, that 'banns had been read. He suggested that you might be a good proposition, that you were gullible and wouldn't guess, and that's why I came to you. I was so frightened of my parents finding out. So I'm sorry too. I've lived in fear these last ten years that you might guess, or that Ralph Pearce might boast about it.'

Jack swallowed and then nodded. 'I think I've always had a feeling that Louisa might not be mine,' he murmured. 'That first night with you, I didn't know what I was doing; it was my first time and I did wonder afterwards how I'd managed to father a child, and I knew that you used to see Ralph Pearce. So I was afraid to love her to begin with. I thought that one day if you were given 'chance you might leave and take her with you.'

'Why would you think I'd do that?'

'I thought you still cared for him. And she looks like

him,' he said. 'Dark eyes and hair. Nothing like me. And he used to turn up sometimes and give one of his sneaky grins as if he had a secret. I thought that if he clicked his fingers you might go running to him. Then, when we had the other bairns, I reckoned that you wouldn't leave them all.'

'I'd never have done that,' she whispered. 'How could you think such a thing?'

He shrugged. 'I was scared, I suppose. I thought I was second best.'

She licked her lips. 'We've both made mistakes.'

'Aye, we have. Is it too late to . . .' He looked pleadingly at her.

'Put things right? No, I don't think so. Can you forgive me? I'm more to blame than you and I'm really sorry.' Her eyes were moist and her words unsteady.

He had never seen her like this before; she was always full of bravado, always quick to find fault. 'Let's not talk about blame.' He reached out to hold her. 'We'll have a fresh start. An honest one.'

'Yes.' She put her head on his chest. 'I'd like that. And shall we tell your folks, just so that they know everything? Mek a clean breast of it.'

'Aye, I reckon so. Just one thing, though. What do we do about Robin?'

CHAPTER THIRTY-SIX

Delia, Peggy and Aaron continued to discuss the situation. Jenny had not interrupted again after her suggestion that Jack and Susan should give their views.

'But we want Robin to stay more than ever,' Peggy said, and there had been more tears when she'd added, 'especially now that we know he's ours.'

'And *you* must come whenever you want to, Delia,' Aaron said gruffly. 'You must think of this as home. We realize that you won't be wanted at 'other place so we'll not include them, but that's their loss.'

Delia had always wanted such a home, one where she would be sure of a welcome, and the idea of it took some getting used to. She had lived an itinerant life, hand to mouth sometimes when the theatre engagements were few, always knowing that what she couldn't provide in her rootless existence was constancy; yet what was remarkable was that in spite of their lifestyle Robin had turned out to be adaptable and well balanced and seemed to be happy.

'I can't thank you enough,' she said tearfully. 'But I think that Jenny is right. First you should hear what Jack and Susan have to say.'

Aaron had shaken his head and said that it wouldn't make any difference, but when Jack and Susan did return Delia went into the parlour and sat with the children whilst the family talked. It was a warm and cosy room, with a log fire and squashy chairs, and books and games scattered over the carpet.

Rosie sidled up to her and leaned on her, then teased her fingers through her dark hair. 'Robin's ma,' she said plaintively, 'we'd like Robin to stay wiv us. We play good games when he's here.'

'Yes, but you don't live here any more,' Molly broke in crossly. '*You* live in your own house, so Robin's *my* friend not yours.'

'I *am* Rosie's friend, Molly.' Robin spoke up from the floor where he and Louisa were engrossed in a noisy game of pick up sticks. 'And Emma's and Louisa's and your cousin Ben's as well.'

'You've got a lot of friends, Robin,' Delia said, and lifted Rosie on to her knee.

He looked up at her. 'I have,' he agreed. 'I only really had one before, didn't I, Arthur Crawshaw, and he was a grown-up friend.' He turned back to the game and shouted with glee when Louisa's pile of sticks collapsed. 'Wouldn't he be surprised if he saw me now? I wish I could write to him and tell him what a good time I'm having, but we don't know where he is.'

After about twenty minutes the door opened and Jenny glanced round at them all, her gaze lingering not on Robin but on Louisa. 'I've made yet more tea, Delia, and we'll have to think about going in an hour or so if we're to catch our train. Jack and Susan are about to go home.'

318

'I'm going with them.' Emma stood up and Rosie slid from Delia's knee and said, 'I fink I will as well.'

Delia got up too. 'I'll come and say goodbye,' she murmured. 'Will that be all right?'

Jenny nodded. 'Yes,' she said, her voice catching. 'I think so.'

Delia approached Susan. 'We haven't been introduced, Susan,' she said quietly. 'I'm Delia, Robin's mother.'

'Yes.' Susan flushed, and seemed embarrassed. 'I'm pleased to meet you.' Her voice was low and husky, as if she had been crying. 'I gather that Robin's going to stay here for a while. My – our girls are really fond of him. Especially Louisa.'

'And me.' Molly had followed behind them. 'He's learned me to read.'

'*Taught* you, Molly,' Emma butted in. 'Not learned.'

'That's what I said!' Molly declared, and Delia understood that a good deal of patience was needed where Molly was concerned.

'We're just off home.' Jack came over to Delia and put his hand on Susan's shoulder. He was very subdued. 'We'll see you again next time you come, won't we? We'll – erm, have a chat and sort things out, mebbe? To see how to go about things? I'm . . .' He heaved a breath. 'I'm – really sorry to have caused you so much—'

'Yes,' Delia broke in. 'We'll talk.' She could barely comprehend that she was speaking almost normally to the man she had reviled in her heart for so long.

Robin came behind her and put his arm round her waist and she looked down and wound hers about him too. 'I'm pleased that you've met my mother, Jack,' he said, smiling up at them both. 'And you too, Susan. Now everybody knows everybody else!'

Delia was proud of him; he behaved perfectly well with adults and wasn't in the least shy, and yet responded well with children too, and it was as if he'd found a niche, as if being part of a family was what he had craved. She looked at Jack, who was observing Robin as if he couldn't quite believe what had happened either, and then he glanced at Louisa and put his hand over his mouth as if he was suddenly overwhelmed by something. A second later he drew the little girl towards him and planted a kiss on the top of her head.

Susan leaned forward and put her cheek against Delia's. 'We'll try to make it work out, Delia,' she whispered. 'Honest we will.'

Jack didn't offer Delia a kiss and she was glad that he didn't, but he held out his hand to her and hurriedly repeated that they'd meet again soon.

When they'd gone, Robin, Louisa and Molly went back into the parlour to clear away their games. Peggy sat down and put her head back on the chair and closed her eyes.

'I feel as if I've been through 'mangle,' she sighed. 'I hope I never have another day like this one.'

'I'm sorry—' Delia began.

Peggy cut her short. 'Don't you dare apologize,' she said. 'Nothing's your fault, and Aaron says we've to get over all our apologies and begin again. As long as 'bairns are all right. That's what's important.'

'Yes,' Delia said quietly. 'I agree.'

'And I mean our Louisa as well as Robin.' Peggy lowered her voice. 'In case Jenny hasn't mentioned anything to you, we now have 'truth about Louisa.'

Delia raised her eyebrows and waited.

'She's not our Jack's child.' There was a note of anguish in Peggy's voice. 'I have to say, it came as no great surprise, and yet . . . 'truth teks some getting used to. But there we are! Jack and Susan mek a good match. It seems,' she went on, wiping a teary eye and seeming to give herself a mental shake, 'that we've lost one grandchild but gained another.'

Delia asked if they might leave ten minutes earlier and drive down to the estuary before they went to catch their train. 'It's been a long time since I last looked at the Humber,' she told Aaron. 'It was part of my life for so long. I watched its moods every day, and every day they changed.'

'I can understand that,' he murmured. 'Having been a fisherman I've a bond with 'river; sometimes . . . well, this might seem strange' – he glanced about the room but only Delia was listening – 'but at one time, when I was a young man, it seemed to talk to me, telling me whether or not to go out or stay ashore, and sometimes when to head home.' He sighed. 'I don't feel it much nowadays, cos I don't go out so often. But I tell you what, that lad of yours, he's got a feel for it too. He's not afraid of it.'

'He must get that from you,' she murmured.

'Aye, mebbe, or . . .' He cast a questioning glance at her and raised his head in the direction of her old home.

She shook her head and said decisively, 'I hope Robin has inherited *nothing* from my side.'

Aaron smiled. 'Except from you, Delia. Bravery and determination are just two qualities I could think of.'

Peggy gave them a blanket to put over their knees as they drove away, as the weather was getting even colder. There was a pale sun and a few patches of blue sky through the dark cloud; Aaron said he thought there might be snow heading their way. Robin had asked if he could come to the station to see his mother off and Peggy gave him a woolly hat to wear and turned up his coat collar, and then brought out another blanket.

They headed down the track towards the village; the river glinted in front of them, and they felt the chill of the wind as they drove nearer. Gulls and other estuarine birds flew low over the water in their hunt for fish.

'See them low clouds, Robin,' Aaron said, 'and how they're flattening out, and feel that Arctic wind coming up 'estuary? That tells you that snow is on 'way.'

'It would be too cold a day to go out fishing then, wouldn't it?' Robin asked. 'Although I thought that there might be plenty of fish coming in from the sea.'

'What meks you think that?'

'Well, didn't you say the other day that the smolt would soon be coming to the estuary to spawn?' He turned to his mother. 'Smolts are a young salmon and spawn means laying their eggs,' he explained.

'I see.' Delia nodded and hid a smile. 'Of course.'

'So I thought that the smolt might be starting to come, to get ready, you know.'

'Ah,' Aaron said. 'But it's not only about 'weather

being warm or cold – and it's still much too cold for them – but it's also about 'condition of 'water. Here at Paull, nearer to 'sea, there's more saline in 'estuary waters and certain types of fish can tolerate it and others can't. So, for instance, you'd find some cod or plaice and turbot round here, but at 'top end of 'estuary where there's fresher water with less saline you'd mebbe find tench or carp or roach.'

'Oh, I see,' Robin murmured. 'There's quite a lot to learn, isn't there?'

There was a heavy swell on the river and brisk white-flecked waves broke over the bank and thrashed on to the road. Delia recalled when she had lived in Paull if the tide had been very high it several times flooded the bottom of her father's land and nothing would grow there. He never built up the bank to avoid the problem; he was a fisherman and didn't seem to care about the land. He kept a mule for pulling his cart which was allowed to graze, but her mother was the one who dug and grew fruit and vegetables, and kept a cow and goats, and hens and ducks with their wings clipped so that they wouldn't fly off, although they often found their way to the waterlogged field and paddled contentedly.

'You, erm, don't go out if the weather's bad, do you?' she asked Aaron, worrying about Robin in the deep water. 'Robin isn't a strong swimmer.'

Aaron shook his head. 'It wouldn't mek any difference if he were a champion swimmer,' he answered. 'With boots and a heavy coat nobody'd stand a chance in that deep water. But you don't need to worry. We don't tek any chances.'

'No, of course you won't,' she murmured. 'I'm sorry. It's just that—'

'That you've allus been there to protect him,' he acknowledged. 'I know. But there're others to look out for him as well now.'

They drove down the long village street and Delia observed that nothing seemed to have changed since she was a girl here; the same village shop where she was sent on errands, women standing on their door-steps with hands in their apron pockets, taking a breath of air or looking to see who was about to chat to; then Aaron took another track back and along to Thorngumbald and on to the Hedon road.

'Will you come back soon?' Robin asked when they arrived at the station. 'I shall miss you.' He clung to her and once more she felt guilty about leaving him behind, even though she knew that it was in his best interests. Peggy and Aaron could do more for his well-being than she could. But it still didn't seem right.

'I'll come back as soon as I can,' she said. 'This run at the theatre is nearly finished so I'll have more time.' Though heaven knows what I'll do for money, she pondered. I still won't have two farthings to rub together.

They climbed aboard the train and Delia felt a lump in her throat as the whistle blew and the engine got up steam and they slowly chuffed out of the station; she thought her heart would break when she saw Aaron put his hand on Robin's shoulder as he waved and waved until she could no longer see him for the pall of steam and smoke that surrounded them.

They sat down and Jenny murmured, 'It seemed to go well, considering.'

It was upsetting for Jack and for me, Delia thought. I was so nervous and he, well, he seemed to have had no thought of the effect his actions might have had. He said he was ashamed, and perhaps now he realizes the enormity of what happened. Susan was pregnant and he thought Louisa was his child, yet the question of my possible pregnancy doesn't seem to have occurred to him.

She gave a deep sigh and Jenny looked at her. 'Yes,' Delia said slowly. 'I suppose we could say that.'

They didn't talk much on the journey; Delia wasn't inclined for conversation and Jenny seemed to understand that. The train drew in to Hull and they stepped down; a train had arrived at another platform and she was reminded of when she'd come back from Hedon after the hiring fair, when she'd left Robin behind and she followed the theatre performers.

They were walking towards the exit and the cab stand when Delia heard a voice calling her name. They both stopped and turned and Delia's face lit into a smile when she saw Giles Dawson striding towards them with luggage in his hand.

'I'm so pleased to see you,' he said to Delia, and then tipped his hat to Jenny, 'Miss Robinson.'

'I'm pleased to see you too,' Delia said, feeling an immediate lifting of spirits. It was true she was delighted to see him; she had missed him when he wasn't there. He looked rather drawn and tired, though, and she hoped he and his wife had managed to sort through their difficulties.

'Can we share a cab?' he asked. 'Miss Robinson, are you staying in town?'

Jenny was about to answer when another voice called out behind them. A man's voice with a distinctive accent, not a northern one.

'Miss Delamour! Delia!'

Delia turned once more and was astonished to see Arthur Crawshaw bearing down on them, looking disgruntled and yet relieved. 'Delia,' he exclaimed as he approached. 'At last! Where on *earth* have you been? I've searched everywhere for you. And *where* is my boy?'

CHAPTER THIRTY-SEVEN

Delia gasped, 'Arthur,' but she also caught sight of the expressions on the faces of her companions: Jenny's of simple astonishment, but Giles' of bewilderment and disbelief, and she realized that he had heard Arthur's words and picked up entirely the wrong implication. Surely he didn't think— But perhaps he did, for he was turning away.

'Jenny, Giles,' she said hurriedly. 'This is an old friend, a fellow performer, Mr Arthur Crawshaw, and a great friend to my son Robin. Arthur, these are my friends Miss Jenny Robinson and Mr Giles Dawson.'

Arthur bowed to Jenny, murmuring 'Delighted', and shook hands with a reluctant Giles, who was resuming his composure.

'But what are you doing here, Arthur?' she asked. 'This is a long way from your usual haunts.'

'Indeed it is,' he boomed, 'and it has taken me all day to get here! That idiot of an agent you employ only told me last week that you had come north, and I asked him weeks ago to find out where you were. Look here, I'm staying here at the hotel; can we go in? I'm desperate to sit somewhere comfortable and have a glass of whisky to revive me.' He turned to Giles. 'What do you say, old chap? Will you join me? And the ladies might perhaps like a glass of sherry?'

'I've only just got off the train myself,' Giles said stiffly. 'I was heading to my lodgings.'

'What about you, Miss Robinson?'

Delia glanced at Jenny; she knew she would be flattered that he remembered her name and then was astounded when Arthur said abruptly, '*Robinson*? Are you a relative of our young Jack?'

Giles looked from one to another, and Delia thought he must be totally confused; by his expression he seemed to be thinking that he'd like to be elsewhere.

'I'll get off, I think,' Giles said bluntly. 'You've probably much to talk about with your . . . friend. Will you be all right to get back to Mrs Benson's, Miss Delamour?'

'Yes,' she answered, 'I will, but I'd like to speak to you. Much has been happening, as I expect it has for you too.'

He hesitated, and then murmured, 'All right, I'll stay. Thank you, Mr Crawshaw, I will avail myself of your hospitality.'

Crawshaw had the hotel staff running hither and thither at his command. He told them to be sure they gave him a good room and to make certain there was plenty of hot water for his bath. Delia asked for a pot of tea, and Arthur commented wryly that he could tell she hadn't taken to drink since coming north; Jenny asked for a glass of port purely because he had suggested sherry; and the two men ordered whisky. Then they all settled back in their chairs, and Arthur turned to Delia.

'Now then, m'dear. Where is young Jack, and why did you come haring up to this godforsaken place?'

'It *isn't* a godforsaken place,' Delia answered. 'It's an old town with lots of theatres and music halls; and,' she added, 'with kind and friendly people. Where are you playing?'

'I'm not,' he said, stretching out his legs. 'I'm finished with all of that – for the time being anyway. But you haven't answered my question. Where is Jack?'

'Jack has changed his name,' she parried. 'He's Robin now.'

'Ah!' he exclaimed. 'I told him he should if he really didn't like being called Jack. *Defy your father and refuse your name.*'

Jenny looked curiously at them. 'Was that really why he changed it? He didn't like to be called Jack?'

Delia shook her head. 'Jack Robinson,' she said. 'Because people teased him about *Before you can say Jack Robinson.* Nothing more than that, Jenny.' She hesitated, and then said, 'He didn't know his father was called Jack Robinson. Still doesn't.' It had been a perverse act on her part to name him after the man who had sired him. She had been young and angry. Now she was older she knew better. The name was a constant reminder.

'So where is he?' Arthur persisted. 'You haven't abandoned him?'

Delia looked horrified. 'No!' she said. 'No,' and then she burst into tears and fished about in her pocket for a handkerchief. 'Yes,' she sobbed. 'I did. But I've been to see him. He's staying with his father's parents, in the village where I once lived. They are Jenny's parents too. Jenny is his aunt.'

Giles leaned forward and handed her a clean handkerchief, and she gave a watery laugh as she took it. 'I must buy you a box of handkerchiefs. I am constantly using yours.'

'Delia,' he said quietly, 'are you sure that you want to discuss this now?'

'Yes,' she said, taking a deep intake of breath. 'I'm with friends I can trust,' and as she said it she was immediately comforted. There had been times in her life when she had no one in whom to confide. 'Although I'm sorry to burden you all.' She wiped her eyes and cheeks and again could smell the refreshing cologne Giles used. She saw the look of concern on his face. 'I'm sorry. I don't know why I'm so upset. Robin is safe; he's with his grandparents, who love him, and I never ever thought I would be able to say that.'

'That's wonderful, m'dear,' Arthur said kindly. 'I'm so very pleased, although I will miss seeing him. I'll write to him, if I may?'

'He would love that, Arthur.' Tears began to flow again. 'He told me that he wished he could write to you and tell you what a good time he was having.'

Arthur nodded. 'So you can begin your life again, travel more and not worry about him,' and Delia was sure that he glanced at Giles as he spoke. 'He will understand, he's a sensible boy.'

After chatting for a while, they broke up. Everyone seemed tired and Giles asked the porter to get a cab

for him and Delia for the short distance to their lodgings, and Jenny chimed in to ask him to order one for
herself to Pearson Park.

Arthur insisted that she shouldn't travel alone, no
matter that it was a Sunday evening and probably quiet
in the town, and that he would be happy to escort her
to her home. 'Miss Delamour will vouch for my morals,
I'm sure,' he added, and Jenny quickly acquiesced,
which Delia thought wasn't at all like her fiercely
independent friend.

Arthur asked Delia to meet him for lunch the next
day, as he had things to discuss with her. There wasn't a
matinee and she willingly agreed. He shook hands with
Giles and said that he had been pleased to meet him
and hoped that they might catch up again; he seemed
to want to add more, but the first cab arrived and he
kissed Delia on both cheeks, saying, 'Goodnight, Delia.
Until tomorrow.'

As he and Jenny waited for the second cab, he said,
'Dawson seems like a decent fellow. Is – does Delia
know him well?'

Jenny gazed at him with interest. 'I understand that
she met him when she first arrived in Hull; that would
be back in November. He's a married man, in case you
were wondering,' she said slyly.

'Oh! That's a great pity,' he said, to her astonishment. 'I thought he seemed rather taken by her. I
worry about her, you know.'

'Do you? Yet you were not able to find her. I thought
perhaps you hadn't looked very hard.'

A grin crossed his face. 'You have a sharp wit, Miss
Robinson.' He took her arm as the porter came to tell

331

them the cab had arrived. 'I like that in a woman. You remind me of my mother.'

She wasn't sure whether to be flattered or annoyed at the comparison, but was mollified when he said, 'I haven't physically looked for Delia, but I wrote to various theatre managers in the south – Brighton, London and so on – to ask if she had appeared with them, and it was only by badgering that damned agent – I do beg your pardon – that I eventually found out where she was.'

He helped her into the carriage, and as they drove to her destination he said, 'There is another reason why it has taken me so long to discover her whereabouts. My father died recently, and there has been much to do regarding his estate. That is why I have given up the theatre. Miss Robinson,' he turned to her, 'I have arranged to meet Delia for lunch tomorrow. I wonder, would you do me the great honour of dining with me tomorrow evening? I shall be leaving the following morning.'

After hesitating for only a brief moment, for convention's sake and because she was perverse, she said yes, she would.

'Delia,' Giles said as he put his key in the lock of the lodging house door, 'I'm sure you've had a harrowing day, but I must beg five more minutes and tell you why I had to leave in such a hurry.'

She nodded. 'Of course. You must have had a good reason for doing so.' She opened the door to the residents' lounge and turned up the lamp, which was burning low. 'You must be tired too, so would you like to begin? You've heard the bones of my story; the rest can wait.'

He sank into a chair and put his hand to his forehead. 'You are the first person I have spoken to about this – I haven't yet told my parents, or even decided whether to tell them at all. In fact I believe I won't, or at least not yet. I have to time it right, and there's no need for them to know anything immediately.'

Delia didn't answer. He was setting his thoughts in order and didn't need a comment from her. But she owed it to him to listen; after all, he had listened to her when she needed a sympathetic ear and he hadn't even met her son.

'I don't want to bore you, Delia, but I think you of all people will understand my dilemma and the decision I have made.'

She simply nodded and let him continue.

He rubbed his fingers wearily over his brow. 'It's as I suspected,' he said. 'Marion is pregnant with her lover's child and that is why she sent for me.' He looked up. 'Have I shocked you?'

'No,' she declared resignedly. 'I've long since stopped being shocked by anything. But I'm sorry if it complicates your life. Does it mean that you have to go back to York and live with her?'

Because, she thought, I would be very sorry indeed to lose our friendship. I have come to value it, more than I thought possible.

'Good heavens. No,' he retorted, 'it does not! When I travelled to York I met her paramour for only the second time. The first time was years ago and he struck me as a principled man, and so he has been. They've

333

somehow contained their love for each other in a platonic way. But it seems that that became impossible and she is now expecting his child; so he's made the decision to emigrate to Canada. That is why I was summoned so urgently.'

'Oh!' Delia drew in a breath. 'He's going to leave her!'

Giles looked up. 'No. He wants her to go with him and they will live as man and wife; they wanted to tell me that they'll do this regardless of whether or not I agree to a divorce.'

'So what will you do?' she whispered.

He relaxed and it appeared as if a great weight had been lifted from his shoulders. 'We talked, the three of us, over various options and I said that to make it easier for them I would divorce her once they'd left England. It will give them a chance to settle in Canada and they can then deliver their decision not only to Marion's parents, but to his too. I will tell my parents only as much as they need to know. That she has run away with the man she has always loved and that I am divorcing her. Marion can inform her parents that she is expecting a child if and when she wishes.'

'You are relieved?' she said.

'I am, enormously.' He gazed at her anxiously. 'Am I doing the right thing, Delia? Does it matter if there is a scandal?'

'You can rise above it,' she said softly, after a moment's deliberation. 'Who's going to be hurt? Her parents, perhaps – or yours. But then they forced both of you into a marriage that neither of you wanted.'

He stood up. 'You're right.' He paused for a moment. 'Will your friend Crawshaw be staying long?'

'I don't know.' She looked up at him curiously. 'I'll know more tomorrow when I meet him for lunch. We've a lot to catch up with. Why?'

'Oh, no reason,' he said hurriedly, giving a forced laugh. 'I only wondered if he was going to monopolize your time! I'm going up to bed now. I'm rehearsing in the morning to catch up with the latest scores.' He bent down, took her hand, giving it a gentle squeeze, and kissed her cheek. 'Thank you, Delia, for being so understanding. I really appreciate your – consideration.'

She gazed after him as he left and touched her cheek and felt a warm glow envelop her. It was a different kiss from the one that Arthur had bestowed; his were always fleeting, a peck merely, a transient acknowledgement of friendship. Giles' kiss had been tender. It was also the first time she had received such a caress from a man.

You're being stupid, she told herself. Don't make anything of it. He's a good friend, nothing more. Don't spoil it. She swallowed hard. I don't want more. I'm afraid of love, afraid of being hurt, of not coming up to expectations. She put her hands to her face. How I wish it were not so.

CHAPTER THIRTY-EIGHT

The Royal Station Hotel was a much grander place than the cosy Maritime and Delia dressed appropriately for her lunch with Arthur. As it was a fine day, though cold, she walked from the lodging house in her old and comfortable boots and fastened a bright silk scarf about her neck to brighten up her grey day dress, with its pearl-buttoned bodice and back pleated skirt. Over it she wore her grey coat and a peacock-feathered hat.

Arthur was waiting for her in the lounge and came to greet her as she came through the entrance into the main hall where they had sat the previous evening. The sun was shining through the domed roof, lighting up the velvet couches and the crystalware.

'I'm so pleased to have found you, Delia,' he said warmly. 'And I'm sorry it has taken so long; my father died at the beginning of December, and I've had a great deal of business to attend to.'

'I'm sorry for your loss, Arthur,' she told him when he had explained the circumstances, and then paused as a waiter swiftly arrived to escort them to the dining room. She marvelled at how Arthur always managed to attract immediate attention wherever he went. The consequence was that she drew herself up and made herself more regal than she knew she was.

'The wine list, if you please,' he said to the head waiter who came to their table. 'You'll take a glass of wine, Delia?'

'Only one glass, Arthur. I'm singing tonight.'

'You'll sing all the more sweetly after a glass of champagne, m'dear. What are you singing?'

She told him about the Cinderella pantomime and that this was the last week of the season.

'So you are not seen on stage?' he queried. 'And what next?' He took the proffered list from the waiter and perused it, chose a bottle of claret for himself and 'a glass of champagne for Miss Delamour', he pronounced grandly. She wondered if his father had been generous in his will, for she couldn't recall his ever being so lavish previously.

He tapped his finger on his mouth as he chose for both of them: lamb cutlets for Delia and rare steak for himself.

Without answering his question, she asked, 'So what has happened, Arthur, since your father's death? Clearly something has.'

'Indeed!' He put his head back as if deciding on the proper way to begin. 'You might think that I have misled you to some degree, Delia, but I assure you that it wasn't intentional. I have long been enamoured of the theatre and in particular with the writings of Shakespeare and Mr Dickens; but of course you know that already, as does your very special son. I wish that I had such a boy,' he said disarmingly. He paused for a moment, and then murmured, 'But perhaps it is not too late; I am not yet forty-five.'

Delia waited. He was in a reflective mood and she had heard these comments before, but something was different this time.

He changed the subject. 'Your friend, Dawson. Have you known him long? What is his occupation?'

She told him briefly of meeting Giles on Hull railway station when she had first come back to the area, and that he was a musician; and then she told him why she had returned. 'I had to take positive action, Arthur,' she explained. 'I was desperate; but also a little mad, I think, expecting to receive any help from my parents when there had been none previously.'

'Indeed you were,' he murmured. 'You were distressed enough to take such drastic measures. I wish you had told me before how grim it was for you. I could have helped in some way.'

'I was too proud to ask. But I think it will come right now. Except,' she added quietly, 'I don't have Robin with me. But don't let's talk about me. Tell me more about you.'

As they ate their starter of smoked salmon with lemon juice, a sorbet and then the main course, he told her of his father's substantial estate in Derbyshire and of his own previous intention of relinquishing his role as heir in favour of his younger brother, who was already married with a young family.

'And then I reconsidered.' He steepled his fingers and paused for a moment, and then continued. 'I was beginning to tire of the theatre world. I have been treading the boards for nearly twenty years now, simply amusing myself if I'm honest, and I thought that perhaps I should settle down after all, look after the estate, maybe marry and have a family and raise an heir to carry on after me. Would I be able to manage that, Delia? Do I have it in me to carry that burden? To make that sort of life a success? My mother wants me to try; she thinks my brother's wife is not up to scratch and won't be able to manage such a grand house.'

'How large is it, Arthur?'

'Mmm, well.' He looked around him. 'We have a small ballroom, I suppose about the size of the hotel lounge, and I think there are twenty bedrooms. Hugh and I had such fun when we were youngsters playing hide and seek. We're not landed gentry, of course,' he laughed as he spoke, 'but the house has been in the family for about a hundred years. Not well managed, I'm afraid; it's badly in need of renovation. Someone with ideas could put it right, but my father was content to leave it unchanged. For instance, it has but one bathroom and three lavatories, which is not sufficient when guests come to stay, which you must, Delia,' he added. 'It's in a delightful part of the county.'

'You'd need help with it, Arthur.' She thought that perhaps he might be rather lazy and not inclined to be businesslike; he most certainly would need an energetic wife if he decided to marry. 'Would your mother stay on in the house if you married?'

'Oh, I shouldn't think so; it isn't the done thing, although it would depend on my wife's inclination. There's a delightful dower house with four bedrooms, a sitting room, a dining room and a garden room that will be perfect for Mother, and rooms for a couple of staff, don't you know.'

Delia's mind was reeling. How could anyone have so much and be so *laissez-faire* about it? He would need to choose a very special kind of wife to be by his side. She hoped she would be able to keep his friendship if he should marry for she was very fond of Arthur.

That evening, Jenny wore a dark green dinner gown of satin and taffeta with a padded bustle, the colour showing off her creamy complexion and flaming red hair to perfection. The sleeves were fitted and ended in a frill at the wrist. Above the low-cut neckline she wore an emerald green necklace, one she had been given by her parents on her twenty-first birthday; a simple emerald jewelled clip was pinned in her hair, which she had twisted into a chignon, with wisps of curl framing her face. She suppressed an excitement she hadn't experienced before when dining out with gentlemen, most of whom had bored her. Nor had she taken so much care over her appearance. She wrapped a fur cape round her shoulders. She was ready.

Arthur had not only sent a cabriolet to collect her but was waiting within it. When she appeared at her door, he went to greet her at the gate wearing an elegant black frock coat, with lapels of satin, and narrow trousers and a gleaming white linen shirt.

At the table in the hotel dining room, where they were shown into a discreet alcove with swagged draped curtains, a bottle of champagne was waiting in an ice bucket and an opened bottle of claret on a side table.

When a waiter took her cape she saw from Arthur's

expression that she had made an impression, and she was pleased with his sincere comments on her appearance.

'Miss Robinson,' he murmured as they sat at their table. 'How delightful; how elegant. It is a pleasure to be in your company and I am grateful that you were able to come at such short notice, when your time must be valuable.'

'I'm a schoolteacher, Mr Crawshaw,' she said disarmingly. 'I do not as a rule dine out on a weekday evening, but as you are a special friend of *my* special friend, Miss Delamour, I made an exception. And,' she added less formally, 'I'm curious. I wanted to ask you, as you know Delia so well, just how she managed to survive alone, with little money and a child, for so many years, and yet still carved out a professional career for herself. She is no longer the girl I remembered.'

The menu was brought and conversation was suspended. Arthur didn't look at it immediately but asked the wine waiter to open the champagne. When it was poured, he said, 'My intention wasn't to talk of Delia this evening, Miss Robinson, but I wonder whether you are trying to discover if she had any monetary help from anyone. I can tell you assuredly that she did not from me, and almost certainly not from anyone else, as most stage performers, unless they are at the top of their particular tree, do not have any money to spare. It is a precarious profession to be in.'

'Please don't misunderstand me,' Jenny said with some unease. 'It is not my intention to pry. She has told me that you've been a good friend to her, as I would have been too, had she not disappeared from my life.

She was a shy, nervous girl when she was young, unlike me, who had the good fortune to come from a strong family background, but she appears to have found extra strength from somewhere and I don't understand where.'

Arthur picked up the menu. 'I would like to think, Miss Robinson, that you and I could have many interesting discussions, but let me tell you this about Delia and then perhaps we could speak of your own ambitions?' Jenny was flummoxed. She hadn't realized that she might be questioned about herself. For goodness' sake, she thought. I've only just met the man.

'Put quite simply,' Arthur Crawshaw went on, 'I believe Delia gained her strength in the age-old manner of a mother protecting her cub. If she had lost her child at birth, which she could well have done under the circumstances, she might not have survived; she might have died of despair as well as hunger. Our friend,' he said softly, 'yours and mine, who appears so vulnerable, has, in my opinion, because of her child, developed an inner tensile strength like nothing else I have ever known; that is why I became her friend and not her benefactor.'

Jenny was silent for a moment, and then she said, 'Do you love her?'

He glanced at the menu, then looked up and smiled disarmingly. 'Of course I do.'

CHAPTER THIRTY-NINE

From behind the thin curtain at her kitchen window, Mrs Deakin watched the man and woman talking in the Robinsons' farmyard. The woman had turned her back so she couldn't see her face, but the man was undoubtedly the Robinsons' son, unmistakable with that head of red hair. The woman wasn't his wife; she was fair and this one was dark. Robinson, his wife and their brood of children now appeared to be living in Foggit's farmhouse next door.

'They'll be trouble,' she mumbled, though there was no one to hear her. 'Deakin isn't happy about it.'

Deakin had gone on a fishing trip early that morning, telling her that he would be home after dark and would want hot food to warm him. 'Make sure there's plenty of hot water for my tub,' he said as he went out, 'and bring the bath in so I'm not sitting on cold metal.'

She'd been outside and lifted the tin bath from the hook on the wall and brought it in to lean against the cupboard door next to the fire, the door sneck-rattling as she did so. The sound startled her. When they had first come here, she kept her spare bed sheets and tablecloth in there. It was a wide and useful cup-board, but when Dorothy at three was old enough to leave her mother's bedside, Deakin decreed that the child could no longer sleep in their bed and that her mother must make her a bed in the cupboard.

She recalled gathering up sheep's wool and duck down, washing and drying it and then filling a bolster case to make a mattress to put on the middle shelf. The child hadn't liked it, of course, and cried piteously, so much so that Deakin had got out of bed and closed both doors on her, fastening them with the wooden sneck and threatening the child with a beating.

I lay all night listening to her cries and that sneck rattling, she remembered now. But what could I do? He was master here. He said she would get used to it and that it would be warm in there. And she did, and it was.

She sat down by the fire and pondered. The child slept in there every night for nigh on eight years, and then one day she asked for an old sheet to make another mattress, and went out that summer and gathered up more sheep wool and down, goat hair and some clean straw, and stitched two sides of the sheet together, filled it, and stitched it up and told me she'd sleep on the floor in front of the fire.

'I told her he'd not let her,' she muttered, 'and she said that he wouldn't know, for she'd be up before him every morning and store the mattress in its usual place in the cupboard. I'm too big to sleep in there now, she said. An' I said do as you please.'

It wasn't until one morning when he rose earlier than usual that he found her and fitted out a space under the eaves so that she might sleep up there; I started to use the cupboard again for storage and discovered that at some time during her night-time imprisonment she'd whittled a gap at the bottom of the door so that she could jiggle it to loosen the latch and open the doors.

She gave a cackling laugh. The girl wasn't dim even though she were only a little biddy; she'd managed to outwit him and he never knew.

She went back to the scullery window to peer out, but the couple had gone. It bothered her as to who the woman was. She saw so few people that when someone new came into her sight she was always curious. This one didn't look like someone from the village; she didn't have the bearing or style of a country woman. She was more of a townie, so why was she here? But wait, mebbe it was the Robinsons' daughter, she worked in town. But no, she then bethought herself; she has red hair too, like her brother and the rest of the clan.

Although Mrs Deakin didn't speak to anyone in the village, on rare occasions she went to the shop to buy flour for baking, and sugar – for if Deakin brought a parcel of tea home, she sometimes indulged herself with a spoonful of sugar in a cup of tea as a treat – and as she waited to be served she would listen to local gossip, which was discussed freely in front of her as she was unresponsive to their nods of greeting and appeared to be completely uninterested in what they were saying. I'll think of an errand and go in again, she thought, and mebbe find out who she is.

She liked the days when Deakin went out on an all-day trip, for she could then please herself with her time;

she'd feed the animals and the poultry, prepare food for the evening for when he returned, then bake herself some biscuits and sit in the easy chair that Deakin claimed as his own. She'd drink tea with a teaspoonful of brandy and eat all the biscuits and think of happier times when she was a child in Brixham, before she met Deakin.

If the weather was good she would put on her working boots and go outside and turn over a plot to grow vegetables. Never flowers, for you couldn't eat them, but she grew enough food to keep them all the year round: potatoes, parsnip, swede and onions, leek and cabbage, peas and beans, carrots and winter sprouts.

I could survive without him if he didn't come home, she often thought; I'm not that fond of fish even though I was brought up on it. I'd rather eat a slice of chicken breast. I'd miss the tea, though, and the brandy. I'm not so bothered about the Genever; the Dutch can keep it as far as I'm concerned, along with their cheese. She would lean back in the chair and occasionally make a plan about how she might live without his brooding presence if by chance he didn't come back from one of his fishing trips.

It was after dark when she was dozing in front of the fire that she heard the muffled clod of the mule and the rattle of the cart as it came along the track, and then the squeak of the gate. He'd never had a horse, always used a mule, a more bad-tempered animal you'd rarely find; he drove it down to the creek where his two boats were kept and tied it on a long rope so that it could graze until his return, knowing that no one would dare go near it without risking a nip from its yellow teeth.

She peered out of the window, and as Deakin drew past the cottage towards the barn she saw a pile of sacks covering a mound in the cart and knew he had had a successful trip. She unbolted the door and then turned to re-heat the kettle and pans of water for his bath.

He came in carrying a wet sack containing shrimps which he passed to her muttering, 'Soup', so she lifted the lid from the cauldron containing the vegetables that had been simmering all day on the flame, put her hand in the sack, brought out a handful of quivering shrimps and tossed them into the bubbling liquid.

'Anybody about?' she asked, referring to the other shrimpers.

'Not sin' this morning,' he mumbled, starting to strip off his wet coat, jumper and heavy trousers. 'They'd finished by dinner time.'

'What about 'Patrington shrimpers?'

'Some, but they'd finished by midday and by four there was a sea fret coming up.'

'Good. All the more for you.' She poured a jug of cold water into the bath and then another, then lifted the steaming kettle and poured that in too. She fetched a thick pad and with it held firmly in two hands lifted the large pan of hot water, muttered, 'Shift yourself,' and poured that in as well, taking a small delight when some of it splashed on to his bare arm and made him splutter. Then she turned her back to refill the kettle whilst he took off his long johns and vest and carefully lowered his backside into the bath.

The next morning, when he had again gone out, she dressed in her boots and a heavy coat, let out the poultry, milked the goats and fed the pigs, and then, first glancing over her shoulder towards the gate, she opened the barn door and peered inside. Everything appeared to be in place; the wheelbarrow hadn't been shifted, spades and forks were hanging on the wall and the straw bedding was stacked as usual, as were the hay-racks and the animal feed.

Yet there was something different, and her sharp eyes narrowed as she stepped inside.

The rully, a flat four-wheeled cart they had inherited from the previous owners, was usually up-ended and leaning on the barn wall but now had all four wheels on the ground and various boxes, crates and sacks piled on it.

'Deakin's allus grubbing about in here,' she muttered. 'He's been in and out for weeks.' She pondered, debating. He kept things in here that she wasn't supposed to know about: wooden crates and old trunks had lobster baskets and trawl nets, sacks of potatoes and heavy objects piled on top of them, making it difficult for anyone to move; but he didn't know her strength and she had soon discovered his cache of spirits and boxes of tea, although when she looked again after a week or so everything had gone.

But something else was going on these days, for he went out for longer periods during the day and night time, and she was convinced that now he wasn't fishing only for shrimp or small batches of tea and spirits, but for something more lucrative.

'I'll not look today,' she mumbled. 'He said he'd

be back by dinner time and he might catch me. But I'll find out, that I will. He's doing a big run and he'll think that Customs won't suspect him in his shrimp boat. The big fellows use their steamboats to avoid capture; but I heard talk down in the village that baccy tax has gone sky high and he'd want to benefit from that.' She sniggered. 'Thinks he's clever, don't he, but he'll not keep owt from me.'

Carefully she fastened the barn door and with a sly grin she went back into the house where he would expect to find her on his return.

CHAPTER FORTY

They were now at the beginning of March and the pantomime was in its final week. It had been an exceptionally long season but extremely successful; the leading lady, aware that Delia had a better singing voice than she had, had asked the management if her substitute might continue until the finale and Delia had been glad of it. But her contract had expired and she was once more running out of time to find a new booking. She had made enquiries at other theatres but there were no vacancies, and fashion shops who were advertising for assistants wanted staff with experience.

One morning she called in at the theatre to ask Mr Rogers what his next show would be. He had talked of putting on another production after the pantomime, but nothing had been said since the run of Cinderella had been extended, and she doubted there would be a role for her even if his plans had not changed.

He was sitting at his office desk with his head in his hands when he looked up, startled, as she knocked gently on his door.

He got to his feet, ever the gentleman. 'Come in, come in, Miss Delamour.'

'Are you unwell, Mr Rogers?' she asked, for he was

ashen-faced and his usual ruddy complexion had quite lost its glow. 'If so I can come back later.' She would have been quite pleased to put off the question she was about to ask.

'No, no, just tired and a little under the weather, you know. And . . .' He heaved a big sigh. 'There's always some issue to complicate the daily grind of theatre management.'

She didn't know what the issue might be, but nodded politely.

'I don't feel well, as a matter of fact,' he confessed suddenly, without any pretext of hiding his anxieties. 'This has been a very long show, and although success-ful you of all people must be aware there have been some trials during its run. Frankly, I'm ready for some time off,' he shuffled papers around his desk, 'but no chance of that, I'm afraid.'

Delia nodded again, sympathetically.

He sat down again and motioned her to take a seat. 'My under-manager has handed in his notice,' he said flatly. 'He's been offered a more lucrative position, and now the ticket cashier has given a week's notice because she's getting married.' He leaned his head against his hands again. 'Finding anyone who under-stands the workings of a theatre is not easy.'

'I see,' she said, thoughtfully. 'What skill does the under-manager need, Mr Rogers? You seem to do most things yourself.'

'I do,' he said mournfully. 'You know how it is; sometimes it's quicker to do something oneself than explain how it should be done. Yet it shouldn't be too difficult.'

'Can I help at all?' she asked. 'I have a good head for figures and could perhaps help in the box office – temporarily, of course, until you find someone.'

Oh, please, she thought. I'll do anything. Then she opened up and confessed. 'It was before your time, Mr Rogers, so you won't know that I once worked at the old theatre, the one that burned down.' She thought back to that time, when she was distraught, knew no one and was given a chance. 'I was in unfortunate circumstances at the time and was offered work as a cleaner and general run-around. I took it, and several months later the manager of the touring company that was performing there heard me singing and gave me a small part to try me out.'

She gave a huge smile. She would bless that man for ever. 'I'm not exaggerating when I say that he saved my life. The theatre and this town have been good to me. They didn't judge me or blame me for my circumstances.'

Dennis Rogers stared at her. 'You had a child!'

Swallowing, and wondering how he had put two and two together, and if he would now want rid of her, she whispered, 'I did.'

'It was born here?'

'Yes. He was. In the old theatre that once stood here.' Her mouth trembled. 'He came so quickly. Everyone looked after me so well. They cleared a dressing room and someone ran for a doctor, but he arrived too late. The woman in the ticket office and the star of the show, a singer, delivered my son.'

She was choked with emotion as she admitted the truth. 'Someone asked where I lived and said they'd arrange to take me home, and I had to explain that I didn't live anywhere and that I'd been sleeping in the theatre.'

'I was working in Hull at another theatre, but I heard about you,' Dennis Rogers said in astonishment. 'The news ran round the theatres like wildfire; everyone wanted to see the baby that was born on stage, that's what the rumour said!' He smiled. 'You were legendary, coping alone without family, and everyone wondered later where you had gone and what had happened to you and your child.'

'I was offered a role with the touring company. I did whatever was needed, including' – she gave a choked laugh – 'including in the ticket office when the theatres were short-staffed.'

She told him many things during the course of the next hour, including the information that her son was presently living with relatives nearby, which was why she wanted to stay in the area. He seemed to understand.

'He'll be of an age when he needs a regular education,' he said, 'and it's fortunate that there's someone to care for him; the theatre is not conducive to learning the three Rs, though many seem to thrive on it. He should be given the chance to choose a career and perhaps he might come back to the theatre one day?'

She told him about Robin's enjoyment of prompting for Arthur Crawshaw and agreed that he might, but not yet. Mr Rogers sat pondering for a moment, and then said, 'My word, Miss Delamour, I think I have little to worry about after hearing your story. You have done remarkably well to survive and thrive.'

He sat thinking for a moment or two longer and Delia suggested that she might make them some coffee or tea rather than bother the caretaker, and he readily agreed. When she returned five minutes later with two steaming hot drinks, he was smiling.

'I should be delighted if you would agree to help,' he said. 'We've booked a variety show in which I couldn't offer you a part in any case; it includes a music hall singer and a rather risqué comedian, so it's not at all the type of show that would interest you. But . . .' He raised his forefinger and took a sip of coffee, and Delia felt her breath quicken. 'I think you might be able to help on several fronts.'

He pulled forward a clean sheet of paper and a pencil. 'You know the workings of the box office, so perhaps you could interview potential staff and find someone who is numerate and able to deal with seating arrangements?' Delia nodded, and he went on, 'And maybe help to arrange forthcoming programmes, enquire about suitable lodging houses that we might recommend for top of the bill, and, most important, remind me to send out contracts to agents and file their return?'

'The usual matters,' she said lightly. 'Yes, there's far too much for one person to deal with.' Privately, she considered that she was quite used to juggling and there was nothing he had mentioned so far that she couldn't do.

'There would be other matters if you took on the role of under-manager, and although the position is normally filled by a man I don't see any reason why a woman can't do it.' He looked at her anxiously. 'But you're a singer; would you not prefer to continue to perform?'

'Normally I would,' she agreed. 'But touring is out of the question whilst my son is still young. I would be anxious if I thought he needed me and I was out of the district, and I have never yet broken a contract. I would relish the chance of being in one place, and, as I said, this town has always been kind to me.'

He stood up and held out his hand. 'Then that's settled. What a relief. Now, Miss Delamour, all we have to do is talk salary.'

She couldn't believe her good fortune and wanted to shout it from the rooftops. Giles was away in York and had been for several days so she couldn't tell him, but she wrote to Robin, and to Peggy and Aaron, to tell them the good news, and travelled to Holderness on the following Sunday to see them. She asked Jenny to go with her but received a postcard in reply saying she couldn't spare the time just now, making the excuse that she was busy with the school schedule. Delia thought that her friend sounded rather preoccupied

She took bonbons to thank the Robinsons, but Peggy said that she mustn't keep bringing presents. 'We don't need a gift whenever you come, Delia,' she'd said. 'We don't expect one from Susan when we look after their bairns; if you want to bring the children something every now and again, that's all right, but I don't want them to expect a present every time. Save your money for a rainy day.'

Giles returned from York a few days later and they bumped into each other in the hall as she was about to go out. He smiled. 'Well met, Miss Delamour. Would you care to partake of luncheon?'

'I would,' she said. 'I have something interesting to tell you.'

The sun came out as they crossed Trinity Square and there was a first fresh hint of spring in the air, a smell of narcissus and crocus and greenery coming from tubs and green growth in the churchyard.

'You seem very animated,' he observed. 'Something momentous has happened?'

He put out his arm and she tucked hers into it. She felt very comfortable with him and was sure he would be pleased with her news.

'Yes, I've been longing to tell you. I've got a job,' she announced. 'Regular everyday work, with a salary!' She paused and turned to look at the surprise on his face, but he seemed more astonished than anything and a little perturbed. 'In the theatre,' she added triumphantly.

'*Our* theatre?'

'Yes, I'm to be under-manager. Isn't it wonderful? Quite by chance I caught Mr Rogers in a dilemma and offered him a solution.'

'That's really good news,' he said, opening the door to what had become their favoured café. 'I'm very pleased for you.'

'Are you?' she asked as she slipped off her coat. 'Am I doing the right thing?'

He took her coat and hung it up for her and pressed his hand to her shoulder before he took his seat.

'A regular income is what you need,' he said. 'Perhaps in time, depending on the hours you work,

Robin might come for a weekend? During the summer holidays, or maybe even at Easter, which is not so far away?'

She looked up from the menu that she was looking at but not reading. 'I was wondering about that, but maybe not at Easter,' she said. 'When I was last in Paull Robin told me they were going to paint hard-boiled eggs and play egg rolling and other games during the Easter holidays. He's never done that before.'

'Then perhaps you could stay there for a day or two,' he said gently. 'They sound like nice people; surely they would welcome you.'

'Yes, they would.' She pondered for a moment. She had always wanted a good life for her boy, yet she still felt a keen sense of loss when she thought of him enjoying that life without her. It was hard to grasp, sometimes.

'Do you think,' he said softly, covering her hand with his, 'that I might meet this wondrous boy of yours one day?'

Her lips parted as she gazed at him. 'Of course you can,' she said. 'I would be so pleased if you did. Arthur said that he'd like to see him again too, but he seems to have disappeared, as does Jenny.'

He withdrew his hand, 'Ah, yes, Arthur! What will you have?' he asked briskly as he saw the proprietor heading towards them. 'I'm having the meat pie.'

CHAPTER FORTY-ONE

Giles seemed preoccupied when they left the café and he asked her to excuse him. He had to make a call at his bank and would catch up with her later.

What had brought on that strange manner? she wondered. Was it something she'd said? She thought back to their conversation, and realized it had been the mention of Arthur Crawshaw's name that had triggered the change. Then she understood. *Giles and I have been good friends ever since we met, but along has come an older friend who, it has to be said, is inclined to monopolize any conversation. It's only natural that Giles might be irritated by him. I do understand that.*

It was still sunny, and she sat on a seat outside Holy Trinity church and put her face up to the sky, closing her eyes. *Most single women with a child might never expect life to be easy,* she contemplated; *and yet I've been so lucky. I've taken care of him when he was vulnerable and loved him, and I've now been given another chance to improve his life; and if it means that we have to live apart I must accept that. Robin is safe and content and I must take comfort even though –* she

358

stifled a sob that had caught in her throat – it hurts.

A shadow fell across her and she opened her eyes to see who was stealing her sunlight. It was Giles.

He sat down beside her. 'I'm sorry to have dashed away. I was rather distracted.'

She shook her head. 'No, I'm the one to be sorry. I shouldn't expect to monopolize every conversation with details of my life. You're always very understanding.'

He patted her hand. 'What you don't seem capable of doing is relinquishing your role of chief protector of your son, when there are now others who are ready and willing to bear the responsibility. You have so much more than other women who might be in a similar situation,' he said, almost echoing her thoughts of a few minutes before. 'You've a new-found family who will love – *do* love – your son, and you should let them; and, although it sticks in my craw to say it, give his father the opportunity to make amends.'

They sat quietly and people around them went about their business, office workers hurrying back to their places of work, women shopping and schoolboys returning to the grammar school after their midday break. Giles commented that it was one of the best schools in England, and then, as if by mutual accord, they rose to wend their way back to their lodgings.

'Did you pick up your post this morning?' Giles asked as they walked, and Delia said no, she hadn't noticed it. She wondered who would write to her; only her agent knew where she was. The thought reminded her that she must write to him to cancel her arrangement with him once and for all.

'I didn't mean to pry,' Giles said. 'I also had post

delivered this morning and happened to see yours. I have a buyer for the York house,' he added, almost as an afterthought.

'Really? So soon!'

'The agents described it as a desirable dwelling, but my only desire was to be rid of it and begin my life again.'

'So you are at a crossroads,' she observed quietly. 'I hope your new life works out the way you want it to, but I also hope that you don't stray too far away. I – I'd miss our friendship,' she said softly, and was struck by an unfamiliar emotion; she realized that she would be very sad if he chose to leave. But I must hold my emotions at bay. There should be no expectation of anything but friendship.

He glanced down at her, his gaze lingering. 'I've been making plans,' he murmured, 'but they depend on circumstances out of my control, although I shall attempt to scupper any opposition.'

'Your divorce?'

'It's too soon, but I've met my lawyers and apprised them of the situation. They've told me that divorce proceedings to make the marriage null and void, from decree nisi to absolute, will take approximately eighteen months to complete. Marion and her . . . paramour, Samuel Ellis, will be arriving in Canada any day now. They travelled separately on the ship, I understand, so as not to precipitate any scandal, but will take the train together to their destination, wherever that might be. I didn't enquire,' he added, 'and therefore will not be able to answer any questions from any parents, hers or mine.'

'Are you bitter?' she asked.

'No!' he exclaimed. Taking off his hat, he threw it in the air and caught it. 'I am not, or at least only for the lost unhappy years.'

She laughed. He managed somehow to be able to rise above any trouble or difficulty, or at least not to show them. And yet he was sensitive towards others' anxieties and not indifferent to their fears – not even, apparently, to those of his wife.

The letter which was waiting for her was from Arthur, with an invitation to pay a weekend visit to his Derbyshire home.

Might I request that you bring our precious boy with you? And as I have also invited your friend Miss Robinson, I would like to ask your friend Dawson if he would be so kind as to be my guest and escort you both. I will of course send the carriage to collect you and bring you home again.

Do say you will come, my dearest Delia. I long to have a fuller conversation with you and welcome you to my home. I wish to introduce you to my mother, and you must promise me that you won't be nervous of her and her acid tongue.

I look forward to hearing from you soon telling me of a suitable date.

Your ever loving friend, Arthur Crawshaw.

She knocked on Giles' door to tell him of the invitation. 'Will you come?' she asked.

They went downstairs into the residents' lounge to discuss dates, and Giles said he'd be pleased to accompany them. He suggested the weekend after the next one and put forward the idea that she should travel to Paull during the coming weekend to make arrangements.

'I'll write to Jenny,' she said excitedly, 'and ask if she's free.'

But there was a note from Jenny in the afternoon post to say that she had received Arthur's invitation and suggested the same weekend.

'I rather think that Jenny received her invitation first,' Delia mused thoughtfully to Giles. 'For how has she replied so quickly?'

'Do you mind?' Giles asked.

'Mind?' Delia looked up. 'Not in the least. In fact,' she said thoughtfully, 'I think they'd make a very good couple. They are both quite self-centred, both enlightened and educated people, and I think if anyone could hold Arthur to account it would be Jenny.' Then she laughed. 'But I don't think there's much chance of that, more's the pity. She told me she was a dyed-in-the-wool spinster and wouldn't ever marry.'

Quizzically he raised his eyebrows. 'So he wouldn't be the man for you, Delia? Not even after your long friendship?'

'No. Ours was a completely platonic friendship, which is all I've ever had with any man.' She spoke without thinking, nor did she notice the easing of tension in his glance. 'I first met Arthur when Jack – *Robin* – was little and beginning to get into mischief. When he was a baby, and then a toddler, everyone kept an eye on him when I was on stage, the women and the men; he was such a sweet and adorable child. I wasn't the only one to think that,' she added, when she spotted his wry grin. 'Occasionally the women would take him shopping with them whilst I was in a rehearsal or a matinee and he'd come back with a new toy, but when he got to be three he sometimes escaped and toddled off backstage on his own to talk to the stage hands. And one evening I'd left him sleeping in the dressing room and during my last song I heard the audience laughing. I wondered why, and then one or two people began to clap and say *Aw*; and when I looked round there was Robin on stage, wandering towards me in his nightgown and rubbing his eyes.'

She put her fingers to her lips as she recalled the memory. 'He put his arms up for me to pick him up, which I did, while I kept on singing; it was "Scarborough Fair", which I often sang to him at bedtime. He put his cheek against mine and so I sang it to him, and then to the audience's delight he began singing it too. He knew all the words.'

She laughed. 'It was the best ovation I've ever received, and I put him down and without any prompting he bowed to the audience and they went wild, standing up and clapping, whistling and cheering.'

'And a star was born,' he murmured.

She brushed away a tear. 'It was fine for just that once, but then I began to worry that he might wander outside and get lost. It was about then that Arthur joined the company and took an interest in him; he began to think of things that Robin could do so that he thought he was part of the company. He asked the ticket office for old ticket stubs and taught him how to count them and put them into sets of colours; and then he began to teach him to read. By the time he was four he could do simple additions and read short words.' She sighed. 'I have many reasons to be grateful to Arthur, for his friendship and advice, but mainly for his interest in Robin.'

Giles nodded. 'You and Robin obviously brought out the best in him,' he said. 'On first meeting he doesn't seem like the fatherly type.'

'He doesn't, does he? But he took a great interest in Robin and that's why he refers to him as *our boy*. And I trusted him completely.'

Jenny called the next day on her way home from school; she was dressed in a plain skirt and jacket and a neat hat with a feather, and Delia could tell that she was full of suppressed excitement.

'How lovely that Arthur has invited us all to stay at his house,' Delia said. 'I'm really looking forward to it. I wonder what we should wear?'

'Well, it's a country estate, isn't it?' Jenny said. 'South of Sheffield and north of Derby. I looked on a map,' she said nonchalantly. 'Just to ascertain its whereabouts. So something practical, I should think.'

'Do you think it will be very grand? I only have plain gowns or my stage ones.'

'One of each then,' Jenny said. 'Why not take that lovely red gown that you wore at Christmas? You could wear that for dinner. We're only there for the Saturday so you won't need anything more. We'll be leaving after Sunday lunch.'

'Yes,' Delia said thoughtfully. 'It's a long way to go for such a short stay.'

She wondered why Arthur had asked them for such

a short visit and then thought that he was taking into account not only her theatre schedule and Giles', but Jenny's and Robin's school schedules too; then she speculated that perhaps it was because of his mother, whose sharp tongue might be best served in small doses.

'It is to introduce us to his mother,' Jenny said casually, and Delia noticed that her cheeks had flushed. 'That is what Arth— Mr Crawshaw said. He has been to Hull again,' she admitted, giving a nervous swallow and lowering her eyes. 'I have joined him twice for dinner.'

'Jenny!' Delia breathed. 'Oh, I'm so pleased.'

'We get along very well,' Jenny admitted, and allowed a smile to slip out. 'It is a very strange sensation for me, Delia. I never thought that – never thought I would meet someone who understood me in the way that he appears to – you know, encouraging me to express my views, taking them seriously, and he does,' she said, as if astonished.

'Perfect!' Delia said. 'You'll be just right for one another.'

'I haven't met his mother yet,' Jenny countered, and then added, 'But he can choose whoever he wants for a wife. He says he is his own master.' She hesitated. 'Nothing is cut and dried, Delia. It's too soon.'

Delia's new managerial post wasn't to start until the following week; the theatre was being cleared after the pantomime and the stage needed repairs, so she decided that she would travel to Paull on Friday as Giles had suggested. She asked if he would like to come too and meet Robin. 'You could stay in the Hedon Arms, perhaps; it's not far from Paull. A nice walk,' she told him.

He hesitated at first, not wanting to intrude, and then agreed, so she immediately sent a postcard to the Robinsons and mentioned that she would like to bring a friend to meet Robin.

Robin was out of school so he accompanied Aaron to meet them off the train. Aaron and Giles shook hands on introduction and then Giles put out his hand to Robin as if he were an adult too. He told him that he had heard much about him and asked how he was settling down to country life after living in towns and cities.

'I've had quite a peripatetic life until recently,' Robin said earnestly, and Aaron glanced at him in astonishment and gave a gentle shake of his head, as if to say he might never quite get a grasp of this boy. 'But I like living in the country very much indeed. I feel very settled and I like school and being with other children.'

Then he frowned a little and took hold of his mother's hand. 'I miss Mother, of course, but I realize that she has to earn a living; when I'm older and can work I can maybe earn enough money to help her. But she does like singing and being on stage, don't you, Mother? What do you do, sir? Are you a performer too?'

'I am,' Giles said, his mouth twitching. 'I'm a musician. A violinist. I have often played for your mother's performances.'

'Oh, I'm so pleased,' Robin enthused. 'And I'm very glad that my mother has a friend she can talk to, because, you know,' he lowered his voice confidentially as if Delia weren't there, 'I think she gets very lonely sometimes.'

Giles nodded and answered gravely, 'Yes, I understand that, Robin; sometimes theatreland can be a very lonely place. But I assure you that I will do my best to counter that.'

Robin then proceeded to advise Giles on the function of the various buildings they passed in Hedon. He pointed out the church and the police station and the Sun Inn where he had first met the Robinson family, and glanced up cheekily at his mother. Then he confessed to Giles that that was where he had decided to change his name and explained why, and Aaron squinted round at Delia and again wryly shook his head.

Robin was first out of the cart. The dog raced towards him and he bent down to pet him. Aaron took hold of the old horse's snaffle, and Giles had just held out his hand to Delia to help her down when there was the crack of a gunshot. Betsy jibbed, the dog sped back towards the house and Delia clung to Giles' hand, her nails digging into his palm and her face suddenly pale.

'What on earth . . .' Giles began, but Aaron said, 'Don't worry, it's just an idiot of a neighbour shooting rats, I expect. I'll have his hide afore long,' he muttered in an undertone. 'He forgets there are bairns about after school.'

'He shoots rats?' Giles asked. 'He must be a good shot.' He could feel Delia's trembling hand in his.

'Aye, I reckon,' Aaron mumbled. He avoided looking

at Delia and ushered them all inside where Peggy was standing by the range with her mass of hair tucked under a white cap, tying the strings of her apron around her waist. A little girl was sitting beneath the table looking at a book and didn't acknowledge them.

Peggy looked up at her guests and said, 'Delia, are you all right? You look very pale.'

Giles ushered Delia towards a chair, then turned to Peggy and put out his hand. He grinned and said, 'A rifle shot to welcome our arrival rather startled us. How do you do? I'm Giles Dawson. Delighted to meet you.'

Peggy put out a clean but floury hand. She immediately liked this man. 'A gunshot?' she said. 'At this time of day? I didn't hear it.'

'Rats, Aaron said,' Delia told her in a trembling voice. 'Sorry, Peggy. Forgive my manners.' She couldn't explain that the sound of the gunshot had brought back dark memories of her father cleaning his rifle and looking at her through narrow eyes as if warning her to beware that it might not only be rats and wildfowl that he aimed at; and she knew with certainty by the long-tailed bodies in the yard, and the mallards, wigeon and teal that hung on a nail outside the door, that he was an accurate and crack shot.

CHAPTER FORTY-TWO

Peggy had made a light lunch of chicken soup, cold meat, pork pie and pickles with warm bread fresh out of the oven. Molly came out from under the table to eat with them; then Aaron and Robin took Giles along the river bank into the village and told him the history of Paull, how since the time of Henry VIII there had been defences to protect the town of Hull, and Aaron promised that the next day, if Giles was interested, they would walk up to the fort which was still manned in case of invasion and show him the high earthen ramparts that protected the cannons and battery.

As they walked towards the long village street Aaron suggested that Giles might care to stay at the Crown Inn that night rather than travel back to Hedon, and Giles immediately went in and booked a room, then bought Aaron and himself a pint of ale and Robin a glass of lemonade.

'My parents' house in York is by the river Ouse,' Giles told Aaron. 'It's where I was born and grew up as a boy.'

'Oh, aye?' Aaron said. 'I've been to York. I was a fisherman afore I met Peggy and became a farmer, and when

I was just a young feller one of my older brothers asked if I'd fancy a trip to York. So off we went, took 'shrimp boat and sailed up 'Humber as far as Trent Falls and Goole and then joined up with 'Ouse and onwards to York. We had a grand few days, looked around York and then set off home again; caught some fish on 'way back.' He grinned. 'I might have passed your folks' house, though you wouldn't have been around back then. Some splendid houses along 'river banks.'

Giles agreed that he wouldn't have been there then, but the house would as it had belonged to his grandparents before his father.

Delia had stayed in to talk to Peggy and told her about the planned trip to Derbyshire; she said she didn't want to walk into the village today as she found the weather rather chilly, although in truth she didn't want to risk seeing either of her parents. The shotgun incident had unsettled her. Louisa came looking for Robin and was disappointed that he was out and said she would stay until he came back. She asked if they'd heard Mr Deakin's gun go off, and told them that her father had said the man was mad.

When the men and Robin came back from their walk, they had a cup of tea and then Aaron slipped out again. When he came back he muttered that there was no sign of anybody about at Deakin's cottage but that he'd catch him the next day and have a word. They had a friendly evening over a hearty supper and then a game of cards before Giles excused himself and set off to walk to the Crown.

The next afternoon Delia and Giles said good-bye and Delia told Robin that they would return the following Friday to collect him for the promised visit to see Arthur Crawshaw.

'Do you think it will be all right for Robin to come back on the Monday morning?' Delia had asked Peggy. 'It will be very late when we return from Derbyshire. We'll miss the last Hedon train.'

'Don't worry,' Peggy had said. 'I'll speak to 'school-mistress. I'll tell her he's been invited to a grand house and that he'll tell them all about it when he comes back.'

On the train to Hull, Giles thanked Delia for inviting him. 'The Robinsons are very nice people,' he said. 'You need have no worries about them taking care of Robin. They obviously love him as their own.'

Delia agreed that they did, but she was very quiet for most of the short journey, so Giles carefully probed a little further.

'Their son?' he said. 'He didn't put in an appearance.'

'He'd be busy on the farm, I expect,' she excused him. 'It's coming up to spring; there's plenty to do in farming even though it's only a small acreage. They always used to have two field horses and they've now got two others for the traps, so they've all to be fed in a morning before they're put to work. Then they've a small herd of cattle to look after. I thought Jack might have come in for something to eat at midday.' She paused. 'I think he makes himself scarce when I come, and he'd know I was bringing a friend; Peggy would have told him. His wife, Susan, has apparently gone to see her parents and taken the other two girls with her.'

'Ah!' he acknowledged. 'And what about the other

incident? The gunshot. What was that about? You seemed nervous.'

She didn't answer immediately but chewed on her lip. Then she murmured, 'It was my father. I could tell by the direction of the shot. He would have been killing rats. Killing something, anyway.'

Deakin had gone off with the mule and cart, a pack of bread and cheese and a bottle of cold tea, and on his return at almost midnight his wife saw from the bedroom window that the cart was again heaped to the top, whatever was in it covered by a rubber tarpaulin. She could hear the barn door crashing against its frame, the mule objecting at being made to stand and Deakin swearing; she wrapped a shawl around her shoulders and went downstairs to wait for him. It was over half an hour before he came into the house.

'What 'you doing up at this hour?' he grunted. 'You should be abed.'

'I was,' she snapped back. 'You woke me with your banging and crashing about. Haven't you brought fish?'

'I threw it back when I reached the landing,' he sneered. 'I've had a better catch than fish.'

'Like what?' she asked slyly.

He looked at her, his eyes narrowing. 'Never you mind; get off to bed.'

'Don't you want tea? Cocoa?'

'If I do I can make it myself. I don't need you for owt.'

And he didn't, she deduced, and was vaguely disturbed.

The next day he was up early again. He hitched the mule to the cart and didn't say when he would be back; he seemed elated over something. She didn't immediately look in the barn, deciding to do her usual jobs first in case he returned and caught her out. She went through her routine of milking the goats and gathering the eggs, and thought that later she'd wring the neck of an old hen and cook it for Sunday dinner. At midday she ate a plate of ham and chutney and began to fidget with indecision. She made a batch of scones and ate one with a pot of tea, and it was after four o'clock before she began looking out of the window again.

'He's gone out on the river, I'll be bound,' she mumbled. 'He'll not be back till tonight. Mebbe I'll just take a look while it's still light,' and with the resolution made, she put on her coat and pulled on a woollen hat and rubber boots and went out to the barn.

There were wooden casks sitting on top of tin trunks on the rully and they were heavy to move, but with much heaving and shoving she managed to roll one to the floor. But she couldn't open it, not without him knowing, as the bung in the top was well and truly sealed and if she broke into it there'd be no sealing it up again. She put her nose to it and sniffed. Baccy? she wondered. There's just a whiff of something. Or mebbe it's brandy. She rolled the cask from side to side and thought that whatever was inside was swilling about.

The metal trunk the cask had been sitting on was easier, as she didn't have to move it; it had a bolt through the catch. Fetching a box to stand on, she took a spanner from a hook on the wall and managed to knock the bolt out and lift the lid. The pungent aroma of tobacco filled her nostrils and she breathed it in. The catchment was covered in sacking and she felt down the sides of the trunk to ascertain if it contained only tobacco. It seemed as if it did, and, nodding her head, she guessed it was worth a fortune. She counted four trunks and six casks and thought that there was no possibility of her seeing any of the profit from it, for Deakin would secrete the money away once the goods were sold on and she wondered where the old miser would hide it.

Mebbe that's where he's gone today, she mused. Gone to Hull or Beverley to haggle with his regular customers. They'll be farmers or bank managers, lawyers or shopkeepers, I expect, thieves the lot of 'em; and because she was trying to think of a way to take some of that profit for herself, and slipping the bolt back into the catch, and then heaving the cask back into its former place, she failed to hear the rag-clad clop of the mule's hooves or the rattle of the cart wheels; nor did she hear the stealthy opening of the barn door.

She got down from the box and turned, dusting her hands together, and almost jumped out of her skin when she saw Deakin standing there. He didn't speak for a moment and she wondered how long he had been watching her. She decided on bravado.

'What's all this lot, then?'

'You're not telling me you haven't looked.' His voice was a sneer 'Don't come all innocent with me.'

'How do you think I could shift any of these on my own?'

'No?' he said. 'Well, we'll see how strong you are. You can help me unload the cart.'

'Righty ho,' she answered with false merriment. 'I'll try, but I don't want to hurt my back. It's been giving me some gyp lately.'

'Has it really?' he asked sardonically. 'First I've heard of it.'

'Don't like to complain,' she remarked, beginning to worry about this cat and mouse game, and walked slowly towards him. He opened the door wider to let her out and she saw the cart once more laden and covered by the tarpaulin, and his rifle on the seat. 'You've been busy,' she observed. 'Fishing's been good, has it?'

He didn't answer but brushed past her and picked up the rifle and she knew it would be loaded. It always was, and she began to shake.

'Lead the mule in,' he said, indicating with a nod. 'And then start unloading.'

She glanced at him but didn't argue. She couldn't possibly lift any casks off the cart, not on her own. If in fact that was what was under the sheeting. He'd taken a risk carrying them in broad daylight. She took hold of the mule's snaffle and he brayed at her. The animal was as bad-tempered as Deakin and she'd had many a nip from his large yellow teeth and kick from his back legs.

But the mule was compliant on this occasion and she was told to uncouple him and let him outside, which she did.

'Come on then,' Deakin told her. 'Start unloading.'

She pulled off the sheeting and saw the casks. 'I

375

can't lift them,' she said. 'How can I? You'll have to help me.'

He came towards her, putting the rifle over one shoulder, and leaned in. 'Course you can,' he said softly, and in one swift movement hit her across the face, knocking her to the ground.

She was stunned for a moment and then staggered to her feet, leaning on the rully to steady herself. 'Why'd you do that?' Her voice shook and she felt blood in her mouth and spat out the remains of a tooth. 'I said I'd help you. I just can't do it by myself.'

A grin crossed his lips. 'I suppose you thought you might have a share in this?' He indicated the haul of goods. 'Thought you'd have a little treat, did you?'

She was watching his hands, ready and waiting for the next blow that she knew would come. 'No, there's nothing I need, is there? I'm so well provided for. A life of luxury is what I've got, isn't it? That's what you promised me, isn't it, all them years ago?'

'Aye, I did. Didn't mean it though, did I? You were just a means to an end; a cover, you and the brat that you brought into the world.'

He lifted his hand again to deliver a blow, but she was ready this time and stepped swiftly to one side, spoiling his aim, and with the spanner that she'd picked up from where she had left it on the rully aimed a swipe at his temple that knocked him to the ground and his rifle with him, and moving fast she picked it up and pointed it at him.

He was stunned, she could tell; it had been a heavier blow than she thought she was capable of and she felt triumphant. But he was heavier and stronger than her even though he wasn't a big man, and he could easily overpower her. But first, she thought, a few home truths no matter what the consequences.

'That brat that you mentioned. That sweet little girl. You didn't want her, did you? But you're right, she was good cover for you too. A family man, weren't you?' She sneered. 'But I wasn't a very good mother either, though not as cruel as you, and at least I never took the strap to her, not that she ever deserved it, poor lass. But then, I wanted a lad. I wanted a lad in his father's image.'

He put his fingers to his brow and she thought that maybe he was concussed; the spanner was heavier than she'd realized.

'He was very handsome, her father. You'd remember him, I expect. Tom Evans? All the girls in Brixham were after him, but Sally Morris got him, her with her blue eyes and pretty blonde curls. But she wasn't his first, oh dear no.' She nodded and smiled even though her mouth throbbed. 'He wouldn't have made a good husband. He had a liking for the ladies, did Tom. He wouldn't ever have been faithful.'

She saw Deakin move as if gathering his wits and guessed that he was about to spring. 'She didn't cost you much, though. She only ate what I provided. Eggs and chicken and vegetables that I grew.'

The rifle felt heavy in her hands but that didn't bother her. Her father had been a poacher as well as a fisherman and had taught her to shoot when she was twelve years old and wanted to catch rabbits and wild-fowl for the pot as he did, for without a mother she was the one who did the cooking and keeping house.

'So have you anything to say, Deakin? I've nothing else to say to you, now that I've got it off my chest about the girl. She has none of your qualities and very few of mine.'

He was frowning and shaking his head as if he didn't understand, but she was pleased when he began to heave himself up from the ground because she would be able to say that he was attacking her and that she'd shot him in self-defence. But on the other hand, she considered, when the resounding crack as she pulled the trigger almost pulled the gun out of her hands, it didn't really matter, as no one was ever likely to find him.

CHAPTER FORTY-THREE

The following weekend Delia, Robin and Jenny were, in their separate ways, in a great state of anticipation over their visit to Derbyshire. It wasn't a county that Delia knew at all. Jenny said she had visited Buxton many years before as a student teacher but didn't know either Sheffield or Derby, except for what she had read.

'I understand that there are many grand houses there,' she said. 'I'm really looking forward to the visit.'

Robin was excited about seeing Arthur Crawshaw again, he told Giles as they waited for the carriage to arrive at the lodging house. 'He's very amusing and clever,' he said. 'He taught me to play cards.'

Giles raised an eyebrow. 'Just what every young man needs to know.' He wondered if it was something the estimable gentleman had done solely for the boy's entertainment, or to give himself a card partner when there was no one else available.

But his original assessment of the man had changed. Crawshaw had befriended Delia when there had been no one else, and had continued to give a faithful though intermittent friendship to a woman who could give nothing in return but the same. Neither of them, he surmised, expected anything more.

The journey in the old brougham was rocky and long, but they had set off at seven, collecting Jenny on the way and expecting to arrive in Derbyshire just after midday. Robin had been looking eagerly from the carriage windows and asking if they thought Arthur Crawshaw might live in a castle.

No one knew, as Arthur hadn't said, but the fact that he had told Delia there was a ballroom and about twenty bedrooms indicated that it was quite large.

They saw it as they turned through wide metal gates and travelled along a drive through the middle of meadows where sheep grazed and spring lambs skipped, much to Robin's joy. Ahead of them stood a gatehouse and an archway through which they drove to see a stone-built three-storey gabled building with two-storey wings on either side.

They were all silent as they approached, and then Delia smiled as Giles hummed in a deep tenor 'I dreamt I dwelt in marble halls'. 'Sixteenth century I'd hazard a guess,' he murmured, and Jenny nodded in agreement. Delia didn't know, but she sensed Jenny's heightened expectation by her bright eyes and bated breath.

'Do you think there might be a ghost?' Robin whispered, and Delia squeezed his hand and whispered back, 'Bound to be, but it will be friendly.'

Arthur was there at the door to welcome them; the driver took down their luggage, though Giles thanked him and said he would carry his violin case. He rarely let anyone else handle it.

'How wonderful to see you,' Arthur enthused. 'Welcome to Holme Manor. But Delia, where is that skinny young lad of yours? I asked especially that you bring him and you've brought some other grown-up young fellow instead.'

Robin looked up open-mouthed. 'No, it's me!' he said. 'Don't you recognize me?' He puffed himself up. 'I've grown and my name is Robin now,' he explained. 'I did away with Jack. Do you remember . . .' He took up a stance and concentrated. '*Deny thy father and*, erm – *What's in a name – that which we call . . .*' He hesitated. 'I've forgotten,' he confessed as he mixed up his quotations.

Arthur broke into a laugh and helped him out. '*Deny thy father and refuse thy name*,' he said, and held out his hand to shake Robin's. 'How good it is to see you again, my dear boy. Introduce me, won't you, to your fine friends.'

'Oh, but you know them.' Robin grinned. 'My mother, Miss Delia Delamour, Miss Jenny Robinson and Mr Giles Dawson. Say how-de-do to Mr Arthur Crawshaw, the celebrated Shakespearean and Dickensian orator!'

To his delight, Delia and Jenny continued with the charade and dropped sweeping curtsies, and Giles gave a deep bow which Crawshaw returned.

'Come along in, come along,' Crawshaw said good-heartedly. 'I'm so very pleased to see you. We decided on a cold collation for luncheon, but first you must see your rooms and freshen up and then I'll introduce you to Mother.'

Two maids were waiting in the wide timber-clad hall

to take them up the curved staircase to their separate rooms, all of which were huge but had fires blazing in the grates to take off the chill; Robin was given a room adjoining his mother's which overlooked the front lawns.

They found a bathroom along the landing and took it in turns to wash their hands. Robin was the first to make his way downstairs to where Arthur Crawshaw was waiting in a room off the hall; sitting in a chair by the fire was an elderly lady dressed in a gown of deep purple with a rope of pearls round her neck.

'Mother,' Arthur Crawshaw said, 'this is the estimable young man of whom I have spoken. Since our last meeting he has changed his name, so may I introduce Master Robin Delamour?'

Robin went towards her; he felt suddenly shy. He gave a short bow and held out his hand. 'I'm very pleased to meet you, Mrs Crawshaw,' he said.

She gave a slight smile and her eyes gleamed as she held out her hand. 'I have heard much about you, Master Delamour, and what a bright child you are.'

If Robin was disenchanted at being described as a child or the fact that he was introduced by his mother's stage name, he didn't show it, but murmured 'Thank you' and smiled as she said, 'I hear that you play a good hand at cards. Perhaps we might have a game of bezique whilst you're here?'

He expressed his disappointment that he didn't know the game but offered to play cribbage. 'I haven't played it in a while,' he said. 'Not since I last saw Mr Arthur Crawshaw, but I think I can remember it.'

'Perhaps we'll all play this evening,' Crawshaw suggested, and then turned to the door as the ladies and Giles entered the room.

Introductions were made and both Delia and Jenny were aware they were under intense scrutiny from Arthur's mother. Delia didn't know how much Mrs Crawshaw knew of her history, and knowing, as Arthur had often told her, that both his parents disapproved of his theatrical life, she behaved with impeccable decorum; Jenny, having only just met Arthur, responded politely as she would as a guest in anyone's home, and with deference to their hostess's seniority, but without any flattery or fussiness as behoved a liberated woman.

Giles conducted himself with charm and courtesy, and it was immediately apparent that he had gained Mrs Crawshaw's approval.

'You have a beautiful home, Mrs Crawshaw,' Jenny commented, as they sat down to await the luncheon bell. 'Have you lived here very long?'

'I came as a bride nearly fifty years ago.' She gave a disheartened sigh. 'But I will be turned out if Arthur should marry, which of course he must, and be confined to the dower house.' She made it sound as if she were to be locked away in the Tower of London.

'Convention must rule, I suppose?' Jenny acknowledged. 'But then,' she paused as if considering, 'might you not find that you're willing to discharge the responsibility to someone else; and as this fine house speaks so beautifully of your hand, would it not be satisfying for you to create a comparable design on a smaller scale and with less effort?'

Mrs Crawshaw's eyes burned into Jenny's but Jenny smiled openly back at her, as if she had spoken from the heart and not with any hidden purpose.

Giles' mouth worked to hide a wry grin. The house had an aged elegance about it, but the furnishings were tired, the curtains faded and the decor in need of several coats of paint; and, he thought, it must be freezing cold in the winter. Arthur Crawshaw, he perceived, was not so much in need of a wife as of an administrator with enough energy to return it to its once regal splendour. He gave a breath of satisfaction. If Miss Robinson kept her wits about her, she could be that person.

During luncheon, Mrs Crawshaw questioned Delia and Giles about their careers and Delia in particular came in for much probing; her hostess wanted to know how she had come to decide on a musical career and about the difficulties of bringing up a child at the same time; at no time did she enquire after the whereabouts of a husband.

'My voice was the only thing I could offer,' Delia explained when she was questioned about her first singing role. 'I wanted a career of my own,' she realigned the truth a little, 'and one day as I passed a Hull theatre I saw an advertisement on their door.' She didn't say that the postcard was asking for a cleaner and not a singer, nor that it was raining and cold and she'd pushed open the door and gone inside and begged for the work. She'd told the manager she was used to cleaning; to sweeping and scrubbing floors, dusting and polishing, and that no job would be too hard for her. The singing had come later.

'Excuse me,' Robin interrupted. 'May I ask a question?'

Mrs Crawshaw looked benevolently at this polite child. 'What is it?'

'I wondered if it would be possible, if I'm very careful, for me to slide down the banister rail?'

Everyone laughed, and he went on. 'I've never seen such a long rail and never ever one with a big curve in the middle of it.' He glanced at his mother and said, 'I'd hold on very tight so that I wouldn't fall off and damage anything. It would be such an exciting thing to do.'

'Well,' said Mrs Crawshaw, and Arthur looked at his mother in astonishment, 'I think that might be possible. Arthur,' she commanded. 'You must put out cushions and rugs to be sure of a soft landing if he should fall.'

Mrs Crawshaw herself took Jenny and Delia on a tour of the house as far as the first floor; she declined to go any further, but said that they could have a wander about themselves if they wished. They peeped into the very top attic where the maids slept and reported back that there were several damp patches on the ceiling, indicating loose roof tiles.

'Well, there you are, you see! Arthur can be quite lax at times,' Mrs Crawshaw said irritably. 'And I can't be expected to be everywhere.'

'Perhaps he doesn't like to look in the servants' quarters, Mrs Crawshaw,' Jenny suggested. 'The housekeeper ought to have noticed, or the maids should have told her.'

'You're quite right.' To Jenny's surprise, her hostess

agreed with her, although she sighed and shook her head.

Robin ran up and down the lawns, turning somersaults and looking for fish in the lake as Arthur took them on a tour of the gardens; they saw parkland, and meadows where cattle grazed, and then they came to the kitchen garden which was overgrown with rampant weeds. Delia noticed that Jenny's eyes gleamed as she came up with various proposals for improvement.

'You sound as if you know what you're talking about, Miss Robinson,' Arthur observed.

'Indeed I do,' she answered. 'I was a country girl before I became a teacher; and although it's a long time since I used a spade or a hoe I do know how to instruct on how they should be used and what should be planted and when.'

Arthur nodded in agreement, and Delia and Giles exchanged a discreet glance. Both knew that an understanding had been reached and wandered off to look elsewhere.

Before dinner Mrs Crawshaw, whose sharp eyes had seen Giles carrying in his violin case on their arrival, requested that he might play for them, and he agreed that he would. 'May I also beg Miss Delamour to entertain us too?' he said. 'We have previously performed together.'

He raised a questioning eyebrow and Delia agreed. 'Perhaps Miss Robinson would play the piano as accompaniment?' she suggested. 'You were once very accomplished, Jenny.'

A memory of a happy time when she had called one

day and been ushered into the Robinsons' parlour where Jenny was playing a merry melody and Jack was blowing a penny whistle came rushing back to her. She hadn't been able to stay long as she was on an errand for her mother, but the recollection was sharp and clear.

'I was,' Jenny agreed, 'but I'm very rusty and only play occasionally on the school piano.'

'The piano needs tuning,' Arthur broke in. 'We'll say it's to blame for any missed notes.'

And so they played and sang several jolly pieces with much laughter at the whines and squeaks of the piano keys, and Giles deliberately misplayed some notes on the violin, until finally he said, 'But now to be serious and to thank you for your kind and generous hospitality.' Here he gave a slight bow to their hostess and a nod in Arthur's direction. 'I thought of this piece of music as we drove towards your beautiful home; it's from *The Bohemian Girl*.'

Delia knew the music, and whilst Jenny sat on the piano stool with her hands calmly folded on her lap, for she did not, Giles played and Delia began the first verse in a low and wistful voice.

> *I dreamt I dwelt in marble halls*
> *With vassals and serfs at my side,*
> *And of all who assembled within those walls*
> *That I was the hope and the pride.*

At the end of the song, Mrs Crawshaw wiped a tear from her cheek and said in a husky voice, 'I recall that beautiful piece of music from many years ago, and loved it then as I do still.' In a reedy quavering voice she sang some of the verse that she remembered.

> *But I also dreamt which pleased me most,*
> *That you loved me still the same.*

CHAPTER FORTY-FOUR

From behind the closed barn door and through a narrow gap in the planks, Mrs Deakin saw the stocky figure of their neighbour Aaron Robinson open the gate and come into the yard and knew he was coming to complain about the rifle shot. Old granfer, he'll be coming to whine that there are children about, she thought contemptuously. But he won't come near the barn. He'll go home when nobody answers his knock.

She'd let the mule into the paddock and then closed the barn doors so that she could decide what to do about Deakin. She thought that she'd load him into the cart and cover him up and then after dark hitch the mule up again, but that was easier said than done, for the animal wasn't always easy to catch and even harder to put in the shafts. 'As bad-tempered as his master,' she muttered, 'but I'll have to do it. I'll sweeten him with a carrot.'

She waited until her neighbour, with a last look about him, walked back to the gate, opened it and closed it behind him, and then she got on with the job in hand. She let down the tailboard of the cart and looked down at her late husband, and then touched his hand, just to be sure. Cold, she thought, and he's not going to warm up. He'll be heavy, a dead weight so to speak. Am I going to be able to lift him? She had often considered a plan for living without him, but hadn't reckoned on having to dispose of him.

She wedged a box under the front wheels of the cart to keep it steady, put her hands beneath Deakin's armpits and with a supreme effort pulled him to a sitting position. Then she bethought herself and felt in his pockets and brought out a bag filled with coins and a wad of paper money. She peered at it and saw the notes were white. Hah! Fivers or tenners; the greedy old miser, and me with never a penny to my name. What was he planning on doing with it? Not sharing it, that's for certain. Mebbe getting rid of me? She stuffed the money bag in her skirt pocket, took a breath and pulled again, moving him nearer the cart so that he was lolling against it, but she had to keep her hand on him to stop him from falling over, then she grimaced as she saw the bullet wound in his chest.

'It was quick,' she muttered. 'You didn't feel a thing; you didn't suffer, though you deserved to, you old devil.'

Another extreme effort and she managed to turn him over on to his knees and heave him half into the cart.

By the time she had hoisted Deakin fully into the cart and covered him with sacks and straw she was exhausted, her back and shoulders red hot with pain. She grumbled and grunted and decided to go inside, make a drink and plan what to do next.

She sat with a cup of strong sweet tea, for now she

knew where there was plenty and she didn't have to skimp with the leaves. She'd bring one of the tea boxes into the house for her future use. She sighed and considered and talked to herself as she so often did.

'If I take him down to the creek about midnight, there'll be nobody about; not any of the other Paull Shrimpers, they'll all be abed by then, and I'll get him into the smaller boat, lie him for'ard and cover him so nobody'll see him should anybody be awake and chance to see a boat drifting by.' She considered the tide and thought it would be running towards the Humber mouth; the wind was freshening, she could hear it, but from which direction? I don't want the boat hitting the lee shore and getting caught up, or somebody will find him come morning.

She poured another cup and sat pondering. It had been a long time since she had sailed; not since she had married Deakin and set sail away from Brixham to a new harbour. It had been hard work, she remembered, especially once they'd reached the sea, but Deakin was strong and she'd been a good sailor, and the weather had been in their favour.

'But can I hoist the sails on my own? I'm thirty years older than I was then. Mebbe – mebbe . . .' She was beginning to have doubts. Once the boat met estuary waters there wouldn't be any difficulty, the tide would carry the boat and its cargo, but – 'I'll need to go aboard and bring her out of the creek,' she mumbled. 'Can I handle her? I wonder if . . . could I . . . yes, that's a possibility.' She was talking to herself and providing the answers. 'If I row her out of the creek into the Humber, keep to the lee side and pull towards the

Pier House jetty where the ferries dock . . . or mebbe the landing near the Humber Tavern, yes, you're right, that might be another option. If I grab hold of one of the staves of the jetty I'll leap out of the boat, shove her off again and set her free.

'Aye, that's what I'll do. Then I'll come back here and hide all of his ill-gotten gains until I can find customers for it. I'll have a couple of days' grace before I report him missing. If anybody sees the mule and cart they'll not think anything of it. He often leaves the mule to graze when he's gone fishing.'

She had several hours to wait so she made herself some food, hid the money bag in a cupboard and then sat down to await the midnight hour when she would bring the mule into the barn, hitch him to the cart and move off. She soon nodded off into a doze, for she had built up the fire and put a blanket over her knees and for once was cosy and warm. When she woke it was half past eleven. She looked out of the window and saw that it was raining hard.

She dressed in one of Deakin's rubber waterproof coats and his cap. She wrapped a scarf round her neck and turned up the coat collar, then lit an oil lamp to take into the barn. She locked the cottage door and put the key under a stone.

The mule brayed at her from the paddock fence and she realized he'd be hungry, but decided not to feed him as she wanted to entice him with carrots. She opened the barn door wide and hooked it back to the wall, then put the lamp down near the rully and took a handful of carrots from a sack.

'Come on then, you old rogue,' she muttered,

holding out a carrot. The animal lunged for it, but she was quicker than he was and she moved backwards so that he would follow her. He kept braying at her and she hoped the neighbours wouldn't hear. She got him into the barn and gave him the carrot. With another dangling above his nose she managed to turn him round so that she could hitch him up to the cart. She then put several on the ground for him to munch whilst she made the cart and traces secure.

For several minutes she stood whilst considering other options for her own well-being, and decided to take a half-anker of brandy with her. She'd put it beside him in case anyone should find the boat, for instance stuck on a sandbank further down the estuary at Sunk Island or Trinity Sand. There were many treacherous sandbanks in the Humber and good navigational skills were required.

She nodded to herself at her ingenuity and fore-sight. This way, if he should be found shot dead with the brandy beside him, the customs men would con-clude there had been a fight amongst the free traders and Deakin had got the worst of it. 'They'd think it was some foreign seaman,' she muttered. 'Not his little wifey at home.' But then she reconsidered. Wouldn't the other smugglers take the brandy with them? She spent a few precious minutes undecided about what to do, but as she'd already loaded it next to him, she decided to leave it there.

'I'm ready, I think.' She urged the mule out of the barn and across the yard and held him by the snaffle until she'd unfastened the gate, but then couldn't close it after her as the mule set off at such a fast trot that she had to grab his neck collar to stop him before climbing on to the wooden box that served as a seat. It was then that she remembered that she hadn't closed the barn door or doused the lantern. 'Oh, well, can't be helped,' she muttered. 'I'll not be long. An hour at most.'

The mule knew his way to the creek and set off down the track towards the village. Mrs Deakin pulled the coat collar up so that it hid her chin and the peak of the cap shielded her face; not that anyone was about on this dark wet night, but she thought that if anyone should see they would think it was Deakin out on his night-time activities.

She reined in as they approached the creek; she wasn't sure where Deakin moored the boats. He had two, one large, one smaller, and she'd decided to use the smaller one as it would be easier to row. The mule, though, kept moving across the grass, and she gave him his head. He would know where the boats were, and besides, she could barely see a hand in front of her. The cloud was thick and dark, heavy with rain. Eventually the animal stopped beside a wooden bollard where presumably Deakin tied him up, and sure enough a long rope was attached to it and this she used to secure him, giving him plenty of space to graze.

She walked along the bank to try to identify Deakin's boats. He'd sold his original and bought two others, then sold those and bought two more, but she'd never seen them, nor had he ever told her what names he'd given them. Then she saw a white-painted bollard with two sailboats attached by a long mooring line which stopped them from bumping into each other; one, larger than the other, was held by two anchors and the smaller boat by only one and she hazarded a guess that they might be his. The smaller boat carried a pair of oars attached to the rowlocks and that decided her. I can manage a boat that size without any difficulty at all, she thought, filled with confidence now that her goal was almost reached.

Yet it was much harder than she'd anticipated as she hauled the boat towards her and wrapped the mooring rope tighter to the bollard before dragging Deakin towards it. 'Oh! What if I drop him in the water,' she moaned. 'What'll I do then?' But she didn't drop him and she stood in the swaying boat and pulled and pulled him from the bank by his feet and legs until she thought her arms would loosen in their sockets and over the bulwark he came, landing with a thud in the stern.

She sat for a moment to get her breath back and thought that now she only had to carry the brandy over and the sacks to cover Deakin's body, unfasten the mooring rope, haul up the anchor and then they'd be away. He'll have to stay in the stern, she decided; she was spent and had no more strength to move him for'ard.

The rain was lessening but the wind becoming stronger, and she reckoned that once in the Humber the boat would be carried swiftly towards the estuary mouth. She brought the brandy and the sacks, staggering now with tiredness, and covered Deakin up so that apart from his boot-clad feet nothing else of him showed; she freed the mooring rope, letting it hang loose, and determining that she was ready began to haul up the anchor, casting a glance at the mule grazing steadily on the muddy bank.

She felt the boat move before she'd stowed the anchor so left it where it was beside Deakin and grabbed the oars ready to push away from the bank and the other vessels that were moored there. It wasn't a very long or wide creek but it was still pitch dark, and there was nothing to identify where she was or what hazards if any were in front of her. She felt the bumps and knocks as they crashed into other boats.

Then she felt the strength and power of the undertow beneath her and the boat began to pitch and roll; she knew she must keep her wits about her when she reached the estuary or she'd miss the jetty, which she must steer towards if she were to get out of the boat safely before the surge bore her away.

The swell of the current caught them, swinging the boat in the direction of the Humber mouth, and she panicked as the oars were almost snatched from her grasp. She pulled hard towards the lee bank, peering into the darkness for signs of habitation and seeing none, and rode on, the wind at her back, until suddenly they were past the Pier House jetty and heading in the direction of the old pub and the landing stage.

'Stop, stop, I must get off,' she shouted in her terror as the swift tide took hold, too strong for her to fight, and she saw the white-painted building stand out in the darkness like a beacon as they were carried past it. 'No. No! I must get off,' but the oars were useless against the spate and she felt the vessel being pulled towards the middle of the estuary and the shipping lane.

'This is all your fault, Deakin,' she screamed. 'This is

your fault, not mine, and I should never have agreed to come with you,' forgetting completely that for reasons of her own she too had had to get away from her home haven so many years ago – a time which for some reason seemed like only yesterday.

'Mebbe when we get near Cherry Cobb Sands we'll get stuck on the marsh land, or mebbe at Keyingham, or Sunk Island; lots of sandbanks there.' She was babbling, she'd heard of these places but had never been, but fear was making her desperate as she abandoned the oars and lay down in the prow of the boat; she saw the tall white lighthouse as they passed and then sat up as she saw flames lighting up the night sky just beyond it.

The surge was getting stronger and the boat rocked and dipped and waves washed over it and she had nothing to bail with but her bare hands; then suddenly there was light and she turned and saw lights behind her. What's this? She was confused. Navigational lights? Were they on ship or shore? They were getting brighter, coming closer. A ship. Or a barge. She stood up and waved her arms.

'Help!' she shouted. 'Can't you see us? Help! Don't run us down!'

The barge, laden with timber or coal, came bearing down and the crew, oblivious of the unlit sailing boat in its path, didn't even feel the bump as it hit the stern, tossing the standing woman into the water and carrying the vessel and its single silent passenger further downriver until they too were flung out of its path to continue a lone journey through the estuary's yawning mouth to the open sea.

CHAPTER FORTY-FIVE

Jack woke during the early hours. Some noise had disturbed him, the wind mebbe; it had been getting up strong and gusty when he'd gone to bed. He turned over and nuzzled closer to Susan; she'd been nicer since they'd moved to Foggit's farm, not as prickly or short-tempered, and seemed to be happier in her own place. No longer did she refuse his loving embraces as sometimes she used to do.

It wasn't time to get up, so what had wakened him? Then he heard a quiet tapping on the door; he lifted his head. 'Who is it?'

Louisa pushed the door open. 'Da,' she whispered. 'I'm frightened. I can smell smoke.'

He was out of bed in an instant. She was right. 'Get into bed with your ma, I'll go and look.'

'I'll go back to mine. Molly's in with me, she might wake up and be upset. The sky's red from my window,' she told him. 'I think it's next door. Mr Deakin's place.'

Jack rushed into Louisa's room, though trying not to waken Molly who had stayed the night; sometimes she did, wanting to be with her sisters, other nights she stayed with her grandparents. Louisa's window overlooked the land behind them, not the estuary; he looked out and took in a sudden breath. There were flames shooting up into the sky, not from the Deakins' cottage but from the building beyond it, the barn, was it? He couldn't recall if the barn was attached to the house or if it stood separate. Callers were not encouraged, and rarely did anyone venture beyond the gate.

He dashed back into their bedroom and began to put on his breeches and jumper. Susan was awake and sitting up. 'What is it?'

'A fire next door, at 'Deakins'. I'll go and tek a look, mek sure they're both all right and nobody's hurt, and then rouse Da. No need for you to get up. It's not going to reach here. I'll come back if there's any fear o' that.'

He ran down the stairs and shrugged into his coat and pulled on rubber boots, then unlocked the door and scooted out into the night. The acrid smell of fire was stronger now, old timbers and straw, he thought, but something else as well, something sweeter. Baccy, he thought, like the one his father and other fishermen favoured; not something he had ever indulged in, though he'd tried it when he was a lad.

He ran across his own land and jumped the fence, crossed the track between the two properties and climbed the other fence too; he could see and feel the heat of the fire now and it was the barn that was well alight, but there was no movement from the cottage which was odd, he thought, as the roar of the flames fanned by the wind was thunderous; perhaps they thought it was just the storm gathering above them, but they should have been able to smell the smoke.

He hammered on the cottage door and shouted; the downstairs curtains were tightly closed. He looked up and saw that the bedroom curtains were not drawn. He hammered again and then went towards the barn.

The building was not attached to the cottage so there was no immediate danger unless the sparks spread; the barn walls were a mixture of brick, stone and boulders, like the cottage, and whatever was inside was burning ferociously, flames licking around whatever was stored in there. Then came an almighty crash that made him flinch as the roof timbers gave way and deposited roof tiles and debris in a great heap on the ground.

'Too late to save owt in there,' he muttered, and wondered again about the sweet aroma, and ran back again to hammer on the cottage door.

He heard someone shout his name and looked back. His father was coming through the gate. 'Is anybody hurt?' he called.

'I can't mek them hear,' Jack called back, hammering on the door again.

'Somebody must be in; Mrs Deakin, even if he's not there. Is there any livestock? The mule, the goats – where are they kept?' Aaron sniffed the air. 'What's that smell? It reminds me of . . .' He sniffed again. 'Rotterdam Shag. He's got a store of baccy – or he did have!' He gave a grim huff. 'Come on, we must try and waken them. If they're out, which is unlikely at this time of a morning, there'll be a key somewhere.'

'Rather you than me,' Jack said grimly.

'If the roof catches . . .' Aaron began to root around near the door and found a flat stone and lifted it to expose a large iron key beneath it. 'Here we are, so where are they if not in 'house?'

He turned the key and pushed open the door. 'Mrs Deakin,' he shouted. 'Mrs Deakin. Get up. There's a fire!'

There was no answer and he stepped into the kitchen. A low fire burned beneath the range and a tray holding a used tea cup and plate was on the table. Only one of each, he noticed.

He called again, and then opened the door to the stairs and shouted more urgently. 'Mrs Deakin!' But there was no answer.

He went outside again and saw Jack by the still burning barn. 'There's a hen house over yonder,' Jack called to him, 'and what looks like a pig pen. I can hear 'goats bleating in yonder shed, but can't see 'mule. Mebbe Deakin's gone out on 'river; he uses 'mule to pull his cart. What do you think we should do? I don't like to leave in case 'cottage roof catches.'

'Tell you what,' his father said. 'Will you ride down to 'village and wake our Harry and get him to stir up 'other fisher lads and see if they're willing to help put 'fire out. If they each bring a bucket we can mek a chain down to 'river and we'll soon have it out. There's going to be nowt of value left anyway now, but we can at least mek sure 'cottage is secure. I'll do what I can wi' bucket and water pump till you get back.'

'Aye.' Jack shot off to harness up one of the horses and Aaron looked round for a pail or bucket to pump water and throw it on to the blazing contents of the barn. When he found one, he looked up and saw Peggy coming through the gate.

'I said there was no need for you to come,' he began.

'I know you did,' she said. 'But I was going to ask Mrs Deakin if she wanted to come back home wi' me.' She started to cough as the smoke hit her throat. 'She must be out of her wits. Where's Deakin?'

'No idea.' Aaron worked the pump handle but no water appeared. It needed priming, so he kept on pumping hard until a rush of water came out. 'We can't mek either of them hear.'

'Have you been inside?'

'Aye, kitchen and from 'bottom of 'stairs. They must be stone deaf if they didn't hear us shouting.'

'I'll go,' she said decisively. 'I don't like 'sound or 'look of this,' and she strode firmly towards the cottage.

'Hey,' he called after her. 'Wait. I'll come with you.' Who knows what's gone on here tonight, he thought. Deakin's not set fire to his own barn, that's for sure. Not with a fortune in baccy sitting in it, so where is he? And where was his wife? He didn't want Peggy coming across anything she shouldn't see.

Peggy opened the cottage door and shouted, 'Mrs Deakin? It's Peggy Robinson. Are you all right?' She took a few steps to the foot of the stairs and shouted up them. 'Mrs Deakin!'

She turned to Aaron, who was right behind her. 'Do you think we should go up?'

'Aye, but there's no light.' He looked round the bare kitchen and saw a candlestick with a stub of candle in it on the mantelpiece. 'Hang on.'

He strode to get it and lit the candle from the low-burning fire. 'I'll go first,' he said, 'but you call, I don't want to scare her.' He was convinced now that Deakin wasn't there and had probably gone out on the river, but he couldn't work out why Mrs Deakin would be locked in.

He held up the candle when they reached the bedroom. It was barely furnished. A chest of drawers and a narrow bed with blankets neatly folded; on the floor beside it was a palliasse, a straw mattress only thinly filled.

They glanced at each other. No comfort in this bedroom, and it hadn't been slept in this night. They turned to go down again.

'We'll have to alert 'authorities first thing,' Aaron murmured. 'There's summat fishy, I reckon.'

Peggy nodded. 'Aye,' she said. 'But it's not fish.'

Before dawn broke, the Paull fishermen and other village men, awakened by the sound of boots, horses and the rumble of carts, managed to douse the fire with river water and drench the cottage roof so that there was no fear of stray sparks catching it. Peggy had gone home and made hot drinks for anyone who wanted them and Susan had come over to ask if there was anything she could do.

'Molly woke up earlier when we went up to bed and said something about Mrs Deakin and 'mule,' she said, sipping on a cup of tea. 'I think she'd been dreaming. She wasn't mekkin' sense, anyway, and then she fell asleep again.'

'Nothing's mekkin' sense,' Peggy said. 'If Deakin was out on 'river he'd have seen there was a fire from his boat, so why didn't he come back to mek sure it wasn't his place? And where's Mrs Deakin? It's five in the morning, so where is she?'

CHAPTER FORTY-SIX

Delia, Robin, Jenny and Giles had all given their warmest thanks to Arthur Crawshaw and his mother for their hospitality, and in return were urged to come again. 'Miss Robinson.' Mrs Crawshaw eyed Jenny as if considering her possibilities. 'I would appreciate your advice on renovating the dower house. You appear to have good taste and common sense for a young woman in your situation. I, of course, have no experience in such workaday matters, and I would wish to follow tradition as a family such as ours has always done.'

The implication that Jenny wasn't of quite the same status as the Crawshaw family was felt by all, and Delia saw the sudden blink of Arthur's eyes, and realized he hadn't even considered the dissimilarity. He had, after all, befriended Delia herself, despite their very obvious differences.

Jenny, however, didn't turn a hair. 'Of course,' she said agreeably. 'I would be glad to; you have such lovely furnishings and will want to take some special pieces with you if you should decide to move there.'

'Yes, that's exactly what I feel,' Mrs Crawshaw said. 'I don't have to move if I don't wish to; but on the other hand, if my son intends to change the way I've always done things, then I shan't wish to stay and impede him.'

Jenny had bent her head to speak confidentially. 'What I would do in your place, Mrs Crawshaw,' she murmured, 'is to start planning and renovating the dower house, fitting a new bathroom, plumbing and so on, *before* he begins on the Manor, then he can devote all his time to your requirements; and then, when he begins the next stage in the main house, you can escape from it. Having workmen in the place will be very disrupting.'

Mrs Crawshaw patted her hand. 'What a wise young woman you are,' she said softly. 'A sensible head on your shoulders.'

As they drove back over the Yorkshire border towards home, Delia noticed the occasional little smiles on her friend's face and the soft flush on her cheeks and was happy for her. I believe that life is going to change for Jenny, she thought. I think that she will become Arthur's wife and be the new mistress of Holme Manor. She will be able to cope with Arthur and he will be pleased to let her organize him and the house. I think they'll be content together. She gave a small sigh. I've never been envious, but although I don't want riches it must be wonderful to have someone in your life who cares.

But then she reproached herself and looked across at Robin, who was falling asleep after an unusually late night, his head lolling on Giles' arm, for he had been allowed to stay up for dinner. I'm so lucky. I have my son. Her gaze caught that of Giles, who was watching her and gave her a gentle smile. Her breath caught in her throat. Could I ever hope?

By the time they arrived in Hull and Jenny was taken home, it was too late for Robin to travel to Paull. Delia was due to start work at the theatre the next morning in her new role as under-manager, so Giles offered to take him.

'I could travel by myself,' Robin insisted. 'I'd be all right.'

'I'd rather you didn't, just yet,' Delia said. 'And as Mr Dawson has offered . . .'

'I'd like to,' Giles told the boy. 'I'd like to have another look at the estuary, and if we catch the early train we could perhaps walk to Paull and along the river bank before you go to school in the afternoon?'

'Oh, yes, we could do that.' Robin was eager at once. 'If we walk past the Hedon Arms we could follow where the old haven used to be. Mother and I went that way when she first brought me to Paull. It was very dark and I couldn't see where we were going.'

Delia had tucked him up in her bed and thought how lovely it would be to have him with her and cuddle up close. She went back downstairs and found that Giles had asked the landlady for a pot of tea for them both, and she had also brought a plate of biscuits and cheese.

'I really appreciate that you have offered to take Robin tomorrow,' she said, but Giles brushed aside her thanks.

'You can hardly ask for time off on your first day as deputy manager,' he smiled.

'Perhaps not,' she agreed. 'I did think I might

let Robin travel alone as he wanted to, but I would have felt nervous, and what would the Robinsons have thought?'

He shook his head in admonishment. 'Delia,' he reproached her, 'you must stop worrying about what people think about you. I, for one, think that you have done splendidly to bring up a well-behaved, well-mannered child. I'm looking forward to getting to know him better, and tomorrow will be a good opportunity.'

'Thank you.' She lowered her head. 'You're a good friend.' I wish, she thought, I wish . . . but no, it cannot be, so I mustn't even think of it.

'Come and sit down, Delia.' He drew a chair out for her. 'I'll pour the tea.'

She laughed. 'You're a very unusual man. Most men would wait for the woman to pour.'

'I've had ten years of pouring tea or coffee for myself,' he said enigmatically. 'It's nice to be able to share with someone.'

'Of course – sorry.'

'You're doing it again, Delia.' He handed her a cup of steaming tea. 'You don't need to apologize.'

The next morning the three of them walked in the direction of the railway station and Delia showed Robin the theatre. When she said goodbye she hugged him and told him how wonderful it had been to have had the weekend with him.

'It's been lovely, Mother,' Robin agreed. 'I've really enjoyed it and I was so pleased to see Mr Arthur Crawshaw again, and I can't wait to tell the girls and

Granny Peg and Aaron all about the big house.' His face creased into a big grin. 'And sliding down the banister!' Then he considered. 'I wondered about asking Aaron if we might go out in his shrimp boat if there's time later.' He turned to Giles. 'Maybe you could come too, Mr Dawson.'

'I'd like that,' Giles said. 'But I understood you were going to school this afternoon?'

'He *is*!' Delia said. 'You're not on holiday yet. Off you go.' She waved them goodbye before turning back to the theatre. She heard Giles telling Robin that he used to sail on the river Ouse when he was a boy and Robin asking what sort of boat he sailed and did he ever go fishing, and with a mixture of sadness and pleasure she realized that her boy could survive without her.

When the train pulled into Hedon station, Aaron was waiting with the horse and trap and if Robin felt any disappointment at not being able to walk to Paull, he didn't show it.

Aaron shook hands with Giles and murmured that he thought Dorothy might have come, then corrected himself and said he meant Delia. When Giles explained about her starting at the theatre that morning, Aaron deliberated for a moment and then said quietly, 'You'll come home with us, will you? Have a bite to eat? We, erm, we need to get an urgent message to her.'

Giles raised his eyebrows in a query, but Aaron nodded towards Robin who was talking to the old horse. 'Summat's happened,' Aaron muttered. 'She might be required back here. But not a word in front of her lad.'

'I'm not in a hurry to get back,' Giles said. 'I told Robin we'd have a walk by the estuary before he goes back to school this afternoon.'

'Mmm, well mebbe not today,' Aaron replied. 'There're things going on down by 'river bank. I'll explain later.'

Robin greeted Peggy with a hug round her waist and told her he couldn't wait to tell the girls about where he'd been.

'Well, as it happens, I've made you some bread and beef to tek to school,' she said. 'And there's a slice of apple pie as well.'

'Oh, do I have to go now?' Robin said. 'I was going to ask if we could go out in Aaron's boat first.'

'He won't have time today. Mebbe next weekend, and mebbe your ma will come again.'

He didn't seem too disappointed, and thanked Giles for bringing him home and went off with Peggy, and was heard asking, 'Have you been having a lot of toast, Granny Peg? I can smell burning.'

'I can smell it too,' Giles observed as he waved good-bye. 'Has someone had a fire?'

'I'd say so.' Aaron dug his hands into his coat pockets. 'Come and have a look. How much do you know about when Delia lived in Paull?'

'Not very much,' Giles admitted as they crossed into the next farmyard. 'But I gather she had a wretched childhood.'

'Aye, she did, but none of us realized,' Aaron said grimly. 'Surprising what goes on beneath our noses, and as for my own lad mekkin' situation worse for her, poor lass. Anyway . . .'

410

They'd come out of the gate and crossed a narrow track, and Giles saw a broken-down cottage with a burnt-out barn. He saw a man with a shock of red hair, the same colour as Jenny's and her mother's, and other men pulling out tin trunks and burnt timber, and when he heard one of the other men call him Jack he guessed that the red-haired man must be Jack Robinson and therefore Robin's father.

'This is the Deakins' place, but there's no sign of either of them. There are fishermen and lifeboat men out on 'estuary trying to find him and folks searching all over 'village in case he's done away wi' her.'

Giles turned a shocked face towards Aaron. 'Why do you think that?'

Aaron didn't look at him as he spoke but kept his eyes firmly in front. 'Back door was locked as if they were both out and there's nobody in 'cottage. Me and Peggy both went upstairs to look for Mrs Deakin when 'fire began, but she wasn't there.'

'But – I still don't understand why you should think . . .' Giles said incredulously.

Aaron muttered glumly, 'Onny good thing I can say about them is that they weren't Paull people; they were from down Devon way. Fisher folk anyway, mebbe Brixham, and mebbe them folk were glad to see 'back of 'em. They turned up nearly thirty years ago, but never mixed wi' villagers. Then one day our Jenny found this little lass lookin' over our fence and brought her to our house to play. A good hour passed and she wasn't missed and Peggy went to tell 'missus that she was with us in case she was worried, but all she did was nod and say send her back when you've

411

had enough of her.' He pursed his lips. 'She'd onny be about three. Poor little lass.'

Jack came over to them and was introduced to Giles. He didn't look Giles in the eye as he reluctantly shook hands, though Giles stared him in the face.

'We can do no more here, Da. I reckon we should leave 'rest to 'police. Harry's been to Hedon and notified them that summat's amiss. There's a boat missing from 'creek and it's not one of Deakin's. His are still tied up. Mebbe, mebbe . . .' His boot scuffed the ground and then he looked up. 'Somebody should tell Delia.'

'What do you mean?' Giles asked him. 'Am I missing something here? Why should Delia be brought into this?'

Both men looked at him. 'Course, you wouldn't know if Delia hasn't mentioned it,' Aaron said. 'And neither does Robin know.' He glanced up at the cottage, then to the smouldering barn. 'Delia was once Dorothy Deakin, and this is where she spent that miserable childhood.'

CHAPTER FORTY-SEVEN

Giles had a midday meal with the Robinsons. Peggy said she'd drive him back to Hedon to catch the afternoon train and asked him if he would explain the situation to Delia.

'She might not want to come back yet,' Giles suggested. 'Not unless the police want to speak to her; and as she hasn't seen her parents for years, there's not much she can tell them.' Then he added, 'Have you thought that her parents might have gone off somewhere for a few days and the fire could have been accidental?'

Peggy nodded. 'Aye, we could all be barking up 'wrong tree,' she said, but her voice indicated that she thought otherwise.

'True,' Aaron acknowledged in the same tone. 'But Deakin wouldn't go anywhere at this time of year; it's a good time for shrimping, and besides how could they have gone anywhere when his mule and cart are tied up at 'creek and his boats are still berthed?'

Giles gave up deducing what might have happened; he didn't know the ins and outs of the fishing timetable or that of country people, but he said that he'd

413

tell Delia about the barn fire and that neighbours were anxious about her parents' whereabouts. I don't think she'll be too concerned about their situation, he decided, and they certainly haven't troubled themselves about hers.

'I don't want to worry Delia unduly,' he told the Robinsons. 'She has had enough to deal with in her life without adding to it.'

Peggy nodded approvingly. 'Quite right,' she murmured. Looking straight at him, she asked, 'Are you fond of her, Mr Dawson?'

He was taken aback by her directness. There was no artifice about this woman, no pretence; it was a straightforward question, so he gave a straightforward answer, but not before Aaron murmured, 'Now then, Mother. Nowt to do wi' you.'

'I'm very fond of Delia, Mrs Robinson, and I don't mind in the least answering your question.' He grinned at Aaron. 'But,' he went on seriously, 'at present I can't make any commitment. I'm not a free man.'

'Oh!' she said, as if disappointed, her voice hardening. 'You're married?'

'Yes. To be brief, my wife and I married to please our parents when we were young, and put under great obligation. Neither of us wanted the marriage and we have both regretted it.'

Peggy nodded. 'Children?'

Giles looked directly into her eyes. This wasn't a subject for discussion. 'No.'

She sighed. 'Delia won't get hurt, will she?'

'Not by me, Mrs Robinson.'

The scullery door crashed open and Jack rushed

in; he looked at all three. 'A woman's body's been found washed up near Sunk Island.' He took a breath. 'Rumour is that it's Mrs Deakin.'

Peggy got up and clasped her hands together. 'Oh, dear God, no.'

'There's been nobody else reported missing. Police are asking for somebody to identify her.'

'Not Delia.' Giles stood up too. 'We don't know where she is, do we?' he said pointedly.

'No, course we don't,' Peggy agreed. 'But anybody down at 'village shop would be able to – or Aaron or me, for that matter.'

'We'll wait till we're asked,' Aaron said sensibly. 'There's no rush.'

From the Hull railway station, Giles walked to the theatre and hoped to find Delia there. He wondered how to break the news about her parents and decided to ask her to come to the Maritime Hotel when she was free. They could speak privately there.

He found her in the small room behind the box office with a pile of papers on the table in front of her. She looked up as he arrived and greeted him with a huge smile; she seemed really happy and he would be sorry to give her sad tidings.

'How are you managing, Miss Under-Manager?' he asked. 'And where's Rogers?'

She laughed and stretched back in her chair. Her hair, which she had fastened loosely behind her neck with a ribbon, hung down her back. 'I've sent him home! He was getting in a state about telling me where everything was and what to do; he was exhausted, poor man. I told him I'd sort out as much as I could and what I couldn't I'd ask him about tomorrow.'

'Good,' he said enthusiastically. 'You are a woman of many parts. Are you almost finished? Can you break off for a cup of tea at the Maritime?'

She hesitated. 'Half an hour? Then I'm finished until this evening.'

'Fine. I'll slip back to Mrs Benson's and get out of my country clothes and into my town ones.' He assumed a serious expression. 'Are you not going to ask me if I lost your son on the way there?'

'Oh!' she gasped. 'How could I forget to ask?'

'What sort of mother are you?' he admonished. 'Peggy took him straight off to school with a parcel of bread and beef, as seemingly everyone was waiting to hear about his adventures in the *big house*. I'd bet he'll tell them a fine tale.'

She sighed. 'Thank you, Giles.'

He headed to the door. 'I'll be back in half an hour.'

Delia finished what she was doing and locked everything away in the huge safe and put the keys safely in her purse. Then she looked in at the auditorium to make sure there was no one in there and called out that she was locking up. There hadn't been anyone in all afternoon, as the joiner had finished the repairs to the stage and the cleaner had finished clearing up. The whole place had been her domain. She fastened the swing doors, and then went to the staff cloakroom to wash her hands and brush and pin up her hair, and as she glanced in the mirror she saw her reflection and smiled back at it. 'I think I'm happy,' she murmured. 'If this is what happiness feels like.'

Giles was waiting outside the front doors of the theatre, as she'd locked them after he'd left. He gazed at her. 'You look nice,' he said. 'Content.'

'I am,' she said. 'I feel as if my life is on an even keel, after being shipwrecked and drowning for so long.'

He nodded, although it was an unfortunate phrase in view of what he had to tell her, and offered his arm after she had locked the double doors behind her. She smiled and went on, 'Even being trusted to do such a simple thing as locking doors is wonderful. I've been in charge of the theatre for most of the day. My son is happy and I have a good friend who is offering his arm to me.'

She flushed as she spoke and hoped he didn't think she was presuming too much, but he smiled and his blue eyes crinkled and she wished for more.

The dining room at the hotel was only partly occupied as it was still quite early; Giles ordered a pot of tea and a plate of sandwiches for them both. When they were brought, she poured the tea and he raised his cup to her. 'Here's to your new career, Miss Delamour. But please don't ever give up singing.'

'I won't,' she said huskily. 'I feel as if I have more to sing about now than I ever had before and it will make a difference to the way I sing, even though this position might only be temporary until Mr Rogers finds someone else.'

They talked of general things as they ate, and Giles told her that he had just opened a letter from his parents telling him that they had received a distraught letter from his wife's parents that they could barely understand.

'I'm so sorry,' Delia commiserated. 'They must all be very unhappy about the situation.'

'I'm sure they are,' he agreed. 'But I wonder if they've ever thought about how unhappy we've been for so many years simply because we obeyed them, honoured our fathers and mothers? Now at last Marion and I have a chance of some happiness in our own lives.'

'Yes.' She drew in a breath and felt suddenly fearful that he might have plans that didn't include her.

'Delia,' he said, leaning towards her. 'I want to tell you something; two things, in fact, but first I must tell you something that might distress you.'

Her heart skipped a beat. He was going away. Leaving. He would soon be a free man able to do whatever he wished with his life. Her eyes suddenly filled with tears and spilled on to her cheeks; happiness wasn't for her after all.

'Don't cry!' he appealed. 'You don't know what I'm going to say!'

She patted her mouth with her napkin, willing her lips not to tremble. 'You're leaving,' she said softly. 'You're pursuing your new life elsewhere?'

'No I'm not.' He gave her a gentle smile. 'How could I? How could I leave without taking you with me?'

Delia's lips parted and her gaze questioned him further. 'What—'

His eyes looked into hers and she saw what she thought was tenderness. 'You know that I'm not yet free and my divorce might take some years. Would it

418

be fair of me if I asked you to wait for me until then?'

Delia shook her head. 'No – I mean yes. Wait?' she said breathlessly. 'Yes, I'll wait, if that's what you're asking me.'

He laughed. 'Was that a yes or a no? But that wasn't the first thing I was going to tell you.' He gazed at her, his blue eyes serious. 'It was the second, but the first can wait. We've known each other for only a short time and I realize I'm being very hasty and you might think it's too soon to make a commitment, but I love you, Delia, and when the time is right I want to ask you to marry me when I'm free.'

'Marry you?' she whispered. 'I never thought that anyone would ever want to marry me!'

'Because?' He shook his head in gentle admonishment. 'Why? Because you have had a child out of wedlock? You are not the first, Delia, and you won't be the last. I'm sure I've already said that.' He took hold of her hand and kissed her fingertips. 'What can I say to convince you that you are worthy of love? But I ask again, will you wait?'

She ran her tongue over her lips as she considered. Would it matter what anyone thought? Whose opinion was of concern to her? She took a deep breath and leaning towards him kissed him on his soft and gentle mouth. 'Do we have to wait?' she murmured. 'I'm already a woman fallen from grace. I'm ready to live with you now in a life of love.'

He returned her kiss, and as they were alone he drew her close and kissed her cheek, eyelids and mouth.

'I want to protect you from scandal,' he whispered. 'I will buy you a ring to prove my love, but we should

419

wait until I'm free and we can be man and wife in law as well as love.'

She smiled and nodded, tears glistening on her cheeks. He was right, of course.

CHAPTER FORTY-EIGHT

Giles decided that he wouldn't speak of the happenings in Paull just yet. The situation there didn't immediately affect Delia. She was happy and so was he, and as they walked hand in hand back to their lodgings he paused as they reached Holy Trinity church and said, 'You realize, Delia, that there can be no church wedding as I'll be a divorced man, unless I can get an annulment.'

Delia nodded. 'If there's a God, as I'm led to believe, I feel He'll let His love fall on us regardless of what went before, and without a church ceremony.'

He turned, and in the shadow of the church put his hands on her face and kissed her lips. 'I've wanted to do that since the day I met you,' he whispered. 'I've wanted to touch your shiny hair and stroke your soft smooth hands.'

Delia lifted her hands, now clad in warm gloves, and spread her fingers. 'My hands were once raw and red from scrubbing and washing and digging in the garden,' she murmured.

'Now they're ready to wear my ring.'

'Yes,' she said, shakily and happily. 'They are.'

She went back to the theatre that evening to sort through more paperwork for the next show in readiness for her new role of under-manager. She felt giddy with happiness, hardly able to concentrate. Giles was in rehearsal, and when it was finished he waited to escort her back to their lodgings.

The next morning when he went down to breakfast, Delia was already sitting at her table drinking her coffee. Two men were sitting at separate tables eating breakfast.

'Good morning, Miss Delamour; gentlemen.' He nodded to the men and then turned to Delia. 'May I join you, Miss Delamour?'

'Please do.' She gave him a beaming smile. 'Did you sleep well, Mr Dawson?'

'Very well, thank you,' he replied, although he hadn't. He'd spent the night tossing about, rehearsing what he should say regarding her parents. In the end he had decided he would state it as a mystery and let the news filter through. 'I hope you did too?'

'No,' she said brightly. 'I was very restless indeed,' and then whispered, 'but full of joy.'

When his coffee had been brought and the two other residents had departed, he began. 'Delia, last night I said I had two things to tell you, but I was rather overtaken by my feelings and somehow they came first, especially when I discovered that we were of the same mind.' He clasped her hand and gently squeezed her fingers.

'Yes,' she breathed. 'I can hardly believe what happened. I have never been in love before.'

'Nor I,' he said solemnly. 'But the – other matter is

rather disturbing. Yesterday, after Robin had gone off to school, I was told, and indeed shown, that a neighbour had had a barn fire.'

'There are often fires in the country,' she commented nonchalantly and sipped her insipid coffee. 'Stooks or ricks set alight accidentally by someone's pipe, or in the summer, if they haven't been stacked properly, haystacks can fire by internal combustion.' She gave a little frown. 'But not usually at this time of year. And in a barn? That's careless. Someone must have knocked a lamp over. What?' She saw the concern in his expression. 'What else?'

'It was your parents' barn,' he said quietly. 'There had been a fire inside and the roof has caved in.'

'And?' She gave a dismissive shrug. 'What has that to do with me? Something else?'

'Yes. According to the Robinsons and apparently other villagers too, your parents seem to be missing. There was no one in the cottage, which hasn't been affected by the fire, by the way.'

She lifted her shoulders again. 'He'd be out shrimping,' she said, unconcerned. 'Shrimping season is about now. No?'

'No. It seems that his boats are still moored in the creek, but someone else's boat is missing; and his mule and cart were still tied up. I'm only telling you what I was told, Delia, but the villagers are concerned about both of them and it was suggested by the Robinsons that I might tell you.'

'I don't know why anyone else would be concerned,' she said slowly. 'They never spoke to anyone unless it was really necessary. I was sent shopping in the village

423

almost from the time I started school, so that my mother didn't have to. They were barely known.'

'Well, you know how rumours can fly,' he remarked. 'But fishermen are out on the estuary looking for them.'

'Well, if the worst should happen,' her voice was cold and devoid of emotion, 'I suppose someone might remember that the Deakins once had a daughter, but as no one but the Robinsons know where I am they won't be able to find me, will they? Does that make me sound hard-hearted?' she asked, looking in his face for a trace of censure, but there was none.

'To anyone else, perhaps,' he said mildly. 'But not to me, and it seems, Miss Delamour, that you have at last left that little girl Dorothy behind you.'

Delia put the news of her missing parents to the back of her mind. She didn't need to think about them. They had cast her off and she was now doing the same to them. Whatever they had done or where they were had nothing to do with her. She had more important things to think about now: her future with Giles, for one, which on the face of it appeared wildly improbable considering the short time they had known each other; but she was deliriously happy, and was loving the work in the theatre and refused to be distracted by thinking of her parents. Dennis Rogers had seen how organized she was and had decided to take time off before the next show began.

'You must take a holiday too, Miss Delamour. Take a holiday at Easter. Go and visit that boy of yours,' he told her, and she said that she would. She had hired a clerk for the ticket office, a Miss Graham, who was so pleased to be offered the position that she practically curtsied to Delia. She would begin the week after Easter when the box office opened for advance bookings of the variety show.

Peggy had sent Delia a letter asking if she would come for the short holiday and said there was news of the Deakins that she should be made aware of. She also said that Mr Dawson would be very welcome and she was hoping that Jenny might be there too.

Delia was curious about Jenny and wondered if Arthur had been to visit, and as the Easter holiday would begin on Thursday hoped that her friend would also travel to Paull to see her family and bring interesting news. Giles had gone to York and on his return the following day called in at the theatre to see her; he told her of his completed house sale, that the money was safely in his bank, and that he had been to his parents' home to explain his wife's circumstances, that she was en route to Canada, if not already there, and finally that she had asked him for a divorce which was now in the hands of their lawyers.

'They were upset, of course,' he said, 'but on hearing that Marion was about to produce a child that wasn't mine they agreed that I must divorce her immediately and said that they wouldn't stand in my way.' He gave a sardonic grimace. 'As if they could! They still regard me as a mere youth unable to make my own decisions. For heaven's sake,' he suddenly burst out, 'I'm thirty-one years old!'

'Did you tell them of any of your plans?' she asked cautiously.

'No, I did not and will not, only what they need to know. And although I had initially thought that I might invite them to our non-wedding celebrations, I have now decided that I won't, but will take you to meet them afterwards and present you as my wife and Robin as my stepson, and completely shock them.' And because they were alone, he put his arms round her. 'Light of my life,' he said, kissing the tip of her nose, 'you won't change your mind, will you? You won't begin to think that everything is far too complicated and happening far too fast?'

'Everything *is* happening too fast,' she laughed. 'But not fast enough and I won't change my mind.'

She wrote back to Peggy telling her that she would be there by late afternoon on Thursday and that Mr Dawson would be pleased to come too, and that he would again stay at one of the hostelries in the village to save them any inconvenience.

'We must do things properly,' Giles said to her. 'We wouldn't wish to cause the Robinsons any embarrassment, and although they might guess the situation between us I'd like to wait for the confirmation of the citation of divorce before we make any announcement.'

'I – I didn't think we'd make an announcement,' she faltered.

'Only to family and friends, to confirm our decision,' he answered. 'And you'll want to explain to Robin? I don't mean make a public announcement, although the divorce will be made public and I don't want your name involved in that. And . . .' He hesitated. 'Would you like to be known as Mrs Dawson?' He saw her confusion. 'It will be an age before it can be official but you can if you want to. It's harder for a woman to deal with such a situation than a man.'

She thought seriously about it. There seemed to be so much happening, and as they travelled to Hedon on Thursday she said, 'I'll explain to Robin, but not immediately, that one day we'll marry and that you'll be his stepfather. It might be confusing for him. He doesn't know that Jack Robinson is his birth father.'

'All in good time, Delia. Robin doesn't need to know the details, but here is another dilemma for you to worry over.' He smiled. 'I thought that now the York house is sold I would buy a house in Hull; there are some good properties in Pearson Park and in Albion Street, and in Parliament Street too. What do you think? Perhaps we might take a look?'

'Oh!' She was astonished. Never in her wildest dreams did she ever think she might live in such elegant housing.

'I've been making plans for a long time, Delia,' he explained. 'Thinking of when I might be free. I've often strolled by such houses, but I always held back, for it seemed pointless when there was no one in my life with whom to share it. But now there is.'

He looked out of the window and took hold of her hand and she realized that he too had been hurting, but hiding it so much better than her.

'Next stop,' he said. 'Will your son, soon to be mine, be waiting for us?'

He was, of course; he was waiting in the trap with Peggy and jumped down to greet his mother with a hug and a kiss and eagerly shook hands with Giles. 'We're painting eggs,' he said excitedly, 'and then we're going to have an Easter egg hunt.'

'Oh, ho! Can anyone join?' Giles asked. 'I remember painting eggs when I was your age, Robin.'

'Oh, yes, you can,' Robin agreed. 'We've got loads of eggs, haven't we, Granny Peg? Some of them are from someone else's hens because they've gone away, so we're looking after them and feeding the goats. Molly's feeding their mule too because she's the only one that can go near him. He doesn't nip her but he nipped through my breeches and I had to run!'

Delia glanced at Peggy, who shrugged and murmured, 'Somebody had to feed 'em, didn't they? We need to discuss some matters, Delia.'

Giles moved closer to the trap. 'Is it essential, Mrs Robinson?' he murmured.

She nodded. 'Yes, I think so,' she said on a breath so that Delia, who was still listening to Robin's chatter, wouldn't hear. 'Identification is proved.'

Delia, Robin and Giles climbed into the trap, and Peggy shook the reins to set off.

'Has Jenny come?' Delia asked.

'No,' Peggy said abruptly. 'And no word from her either; not that she needs to say she's coming, but I would have liked to know.'

As they drove along the Thorngumbald road, Giles commented on the wide evening sky. It had been a dry and bright day and the sky reflected it. Though the sun was setting behind them in the west, great swathes of purple, red and gold were interspersed with the darkening wave-like clouds that passed over them, creating a landscape of images in the sky.

'Look at that,' he said, pointing. 'It looks like the sea or a great river.'

'Aye,' Peggy answered. 'It's as if 'world has turned upside down and 'estuary is above us. There's nothing like a Holderness sky for drama and spectacle,' she said complacently, and even though she had never once stirred from her home county she added, 'Nothing in 'world to touch it.'

'Sometimes you can see castles and turrets and ships,' Robin stretched his neck back to look up. 'I'm going to make up a story about them.'

As they reached Thorngumbald and neared their turning, Peggy pointed ahead to where a carriage was bearing in the same direction. 'Look there,' she said. 'Who round here can afford a carriage like that?'

Giles turned his head to grin at Delia, who smiled back. 'Looks as if you might be having more company, Mrs Robinson,' he commented.

Robin stood up to look. 'I know who it is,' he said excitedly, and his mother put her finger to her lips to silence him. He clapped his hand over his mouth, his eyes bright with laughter.

CHAPTER FORTY-NINE

'I knew that if I told you I was bringing someone home you'd clean the house from top to bottom, Ma.' Jenny kissed her mother on the cheek when they arrived in the trap. 'And there was no need. The house is perfect and Arthur must accept me, us, just as we are.'

'Arthur? But – who is he?' Peggy's bewildered gaze cut across the yard to where Aaron was standing by the fence in his baggy old cords with his arms folded across his chest, talking to a man in a top hat with his well-coated back to them as he gazed towards the estuary.

'He's a great friend of Delia's,' Jenny smiled at her friend, 'so that is a very high recommendation, and . . .' She paused for effect. 'He's the man I'm going to marry.'

Peggy put both hands over her mouth and looked at her daughter. 'But we don't know him. He's a toff! Look at his clothes, look at his carriage.'

'I know.' Jenny sighed ruefully. 'But it can't be helped. You'll get used to the idea. And by the way, he lives in a huge manor house with servants.'

Then she laughed as she saw Robin race across

the yard towards the two men, calling, 'Mr Arthur Crawshaw!'

'You see,' she said. 'Robin has no difficulty with his status.'

Giles folded his arms across his chest and turning to Delia said wryly, 'Why do I feel that my nose has been pushed completely out of joint?'

'Is this 'great speaker that we've been hearing about?' Peggy also turned towards Delia. 'The one who quotes Shakespeare?' and at Delia's merry nod she said, 'I thought he was a made-up person, someone out of Robin's imagination! Well,' she exclaimed. 'I'd better go inside and get myself ready to greet him, but as for you marrying him, Jenny, I don't know about that!'

'I think you'll find, Ma' – Jenny laughed – 'that although there wasn't any necessity, Arthur has already spoken to my father.'

Later, after Arthur had been introduced to Peggy and remarked that now he knew where Jenny's glorious hair had come from, had shaken hands with Giles and kissed Delia on her cheek and said how radiant she looked, he sent his driver to book rooms at one of the pubs in the village, telling him to get himself a meal and return at nine o'clock to collect him. Arthur and Giles, clad in an assortment of rubber boots and old coats, then went out with Aaron, Robin and an uncommunicative Jack to look over the farm. There were new spring lambs still undercover that Robin wanted to show them; young piglets still suckling and weaners who had been separated from their mothers who were snuffling about out on grass, and land that was showing new spring growth.

'I'm pleased that you could come, Delia,' Peggy said, whilst Jenny made them another pot of tea. 'I want to talk to you later and I know it will be a difficult matter for you to discuss, but it must be done.'

Jenny came in carrying a tray of tea and cake. 'I found this cake in a tin, Ma,' she said. 'Is it all right that I've cut into it?'

'Of course it is, but don't eat too much as I'm cooking lamb. It's ready to put in 'oven, but I might need to do more vegetables,' she said meaningfully, still reeling from the sight of the unexpected visitor.

'There will be enough,' Jenny said pragmatically, and poured them each a cup of tea. 'You always do more than we need. Incidentally, we have to return tomorrow morning as we're travelling to Derbyshire. Delia,' she changed the subject, 'you and Giles both look very happy. Is there a reason?'

'We are happy,' Delia said contentedly. 'And we weren't going to say anything yet, but Giles has filed for divorce and although it might be a while before he's free, he's asked me to marry him and I've said yes!'

'Good heavens! How long have you known each other?' Peggy asked. 'And as for you, Jenny, you haven't known Mr Crawshaw more than five minutes! What's the rush?' Then she gave a gasp and looked at them both. 'There isn't one, is there?'

Delia and Jenny both laughed and shook their heads. 'I didn't think it would ever happen to me, Peggy,' Delia said wistfully, and Jenny responded by saying, 'And I decided to catch Arthur before he had the chance to change his mind! And, Ma, you forget that you once told me that you fell in love with Da the first time you met him and were married before you reached eighteen.'

Peggy nodded. 'It's true, I did. We were both young but I was determined to have him.'

'Well, there you are then,' Jenny said. 'I'm following in your footsteps, but I'm not eighteen so why would I wait?'

Supper was a jolly affair and all the girls came along with Susan to be introduced by Robin to Mr Arthur Crawshaw, whom they hadn't believed to be real either, just as their grandmother hadn't. They didn't stay to eat but were coming for lunch the next day.

On the stroke of nine, Arthur's driver returned and Giles was offered a lift back to the village, where he and Arthur retired to the best room in the Humber Tavern and consumed several glasses of whisky, discovering that they knew many of the same theatrical people; they then discussed various aspects of marriage, of which Crawshaw knew nothing. It was then that Giles finally appreciated that his companion had never had any romantic notions towards Delia, and had regarded her as someone who was badly in need of a good and reliable friend. 'I was there at the right time, old chap,' he said. 'She was pretty desperate, poor girl.'

Peggy and Delia were the last to go to bed. Delia was sharing Robin's room but wasn't tired and she'd hung back, helping Peggy to put dishes away, preparing the breakfast table and ignoring Peggy's entreaties that she would see to everything. Finally, she sat down by the banked-up fire and said, 'What was it in particular that you thought we should discuss, Peggy?'

'Oh, not tonight, honey,' Peggy said. 'Tomorrow, mebbe, when Jenny and Mr Crawshaw have left. I want you to have a pleasant weekend.'

'We are having a lovely weekend,' Delia told her. 'And we don't have to rush back. The theatre is closed for the holiday. But I won't sleep tonight unless you tell me what it is we need to discuss. It's about my parents, isn't it? Have they been found?'

Peggy sat down opposite her and took off her cap. Pulling the pins out of her hair, she ran her fingers through it so that her curls fell on to her shoulders.

'You're lovely, Peggy.' Delia smiled at her and her eyes prickled. 'You've no idea how much I used to wish that you were my mother. I always wanted to call you Ma, like Jenny.'

Peggy leaned forward and grasped her hands. 'You can, m'darling. I'd like you to.'

Delia swallowed and nodded. 'Have they been found?' she repeated.

'Mrs Deakin has.' Peggy carefully avoided calling her Delia's mother; neither did she mention that Giles already knew, for she guessed that he had had his own reasons for not telling Delia. 'She's been identified by several people, including Aaron. She was found on a sandbank somewhere near Sunk Island, but there's no news of Deakin or of 'fishing boat he took that wasn't his.'

Delia shook her head. 'I don't understand why he would take anyone else's boat. He was so very particular about his own.'

434

'Could your mother sail?' Peggy asked.

'She did when she was a girl. Her father had been a fisherman and had taught her to sail when she was very young.' Suddenly she recalled the day when she had caught her mother gazing out at the shrimpers' sailboats on the estuary and in a moment of rare conversation had told her that she and Deakin had sailed there from the Devon coast. 'She told me that she'd helped to sail the boat here from Brixham,' she continued. 'But never in my life did I hear her mention Paull creek or the boats and she never again talked of sailing.'

'Mmm. I wonder why they left their own harbour?' Peggy probed, but Delia didn't know. She knew nothing of their past, and, she thought, she didn't want to; they were strangers to her now as much as they had been when she was a child and a young woman.

'It's just,' Peggy continued, 'well, there's the matter of 'cottage and 'smallholding. Who it belongs to.'

Delia looked at her. 'I don't know. It might be rented, though I never saw anyone call at the house.' She shrugged. 'Not that I care. I don't want it.'

'Mebbe you don't,' Peggy said persuasively, 'but 'rumour is that Deakin bought it cheap for cash when they first came here.'

Delia frowned. 'Rumour? What rumour?'

'Aye.' Peggy nodded. 'It's been talked about for years. Somebody spilt the beans, and buying a property for a wodge of cash isn't something that folk would forget easily, even after nearly thirty years; not in a small village like this one.' She took a deep breath. 'And even if you don't want it, mebbe it'd be a good nest egg for your son?'

Delia licked her lips. She didn't want any part of it, but for Robin? If it had been her parents' property it could be sold to ensure his future. 'Yes,' she breathed. 'I suppose so. What should I do, Peggy? The property would be in *his* name, I expect, and if he hasn't been found . . .'

'Mebbe have a look round 'cottage, if you can face it? See if there's any place where deeds would be kept.'

Delia gave a dry and ironic scoff. 'He kept money under the floorboards. Under a rug in the kitchen. I stole from it when I left. I would have been completely destitute if I hadn't.' She remained silent for a moment as she considered. 'Will you come with me?' she asked. 'I daren't go in alone; too many shadows from the past.'

Jenny and Arthur were waved off after a fish luncheon at midday on Good Friday. Peggy had baked a large cod and served it with a batch of shrimps and parsley sauce. Arthur and Giles agreed that they had never before eaten such tasty fish.

'That's because it was swimming in 'estuary only this morning and brought home by Aaron before you were out of bed,' Peggy told them.

Aaron grinned and bashfully agreed that she was right. 'Tide had been high,' he said. 'Though I sailed almost to 'mouth of 'Humber to catch it. Plenty o' fish about. No need for anybody to be hungry.'

After Jenny and Arthur left, Giles agreed that he'd join the children at the kitchen table to paint eggs and to the children's amusement wore one of Peggy's aprons to cover him; Aaron went out into the fields to find Jack, and Delia had already whispered to Giles that she was going with Peggy to look at the burnt-out barn and didn't want Robin there. He nodded in understanding and pressed her hand.

Delia shivered as they opened the gate into the Deakins' yard; it felt to her that it was like a ghost farm, quite unreal and nothing to do with her. When she'd first come back with Robin that dark night in November, she hadn't seen anything but a chink of lamplight at the window and a mere slit of light at the door when her mother had opened it.

Now she saw it as it was: the cottage looked derelict, with cracked window panes and unpainted window frames and door; the yard had weeds growing through the cracks of paving slabs and puddles of dirty water they had to step over. The grass in the paddock was uncut and two thin goats bleated at them. Was it always like this? she thought. Did I not see it before or did I simply accept it?

There was still a strong smell of burning wood and straw and an underlying aroma of something else, a pungent sweetness that Peggy said Aaron thought was tobacco. 'But something else too,' Delia said, sniffing the air.

They crossed to the barn and saw the damage. 'It'll have to come down,' Delia remarked, 'and I've been thinking that if the property didn't belong to them, why hasn't an agent or the owner come to look at the damage? Everyone must have heard about the fire.'

'It was 'talk of 'village for a couple of days,' Peggy told her, 'and you're quite right, I don't recall anyone saying that it belonged to anybody else, and somebody would have known. If you can't find any documents we'll have to mek enquiries wi' authorities.' She heaved a sigh. 'Have you seen enough here?'

'No.' Delia stepped into the barn. The floor was still wet from when the locals had doused the fire with river water. 'That smell? It's alcohol, isn't it? Brandy! I remember now; sometimes he – Deakin – smelled of it. He'd go outside of an evening and when he came back in we could smell it on him.' She turned to Peggy. 'He was smuggling, wasn't he? How else could he afford brandy? Not from shrimping.'

Peggy nodded. 'Yes, that's what we thought. Me and Aaron. Do you think that's why he came to live here on 'estuary? Because of being nearer to 'Netherlands? Brandy and tobacco? Aaron said there were casks and crates in here that were going off like Chinese crackers once 'fire had tekken hold.'

'I don't know,' Delia admitted. 'I know nothing of his life; he barely spoke to me except to tell me to fetch him something, or clean his boots.'

She walked carefully to where the metal trunks were stacked. Some had collapsed on to their sides as if they'd fallen over; a pile of soft grey ash was scattered over the floor. 'They used to have an old rully,' she said. 'And boxes and trunks were always stacked on top of it. I never knew what was in them and I didn't dare look.'

A spanner was lying on the floor and she bent to pick it up and hit the bolt on one of the upright trunks to open it. It didn't budge and she hit it again and still it wouldn't move.

'There used to be a can of oil for oiling hinges or

shears,' she said, looking about her, 'but I expect that went up in flames too.' In exasperation she held the spanner with both hands and hit the bolt again and this time it slid across. 'Hah,' she said. 'Now let's see.' She lifted the lid and her hands were immediately black with soot. There were layers of cardboard and beneath that several sheets of paper. With the tips of her blackened fingers she lifted those and beneath found two metal boxes. She lifted out one of them and raised the lid. Inside was a stack of white five pound notes, and beneath that another wad of ten pound ones.

Delia said nothing but looked at Peggy, who stood staring. Then she lifted the other box. It was heavy and locked. She shook it and it rattled. 'Coins,' she whispered. 'Ill-gotten gains. What do I do with these? I don't want them. They haven't been come by honestly.'

'You don't know how they've been come by,' Peggy murmured. 'So who would you give them back to?'

Delia shook her head; she only knew she didn't want them.

Then Peggy said slowly, 'There's a young fisherman in 'village deprived of his living because *somebody* took his boat out and it's apparently now lost. You could give some of it to him to buy another, or give him one of Deakin's boats that were left behind.'

Delia looked about her. 'Yes,' she said vaguely. 'I could do that. But what if he comes back? And I still don't understand why he would take a boat that wasn't his. Or maybe it wasn't him; maybe it was my mother who decided to leave him and didn't realize it was the wrong boat. But if so, where is he and where is the boat?' She sighed. 'We'll never know. Help me, Peggy. We'd better take these to the cottage and hide them.'

'Not safe there,' Peggy said. 'We'd best tek them to our house. Nobody would think of looking there and we're allus about the place. Shall I fetch Mr Dawson to carry them? Do you trust him enough?'

Delia gave a wistful smile. 'With my life, Peggy,' she said. 'With my life.'

CHAPTER FIFTY

Delia rose early the next morning. Robin was still sleeping and she gazed at him before dressing and going down. Peggy was already up and putting bread in the oven, and looked in surprise at Delia.

'I thought you'd have had a sleep-in this morning. Would you like tea?'

'No, thank you, not just now. I'm going across to the cottage. If I don't go now, then I won't go at all.'

Peggy put her hands on her hips. 'On your own?'

'Yes; I thought about it in bed last night, and decided it's what I have to do.' Delia gave a little huff of breath. 'Get rid of the final ghosts.'

Peggy slung the oven cloth over her shoulder. 'Sometimes we have to be brave enough to do things on our own, but you don't need to prove anything any more, Delia. You've shown your courage since you were seventeen years old and made a future for yourself and your son. Now you have friends and family who'll stand by your side.'

Delia went towards her and kissed her. 'I know,' she said, her voice cracking. 'But this is the very last thing and then I'll know that I'm whole again.'

Buffeted by a brisk wind, white clouds scudded across the sky above the estuary, which still showed silver and gold streaks of dawn. The estuary too was running fast, and white-crested waves tossed and churned on their irresistible journey to the sea.

Delia crossed the yard and over into old Foggit's farm. The fence dividing the two properties had been taken down by Aaron and Jack and she didn't see Jack straighten up from behind the pigsties as she passed through. She came to the fence where a wooden gate led onto the track and paused for a moment, then went through and closed it behind her and walked down the track to the old cottage with the squeaking gate.

The smell of burnt timbers still lingered but she didn't look towards the barn and went purposefully towards the cottage door. Peggy had told her that the key was under a stone and she'd given a slight nod; that was where it had always been hidden.

The iron key was large and heavy in her hand but it turned easily enough though the door creaked as she pushed it. A heavy dusty curtain hung behind it and she wondered if it was the same one that had always been there. She hesitated before entering the kitchen, almost expecting to see her father sitting by the fireside, but the room was empty and cold and any fire that had been there had burned down to a muddy grey ash.

Her eyes went to the cupboard at the side of the range; she had spent many hours in there in her childhood until she grew too big to sleep in it, when she had rebelled and asked her mother for a cotton sheet so that she could stuff it to make a mattress she could

442

use on the floor. It was sleeping here that she had discovered the loose floorboard and what lay beneath it.
Too late, her father must have been fearful of her discovering his secret hoard of money and had made her
a place in the roof space.

Slowly she mounted the stairs to the small square
landing and glanced into her parents' bedroom, which
looked exactly as it had always done and had the same
stale odour. She then took the three steps up and bent
her head as she pushed open the low door to the loft
which had eventually become her bedroom. It had
been draughty and freezing cold in the winter, but this
place had felt like her private abode. Here she'd kept a
sparrow with a broken wing, making it a box filled with
straw and bringing breadcrumbs every day until one
morning she found it dead, when she had cried and
buried it under a hedge.

Her mother sometimes came up here when she
was at school; she always knew when she had been for
things had been moved. A rickety cane chair which
sat against the wall was shifted mere inches, but Delia
always knew. There were two small cupboards built
into the base of the wall; one of them was crammed
with old curtains and sheets, the other was empty
apart from a wooden button box filled with all kinds
of paraphernalia: string, bobbins of strong thread,
pieces of frayed ribbon and unfinished tatting, but
no buttons. But this cupboard was the one blocked by
the chair and therefore, Delia had reasoned, the one
her mother had always looked in, but she had never
fathomed out why.

She shifted the chair away now and took a curtain

from the other cupboard, spreading it on the dusty floor to sit on; it seemed as if there hadn't been a duster or brush up here since she had left. She opened the cupboard door and took out the button box and gazed at the empty space. Then she noticed for the first time that the flooring in this cupboard was higher than in the other, as deep as a step and made from a different kind of wood, thinner and more pliable, with a narrower plank and a gap at the back just wide enough to fit in a screwdriver or a chisel.

Delia pulled the button box towards her and opened it again, rummaging in it until she found what she was looking for. A small thin chisel lay at the bottom of the box as it always had, and she took it out, leaned inside to the back of the cupboard and slotted the chisel into the gap. Perfect!

She got on to her knees and prised the tool towards her, jiggling it about to get purchase, and although it was a tight fit she drew up the plank, put her hand inside the gap and brought out a parcel of some kind, wrapped in a cloth that might once have been part of a curtain.

'So, Ma,' she murmured. 'What fine thing have we here?'

She carefully unwrapped the cloth and drew out a roll of documents fastened with a ribbon; she unfastened it and smoothed out the parchment. These, she thought, and confirmed as she scanned them, were the property documents. Davis Deakin's name was on them and they were copies of those held by a Hedon lawyer. Her eyes widened when she saw the amount the farm cottage and buildings were bought for and paid in full.

'So it was true, he did pay in cash!' she muttered. 'Money from smuggled goods?' But not from round here, she considered. He must have brought the money with him from his former fishing ground; perhaps he had the Customs men looking for him down Devon way and decided to come to fresh waters, and Ma came with him.

She carefully rolled up the documents again, laid them to one side and put her hand inside the aperture again; she searched about with her fingers and brought out a large envelope. Inside were letters and some early grainy and faded photographs. One showed a group of young people near a harbour wall, and in the middle of them a tall handsome fisherman with a dark beard and hair and a big smile on his face holding a huge tunny fish within both arms. Above him someone had marked in pencil a small x. A dark-haired girl dressed in a man's fishing smock stood smiling to one side of him and it looked as if she had her arm round him; on his other side stood a fair-haired pretty girl in a summer dress. Other young men were holding fishing rods, and an older man had turned his head and hidden his face from the camera; all wore long fishermen boots.

Delia turned the photograph over. Written in pencil, so faded she could barely make it out, she read, *Me with x – my sweetheart Tom Evans, and the other fisher lads, and his soon to be wife Sally Morris. Deakin hiding his face as usual.*

Then there was a studio photograph, clearer than the other, with just the dark-haired girl wearing a long dark skirt and white blouse and the handsome fisherman with their arms around each other's waist and a message on the back reading, *Saying goodbye to my lovely Tom. I think my heart will break.*

She looked closely at both photographs. So who were they? She had never heard of Tom Evans or Sally Morris, but the man who had covered his face could well have been her father; she recognized a similarity in his bearing. But the dark-haired girl? Was it her mother?

She tipped out all the contents on to her lap and at the bottom was a small notebook, not a diary, but dates were written in it in what was clearly her mother's hand. The first page was dated 1850 and written beneath were the words:

The deed is done, my father is put to rest and I'm tying my life to Deakin, leaving behind my sweetheart Tom. I'm taking with me his most precious gift and the memory of his beautiful lilting Welsh voice which has so often sung love songs to me. What else can I do? He's promised to another and needs her father's wealth and my father has left me none.

If Deakin should ever discover this he'd kill me. That he can't read is to my advantage. He has to leave soon or he'll be caught and jailed and I'll have no option but the workhouse, me and my unborn child. He's offered me a chance of a new life away from all I've ever known, but from what motive? Not for love. He doesn't care for me nor I for him. We sail tomorrow.

Delia felt breathless, confused. Did it mean what she thought it meant? She turned several blank pages, others with scribbling on them relating to a good catch, or a bad one, and then another at the back of the notebook, which read:

The child has got herself into trouble. There'll be no hiding it and he'll turn her out. It's best that she goes; she'll have the chance of a better life than one with us. We've never done right by her and I'd rather she left, for each day she reminds me of the man I loved and lost, and there'll come a time when I might have had more than I can bear with Deakin.

She heard the rattle of the cottage door and jumped, suddenly fearful, as she had been when a young girl, that it was Deakin returning, but then she heard an anxious voice calling, 'Delia! Delia! Where are you?'

She went to the top of the staircase. 'Up here, Giles,' she said. 'Come up.'

He bent his head as he came in through the low door. 'What are you doing up here all on your own?' His voice was concerned. 'I was worried about you. Mrs Robinson said you'd come here an hour ago and Jack said he'd seen you pass by.'

She gazed at him. 'Is it so long?' She looked down at the documents and the jumble of papers and photographs.

'What was this room?' Giles looked round. 'A storage room? A glory hole? Everyone needs somewhere to put things they can't decide whether to keep or not.' He looked out of the small roof window and murmured, 'A good view of the estuary, though.'

447

'A good description of my bedroom,' she commented.

He turned to look at her. 'Your bedroom? No, surely not?' His expression was troubled. 'You're not serious, are you?'

'It's a better room than the cupboard I had before it.'

He stared at her and then said, 'Come on,' and gathered up all the papers, documents and photographs. 'We'll take them and you can look at them at the Robinsons'. The kettle's on the boil and the children are all waiting to show you their painted Easter eggs, and so am I.'

'First, will you read this and tell me what you think it means?' She handed him the notebook and one page in particular.

He read it and then said, 'Is this your mother's hand?'

'Yes, I think so,' she said on a breath, and then showed him the photograph of her mother and the fisherman.

He looked at them and then at her and lifted his eyebrows. 'This is not Mr Deakin, I gather?'

She shook her head. 'No.'

'Your real father then? At least – you have a look of him.' He gazed at her. 'And with a beautiful voice?'

Delia nodded. She couldn't speak and her eyes were awash with tears.

Carrying the papers, documents and photographs, Giles led her downstairs and out of the cottage; he locked the door after them and put the key in his jacket pocket, then with his hand firmly on her elbow he steered her towards the gate, closing it behind him, and down the track to Foggit's where Jack was

448

standing by the fence with an anxious expression on his face.

'You all right, Delia?' He ran his hand over his chin. 'Can I – is there owt I can do?'

'Yes,' Giles answered for her. 'You can carry these,' and he handed the roll of paperwork to him. 'Don't drop them, they're important.'

Jack held the bundle as if it were a precious baby and led the way across the yard towards the other farmhouse, whilst Giles kept his arm firmly around Delia. As they approached, the door opened and Robin came out.

'I was just coming to find you,' he said, rushing up to her and putting his arms round her waist. 'I thought you were lost.'

A tear ran down her cheek. 'I think I might have been, but now I'm not.' She dropped a kiss on the top of his head. 'I'm found again.'

All the other children and Susan were sitting at Peggy's table with a basket of painted eggs in the middle. Aaron was standing with a mug of tea in his hand and Peggy was putting a batch of bread rolls in the oven. She closed the oven door and straightened up, a question on her lips which she didn't utter.

'Deakin wasn't my father!' Delia said, triumphant yet emotional. 'Though I was given his name. Whether he knew or guessed, we'll never know.'

'*What's in a name?*' Robin struck a theatrical pose, though he didn't know what his mother meant or understand why she had tears streaming down her face. '*That which we call a rose* – Ma, don't cry. You never cry. Why are you crying now?'

449

She gave a choking laugh. 'Ma?' she said. 'You've never called me Ma before!'

'I like it,' he said, coming towards her and hugging her. 'Why are you crying?'

She bent and dropped another kiss on the top of his head. 'I like it too. And I'm crying because I'm happy.'

It was mid-May when the battered fishing boat was washed up on rocks near Cayton Bay just below Scarborough. Deakin's body and a rifle were trapped between the bench seat and the anchor which had held him down. A half-anker of brandy was rolling about, but it disappeared shortly after the discovery of the boat and before the police arrived. The coroner was informed and an inquest arranged when it was found that a bullet in his chest had killed him. The conclusion was drawn that he had probably been killed by fellow smugglers after a disagreement over payment for illicit goods. The deceased was known to the authorities, who had been hoping to make an arrest.

The Customs and Excise men descended on the cottage and burnt-out barn shortly afterwards, but expected to find nothing and were not disappointed. The trunks were empty and they agreed that there was a faint lingering odour of tobacco and brandy which must have gone up in the fire. In the inquest on Mrs Deakin no conclusion was reached except that she might have been complicit in the smuggling trade, although there was nothing in the cottage that implied she had benefited from it. It was believed she had been washed overboard during the fracas.

Three months later the lawyers ruled that the property rightly belonged to the next of kin, a daughter Miss Dorothy Deakin, and as she was apparently living elsewhere at present, documentation would be held in the lawyers' vaults until she claimed it.

Although Delia had said she didn't want anything to do with the proceeds of smuggling, immediately after she and Giles had returned to Hull following the Easter holiday Peggy, Aaron and Jack had done a systematic search of the property and the barn; in the cottage they had found the loose floorboard where Delia said it was and unearthed a tin box filled with paper money and cash in coins both silver and gold. On searching the barn and moving the trunks and other rubbish, they discovered a metal ring sealed in the ground and the small pit that had been dug beneath it. This too contained paper money and gold coins, some foreign.

Much to Peggy's disquiet and at Aaron's insistence, the tin box was kept beneath their bed until it was decided what should happen to it. Then one day at the end of April, Aaron took some of the ten pound notes to the young fisherman whose boat had been stolen, and mentally crossing his fingers, because untruths didn't come easily to this honest man, he said that insurance money had been paid out and he was directed to pay him back for the loss of his boat.

Molly still insisted on the story that she had seen Mrs Deakin driving the mule and cart down the track on the night of the fire, but she didn't bother to tell anyone that she had also seen a booted foot sticking out from under a tarpaulin in the back of the cart, because she knew no one would believe her. In any case, she was bored with the story now, and had another interest as her father had given her two piglets of her own to look after. She told everyone that she was going to breed from them.

ENDING

It was in August that year that Delia's very best friends Miss Jenny Robinson and Mr Arthur Crawshaw dispensed with the convention of marrying in the bride's local church and were wed in the village church close by the groom's home, where a guest reception and wedding breakfast was held in the great hall with a marquee on the lawns for the staff and villagers with food and drink and dancing in the evening.

A moist-eyed Aaron led his Paris-dressed daughter down the aisle; Delia in deep rose satin with a white chiffon overskirt was chief attendant. Arthur's brother was his best man, Jenny's four nieces were bridesmaids in yellow and pink silk dresses with flowered head-dresses, and Robin was asked to read a lesson which he was very pleased to do, as he said it would be good practice in case he decided to be an actor rather than a fisherman after all. Delia smiled to see her young son, whose head only just showed above the pulpit, proclaiming the words without a touch of nervousness.

Jack was a groomsman, and as Delia watched him, nervous in his unaccustomed finery of hired morning suit and silk cravat, she wondered if now was the time for forgiveness. Peggy, who was splendidly attired in a green silk gown with a large bustle and short train and a matching silk hat set on her red curls, wept throughout the service, not, she explained, because she was sad but because she was happy, as she had always thought that her independent daughter would never marry.

Arthur's mother was regal in deep purple and told anyone who asked, or even those who didn't, how very pleased she was with the progress being made in the dower house and that she was looking forward to her residency there.

Giles had brought his violin and at the reception played several merry jigs and reels that the guests danced to, and there were a few sighs from unattached young ladies of distinction who had eyed him as a potential suitor until he began to play for Delia as she sang 'I Dreamt I Dwelt in Marble Halls' and realized that he was spoken for.

'Won't you play some more romantic music?' Delia asked as they sat drinking champagne whilst a string quartet played.

'No.' He gently squeezed her hand. 'I'm saving that for someone special once I'm free.'

Giles had seen an elegant house in Hull's Albion Street that he said Delia would love. She'd visited it and thought it wonderful, and when Giles suggested that they could convert one or two rooms to music rooms so that they could improve their singing and playing, and perhaps give recitals, she felt as if she must be dreaming.

Robin approved of the house too and had chosen his room on the top floor for when he came to stay.

It had a good view of the museum on the opposite side of the street, which he had found was full of the most interesting objects. He had asked his mother if she would mind very much if he continued to live with Peggy and Aaron for he liked it there, and if he left he would miss them and all the little girls, especially Louisa. And then he had added, 'I'm very useful to them.'

Delia felt torn and she felt Robin must be too, but she also realized how content he was with his settled existence, even though she hadn't yet told him that Peggy and Aaron were his grandparents. It was his choice, she decided, and because he had asked and they had had a discussion, she didn't feel that she was forsaking him. He also seemed to be getting along well with Jack, who was teaching him about animal husbandry and had let him help with calving and shown him how to milk a cow.

After discussion with Peggy and Aaron, Jack and Susan had suggested that Robin could stay with them at Foggit farm sometimes, just as the girls stayed with their grandparents. 'It means,' Susan had said hesitantly, 'that we'll become used to him as family and when 'time comes he can be told that he's Jack's son.'

Mr Rogers said he didn't know how he had ever managed without Delia as under-manager at the theatre. She'd thanked him, but didn't mention that soon he would have to, as she and Giles were planning on going on tour as a duo in northern theatres and festival halls; that was also their intention after their marriage, which was still some time away. She was, however, advising Miss Graham the ticket clerk on other tasks, and as the woman had a good head for figures was sure she would be a great help to Mr Rogers.

When Robin's eleventh birthday came along in November Delia and Giles stayed in Paull, Giles in one of the hostelries and Delia with the Robinsons, for she had decided that she would, after all, wait a little longer in a state of celibacy until Giles was completely free.

Then on the day of the Hedon hirings the whole family gathered to mark the ending of a rather special year, and booked a midday meal at the Sun Inn; Delia, Jack and Susan had come to an amicable understanding, but the main focus was that although they all agreed that much had happened in a very short time, Giles and Delia had met on that same day too and it should be a day of celebration.

Christmas came and they spent another very happy time in Paull, with Delia rejoicing that at last she had the family that she had only dreamed of when she was young. On Boxing Day Jack asked her if she would come and look at the site where Deakin's cottage stood. The Robinsons had emptied it completely, as Delia had said she wanted nothing from it, and they had had a great bonfire of the old furniture and everything that was of no value.

Jack took a sledgehammer and aimed the first great blow to the cottage walls and said he hoped he had made amends and that he would consider Robin as his son, the son he had always wanted.

They gazed together at the mound of brick and stone and boulders that had fallen and Jack muttered sheepishly, 'Mebbe one day, Delia, you'll think of building another house here? One where you and Giles could come and stop sometimes when you want some peace and quiet from town or travelling; and mebbe when Robin's older he might like to keep some sheep and pigs an' have a proper smallholding.'

He pointed down to the bottom of the paddock, where the two goats still bleated and the mule brayed at them and the estuary ran swift and constant. 'You could even mek a small lagoon where seabirds'd come: avocets, shelduck, curlew, grebes and mallard; there'd be all manner of wildfowl flying in.'

As she heard the enthusiasm in his voice, Delia remembered what Jack had been like when he was just a boy, spotting different species of wildfowl, nurturing a litter of kittens, birthing a calf, and sometimes telling her he had seen seals and once a dead whale off Spurn; he'd been a quiet shy country lad then, seemingly without any anger in him.

'Louisa would like that.' Robin had come to join them and caught the end of Jack's suggestion. He ran off to find Louisa and tell her.

Giles came looking for her and Jack, turning pink with embarrassment, looked down at his feet. 'In a few years' time there'll be some explaining to do,' he muttered. 'I overheard Robin telling Louisa that they could get married when they're old enough.'

Delia and Giles both smiled. Delia couldn't comprehend that her young son would even think of such a thing, but then sighed and thought that in ten years' time he would be an adult. She gazed at Jack, who still couldn't meet her eyes. 'I think, Jack,' she said, addressing him easily by name for the first time, 'that next year, when they're twelve, we must tell them their own stories.'

In January of the following year, Giles received a letter from his wife to tell him she had been safely delivered of a daughter and that she would be for ever grateful that Giles had been willing to set her free to marry again; she asked if he would consider being a god-father by proxy to their baby girl whom they were naming Gloria. He asked Delia what she thought and she said that it was a lovely request to make and good that they could remain friends after they had both been through such a troubled time.

In June, his decree absolute was granted, and as he and Delia were both living in the town of Kingston upon Hull their marriage licence was approved at the register office in Parliament Street; a wedding was arranged within the month as Giles said he couldn't possibly wait any longer to marry the woman he had loved since their very first meeting, when they had shared a carriage ride to the theatre.

Giles looked out of the window of the reception room in the elegant register office and saw the barouche arrive with Delia, Robin, Louisa, Peggy and Aaron. Behind them in a smart curricle were Jenny and Arthur Crawshaw. They had all been staying at the Maritime Hotel, where later they would have the wedding break-fast. Peggy had promised the little girls that they would have a party at the farm the following day, and at the last minute Delia had decided that it would be nice to ask Louisa to come as company for Robin.

Giles had kept his vow of not telling his parents about their wedding. He wanted no one there who might disapprove even in the slightest, and he knew they would offer him their opinions and recommendations regarding the way he should conduct his life; they had ruined ten years of it, and he wanted nothing to mar this special day. Both he and Delia had survived a difficult time and he felt they deserved the happiness that they would now share.

Giles watched as Robin, dressed in a grey velvet jacket and grey trousers, detached himself from the group and ran up the steps and through the open door; Giles went to greet him.

'Mr Dawson, sir, might I have a few words?'

Giles looked down at the young boy, who was desperately trying not to spill the tears that were gathering. 'Of course, Robin. Is something bothering you?'

Robin shook his head and swallowed. 'No, no. It's just – just that I must ask you something. I want to ask – if you will promise to always take care of my mother. You see, she's only ever had me to look out for her before.' He sniffed and fished in his trouser pocket for a handkerchief. 'And I want to be sure that I can rely on you to do that as well as I have, even though I know that sometimes I wasn't very good at it.'

Giles gave a little frown. 'I've never heard any complaints in that regard, Robin,' he assured him. 'Excellent reports, in fact, and I have been rather anxious that I might not achieve such high standards as the ones you have set.'

'Oh, I think if you try hard you'll do all right.' Robin blew his nose. 'Before we left Paull yesterday, Jack took me on one side and said that my mother was a very special lady and deserved only the best, which is why I thought I'd mention it.'

'Did he really?' Giles murmured. 'Well, that was very' – he searched for an appropriate word – '*thoughtful* of Jack.' From the corner of his eye he saw Aaron helping Peggy and then Delia down from the carriage. 'But let me assure you, Robin, I will love and protect your mother with my life.'

Robin gave a watery grin. 'I couldn't have put it better myself,' he said, and turning towards his mother, who was ascending the steps towards a new life, he approached her, took her hand, and led her towards Giles.

Giles gently held her ringless fingers. 'You are so beautiful,' he murmured. Delia was dressed in a silver-grey gown with a train and a short whisper of a veil fastened with silver clips to her dark hair.

'I am full of joy and happiness,' she whispered. 'I feel as if I'm living a dream and in a moment I shall wake up.'

'No dream,' he said softly. 'Pure and perfect reality. Miss Delamour,' his eyes were on hers, 'shall we make harmonious and lovely music together?'

Delia smiled happily, her eyes bright and moist and loving. 'Yes, Mr Dawson. I think that perhaps we should.'

ACKNOWLEDGEMENTS

With grateful thanks to Dr Martin T. Craven B.Sc. for the generous gift of his book *A New and Complete History of the Borough of Hedon*, The Ridings Publishing Company, Driffield, 1972. At last I have a copy of my own!

The generous loan of books from Brian Dornan: *Smuggling in Yorkshire 1700–1850* by Graham Smith, Country Side Books, 1994; and *Paull Heritage Trail* by Paul Cross, Highgate Print Ltd, 24 Wylies Road, Beverley.

As always, appreciative thanks are due to my ever supportive publishing team. You all know who you are. Thank you.

I was born in the mining town of Castleford, spending my formative years there before coming to live in East Yorkshire as a young girl, and just like a stick of Scarborough rock I'm Yorkshire through and through.

I was such a dreaming child, living in my imagination and through books. My education was dire, and I had the distinction of failing my Eleven Plus – twice. My saving grace was my writing and reading ability; given an essay to write I was in my element, and as for books, I couldn't get enough of them.

In my adult life I took myself off for Further Education to achieve for myself what my teachers couldn't teach me. But, rather than go on to take a university degree which had been my original intention and because I had re-discovered my love of writing, I joined a writers' workshop to polish and hone my writing skills and importantly be with like-minded people.

Prior to this I had in the meantime worked in fashion, trod the catwalk, danced ballroom competitions, married Peter and had two daughters and a grandson. I had lived a full life before taking my writing seriously, but once I did it became my passion. This was the time too when I became a hands-on volunteer and a supporter of various charities, some of which I still support today.

I began my first novel, *The Hungry Tide*, in about 1988 and in the several years of writing it I became completely absorbed in the nineteenth century and the way of life. That novel became the catalyst of what was to come; in 1993 I entered and won the Catherine Cookson Prize for Fiction and was propelled into becoming an author of regional historical novels.

Having lived in the country district of Holderness for most of my married life, I now live in the lovely old market town of Beverley. It featured in my book *The Kitchen Maid*; I've always had a soft spot for Beverley and I have the advantage of both town and country on my doorstep. I have a small gravel garden where I can sit and ponder or retreat to my summerhouse, and I always have a book with me. Old habits die hard.

Interview with Val

1. Did you always know you wanted to be a writer?

I had never thought of being a writer even though as a child I loved to write and always had a story in my head. I didn't know any writers except for two aunts who when they were children had stories published in a Scarborough newspaper's Children's Corner. I remember being very impressed by that.

2. Where do you get your inspiration from?

Inspiration? Well it's all around us if we choose to look and I'm lucky enough to have an enquiring mind and a fertile imagination. I only need to look and listen and think 'Just suppose' or 'What if', and I can be off on an idea. I live quite close to the east coast and the Humber estuary and those are powerful elements, but ordinary people's achievements inspire me too.

3. Do you have any favourite characters you'd love to write about again?

Sometimes a character stays with me long after I have finished a book, and not always the chief protagonist. This happened in *The Hungry Tide* and the character Annie, who, in spite of appearing to be weak and a hopeless case, I felt had more to offer given the chance, and she had, in her own book in her own name Annie became strong, warm and with a great humour that hadn't been apparent in the first book. In *His Brother's Wife* there is a child, Daniel, whose forebears were unknown. I had to write about him in order to find out just who he was and what had gone before. This became *His Mother's Son*.

4. What books do you read in your spare time?

For my reading now, I have a comprehensive taste in
books from C.J. Sansom's series of fictional historicals,
Tracey Chevalier, Kate Atkinson, Sarah Waters, and
books about the Orient and Afghanistan, to Lynda La
Plante. So many choices and all make me want to do
better.

5. What themes are important to you when you write?

Poverty and injustice are my pet hates and these were
prevalent in the 19th century. I also like to write about
strong women. They had to be strong in order to survive.

Fall in love with
Fallen Angels
by Val Wood

After her devious husband Billy tries to sell her at a
wife sale, Lily Fowler finds herself alone, frightened
and heavily pregnant on the streets of Hull.

Running out of options when even the workhouse
turns her away, Lily is forced to swallow what little
pride she has left and accept work in a once-grand
mansion in Leadenhall Square – now a brothel.

Unexpectedly, she soon forges a strong bond with
the group of people she finds there, all good-hearted
women who have simply fallen on hard times. Seeing
potential where others see only destitution, Lily and
her 'fallen angels' join forces to outwit the low-life
brothel-keeper.

In working to transform the house in Leadenhall
Square into something more respectable, doors to
new opportunities are opened and lost loves are
rekindled.

**Can the happy endings the fallen angels never dared
to dream of finally come true?**

Fallen Angels is available in paperback now

No Place for a Woman
by Val Wood

When Lucy's parents are killed in a train crash, her kindly uncle steps in to look after the little girl – to the initial apprehension of his wife and her son. However, Lucy's sweet, spirited charm slowly wins over her new family, and as she overcomes the trauma of her childhood, she grows up inspired to become a doctor, just like her father.

But studying medicine in London takes Lucy far from her home in Hull and the people she loves, and she has to battle to be accepted in a man's world.

With the dark clouds of the First World War gathering on the horizon, an even greater challenge approaches. Can a woman find her place on the front line of battle? Will Lucy be able to follow her dreams – and find love – in a world shattered by war?

No Place for a Woman available in paperback now

The Kitchen Maid
by Val Wood

Jenny is determined to make her own way in the world, and she secures a job as the kitchen maid in a grand house in Yorkshire. Gradually, she gains the attention of the young master of the house, and they fall in love. But slowly their dreams turn to nightmares, culminating in a scandal that will force Jenny to leave behind everything she knows.

Cast aside by her own family, Jenny faces many difficulties until an unusual promise changes the course of her life: Jenny the kitchen maid becomes mistress of her own grand house. Although she tries to fit in with this new world, however, she never forgets the words a gypsy once told her: that one day she will return to where she was happy – and discover her true love . . .

But will the tragedy of her past stand in the way of her happiness?

The Kitchen Maid available in paperback with a beautiful new cover now

Little Girl Lost

by Val Wood

Will the troubles in her past break her spirit?

Margriet grew up as a lonely child in the old town of Hull. Her adored father often travelled by sea to the Netherlands, leaving her with an unaffectionate mother and only her imagination of a little Dutch girl, Annelise, to keep her company. When devastation ravages her tiny family. Annelise becomes the comforting friend Margriet needs for a long time to come.

A few years later, Margriet is blossoming into a kind young lady. Keen to escape her mother and strike out on her own, she forms an unlikely friendship with some of the street children who roam the town.

As Margriet acts upon her inspiration to help them, will the troubles of her past break her spirit, or will she be able to overcome them?

Little Girl Lost available in paperback now

Far From Home
by Val Wood

**Can she make a new life away from
everything she knows?**

When Georgiana Gregory and her maid, Kitty, make
the long sea journey from their native Hull for New
York, they hope to escape the confines of English life
and savour a land of opportunity.

But in New York, Georgiana finds she isn't far from
home when she encounters a man passing himself
off as a local mill-owner's son, Edward, who has fled
to America. Georgiana recognizes the man standing
before her as Edward's valet Robert – Edward himself
appears to have vanished.

As Georgiana and Kitty pursue the adventures of the
frontier, and Edward tries to flee his enemies, are the
dangers of this new country too much to cope with?

Far From Home out now in paperback with
stunning new cover

Join
Val Wood
online

Find out more about Val and her novels at

www.valeriewood.co.uk